*She took herself
out of her body,
soaring free . . .*

Joie felt weightless, free, skimming through
the mountains she had studied so carefully.
She crossed space. Smelled the rain. Felt
cool and moist in the mist of the mountains.
Far below her, she saw the entrance to a cave,
spotlighted by the small sliver of moon that
managed to peek around the thick cloud
cover. Smiling, she dropped down to enter
a world of crystal and ice. Whether she was
dreaming or hallucinating didn't matter; all
she cared about was escaping from the pain
of her wounds and the smell of the hospital.

DARK NIGHTS

By Christine Feehan

DARK PRINCE • DARK DESIRE
DARK GOLD • DARK MAGIC
DARK CHALLENGE • DARK FIRE
DARK LEGEND • DARK GUARDIAN
DARK SYMPHONY • DARK MELODY
DARK DESTINY • DARK SECRET
DARK DEMON • DARK CELEBRATION
DARK POSSESSION • DARK HUNGER
DARK CURSE • DARK SLAYER
DARK PERIL

WILD RAIN • BURNING WILD
WILD FIRE

MAGIC IN THE WIND • TWILIGHT BEFORE CHRISTMAS
OCEANS OF FIRE • DANGEROUS TIDES
SAFE HARBOR • TURBULENT SEA
HIDDEN CURRENTS

WATERBOUND • SPIRIT BOUND

SHADOW GAME • MIND GAME
NIGHT GAME • CONSPIRACY GAME
DEADLY GAME • PREDATORY GAME
MURDER GAME • STREET GAME

LAIR OF THE LION • THE SCARLETTI CURSE

CHRISTINE FEEHAN

DARK NIGHTS

A V O N

An Imprint of HarperCollins*Publishers*

A previous version of "Dark Descent" appeared in *The Only One* copyright © 2003 by Dorchester Publishing Co., Inc.

"Dark Dream" appeared in *After Twilight* copyright © 2001 by Dorchester Publishing Co., Inc. and *Dark Dreamers* copyright © 2006 by Dorchester Publishing Co., Inc.

AVON BOOKS
An Imprint of HarperCollins*Publishers*
10 East 53rd Street
New York, New York 10022-5299

Dark Nights copyright © 2012 by Christine Feehan
"Dark Descent" copyright © 2003, 2012 by Christine Feehan
"Dark Dream" copyright © 2001 by Christine Feehan
ISBN 978-0-06-221902-2
www.avonromance.com

First Avon Books mass market printing: November 2012

Avon Trademark Reg. U.S. Pat. Off. and in Other Countries, Marca Registrada, Hecho en U.S.A.
HarperCollins® is a registered trademark of HarperCollins Publishers.

Printed in the U.S.A.

10 9 8 7 6 5 4 3 2 1

To Brooke Borneman and Diane Stacy.
In appreciation for all you do.

Acknowledgments

A big, huge Thank You to my agent, Steve Axelrod, for getting me this opportunity. This book wouldn't have been written without Brian Feehan, who helped with battle planning and every other aspect. Thank you so much the hours of brainstorming!

DARK DESCENT

Chapter One

Veins of lightning lit the clouds, dancing whips of white-hot energy illuminating the midnight sky. The earth rumbled and rolled, unsettled and flinching as the creature clawed its way through the soil to burst into the air, instantly fouling every living thing it touched. Leaves shriveled and blackened. The air vibrated with alarm. The vampire settled to earth, turning its head this way and that, listening, waiting, its cunning mind racing, its rotten heart beating with a mixture of triumph and fear. He was the bait, and he knew the hunter was not far behind, close on his trail, drawn straight into the heart of the trap.

Traian Trigovise burrowed through the soil, following the stench of the undead. It was too easy, the trail too well marked. No vampire would be so obvious unless he was a rank fledgling, and Traian was certain he was dealing with strength and cunning. He was an ancient Carpathian hunter, a species nearly immortal, blessed and cursed with longevity, with timeless gifts and the need for a lifemate to make him complete. He was first and foremost a predator, capable of becoming the most loathsome and evil of all creatures, the undead. It was his sheer strength of will and duty to his race that kept him from falling prey to the insidious whispers and call of power.

When the tunnel veered upward toward the sky, Traian continued onward, pushing deeper into the dirt, feeling his way, listening to the heartbeat and energy of the earth around him. All was silent, even the insects, creatures often summoned by the evil ones. He scanned the surface, taking in a large area, and discovered three blank spots, evidence that more than one vampire was close.

He found a web of roots, thick and gnarled, humming with life, reaching deep into the earth. He whispered softly, respectfully, touching the longest, deepest artery, feeling its life force. He chanted softly in the ancient language, asking for entrance, and felt the response moving through the thick old tree. Leaves shivered as the tree reached toward the moon, embracing the night even as it shrank from the presence of the foul beings. Imparting secrets and conspiring to help, the tree spread its roots to allow Traian into the intricate system protecting and nourishing the wide trunk.

The hunter was careful not to disturb the soil or the root system as he maneuvered his way through the labyrinth, pushing through the surface just far enough to scan his surroundings from inside the cage of safety of the overlapping roots above ground. Stealthily, he shape-shifted as he emerged, nothing more than a shadow hidden amongst the thick branches and leaves.

For one moment he could see only his prey, the tall, thin figure of Gallent. He recognized the vampire as one of the ancients sent out by their prince so many centuries earlier, just as he had been. The undead continually twisted, sniffing the air suspiciously, his gaze darting along the ground. He clicked his long fingernails together in a peculiar repeated rhythm.

The wind rushed through the grove of trees, and the

leaves rustled and whispered. Traian allowed his gaze to shift, quartering the area, searching with his mind more than with his acute vision. The breeze brought the echo of that strange rhythm to him, coming from his left. Those blank spots—the undead protecting their foul presence from nature—came from his right. It took a few more moments to detect the other two undead waiting to fall upon him and rip him to pieces. He shifted again, drifting with the breeze through the cage of roots, rising as molecules into the night, allowing the friendly wind to take him higher into the cover of leaves.

Dark clouds swirled into a boiling cauldron. Lightning veined the murky, spinning mass. He hovered there with a small, humorless smile in his mind. Discretion really was the better part of valor in some circumstances. The band of vampires had been following him, first one group and then another, attacking and retreating each time he got the upper hand in the battle. This time, they appeared to have the advantage and in any case, he was already exhausted. Like a pack of dogs wearing down prey, they had been nipping at his heels for several risings, inflicting damage here and there, nothing huge, but enough to wear him down. He would pick his own battleground.

As he turned away, the sound of the clicking fingernails came again. The sound grew louder. With each click, droplets of water fell from the clouds—tiny droplets that never quite reached the ground. The beads collected in midair, formed a large, shimmering pool. Shocked, he could see his own reflection clearly in the pool. Not the scattered molecules, or an illusion, but the real man amongst the leaves. If he could see himself, so could the enemy. It was his only warning, and it came just a heartbeat before the attack.

He caught movement from the corner of his eye and instantly reacted, somersaulting through the sky, shifting into his true form, grateful for the leaves that hampered the nearly invisible silvery net meant to entangle him. Spears spiraled through the air, along with tiny darts tipped with poison from the tree frog, and showers of red-hot embers that burrowed into the skin and burned for weeks, engulfed him in a fiery cloud, penetrating deep. Pain slammed through him, but Traian shoved it aside, turning to face the enemy. Insects clouded the skies, and all the while the clicking of the fingernails went on relentlessly.

He launched himself at the shadowy figure orchestrating the fight, ignoring the two lesser vampires. Gallent seemed to be directing the action, a leader in evil, as he had been a leader among Carpathians. The ancient Carpathian-turned-vampire was a master at planning cunning traps and with the poison working its way through his system, Traian knew he was in serious trouble. He couldn't allow Gallent room to think. His lesser vampires were considered fodder, merely pawns in his scheme to kill a Carpathian hunter. It was Gallent, Traian had to destroy.

Traian burst through the sky, his fist already snapping out, driving toward the vampire's chest, intending to smash through the rotting shell of bone and tissue for the blackened heart.

Gallent shimmered transparently. The fist passed through his body harmlessly even as the undead struck back with razor-sharp talons. The hand came from Traian's left, the swift, sure movement of a full-fledged master. The knife-like nails drove deep through flesh and muscle, all the way to the bone. One of the lesser vampires hurled himself onto Traian's back, sinking his teeth into his target's exposed neck.

Dissolving into mist, Traian streaked toward the ancient vampire, at the last moment shifting back to solid form, his fist slamming deep into the chest of the undead. Gallent shrieked. Black blood sprayed over the hunter, burning through flesh to bone, the poisonous acid pouring over Traian's arm and hand.

Gallent retaliated with a swipe of his vicious claws at Traian's eyes, attempting to blind the hunter. A brutal head-butt followed, and the vampire rolled his head to one side, teeth tearing into Traian's neck, right over his vulnerable artery. Pain streaked up his neck and radiated through his body as the vampire's serrated teeth viciously sawed through flesh to get at the enticing banquet of pure ancient blood.

Traian set his teeth, pushing aside the fierce pain to burrow deeper, tunneling towards the blackened heart. His flesh tore and the vampire spit it out, gulping at his spraying blood. The two lesser vampires shrieked in glee and leapt at him, dragging him to the ground, ripping his arm back away from their master, teeth burying into his body, desperate to get at his blood. Gallent kicked at them as they tried to devour him, teeth ripping through skin to get at the precious treasure.

The pain level became agony, nearly impossible to block out. Traian knew he had to retreat to give himself enough time to repair the damage to his neck and body. With such a blood loss, he was weakening fast. He twice tried to throw off the lesser vampires, but they stuck to him like glue. Gallent's furious orders and vicious kicks couldn't dislodge his minions either. The lure of pure blood was too strong.

Gallent abandoned his tactics, saliva dripping in long, slobbery strands from his mouth, as the need for Carpathian blood overcame his discipline, won over hundreds of years of being vampire. He threw himself on Traian, talons raking and teeth biting, trying, like his underlings, to strip flesh away and get at the blood. So rich and pure, the feast would boost strength and give the vampires not only a further advantage, but a rush of feeling they were so desperate to have.

Weakened, Traian took the only way out left to him, evaporating and taking to the air, streaking away from the frenzied undead. Shrieking, the three followed him, unwilling to lose their prey when they were so close to victory. Killing a hunter of Traian's stature would be a significant victory, and with the taste of blood already in their mouths, they refused to allow such a prize to escape. Traian's blood rained down on the shivering leaves, the scent of the ancient gift driving the vampires into a frenzy of rage and hunger.

Traian had long been fighting these battles and weariness settled over him even as he raced across the night sky, forced to flee with the poisonous acid working its way through his body and his blood spraying across the forest, the hounds of hell nipping at his heels. He glanced up at the sky. Sunrise was still a good hour away. The vampires would pursue him until they had no other recourse than to go to ground to avoid burning in the sun.

Cursing under his breath, he used a flash of tremendous energy to cut off the bleeding and repair his torn neck as best he could in flight. He needed soil and saliva, but flying as mist precluded both. Shifting took energy as did staying in the air, and he was running on empty. He needed to shake his pursuers fast. The hounds had become the hunters and they had a pack.

He glanced at the sky, calling softly for aid. Clouds responded, moving across the stars, dark and boiling, lightning edging the bottoms, the energy building fast, looking for targets. Deliberately he slowed just a little, just enough to draw excited, triumphant shrieks from the lesser vampires. They increased their speed in an effort to capture him.

Traian dove toward earth, the three vampires spreading out like a vee behind him, Gallent leading the way. Heavy forest rose up to meet him. Fog lay along the ground, thick and heavy, a dense mat of mist obscuring the thick vegetation of rotting trunks and leaves. He slipped into the layers of fog, turned sharply to slide behind a large rock basin hanging over a stream. Casting a trail of running footsteps leading away from his actual position, he stayed very still, waiting for the three vampires to descend.

Gallent, with his years of experience, dropped back to allow his hounds to sniff the ground and rout around for the scent of the wounded Carpathian. Eager to find the treasure of rich blood, the two grotesque creatures crawled on the ground. One whined eagerly, finding the faint trail of kicked up leaves. He rushed after his prey. The other abandoned his sniffing just a few feet from where Traian was concealed in the layers of fog. He'd cut off the spraying arc of blood from his torn neck, but there were hundreds of bloody bites covering his body and the vampire had only to take another couple of steps and he would have scented his prey. Fortunately, the undead was far too greedy and didn't want his companion to get the jump on him.

Gallent hesitated, torn between caution and greed. The first lesser vampire shrieked again with joy as he discovered a twisted piece of moss right on the bank of the stream. Gallent made his decision and followed, dropping to earth, shoving aside his two underlings to peer down at the trail.

Traian struck hard and fast, slamming bolt after bolt of lightning into the area, blanketing the forest and stream with forks and whips of white-hot spears burning through the sky to earth. Thunder shook the forest, reverberating through the night. The trees lit up in macabre orange and red, glowing hot.

The vampires screamed horribly as fire ravaged the earth around them, burning pure, turning foul breath to ash. On the other side of the ferocious storm, Traian once again took to the sky, retreating to find a place to rest and heal before he returned to the hunt. It was his way of life, one he had known for far too long now.

He traveled quickly through the night. The Carpathian Mountains were riddled with networks of caves, where rich soil deep beneath the earth waited to welcome him. He was close to home. He had been steadily traveling back to his homeland to see his prince but had become sidetracked when he came across the vampires. He had spent the last few risings leading them away from the area where Mikhail Dubrinsky and his lifemate, Raven, were known to dwell.

His shoulder throbbed and burned. His neck was a fierce torment. There were a hundred places on his body that ached from the embers and darts and the terrible bites where chunks of flesh were missing. He found an opening into the cool interior of the mountain, went deeper still, through a labyrinth of tunnels into the earth. He floated down into the bed of rich soil and just lay there, feeling a sense of peace and solace in the wealth of welcoming minerals.

He would need blood to recoup. But for now, the earth welcomed him, would do its best to aid in his healing. He closed his eyes and allowed sleep to take him.

Austria

The theater doors opened to allow the smartly dressed crowd out. They emerged laughing and talking, a crush of happy people pleased with the performance they had witnessed. Lightning forked across the sky, a brilliant, dazzling display of elemental nature. For a moment the long, sequined gowns, furs and suits of varying color were lit up as if caught in a spotlight. Thunder crashed directly overhead, and the ground and buildings shook under the assault. The light faded, leaving the night nearly black and the crowd almost blind. The throng broke into couples or groups, hurrying to their limousines and cars, while valets tried to work fast before the rain began to fall.

Senator Thomas Goodvine stayed beneath the entrance archway, bending his head toward his wife to hear her over the buzz of the crowd, laughing at her softly spoken words, nodding in agreement. He pulled her beneath his shoulder to prevent her from being jostled by the steady stream of people hurrying to avoid the weather.

Two trees formed the unique archway to the theater, the branches interlocking overhead to form a small protection against the elements. The leaves rustled and the branches clicked together in the rushing wind. Clouds whirled and spun, weaving dark, ominous threads across the moon.

Another burst of lightning illuminated two large men pushing against the stream of theatergoers, apparently determined to gain shelter in the building. The flash of light faded, leaving only the dim lighting of the archway and the streetlights flickering ominously. Thelma Goodvine tugged at her husband's jacket to bring his attention back to her.

"Gun! Down! Get down!" Joie Sanders plowed into the senator and his wife, her arms outspread, sweeping them both to the ground. In one move she rolled up on her knee in front of them, a gun in her outstretched hand. "Gun, gun, everybody down!" she shouted.

An orange-red flame burst from two revolvers in a steady stream toward the couple she'd been assigned to protect. Joie returned fire with her usual calm and dead-on accuracy, watching one man begin to topple, almost in slow motion, his gun still firing but up into the air.

People screamed, ran in every direction, fell to the ground, and crouched behind flimsy cover. The second gunman grabbed a woman in a long fur and dragged her in front of him as a shield. Joie was already pushing at the senator and his wife in an effort to get them to crawl back inside the relative safety of the theater. The second gunman propelled the sobbing woman forward as he fired at Joie, who rolled again to cover her charges' line of retreat.

A bullet sliced through the flesh of her shoulder, burning a path of pain and spraying blood over the senator's trousers. Joie cried out, but steadied her aim, ignoring the churning in her stomach. Her world narrowed to one man, one target. She squeezed the trigger slowly, precisely, watched the ugly little hole blossom in the middle of the man's forehead. He went down like a rock, taking his hostage with him, falling in a tangle of arms and legs.

There was a small silence. Only the clicking of the branches could be heard, a strange, disquieting rhythm. Joie blinked, trying to clear her vision. She seemed to be looking into a large, shimmering pool, staring at a man with flat, cold eyes and something metal glinting in his hand. He rose up out of the crowd, slamming into Joie before she could scramble out of the way. She twisted just enough to escape the lethal blade, driving the butt of her gun upward into his jaw, then slamming it back down on his knife hand. He screamed, dropping the blade so that it went skittering along the sidewalk. His fist found her face, driving her backward. The man followed her down, his face a mask of hatred.

Something hit the back of his head hard, and Joie found herself staring up at one of her men. "Thanks, John. I think he smashed every bone in my body when he fell on me."

She took John's outstretched hand, and allowed him to help her out from under the large body. Joie kicked the gun from the limp hand of the first man she'd shot, even as weakness overwhelmed her. She sat down abruptly as her legs turned to rubber. "Get the senator and Mrs. Goodvine to safety, John." The wailing sirens were fading in and out. "Someone help that poor woman up."

"We've got it, Joie," one of the agents assured her. "We have the driver. How bad are you hurt? How many hits did you take? Give me your gun."

Joie looked down at the gun in her hand and noted with surprise she was aiming it at the motionless attacker. "Thanks, Robert. I think I'll just let you and John handle things for a while."

"Is she all right?" She could hear the senator's anxious voice. "Sanders? Are you hurt? I don't want to just leave her there; where are you taking us?"

Joie tried to lift her arm to indicate she was fine, but her arm seemed heavy and uncooperative. She closed her eyes and breathed deeply. She just needed to be somewhere else, just for a short time while the medics fixed her up. It wasn't the first time she'd taken a hit and she doubted it would be the last. She had certain instincts that had taken her to the top of her profession. It was very dangerous at the top.

Joie could blend in. Some of the men liked to call her the chameleon. She could look strikingly beautiful, plain, or just average. She could blend in with the tough crowd, the homeless, or the rich and glamorous. It was a valuable gift, and she used it willingly. She was called in for the difficult assignments, the ones where action was inevitable. Few others had her skill with knives or guns, and no one could disappear into a crowd the way she could.

She took herself out of her body, watched the frantic scene around her with interest for a few minutes. The others assigned to the senator and the Austrian agents had everything under control. She was being put into an ambulance and hustled away from the scene. More than anything, she detested hospitals. She'd seen too many of them and associated the smells with death. More than a few of her coworkers—her friends—had gone through hospital doors and had not ever left.

Joie didn't know if she truly believed in astral projection, but she had been having out-of-body experiences from the time she was a toddler. She had perfected her craft over the years, directing herself to fly away and leave her physical body behind when she didn't want to be where she was. It was a useful, exhilarating gift, and all too real. Sometimes too real. Many times the places she found herself in were far more intriguing than where she'd left her body and of course, the danger was always in not finding her way back.

She'd read numerous articles about astral projection and most seemed to happen to enlightened people, people of faith who believed in a higher, better realm. She was far more practical, dealing with the seamier side of life and finding her faith was in nature and the beauty of the wild, untouched places she sought out both on an astral plane and with her physical body when she had time off.

The smell of the hospital was overpowering, making her stomach lurch. People moved around her fast, poking needles into her, talking in low voices, cutting her shirt away. She didn't take painkillers as a rule and tried to tell them, but no one listened to her. An oxygen mask was slapped over her face. What was the use in staying in a place she didn't want to be when she could roam the world in her mind? Whether she was actually there or not mattered very little. It *felt* real when she journeyed out of her body. She took a deep breath of the oxygen and let go of her physical body.

She simply took herself away now, soaring free. She wanted to be outdoors, under the sky or beneath the earth in a world of subterranean beauty—it didn't matter, as long as it wasn't within the walls of a hospital.

Joie felt weightless, free, skimming through the mountains she had studied so carefully. As she soared free, she planned a trip caving with her brother and sister as soon as the senator and his wife were safely back home. She crossed space. Smelled the rain. Felt cool and moist in the mist of the mountains. Far below her, she saw the entrance to a cave, spotlighted by the small sliver of moon that managed to peek around the thick cloud cover. Smiling, she dropped down to enter a world of crystal and ice. Whether she was dreaming or hallucinating didn't matter; all she cared about was escaping from the pain of her wounds and the smell of the hospital.

Carpathian Mountains

Traian lay in the cool earth, gazing up at the high, cathedral-like ceiling. His body hurt in so many places, he just wanted to rest. The beauty of the cave was breathtaking and took his mind off his physical pain. The network of caves he'd entered deep beneath the earth was part of a huge subterranean city. Great waterfalls of ice cascaded down from ceiling to floor, some lapping around one another until it looked as if great bows of thick ice had gift-wrapped the entire cave he lay in.

Despite the cold, some insects and bats dwelled in the realms above him, but he had gone deep, where few living creatures could exist. The cold helped to numb the pain and bring him a soothing sense of peace he so badly needed after the last few risings. In the far corner of the cave the formation actually looked like thick ice walls with a covering of ice clouds over them. As he worked at forcing some of the burning embers from his body he tried to imagine the forces it would take to forge such a dramatic thing of beauty deep beneath the earth.

Traian turned his head and saw her. His heart nearly stopped and then began pounding. The breath left his lungs in a long rush. She was hovering just overhead to his left. She'd entered silently and somehow gotten past his safeguards. Had he been so exhausted that he'd forgotten such an important life-saving detail? Impossible. He could feel the weave, strong and in place. No one—*nothing*—should be able to get passed his safeguards.

He studied the woman. She had a cap of dark, glossy hair, very thick—the kind a man would want to run his fingers through. The thought brought him up short. He didn't have thoughts like that about women—at least any that he could remember—and he had lived a very long existence. Her eyes were large and gray, heavily fringed with thick lashes. She stared back at him with complete astonishment.

"You're hurt," she said. "If you were real, I'd send the paramedics."

Her voice seemed to go right through his skin, wrap itself around his heart and squeeze so tightly he lost his breath. His vision blurred. Tiny pinpoints of light burst behind his eyes, a light show of colors. Pastels at first so that some of the ice formations took on subtle blues and greens.

"What makes you think I am not real?" He tested his voice, not certain if she was real or if he'd dreamt her up. He'd been wounded a thousand times and *nothing* like this had ever happened to him before. A woman hovering above his head? Floating in the air like an angel? He was so far removed from heaven none of this made sense. He wasn't a man to panic and was willing to see what she would do. He had no doubts that he could kill her if she made a wrong move.

"Because I'm not really here," she answered. "I'm in a hospital many miles away. I don't even know where here is."

Traian frowned and rubbed his eyes. Colors shot at him like sparks, a fireworks show inside of his head. Great. The last thing he needed with a new, potential threat was to lose his vision. She didn't feel like a threat. If anything, there was a sense of amusement and serenity about her. She didn't look transparent, but it was possible she was telling the truth. Her voice had a soft melodic echo to it, as though it was disembodied.

"You look real enough to me."

"What in the world are you doing lying in the mud in the middle of a cave?" Her soft laughter rippled through him. "You didn't mistake this for a beauty spa, did you?"

His heart nearly ceased beating. He blinked several times as the colors behind his eyes burst into a spectacular display of raining drops of dark color. When he stared at her his world was upside down. Her simple questions had wrought a change that would never be undone.

He was aware of everything—the coolness of the interior, the blue of the ice, the dramatic sweep of architecture formed thousands of years earlier. He was mostly aware that her hair was a rich brown, dark and glossy, the strands, several shades of brown, so many he hadn't even known the colors existed. Her eyes were a cool gray and her lashes and brows matched her hair color. Her mouth was wide and curved at the corners, teeth small and very white. There were laugh lines around her mouth and eyes hinting at her sense of humor. Her skin was light gold, burnished by the sun.

He was seeing in color. After hundreds of years of a bleak, gray existence, living in a world without color or emotion, there she was. The other half of his soul. Staring down at him with curious eyes and an amused grin. There was blood on her shoulder and bruises on her face, and she seemed to be wearing a bizarre, thin-looking gown that didn't cover much.

His eyes narrowed, trying to see what injuries she had. She'd mentioned a hospital. "What happened to you?"

She smiled at him as if those injuries were nothing at all when they'd set his heart pounding in fear and dread coiled his belly into tight hard knots. She had no idea how important she was. His lifemate. After so many endless years.

"I was shot." She touched her face, wincing as if it hurt. "Someone smashed me in the face. It's all a little hazy. They're giving me drugs and I've never reacted well to them."

For the first time her body shimmered and she appeared transparent.

"Wait! Don't go." He nearly leapt to catch her, but knew his hand would pass right through her if she wasn't really there.

Traian had never panicked in his life. Not that he could remember. He'd been in countless battles, but whether she was real or not, he was seeing in color. He was *feeling*. Emotion. Real emotion. He knew that much was real. Was it possible he was caught in a hallucination? He had lost a lot of blood—too much blood—and there was nothing in the cave to replenish the amount he'd left in the ground. He couldn't imagine that he could ever conjure something like this up.

Fear. Elation. Shock. The emotions were far too strong to be memories. She had to be real. He had no idea how she'd traveled to the cave, but she was real enough to bring him color and emotion. He couldn't lose her. Not now. Not after searching the world over for her. He had to find a way to keep her with him.

A small shudder went through her body as she made a visual effort to stay with him. "I can't do this for too long. But," she frowned at him, "you're hurt too. Do you often go swimming in the mud with a gaping hole in your shoulder? You have heard of infection and gangrene, haven't you?"

"A small run-in with a group of unsavory ruffians. I was uncharacteristically slow." He kept his voice light, dismissing of his own wounds.

"Does this sort of thing happen often?"

He knew she had a good sense of humor from the laugh lines around her mouth. He liked her mouth, that quirky little smile that reached her eyes. "Unfortunately very often. And you?" He felt himself go very still waiting for her answer.

"Same thing. In my line of work, it's one of the hazards you just live with."

He inhaled but couldn't catch her scent, telling him she truly didn't have a physical body present in the cave. "We must do similar work."

"*But,*" she flashed another wide smile, "you're here in this cave and I'm in a hospital. What does that say about you?"

His own sense of humor welled up. He hadn't bantered with anyone since his childhood and he barely had managed to remember those days. "I'm eccentric?"

Her laughter seemed a melody playing over his body like the soft brush of fingers. "You seem a bit underdressed for a cave," he pointed out.

She looked down at her body, one eyebrow arching. She seemed to be in some sort of a hospital gown. She'd forgotten to clothe herself properly in her astral flight. She shrugged, her laughter soft and inviting. "Yes, well, a lady likes to know she looks her best when the cave crickets come calling."

Joie studied the man below her. He was the most handsome man she'd ever seen. *Ever.* And she trained with some fairly hot men. He had a rock-hard body. Plenty of defined muscle and she was a darned good judge of such things. He exuded power, despite the fact that he was obviously severely injured. He was making light of it, but when she really studied him, she could see a horrific tear in his neck and bite marks all over his shoulders and running down his arms. When he eased his position slightly, she caught sight of more on his back.

"You look like you ran into a pack of wolves."

She bit her lip hard, waiting for an answer. She found, when she took herself out of her body, that she didn't feel pain, but she did feel cold, and this time, she was colder than usual and it had nothing to do with being in an ice cave. She had never held a projection for an extended period of time, certainly not over a great distance, and she'd chosen a mountain range she'd been studying with the idea of vacationing there.

The biting cold pierced her through and through. She was worried about this man. Where her body was barely there, and he couldn't really see the damage to it, with all the blood and gore, she could see the wounds on him easily and the evidence all over the ice where he'd come in. He was really injured. Without a real body she couldn't help him.

"More like dogs than wolves. I wouldn't give my brethren such an insult."

She loved the sound of his voice. "You have an incredibly sexy accent. Do women fall all over you just at the sound of your voice?" She was very good at placing people by their accents, but his was different; there was a rich turn to his words. As astral dreaming went, this one was fascinating. The longer she stayed, the more real he seemed to her.

"I have not actually noticed such a phenomenon," he replied, his eyes glinting with amusement, "but I will watch for it in the future."

The idea of women falling all over him irritated her on a

primal feminine level which surprised her. She wasn't that kind of person. She worked with men every day and never once had she decided she wanted one permanently. How strange that during an astral projection she would run into a man she found attractive. She loved his sexy voice, and hard, firm body. He was definitely European. His hair was longer than she usually liked on a man, but he wore it exceptionally well and it suited his aristocratic face.

She couldn't determine his age, but he was definitely all man. A warrior. The type of man who really appealed to her. She realized she was staring at him and sent a small smile his way, trying not to let her teeth chatter. The cold was worse, deep inside her as if her core temperature had dropped alarmingly.

"You're too charming not to have noticed," she pointed out. "You seem a very experienced man to me." She looked around her. "Nice cave. I love caves. This one looks like a wonderful place to explore."

"I do not believe it has been discovered yet," he replied pleasantly.

"Really? You just sort of stumbled in blindfolded, did you? An interesting way to explore caves. Where am I? I'd like to come back here."

"If you did not know about these caves, how could you find them? Did you float through the air blindfolded?"

She grinned at him. "I do that sometimes when I don't want to be wherever I am. A bad habit."

Traian studied her. She was beautiful, even though at times her form seemed to fade in and out. "You're in a network of ice caves in the Carpathian Mountains. This mountain range is considered home to my people. The wilds of the forest, and the deep of the earth."

She frowned at him. "I like the way you talk, I really do, very old-fashioned and courtly, but also, you managed to neatly avoid my question. The Carpathian Mountains happen to be a very large range and run through many countries."

Traian's way of life had been deception for as long as he could remember. Carpathians left no traces of themselves behind, no trail, nothing that might indicate they were not human. And they certainly didn't give the location of their homeland away. He hesitated. The prince was close by and had to be protected at all costs.

Her form shimmered and her smile faded. "They're doing something nasty to me, I can't hold the projection."

He sat up, bit back a groan as the embers beneath his skin burned fiercely. "Do not go yet."

"I'm sorry." She looked down at her arm, looked back at him, tears swimming in her eyes. "They're cleaning my wound. It hurts like a bear."

"I have to be able to find you. Where are you?"

She frowned again. "I don't know. The hospital."

"Romania. These caves are in Romania. I can't lose you." He held out his hand to stop her.

She tried. He could see her make an effort. She said something he couldn't hear, her body fragmenting.

"I *have* to be able to find you. Tell me your name. Your name." He could find her with that.

She opened her mouth, but nothing came out and then she was gone. That fast. Vanishing without a trace. He sat there alone in the dark of the cave, astonished at how life could change in the blink of an eye. She was real. Her psychic abilities were strong. He had shared her space, shared her mind, and the path was imprinted on his brain. She would not escape him, but it wouldn't be easy without her name, with no starting point.

He became aware of his heart hammering out a rhythm of joy. A lifemate. It was the last thing he had expected on this long journey back to his homeland. She wasn't Carpathian, which was shocking, but the prince had been mated to a human so it was possible. He needed this woman to survive. He *had* to find her. It was difficult to force discipline on himself and not try to rush like a madman out of the cave into the rising sun.

He let his breath out with a long slow hiss of promise. The woman belonged to him. She had the other half to his soul. He should have bound her to him right then, but the distance was too great and if it took too long to find her, the ritual words would wreak havoc with both of them. No, he had to heal first and then his only mission would be to find her.

Traian lay back and waved his hand to close the small amount of soil and mud he'd discovered over him, stilling his heart, his breath, allowing the song of the earth to send him into a deep, healing sleep.

Chapter Two

Jubal Sanders glanced up at the sky, heavy with clouds, the temperature dropping alarmingly. "Night's going to come fast when it does," he announced. "Maybe two hours to sunset. If we don't want to camp up here on the side of the mountain, we've got to start down."

"You're losing it, Joie, there's nothing here." Gabrielle Sanders sank gracefully to the ground and drew up her knees as she regarded her sister with cool gray eyes. "Stop making yourself crazy and enjoy the view. It's breathtaking up here. You've been in a frenzy for hours now." Tipping her head back, she stared up at the sky. "We've been climbing forever. If you were going to find anything, you would have done so by now."

"I'm not losing my mind, Gabrielle," Joie insisted. "Or, truthfully, maybe I've already lost it."

There was a sudden silence. The wind paused. A hawk screamed as it missed its prey. Gabrielle exchanged a long look with her brother. They both stared at their younger sister. She seemed focused entirely on the rock surface she was studying.

"Well, that's a relief," Gabrielle replied, laughing. "All this time I thought I was the abnormal one."

Joie let her breath out slowly. She knew she was acting crazy, almost out of control. What was she going to tell Gabrielle and Jubal? That she really had lost her mind some weeks ago and this was a last-ditch effort to hold on to her sanity? That she wasn't joking, and she belonged locked up somewhere on heavy medication?

She'd woken up in the hospital in Austria with a strange buzzing in her head. Whispers that never ceased. A man's voice, not just any man's voice, but *his* voice, her mysterious, sexy stranger. She could imagine telling Gabrielle and Jubal she'd met a hot man during one of her numerous astral projection jaunts. Oh, yeah, and he was deep beneath the earth in a network of unexplored caves in Romania. They'd lock her up and throw away the key.

She couldn't stop thinking about him. She was certain she was clinically obsessed with an apparition. How could he have been real? The doctors had told her she was out a long time. Who knew what went on in one's brain when they were under anesthesia? If she told her sister and brother she wasn't so much looking for the perfect cave as she was the man trapped in one, they'd definitely haul her butt to a head doctor. There was no way to explain her need to find him to anyone.

She'd been placed on leave, as was typical when one of the professional protectors was injured on the job. She hadn't gone back to the States, but when Gabrielle and Jubal had come to visit her, to help her with physical therapy, she convinced them to go to the Carpathian Mountains and go caving with her.

In the beginning she'd tried to ignore the whispered intimacy, but eventually she'd succumbed to the sheer lure of it. She'd carried on silly conversations with him, sometimes philosophical ones, and God help her, sexy, nearly erotic exchanges she couldn't imagine herself having with anyone else. The voice in her head had been growing stronger since she'd entered Romania, as if, finally, she was much closer to him.

What are you doing?

The voice came out of nowhere, unexpectedly as it always did, catching her by surprise. Masculine. Sometimes amused. Sometimes teasing. Always alluring. She tried not to hear it. Tried not to respond. But she could never help herself. She always talked to him. Laughed with him. Wanted him.

In spite of the beauty of his voice, this time he sounded infinitely weary, strained, as if he were in pain. She'd never heard that particular note in his voice and it alarmed her. Was he hurt? Could he be hurt? If she wasn't crazy, that meant he was real and she didn't need to feel crazy most of the time. Right now, maybe a little bit.

"Come on, I'm so close to the entrance I should be able to see it. Jubal," Joie appealed to her brother. "You know I'm right. I'm always right. There's a network of caves, most of them unexplored, and we're right on top of it."

Okay, not a little crazy. Joie was certain she'd already begun her descent into madness. She'd rather be with that voice in her head than with any real person in the world. She lived to hear that voice. She thought about him day and night, had become consumed by him.

Joie lifted her chin a little defiantly and reached for him—her imaginary friend who was fast becoming an imaginary lover.

I'm proving you don't exist so I can get over you. I have a list of would-be lovers a mile long, and I'd like to have a little fun for a change.

You're too close. I can feel you. You have to leave. This mountain is dangerous.

Joie frowned, studying the snow-capped rock face. She

was so close to the hidden entrance. So close. The mountain needed to breathe, a soft sigh of air and she would have it.

Of course you would say that. You don't want me to know you aren't real. She stepped to her left, skirting around an outcropping. She could feel the entrance now. Her body responded, excited. Eager. And it had *nothing* to do with him. *Look, honey, it's been fun, but we have to break up. I can't have a mythical lover, even if you're an awesome lover in my dreams. A girl wants to have the real thing once in a while. It isn't like I can introduce you to my family. Hey, guys, this is my invisible pal, Traian. He has a name like a locomotive, but that's my fantastic imagination.*

Traian is a very old and respected name.

She heard the amusement seep into his voice, but it was still very strained and a terrible urgency to get to him fast took seed in her heart.

Go away from here, Joie. I will not comment on your name, as it would be considered extremely rude.

Comment away, Traian. You're not real and neither is this conversation, so insult me all you want.

"You're always looking down when you should be looking up, Joie," Gabrielle said with a sigh. "If you reach straight up, you might be able to catch a cloud. Have you even noticed the flowers? They're gorgeous. I wish I knew what they were called. For once in your life, think of something besides caves." She waved her arms to encompass the countryside. "This is Dracula country. If you'd forget your obsession with caves, we might be able to explore the old castles for a change."

The flowers that are pink with a yellow middle are called Tratina. The white daisies are Marguarete. I cannot remember offhand what the blue ones are called, but it will come to me.

Are you eavesdropping on our conversation?

You are thinking loudly—and denying my existence—which seems to be a habit of yours lately.

Joie gave a little sniff. He was a figment of her imagination and he knew the names of the flowers. She glanced over her shoulder at her sister.

"Gabrielle, the pink ones are *Tratina*, and the white daisies are *Marguarete*. I have no idea what the blue ones are called."

"You're a walking encyclopedia," Gabrielle said, impressed.

"That should teach you to tell me I have no interest in anything but caves," Joie said. She shivered, although she was dressed for the cold. There was just something a little off about the place and a part of her felt as if they needed to get off the mountain fast. She glanced up at the sky. Maybe there was a storm coming.

Jubal stared at the wild countryside surrounding them, on either side and below. There were many deep gorges and several caves. Green valleys and plateaus made the view breathtaking. Below them, in the heavier depressions, water had soaked the ground, causing peat bogs. There were vivid green beds of moss and numerous shallow ponds winding their way around stands of birch and pine. The area was magical, and yet Jubal was uneasy. The air was crisp and cold and the sky seemed clear, yet a strange mist covered the surfaces above them. At times he thought something moved in the mist, something alive and terrifying.

He studied the towering heights rising above them. They were halfway up the mountain and the mist seemed to be slowly descending. If they were caught out in the open, they had the equipment to spend the night, but it would be a nasty night.

"Joie, give it up and let's get out of here," he said. "This place feels haunted to me. I don't like the vibes."

Gabrielle turned her head to stare at her brother. "Really, Jubal?" She arched a winged brow at him. "That's strange, because I feel exactly the same way—like we shouldn't be here, or that we're intruding in some way. Do you suppose it's all the vampire stories we were listening to at the inn last night that's made both of us jumpy? Normally, creepy stories are amusing, but I definitely feel apprehensive." She raised her voice. Her younger sister had moved around the outcropping and appeared to be examining another limestone boulder jutting out of the side of the mountain. "What about you, Joie? Does this place give you the creeps?"

"We came here to explore the caves," Joie said firmly. "We're always very respectful when we're on the mountain and never leave anything behind, so there's no reason to be nervous. The mountain gods have no reason to be angry with us, if there are such things. I know the opening is here. I'm feeling it very strongly. I know I'm close."

Joie ran her hand up a long crack and then walked carefully back around the outcropping of the mountain, stepping over her brother's outstretched legs without even glancing at him. Her heart began to pound, a sure sign that she was close. She closed her eyes and tried to image the opening, to "feel" her way with her mind. Her obsession was growing stronger and with it, the conviction that this was the place.

"The entrance is here, I know it is," she muttered aloud.

The others feel the threat of the vampires. You must go, Joie. Traian's voice came to her softly in warning, slipping into her mind, bringing with it an ominous chill.

Oh, now you're going to tell me you believe in vampires. I just picked up that thought from Gabrielle. You aren't real, so be quiet and stop trying to frighten me away. I'm not leaving until I know for certain. She was not buying a vampire story to scare them all away.

You already know; you just cannot admit the truth. I am trapped and will not be able to rescue you should you come upon them.

"Rescue me?" Joie nearly shouted the words, her eyes flashing with indignation. She turned her head to smile in reassurance at her brother and sister.

Gabrielle and Jubal exchanged a long, amused glance, used to Joie and her ramblings when she was on the scent of a new cave. Few people were as adept as their youngest sibling at discovering magical worlds below the surface.

Rescue me? She hissed it into his mind. *You can just bite me, Traian. Do you have any idea how annoying it is for someone like me to be treated like a ditzy little woman who can't fend for herself?* The trouble with arguing with the voice in her head, Joie decided, was trying to determine whether it was all imagination or real.

I would not mind biting you. This time his voice purred with sexual innuendo. *But another time would be better. Seriously, I'm in some trouble and if you managed, by some fluke to actually join me, I am not certain I could adequately protect your party from harm.*

Joie shivered in spite of herself, yet heat curled deep inside her. *If you keep this up, my brother and sister are going to figure out I'm crazy and have me committed. Then where will you be?* Strands of dark hair blew across her face, hiding her expression from her siblings.

And just for your information, Sir Galahad, I am not the "in need of rescue" type, so get over that one fast. Sheesh. First it's vampires and now it's rescuing. Will you just be quiet and let me figure this out? I don't suppose you want to tell me, give me a hint or two, if you're really down there and know where the opening is.

Jubal leaned back in the tall grass with his hands behind his head, studying the cloud formations. The mist had begun to reach them, long streaming tendrils that looked as if giant hands were reaching for them. A few of the thicker streams had dropped low and looked almost as if they were winding their way around Joie's legs as she made her way back around the outcropping, drawn again and again to the same place.

"You're like a hound dog on the scent of a criminal, Joie," he said, narrowing his eyes, watching the snake-like ribbons of mist. "You would have made a great detective."

"She would have," Gabrielle agreed with a little grin. She concentrated on the bright blue flowers with their symmetric petals, lying on her back waiting for her sister to call it a day. The beautiful masses of flowers were unusual, yet something sinister seemed to lie beneath the ground, just inches from the soft petals, an obscene, malicious presence.

The wind rushed over the mountainside. The flowers shook, some closing quickly. Gabrielle gasped and drew her feet up. She sat up quickly, blinking rapidly.

"What is it?" Jubal asked.

"I don't know. For a moment I thought I saw something moving beneath the soil. I know this sounds crazy, Jubal but the soil rose up an inch or so as if something alive tunneled beneath it." She looked around her, noting the mist streaming down toward them. "This place definitely gives me the creeps."

"Joie, come on. We're getting out of here," Jubal decided, reaching a long arm to gather their gear. "The sun will be down in a couple of hours anyway."

Joie examined every inch of the outcropping and the niche on either side. The rock was grown over with scrub and grasses. Wildflowers lifted their bright heads toward the diminishing sun as if soaking up the last of the rays.

Joie narrowed her gaze and stepped up as close as possible to the large outcropping, focusing completely on the jutting surface and every crack and shadow. "I've never felt so driven in my life. I don't think I can leave without finding it," she admitted honestly. "I'm sorry—if you two want to take off, go ahead. I'll come along as soon as I can."

Jubal and Gabrielle exchanged a long, knowing look. "Sure thing, sis, we'll just leave you up here all by yourself. Knowing you, you'd disappear into a cave and mate with a troll," Gabrielle said. "Just like Mom is always saying is going to happen."

"Ha ha," Joie answered, the frown still on her face as she studied the outcropping.

"What's the name of this mountain range?" Jubal asked idly, but his gaze was on Joie as she scanned the rock surface. "The bogs are even beautiful. If it wasn't so freaky up here, I could live in this area." When Gabrielle arched a black eyebrow at him, he laughed. "I could. I don't need to live in a city. I've got the same genes as the two of you. I just like to have money, you know. I need it for the two of you, to bail you out of all the trouble you get into."

"You idiot," Joie said affectionately, although she didn't look at him. "You have enough money to retire from that silly job of yours and do something useful with your life. Something *humanitarian*. There's a small crack running the length of the rock here. There's something funny about this, Jubal, come look at it. It just isn't right the way it is and you're exceptionally good with puzzles."

"My *humanitarian* contribution to the world is looking after you two thrill seekers," Jubal pointed out as he got lazily to his feet. "Without me to curb your antics, the world would be a frightening place." He looked up at the strange, moving mist. "Rather like this place." He sauntered slowly over to examine the surface of the outcropping.

"We're in the Apuseni Mountains, part of the Carpathians, you heathen," Gabrielle informed her brother. "If you paid even the slightest attention to anything we said, you'd know that. And you could no more give up your luxury condo and live in the mountains than you could swim the English Channel. And, I might add, we take care of you."

"Here," Joie said triumphantly. "I feel the cave's breath on my face. It's here. I just can't figure out how to get in."

"Hey! I can swim," Jubal objected. He ran his hand over the rocks, frowning as he did so. "Just because I don't like to swim doesn't mean I can't. I wasn't born with gills like the two of you. She's found something, Gabrielle. This is a pattern, but it needs to be . . ." He trailed off, dug his fingers around several of the smaller rocks, and began to rearrange them.

"There's a surprise," Gabrielle said and rose to her feet also. The cool mountain air fairly vibrated with excitement. "You could always come and research hot viruses with me," she invited, slinging her arm around her brother.

"Yeah, I'll get right on that, Gabrielle, because I'm a crazy man and want to die a miserable, but noble, death," Jubal said, ruffling his sister's dark hair. "I think I'll stick to my stocks and bonds and let you do your wacko research all by yourself."

"Feel that," Joie spun around to face her brother. "The mountain is exhaling into the cave's entrance."

Jubal nodded in satisfaction. "There it goes. Wow, look at that. As usual, Joie finds the entrance and this one is damned strange."

The mountain shivered. Creaked. He placed the last rock in the sequence he saw as a pattern. The crack widened, the rock grinding with a loud groan. Ice cold air rushed out as if the mountain had exhaled.

"This is man-made, not natural. Damn it, Joie, don't go

in." He snagged his backpack and pulled out a logbook, carefully entering the time. "We're just doing a cursory exploration, and it's nearly sunset. No one knows where we are."

It was too late. Joie was too driven to wait for anything, ignoring the time-honored rules they always followed for safety. She squeezed into the crack, dragging her gear behind her.

Cursing, Jubal hastily anchored the logbook near the crack with a couple of rocks, marking the entrance for a rescue team to find should they get lost inside the network of caves he was certain they were about to descend into.

Gabrielle shouldered her gear and followed. "It's extremely tight, Jubal," she cautioned. "Pass me your gear; it's the only way you're going to get through."

Jubal took one last look at the sky, noting that the clouds that had been floating so lazily overhead were spinning ominously, a gathering of a great force. Mist now shrouded the entire upper half of the mountain, looking for all the world like a great white veil slowly being drawn over the entire towering mass. They were in the clouds, cut off from below. The mist had gone beneath them as well, searching out the lower fields, covering their descent, the weather turning on them fast.

Resolutely, Jubal pushed into the jagged crack, his chest scraping against the limestone as he forced his larger body into the narrow hall.

Behind him the wind rose in a sudden shriek, lashing at the mountain, while strange, haunting cries echoed off the peaks. Mist swirled around the mountaintop, a mini tornado that snatched the logbook and sent it skittering down the hillside to land in one of the many bogs, where it slowly sank beneath the dark waters.

The mountain groaned, rocks creaking. The floor beneath their feet trembled, shuddered and rippled with sudden life.

"Hold on," Jubal called to his sisters. "Earthquake."

They all reached to grab any hold they could. Joie found a couple of finger pockets to stick her fingers in and hoped that terrible dread filling her stomach didn't mean the passage itself would shift and narrow. Gabrielle placed her fist into a tight fist jam with one hand and braced herself with a flat palm with the other, biting her lip, afraid the ceiling would cave in. Jubal had to use an under-cling, praying the floor wouldn't drop from beneath him as the ground shook.

Outside the passage, the rocks rolled away from the outcropping, settling into a random pile of innocent-looking stones just at the base of the slowly narrowing crack. The grinding of rock echoed through the cave, a terrible ominous sound that reverberated down the tight passage. Darkness settled into the entryway of the cave and the siblings immediately switched on the lights built into their helmets.

Joie moved quickly through the narrow hall, well ahead of her brother and sister. The ceiling dropped with every foot, so she was forced to bend over, eventually crawling on all fours and then sliding on her stomach.

"It's tight here, Jubal," she called back to her brother. The sense of urgency driving her was tempered by the building knots in her stomach. The cave didn't feel right to her.

Normally, caves were a place of absolute wonder. Fascinating, mysterious, the last frontier for those like Joie, who needed to walk where no one else had gone, to discover things and see things no one else had dared to see.

Around her, the coolness of the rock called to her; the steady sound of water streaming from numerous cracks and the sudden chasms plunging into darkness below added to the surreal experience of pushing through a tight crevice on her stomach. She wiggled through until she could feel the cool air coming from a subterranean chamber.

Just up ahead was a perfect tube where powerful, swirling

water had blasted through the limestone for hundreds of years, carving an opening. She entered it without hesitation, ignoring the flashing warning sign deep in her stomach. Hard knots coiled tighter, becoming the herald of dark dread. Everything inside her demanded she keep going, even when she had to maneuver her body at odd angles to slither through the tunnel.

"Slow down, Joie," Jubal cautioned. "Stay within sight of us."

"I don't like the way she's acting," Gabrielle whispered. "I've never seen her like this. She always obeys the safety rules, you know that, Jubal. Something is really wrong." She felt sick, her stomach churning, her mind filled with a terrible trepidation. "Something terrible is going to happen if we don't stop her."

Jubal waited, but Gabrielle didn't move; she remained wedged in the narrow hall, blocking him from continuing. "Keep going, Gabrielle," he said. "We'll catch up to her and talk sense to her. She's been caving for years. She's not going to forget everything she's ever learned."

"Ever since she was hurt in Austria, she's been different," Gabrielle pointed out. "Distracted. Driven."

"She's always very focused when she's going into a cave. And this is a big discovery, an unexplored cave. We have no idea what we're going to find. Of course she's excited."

"You know it isn't just that; she's been different this entire trip. Even before that. She's quieter. Joie isn't quiet. Now she seems to be somewhere else half the time. I feel like we're losing her, Jubal—as if something is pulling her into another world where we can't follow."

Jubal sighed loudly. "I wish I could say I don't know what you mean, but that's why I came on this trip. I've been worried about her too." He reached out and pushed at his sister. "Move it. I can't even hear her now."

"I can't move, Jubal." Gabrielle sounded scared. "I really can't."

"Are you stuck?" Jubal was very calm, but inside that insidious dark dread was stealing over him.

"No," Gabrielle whispered. "I just can't move. Have you ever heard the term 'paralyzed with fear'? I think I really am."

"Gabby," Jubal said, his voice very quiet. "What are you afraid of?"

"I don't know. Joie's acting so out of control and . . . can't you *feel* it? The cave doesn't want us in here. Listen to the sound of the water. The cave feels evil, Jubal."

"You're letting your imagination get the better of you, Gabrielle. Just take a breath. You're not claustrophobic and you're not superstitious. If Joie's in trouble, we have to help her. The only way we're going to do that is to stick with her and get her through this."

"I'm trying," Gabrielle said, pushing with her toes in an effort to break the paralysis.

Joie pushed forward as the ceiling lifted, allowing her to walk once again. Eventually the hall opened into a large chamber.

"Hey, you two, it's much better in here. There's a large gallery." She shone her light around the area, noting the finger-like formations surrounding a large abyss that yawned in the middle of the chamber. "Looks like a cathedral in here. Ice balls have formed everywhere here and the sculpted ice is fantastic below, layered in blues and greens."

She peered down into the seemingly bottomless abyss, her heart drumming hard, a breathless anticipation, half for the discovery of a cave no one had walked in and half about a mythical man who refused to go away.

"Ice stalagmites are in abundance, Gabrielle, they're everywhere on the floor, but that means the temperature here goes above freezing. We're going to have to be careful," she called back over her shoulder, all the while study-ing the deep hole.

The allure of the unknown was always on her when she came into a cave. The idea that she might be where no one had ever been was a feeling indescribable and she rarely tried putting it in words. She *had* to explore the unknown. She was driven to do so. She had acquired a good reputa-tion and many countries allowed her permits to explore and map caves. She often brought out samples for researchers. That was Gabrielle's department, not hers, but she assisted her whenever she could.

"There's a few ice boulders here, scattered around the top. I'm going to dislodge them. We can't have that kind of threat hanging over us when we descend." She used her ice pick to clear away as many of the boulders as she could. Occasion-ally she could hear the cracks and creaks that told her the ice was weighing itself down and the pressure could send a large piece bursting forth like a rocket, to hurl itself across the empty space with enough force to kill one of them.

"Hurry up, Jubal," she called. "What's the hold-up?"

"Gabby's having to take a moment. Just relax, Joie. Take a breath while I talk her through it."

She *couldn't* wait. Every cell in her body screamed at her to hurry. There was little time. The urgency settled deep into the middle of that terrible cloud of dread she couldn't stop. She climbed into her rigging as she struggled to hold on to reality. *He* needed her. Something was terribly wrong. She had to get to him fast.

"Gabrielle! Jubal! I'm going to begin my descent." Joie tested her harness and glanced back toward the tube. "Gabrielle! Jubal! Are you two okay?"

"Wait for us, Joie," Jubal ordered. "Gabrielle has a bad feeling about this and so do I. I'm thinking we should regroup for a few minutes and talk this over. This could be more trouble than we want."

Joie fought back hysterical laughter that bubbled up out of nowhere. "Talk it over? Nobody's in more trouble than I am right now, Jubal. I can't turn back. I have to make this descent or go live in a padded cell for the rest of my life. I am not kidding you."

Jubal caught at Gabrielle's leg. "She isn't joking; she sounds on the verge of hysteria."

"I can't," Gabrielle began to cry.

"Move your ass. Right now," he ordered Gabrielle, and then raised his voice to make certain his youngest sister could hear him. "Joie, don't you *dare* start that descent without us. You stay right where you are until we get there. If you don't listen to me, I'm going to haul your ass back to the surface and take you out of here."

Jubal rarely used that tone with either of his independent sisters, but it had the desired effect. Gabrielle scooted forward, driven by the fact that her brother obviously shared her growing fears for Joie.

Shaken, Joie pulled back from the abyss, shocked at herself that she would have started without Gabrielle and Jubal. She always put safety first. *Always.* She was an expert climber and caver. It made no sense that she was acting so insane. She was in dangerous territory. An unexplored ice cave was a disaster waiting to happen for anyone not paying attention to what they were doing.

She pressed her fingertips to her eyes, taking in great gulps of air, trying to find a balance. She couldn't risk the lives of her brother and sister. She knew they'd come exploring with her because they were concerned about her. She was just as worried as they were for her sanity.

Joie. You must listen to me. You and your siblings are in

mortal danger. There is evil here and you must leave before it is too late.

She drew in her breath sharply. There he was again—her mythical man. His voice was commanding. Firm. His tone held absolute conviction. But it also held pain. He was somewhere down below her suffering. She could feel him close to her. He needed her, whether he wanted to admit it or not. He *needed* her. She had been on rescue teams many times, even led a few herself, but this was different. Whatever his injuries, they hadn't been sustained in a climbing accident.

His fear for her—for all of them—beat at her, impossible to ignore. Joie sat on the edge of the precipice, staring down into the black abyss. The walls of ice belled outward away from any rope, creating a free rappel. It would be difficult to slow down. They'd have to work to control speed on their descent on an ice-slick rope. Jubal and she both were expert at handling a descent bobbin, but Gabrielle might have a little more trouble. She didn't look up when her brother and sister joined her.

Jubal rested his hands on her shoulders. He took a long slow look around the large chamber, shining his light up along the vaulted ceilings and studying the edges of the abyss to assess their safety should they choose to make the descent.

"Joie," he said, as gently as possible. "You're going to have to talk to us. We have to know what's going on with you. Exploring caves is something we all enjoy together, we have for a lot of years, since Mom and Dad rigged harnesses for us when we were toddlers. But this isn't fun. It isn't even safe and I think you know that. We're willing to follow you and help you any way we can, but we have to understand what's going on."

Gabrielle sat cautiously beside her and took her hand.

"So tell us. We'll help. We always stick together. There's no need to hide anything from us."

There was a small silence. Finally Joie sighed, her shoulders sagging. She had to tell someone—and besides—she owed them an explanation. "Does insanity run in the family?" Joie continued to stare down into the well of darkness. "Because if it does, someone should have warned us."

"You think you're insane?" Jubal struggled to understand. Joie was the one who laughed all the time, who found humor in everything. She lit up the world with her smile, and she certainly never seemed to suffer from depression.

"I hear voices. Well . . ." she hedged, "*a* voice. One voice. Mostly at night or in the early morning hours. We have conversations. Long conversations. Sometimes very intense and sometimes humorous." She felt the color rise beneath her skin and was grateful it was dark in the gallery. "Sometimes sexy. I find myself staying up all night just to be able to hear his voice and spend time with him." She shrugged her shoulders. "He even has a name. Traian Trigovise. How could I think up a name like that? I've never even heard of a name like that. He has an accent—a European, very sexy accent. He'd old world and charming and I can't stop obsessing over him."

Gabrielle tightened her fingers around Joie's hand. "When did this start? When did you first hear this voice?"

Joie shrugged, remaining silent. Neither Jubal nor Gabrielle spoke, waiting her out. Finally she sighed again, hating to admit when the voice had first begun. She knew what they would think, but to her, he was real and he was in trouble. She *had* to find him.

"When I was shot in Austria. You know how much I hate hospitals. When they took me there, I did my little disappearing act." She looked at her brother and sister briefly and then away again. "It isn't as if I didn't consider that I was dreaming when I first saw him—you know feeling the effects of the anesthesia, but it's so much more than that."

She stole another quick look at both of her siblings. She had their attention and clearly they were trying to understand.

"I've practiced astral projection for a long time. Remember all the stories I told you as a child about flying?"

"In your dreams," Gabrielle said.

Jubal shook his head in warning. "Keep talking, Joie."

"I guess I really succeeded. It really happened. This has to be real. I think we connected because we'd both been in a storm, in a battle and wounded at the same time." She shrugged helplessly. "It's the only reasonable explanation to me. He didn't go away. I could hear him talking to me in my mind. He found something important in the caves. I was already planning a trip here with you two, so I figured I could see if he was real."

"Joie," Jubal reprimanded gently. "Telepathic communication? With someone else? I know we can use telepathy, but we've never met anyone else who can."

"Is it really that far-fetched? I can take myself somewhere else. I know when I'm in danger. You're weird with patterns, and Gabrielle can do all sorts of strange things. We're all able to use telepathy with each other. Is it such a stretch to believe others can use it, too? I have to go down there. I have to know if he's real, if he's here, in this place. I feel him. I can't explain it, but it's like he's crawled inside of me somehow and I need him. I need to prove this to myself. And I'm afraid he's injured."

"Why didn't you tell us right away, Joie?" Jubal asked.

"Because I don't want the voice to go away," Joie admitted with stark truth. "I saw a counselor. He said I was having a break with reality, schizophrenia, probably brought on by the trauma of being shot. I didn't want to point out it wasn't the first time I've taken a bullet; it wasn't the worst injury and it won't be the last. I didn't take the medication the counselor prescribed. I thought maybe it wasn't so bad to live in a fantasy world part of the time. I still function and do my job." She managed a faint smile, her sense of humor rising even in the middle of such a serious conversation. "Do you think many people want a schizophrenic bodyguard? They get two for the price of one."

"Come on, Joie, you can't believe you're going crazy. You're . . ." Gabrielle paused in search of the right words. "You're *you*. You can do anything. You excel at everything. You *can't* hear voices. You're the most stable person I know. Out of your mind for loving this kind of thing, but still . . . stable."

Joie smiled up at her sister. "I'm definitely hearing a voice. Right now he's telling me to get out of here. He's saying it's dangerous and that we're all in mortal danger. He actually used the word *mortal*. I don't use that word. Do you think I have a split personality? I've always preferred male activities. I've always been such a tomboy. Maybe this is just my male side coming out. And just so you know how really screwed up my mind is, he's sexier than I am."

"Maybe your intuition is telling you not to make the descent, Joie," Jubal cautioned. "We haven't planned this out adequately."

"I don't have a choice," Joie said sadly. "Not this time. We have the rigging. We have the supplies. We're all dressed warmly enough. I can go down and look around. If I'm not back in a couple of hours, you can go for help."

"You didn't let me finish. If he isn't real, we should find out, and if he is real, logic would say we need to help him if he's hurt. Besides, we're a family and as Dad always says, 'in for a penny, in for a pound.' "

Gabrielle shook her head. "We all go. We stick together,

Joie. If you have to do this, then we do it together like we always have."

"Then we should stop talking and get moving," Jubal said decisively.

Joie wasn't going to change her mind. Whatever was compelling her into that black abyss was too strong to fight. Worse, the dread was still growing inside him. Jubal glanced down into the dark hole. Evil lurked close by, and he had the feeling they were going to come face to face with it.

Chapter Three

"Joie, this is out of this world," Jubal said softly, in awe. He turned in a full circle, shining his light on the walls of the gallery. The descent had been a long one, well over three hundred feet. "I've never seen anything like it. What a find. The ice formations are incredible. I swear I actually saw a vein of gold in more than one place. There are so many halls and galleries to explore."

The century-long hidden domain was breathtaking. Despite the urgency she was feeling, Joie allowed herself a brief moment of wonderment, looking around her into twisted corridors and tunnels, shadowed pools lined with gem-like crystals and a network of narrow crevices and grottoes. The gallery opened up into an entire underground world. If they hadn't found that strange crack allowing them inside, they would never have seen the sparkling world deep beneath the earth.

Small ice balls and ice draped the ceiling and walls, shimmering all hues of blue; steep slopes and wide outcroppings marked the magnificent gallery. Inside the subterranean world were peaks and crags, the ice forming mountains and valleys, ridges and gorges. Underground rivers were frozen after carving out tunnels and shapes. "Windows" gave glimpses of *moulins* deep beneath them.

Gabrielle cautiously moved around an ice sculpture that rose like a living flame from the floor. "Look at this. When I shine my light on it from this angle, I'd swear the thing had gems in it. It's as brilliant as a polished diamond but reflects the light as if it were red like a ruby."

Movement caught her attention, and she turned her head to watch Joie as she examined the glacial ice that formed the gallery. "Be careful, I suspect that a good number of viruses previously unknown to us come from insects and even perhaps the fungi in caves such as this one. These microorganisms exist with no light and few nutrients, locked inside the ice, yet still capable of living. There's such a wealth of information down here." She gave Joie a quick, excited grin. "No one has probably ever touched this ice. Can you imagine the microbes living down here? This is a scientist's dream."

Joie took a long breath and let it out, looking around at each of the tunnels leading to other chambers. She was so close now, she could almost feel him breathing. Somewhere in this labyrinth of halls he was waiting for her. Smoldering. Angry that she had disobeyed him and put herself and her siblings in danger. He was real, not a voice in her head, not a part of a split personality. He was real and alive and in pain. She could feel his pain, throbbing through her body, beating at her head.

Tell me. She demanded it. Forced him to deal with who she really was, not who he thought she should be.

Tell the others to be quiet. They are in danger. I have battled the same enemy three times since you first found me in the cave weeks ago. I am a prisoner and wounded and extremely weak. I cannot aid you much in the battle, and the enemy has powers you cannot possibly comprehend.

Joie pressed her lips together, her heart suddenly pounding. His tone rang with truth. He believed in what he was saying. Joie tended to keep her cool with humor. She gave him a mental image of rolling her eyes in exasperation.

Sorry for the fluff in my head, but I'm usually found wrapped in cotton or bubble wrap to protect me from all the evil people in the world.

"Jubal, Gabby, we have to be quiet. Something's in here with us and it isn't good."

She took the lead and Jubal dropped back to protect his sisters, neither sibling asking questions. They knew Joie, knew she was good at her job and she had switched easily into hunter/protector mode. She trusted Jubal. He was the steadiest man she knew in a fight, and she worked with a lot of good men.

"Tell us what's happening, Joie," Jubal demanded.

She shook her head and placed a finger to her lips. "He's telepathic. I don't want to chance communication he might overhear until we know what's really going on." She mouthed the words to her brother and sister and waited for them to nod in understanding before she continued. *She* was ready to trust the stranger in her head, but she wouldn't risk Gabrielle and Jubal without knowing what they were getting into.

There were several halls and tubes leading away from the open gallery they had descended into. She moved slowly to stand in front of each to feel her way. The pull of Traian was strong and she knew the moment she was at an entrance that he was somewhere in that direction. Using hand signals, she started down the hall, as stealthy as one could in climbing gear. The long hallway continued forward but two other tunnels branched off from it, one leading down and the other appearing to climb upward. The pull to go down was strong.

Joie, Traian's voice seemed weaker. *I'm asking you one*

last time to get out of here. You're risking your life and the lives of your companions.

She moved through the halls with confidence, recognizing the feel of him now, knowing she was moving toward him. She picked up the pace, although she remained very conscious of the layers of ice surrounding them. The walls appeared thick, but they creaked and cracked, loud popping noises signaling ice falling or shooting out of the walls from the weight above them.

I doubt very much if I'll need your aid, Mr. Brawny, but I'll keep it in mind. How many?

Traian sighed, obviously unwilling to argue with her anymore. Worse, she felt his strength draining away and had to fight the need to run to him.

There is one with me now. The others will return well fed and high with a lust for killing.

Joie didn't like the sound of that. Lust for killing held very bad implications. *Could you be exaggerating just a little?* She desperately hoped he was.

You do not want to meet them.

Joie gave a little sniff, her heart slamming hard just once at his tone. He wasn't joking about his enemies. She took a deep breath and let it out. *Isn't that the truth. Anyone with a lust for killing isn't going to be invited for Sunday dinner.*

She glanced back at her brother and sister, frowning, suddenly afraid for them. What was she getting them all into with her obsessive behavior? She hesitated at the next twisting tunnel. He was so close now, and so was danger. She felt it and she could tell Gabrielle felt it as well. Her sensitive sister pressed her hand hard into her stomach and had a look of fear stamped on her face. Behind her, Jubal had produced a gun, his features hard-edged and sober. They would stand with her, back her up under any circumstances, but she didn't feel it was right to force them—through their love of her—into a dangerous and unknown situation.

"Let me go in alone, figure out what's wrong and . . ." She began, mouthing the words rather than speaking them aloud or telepathically. She still didn't want Traian to be privy to her private conversation with her siblings and she didn't know how strong his psychic abilities were—but he felt powerful. *She* had to find the man, but she didn't trust strangers with her siblings' lives.

Jubal held up his hand to stop her and indicated with a hand signal for her to proceed. She looked at Gabrielle's resolute expression. No, they weren't going to leave her. They were in it together, good or bad, they stood with her. She took a breath, nodded and stepped into the water-carved tunnel.

Bands of green and blue in wide circular stripes surrounded them and ordinarily would have had all three examining the beautifully constructed tube, but the moment they entered the hallway, all of them felt the presence of evil. Joie's mouth went dry. She touched her belt, assuring herself her knife was close at hand.

I guess I'd best pull your butt out of trouble and get the heck out of Dodge.

Traian sighed. *You do not act like any of the women I know.*

Thank you, I appreciate your saying so. Her stomach was in knots.

Evil permeated the narrowing hallway, so that every breath drawn in was foul, the air dense—thick with poisonous breath. The tunnel narrowed and the ceiling dropped considerably, making it impossible to walk upright. Joie dropped to her knees and crawled through the tube on her hands and knees. Jubal and Gabrielle followed close behind. The steady drip of water reminded Joie of the clicking of the branches at the theater the night she was shot. There was a peculiar rhythm to the drops, almost as if some unseen hand, not nature, guided the water's descent. The tube began to widen until she could once again stand.

A strange growling noise assaulted her ears, sounding like a cross between a hyena laughing and a dog growling viciously. Immediately she held up her hand behind her, signaling Jubal and Gabrielle to stop while she scooted closer. She used the tall columns of rock and ice formations as cover as she worked her way into a position to be able to see into the chamber.

A man—and it had to be Traian—was literally pinned like an insect to a wall of ice, his feet actually off the floor. Blood ran down from each shoulder and leg where sharp, twisted stakes had been thrust through his body. It was the most horrific form of torture she'd ever seen. Joie held her breath to keep from crying out in dismay. It was no wonder she could feel the pain radiating from him. Every movement of his body had to be excruciating. Who would do such a thing? And far beneath the earth in an ice cave, it was bizarre, unreal and too cruel.

She could see something that resembled a man—or at least had a man's shape—prodding at Traian's wounds with a bony finger, dipping it in blood and licking with a grotesque, purple tongue. A shudder ran through her body.

She forced herself to look at the terrifying apparition holding Traian prisoner. He was nearly as tall as Traian, but his body appeared skeleton-like, as if his skin had shrunk over bones. His clothes were filthy and tattered, thin strips of material that should never have been worn in an ice cave. The *thing*—she had no other name for it—had longish strands of hair sticking out haphazardly in all directions over his misshapen skull.

The thick perversion of evil emanated from the creature.

The apparition turned slightly and she could see the fingers ended in long, wicked-looking nails, almost like a bird's talons, very sharp and yellowed and stained. It was hard to control the pounding of her heart. She'd faced many human monsters, but this—this *thing*—was not human, at least not any more.

She knew Traian was aware of her presence, but he didn't make the mistake of giving away her position by so much as glancing toward her. He watched the creature hovering over him with cool eyes.

"You seem nervous, Lamont," Traian observed in a low, amicable tone. He sounded polite, almost friendly and just a little bit amused.

The creature hissed, a low, ugly expression of hatred. Without preamble he bent his head to Traian's neck and sank his teeth into the pulse beating there. Joie could easily see the long canines stabbing into flesh; something she'd only seen before in films. Her heart pounded so loud she was afraid the thing would hear the drumming even above the sound of water and cracking ice.

She dropped to the ground, crawling on her stomach, using her elbows to propel herself across the floor between two columns of ice to get into a better position for attack. She came up on her knees behind a large ice formation, her gaze fixed on her target. It took her a couple of tense moments to quiet her shaking hands. She'd been afraid many times in her life, but always—*always*—her body was as steady as a rock. Facing this hideous apparition, not knowing what it was or how to kill it, was quite frankly terrifying.

He is very dangerous, especially now when he is filled with the blood of an ancient. Traian's voice was calm in spite of the ghastly creature tormenting him. *He is very angry with me because I killed his master, Gallent.*

Joie stared at the hideous thing closely now that she could

see more of it, grateful for the steadying sound of Traian's voice in her head. The creature was tall and emaciated, the skin shrunken around its skull, almost as if it were dead. Tufts of hair stood straight out, a curious gray-white color, while the rest of the hair hung in oily, twisted ropes. He gulped down the blood, smearing it on his lips and stained teeth, all the while making growling noises in his throat. Definitely more animal than man.

My family always warned me if I hung out underground too long I could end up with a troll. At the risk of seeming shallow, I have to say he isn't very handsome and doesn't appeal at all to me. She was rather proud of the fact that she managed to sound amused instead of slightly hysterical, which was exactly how she felt.

Her hand went up to the back of her neck, sliding down between her shoulder blades in a well-practiced move, and came out with one of the knives she always carried.

The creature lifted his head alertly and looked around the large gallery with suspicious eyes. Joie froze, remaining motionless, hardly daring to breathe, praying her brother and sister wouldn't make a sound. They were still safe in the twisted tunnel, but Jubal would be worried by now. The cold air rushed through the chamber and touched Traian and the creature with icy fingers. Immediately Lamont caught at one of the stakes pinning his victim to the ice floe, pushing at it viciously.

"None of your tricks, ancient one. Your blood belongs to us now. The others will be back soon with a victim to force you to do our bidding. You are far too weak to resist."

Joie closed her eyes against the ripple of pain on Traian's face. She swallowed bile and forced air through her lungs. *What is he?*

He is vampire. The undead. And there are several more. You must get your family out before the others return.

Traian watched his tormentor intently. The vampire leaned close to the gaping wound in Traian's neck, his breath a sickly green vapor as he licked at the blood with a thick, dark tongue. "I just might kill you instead. A stake through the heart for what you did to my master." He lifted a lethal-looking stake over his head and gave a maniacal laugh.

Vampires are difficult to kill. You will only get one chance. Go for his heart.

Joie didn't dare hesitate. She didn't want to lose her nerve, or risk waiting and allowing the terrible creature to kill Traian. She threw the knife with deadly accuracy. It hummed as it rocketed across the chamber and buried itself deep in the vampire's chest. The creature screamed, the sound cracking the ice so that sharp daggers broke from the high ceiling and rained down like deadly missiles. Joie flung her body against Traian's, in an effort to protect him from the falling ice. The vampire went down hard, thrashing wildly, the sounds echoing through the cavern, and then there was sudden silence. Once again the sound of water was overloud in the chamber.

Joie moved back slowly, slipping a second knife from the scabbard on her calf. "That didn't look so difficult to me." She drew in a couple of deep, shuddering breaths and managed a small, tentative smile. "If you want, I'll give you a lesson or two."

"What took you so long?" Traian asked.

She made her way cautiously around him, kicking aside the bigger chunks of ice. "Bad directions. You know how traffic in these places can be." She leaned close to study one of the stakes slicing through his shoulder to hold him to the wall. "I hate to point this out to you, but you're in a bit of a mess. What was all that he-man macho crap telling me to stay away? If you ask me, you're in serious need of rescuing."

Joie! Answer me now, Jubal demanded.

I'm good. You'd better come in here, she assured him. How was she going to explain any of this to him?

Traian arched an eyebrow. His skin appeared pale, and he was clearly weak from loss of blood. Unattended wounds from a recent battle leeched away more of his precious life fluid. He shook uncontrollably, unable to maintain his body's temperature. His hair was black and matted with blood. "I am certain I would have thought of something. He has friends. They will be returning soon, and when they see him, they are not going to be happy. And if I do not incinerate his body immediately, he will rise again."

"Lovely thought," Joie said and turned to keep a wary eye on the repulsive corpse. "Lucky for you I travel with a doctor. My sister Gabrielle is quite mad, always peering into microscopes and lecturing us about how we're parasites on earth, but she does have certain skills."

Jubal entered, coming in low, gun in his fist, his features hard and determined. Gabrielle peered into the chamber and gave a soft cry when she saw Traian's bloody body. Immediately she started across the floor to him, but Jubal caught her arm, halting her.

"Explain." A single word. A command.

Joie did so quickly, stumbling over the word *vampire*. The creature lay on the floor, looking foul and scary, but her brother hadn't seen his teeth tearing into Traian's neck as she had. She pressed her lips together, watching Jubal closely.

"We have to hurry, Jubal," Gabrielle said. "He can't stay like that. He needs medical attention right now."

Joie noticed Traian didn't attempt to plead his case to either of her siblings, he was conserving energy and leaving her to do the explanations.

Gabrielle made the first move, her compassionate nature getting the better of her. She pushed past Jubal and, carefully avoiding looking at the vampire, stepped right up to Traian, studying the wicked stakes pinning him to the wall.

"You do know the strangest people, Joie," she murmured softly. "I don't even want to ask where you met him."

Does everyone in your family have the same weird sense of humor?

Joie nodded. *Pretty much. We've had to find humor in everything to get by. It's that or cry. Laughing is better.*

Gabrielle frowned and stepped closer. "I'm going to touch this. I'm sorry if it hurts you." Her fingers probed gently around the wound in his shoulder where the stake had gone through his body. "Jubal, you'll have to pull these out. They go all the way through and are buried pretty deep into the ice."

"If I pull out the stake, is he going to bleed to death?" Jubal inquired. He had followed Gabrielle into the middle of the chamber, but stopped beside the vampire, crouching down to study the undead. "This guy is twitching. I don't think he's dead."

"Twist the knife in deeper and cut out the heart. That will buy us a little more time," Traian suggested.

Jubal's gaze jumped to his face. "Are you kidding me?"

"No, he's going to rise again and soon. The only way to kill one permanently is to incinerate the heart." Traian closed his eyes, took a breath and slammed his body forward against the stakes holding him.

Blood oozed around each of the stakes and Gabrielle jumped back, nearly tripping over Joie. "Don't! You're going to make it worse. Jubal, you have to help us."

"You have to cut the heart out of his body and do not get any of his blood on you. It acts as an acid and burns through flesh and eventually bone."

Jubal's eyes met Traian's.

"If you cannot," Traian continued calmly, "then your sister must. That blood will eat through the blade and he will be free."

"I'll do it, Jubal," Joie said, her stomach churning madly. She wasn't certain she could find the courage to touch the hideous creature, not now that he was twitching.

"Like hell," Jubal said and grasped the hilt of Joie's knife, glancing back at Traian, over his shoulder. "But you had better be telling the truth. If you lay one finger on my sisters, I'll shoot you right between the eyes."

Sickened, Joie looked away from the black thick goo bubbling up around the blade of the knife to look once more at Traian.

"We have to get the stakes out of him one at a time," Gabrielle said. "I think we can do it, Joie. As soon as we do, I'll apply pressure and you'll have to find something to pack the wound to stop the bleeding. He can't afford any more blood loss."

"You'll have to pack it with a mixture of my saliva and any dirt you can find."

Gabrielle made a face, and pointed to her pack. "The first-aid kit is in my pack, Joie, but I don't know how we're going to get him to the surface." *I think he's in so much pain, Joie, that he's delusional. Saliva is not going to save him.*

Joie looked around the cave. "If there's dirt, it's under fifty feet of solid ice. It will have to be my shirt." She opened her jacket, stripped quickly down to her Patagonia tee shirt and quickly cut it into strips before retrieving the first aid kit.

When she would have put the cream onto the material, impatience crossed Traian's face. "I told you what to do, Joie."

"Do you really want your saliva on the strips?" Caught between Gabrielle and Traian, Joie didn't know what to do.

"Yes. My saliva will heal me faster. Hurry," Traian advised. "Or we are all going to die. Vampires are very dangerous and extremely hard to kill. You were lucky."

Joie hastily donned her jacket, zipping it up tight, and shoved the strips of cloth into his hand, his urgency catching at her. Clenching her teeth, she grasped the stake in his shoulder. "Are you ready for this?" The question was more for herself than for him. She glanced at Gabrielle, who nodded.

"Just do it."

Her stomach lurched as her fingers curled around the thick stake. She closed her eyes, took a breath and yanked. Traian grunted, his face going white. Tiny lines appeared around his mouth. Joie felt the stake slide a couple of inches out, so it was no longer stuck in the ice behind him, but it was still through his shoulder.

"Jubal, I need you." She looked over her shoulder at her brother.

"I'm trying," Jubal bit out between his teeth.

The moment she saw what he rolled across the floor, she was afraid she was going to vomit. A blackened, shriveled heart left a trail of smoking acid across the ice, etching a trail of dark gooey liquid into the floor of the chamber. Jubal stood up slowly, a grim expression on his face. He tossed the hilt of Joie's blade after the rolling heart. The metal was pitted and breaking just as Traian had warned what would happen.

"Did you get any of it on you?" Traian asked. "It will burn right to the bone."

Jubal shook his head. "I used her knife and mine to carve it out of his chest." There was distaste in Jubal's voice. He moved Joie out of his way and grasped the stake with both hands and yanked hard.

Blood spurted, but Gabrielle pressed her palms over the

wound hard. "Stuff that strip of material into the wound. Did you put antibiotic cream on it? He needs blood as quickly as possible."

Joie held the material up to Traian's mouth, ignoring Gabrielle's gasp. She stuffed the rag into his shoulder. Traian broke out into a sweat.

"There will be others. Try to go for the heart. You will not kill them unless the heart is incinerated. They are masters of illusion. They can shape-shift. Do not look them directly in the eyes and beware of any pattern. They can trap you with their voice. If one of you becomes trapped, break off all connection and no matter how difficult, leave them. You will not be able to save them."

Jubal grasped the second stake and yanked hard. Traian slumped forward before he could catch himself. The strain against his legs had to be excruciating. He gasped and caught Jubal's shoulder to steady himself.

"Keep talking," Jubal advised as Joie pressed the strip to Traian's mouth while Gabrielle applied pressure to the wound. "Tell us more."

Traian took a breath and righted himself. "I am sorry. They took a large amount of my blood and I am very weak."

"You don't have to apologize," Jubal pointed out, his hands already grasping the third stake while his sisters attended Traian's shoulder. "Just tell us what to expect."

"Wounds will slow them down, but not stop them. Attacking the heart buys you a few minutes at most, but it isn't permanent."

He indicated with his chin the blackened heart. To Joie's horror the shriveled organ rocked. With every movement, the vampire stirred, those long talons slowly unfolding, the bony fingers beckoning toward the heart.

Jubal swore. "Do bullets stop them?"

"They'll slow them down. You can't allow that heart near him."

Jubal yanked the third stake free and crossed the ice floor with long, deliberate strides. "Damn it, die already," he snapped as he slammed the stake through the middle of the pulsating organ, pinning it to the floor of the ice cave.

The vampire's mouth gaped open in a silent scream. He bared blood-stained, pointed teeth as he expelled his foul breath in a kind of promise of retaliation.

"Never show them emotion. They feed off of fear. They want adrenaline-laced blood. It gives them a bigger rush," Traian continued.

Jubal glared at him. "You might have considered the danger to my sister before you decided to lure her down here," he pointed out, grasping the last stake in Traian's leg. "How the hell could you live through this?"

"Just get it out," Traian instructed. "We really have to hurry."

"Do what he says, Jubal." Joie caught the sense of urgency emanating from Traian. Little white lines were etched around his perfectly sculpted mouth. "Vampire babe is beginning to find his legs." To her horror, the heart, even with the stake through the middle of it, was vibrating, wiggling back and forth as if slowly emerging from the rotted flesh. "Hurry—we may have a little problem with handsome. He seems to be coming back to life."

Joie's mouth went dry. No matter what Jubal had done, the creature kept coming back.

"Pack the last wound. Hurry," Traian instructed.

She didn't want to take her eyes off the ghoulish creature, but the dark compulsion in Traian's voice alarmed her; she obeyed, trusting her brother to keep an eye on the vampire while she and Gabrielle pushed the strip of cloth into the wound in an effort to stop the bleeding in the gaping holes in his flesh.

Jubal had his back to them, his eyes on the foul creature thrashing on the floor. Without warning, Traian reached out and dragged Jubal close to him, murmuring something Joie couldn't quite catch. He bent his head toward Jubal's exposed throat.

Gabrielle screamed and rushed to her brother's aid, but Traian lifted his hand and murmured something aloud, the words in a language she didn't know. Gabrielle stopped abruptly and stood absolutely still as if under a sorcerer's spell.

Fury burned through Joie. "You blood-sucking fiend! Let him go or you die. I'm not kidding you. Let him go or I'll tear your heart out. And don't try using your voice on me, because it won't work." As she hissed the words in a low, smoldering voice, she pulled her knife from the sheath strapped to her calf. At the same time, she tried to keep the vampire in sight.

"If I do not get blood, we are all going to die," Traian said calmly. "That is a fact. You need me to get all of you out of here and I need blood." He looked at her, his gaze steady and honest.

She let her breath escape between her teeth as she reached out and jerked Gabrielle away from him, thrusting her sister behind her. "Release them now."

"We have only minutes."

"Then don't waste time." Her hand didn't waver. Neither did her stare.

Traian spoke softly to Gabrielle and Jubal. Jubal jerked away from the man, drawing his gun as he did so. He put his arm around Gabrielle's. Tears swam in her eyes and she hid her face in his shoulder.

"For someone who is supposed to be so damned weak from blood loss, you felt strong enough to me."

I've never run across anyone with that kind of strength, Joie. If he gets any stronger and he turns on us, we're in serious trouble.

We're already in serious trouble, Joie pointed out.

She studied Traian. His expression hadn't changed at all, even with Jubal's gun and her knife. He just looked back with his steady expression.

"Tell us what's going on," Joie suggested. "It isn't as if we didn't witness the zombie man on the ground here, doing his sorry imitation of Dracula. You forgot to mention you're a little vampish yourself, dragging my brother to you and wanting to bite his neck."

"I am Carpathian, of the Earth, a species that has the unfortunate capability to turn wholly vampire. All the stories I told you were true when we had conversations at night. I did not make them up to entertain you. I lived the battles; they were not fiction. I need blood to survive, but we do not kill for sustenance. I have fought the vampire for hundreds of years." His voice was every bit as steady as his gaze. "This one will rise again, and he has friends. You cannot stop them, nor can I without blood to build my strength."

Jubal caught at Joie and tried to drag her backward, away from the wounded man when she took a step toward him. "This is bullshit, Joie."

"Take a look at Lamont and tell me I do not speak the truth," Traian said.

Joie held up her hand. "I have to believe him, Jubal. There's a terrible dread building in my stomach. I can feel others coming—can't you?" She handed her knife to her brother, ignoring her trembling hand. "If I'm making the biggest mistake of my life, I expect you to avenge me."

She made her way to where Traian remained slumped against the blue ice, pulling off her helmet as she did so. "Go for it, but remember, my brother can hit his mark every time, and if you're like these creatures, you taught us how to kill you."

Traian touched her then, circling her wrist with his long fingers and drawing her slowly, inexorably to him. Joie's heart skipped a beat, and then began to pound, whether in fear or excitement, she didn't know. She knew only that her mouth went dry and her insides were melting at an alarming rate. His eyes went dark, focused on her completely, shutting out everything else. Everyone else. He pulled her into the shelter of his large frame.

Joie felt his every muscle, hard, defined, rippling with power. He should have smelled of sweat and blood, but his scent was masculine, clean, inviting. Sexy. The world seemed to drop away. Danger didn't matter. His arms swept around her, held her close so that her heart beat with the same rhythm as his. She placed her hand over his chest, felt his heart beat strongly against her palm. She lifted her gaze to his and was instantly lost in the burning intensity she saw there.

There was a storm of emotion between them, a dark cauldron every bit as roiling and wild as the gale raging above ground. Mesmerized, she could only stare up at him. His fingertips brushed the hair from her neck—sent fire racing through her bloodstream. Where he had been businesslike and abrupt with Jubal, he was gentle, even tender as he enfolded Joie closer. He bent his head to hers.

Gabrielle made a small cry of protest, and stepped toward them with every intention of stopping him. Traian lifted his head, his eyes glowing with a strange fiery red, halting her in her tracks. His eyelids drifted down, his arm curling around Joie possessively so that she nearly disappeared from sight, completely engulfed in his embrace.

There was something very protective, yet predatory, in his posture.

His lips barely skimmed over Joie's skin. She felt it. A brush of butterfly wings, no more, yet that slight touch sent heat spreading through her body. He kissed her eyes until she closed them. Sensations increased. He whispered to her, in her mind an intimate, soft litany of words in an ancient tongue.

"Te avio päläfertiilam." The seductive ancient language wrapped her in velvet, an erotic spell of enchantment she willingly embraced.

Joie felt his breath warm on her neck. His tongue swirled over her pulse. Once. Twice. Her entire body clenched, every muscle contracting breathlessly. Waiting. Wanting. His lips feathering over her neck sent heat pooling low, and her legs went weak. One arm, of its own accord, slid upward to curl around his head, to draw him closer, cradle him to her. White-hot lightning pierced her skin and sent whips of lightning dancing in her bloodstream, a pleasure bordering on pain. Nothing had prepared her for the sheer erotic fire coursing through her body. A soft moan escaped her. She moved restlessly against him.

Traian pulled her closer, imprinting his body against hers, feeling every lush curve and soft, rounded line. *Lifemate.* He had waited so long. Endured so much. There was no shield providing her with a protective barrier. She knew exactly what he was doing and yet she accepted him, accepted his need for her blood. That rich life-giving liquid rushed through his body with the force of a freight train; his shrunken, starving cells soaked it up; tissue and muscle and damaged organs demanded sustenance. He wanted to savor the moment, savor his first taste of her, his first touch on her skin.

Even as Traian struggled for sufficient control to blur the

horrified gazes of her siblings, he was aware of the undead struggling to rise again and at least two vampires rushing through the maze of halls to reach him before he could escape. He took from Joie only what he needed to have strength when the battle came. He couldn't risk her being too weak to defend herself. They would have more than one skirmish with the undead before they were out of the labyrinth of caves.

Very gently, almost reverently, he swept his tongue across the pinpricks to close and heal her skin. "Thank you, Joie." His arms held her up, his body taking her weight.

She shivered as she lifted her lashes to study his face. At once she was caught and held in the dark depths of his eyes. "You're welcome."

"I hate to break up the love fest the two of you are having," Jubal snapped, "but we've got a little problem. The stake just fell out of the dead thing's heart. It's rocking, which is gross, by the way, and he's beginning to crawl around. With a big hole in his chest and black acid dripping everywhere, it isn't a pretty sight."

Jubal's voice broke the spell Traian seemed to have woven around Joie. She pulled her gaze away with an effort and looked over at the creature clawing the floor of the cave in desperation, looking for his shriveled heart.

"He looks angry," she observed.

Chapter Four

"Lamont is not the only one," Traian agreed. "His friends are coming this way fast, and they have murder on their minds."

He had to get Joie and her siblings to safety. The network of caves was a huge maze. How was he going to quickly explain a concept to them they all found impossible to believe? He looked at Joie. She was a miracle to him, an impossibility, just like the vampires and his need of blood must seem to them—as if they were caught in a nightmare and he was caught in a dream.

The vampire struggled to a half-sitting position on the floor, black blood and spittle running down his chin. His red-rimmed eyes fixed on Joie with a mixture of hate and fear. Long fingernails dug into the ice and he dragged himself another inch toward the blackened heart, all the while staring directly at Joie.

Traian's heart jumped, and then began to accelerate. He tasted fear in his mouth. Apprehension was alien to him, an emotion he hadn't felt in hundreds of years. Now, with the vampire silently vowing revenge on the one woman who mattered to him, Traian found dread filling him. Of all places for his lifemate to show up—in a labyrinth of caves when he was drained of his enormous strength—with a brother and sister in tow. He'd searched centuries for her and when he was at his most vulnerable, she appeared. Fate was a terrible jokester.

Joie! Do not look at him directly like that. It is easy to become ensnared.

She pulled her gaze away with an effort. "What the hell did you do to my knife, you fiend? Do you have any idea what a blade like that costs?" She held out her hand to Jubal for the knife she had given him. "Give that to me. I think I'm going to need it."

The vampire snarled, spraying foul blood across the ice, where it burned deep. His fiery eyes promised a vicious revenge.

Gabrielle gasped and covered her face. "I want to go, Joie. I'm not like you and Jubal. I can't do this."

Jubal immediately put his arm around her. "We'll get out of here, honey." He looked at Traian. "Can you kill it? We've got matches in our pack, so we can set the thing on fire."

Gabrielle made a sound of horror in the back of her throat. "We're going to burn it alive?"

"We have to do something," Joie said, taking a step toward the creature.

Traian swept her firmly behind him with a strong arm. She was worried about her sister and feeling guilty that she'd brought her siblings into such a dangerous situation, but he couldn't allow her to place herself into danger when he could kill the foul creature. He signaled to Jubal and Gabrielle to move away from the vampire. They did so carefully.

Lamont continued to make hideous noises, his talons cutting deep gouges into the ice. The blackened heart wriggled and rolled a couple of inches toward the outstretched hand.

Jubal handed his sister the knife. "Let's get out of here

while we can. I don't think I want to meet any more of these things."

"I'm going to pretend I never met this one," Gabrielle said firmly. She shuddered, and took a deep breath. "Just do it. If we're going to kill the thing, do it fast please."

Traian nodded and stepped in front of all three of them. Joie watched him closely. He seemed to be gathering something unseen into his hands. She could feel the buildup of energy in the chamber. The gallery was actually warming, increasing the dripping of the water dramatically. Between Traian's palms, light glowed, a bright orange-red, emitting heat. It appeared just smaller than a basketball, the energy coiling and spinning.

The vampire screamed in rage and attempted to rise, desperate to attack the hunter. When he couldn't make it to his feet, he threw himself forward across the floor of thick ice, and reached for his twisted heart. The blackened organ responded to his desperation, rolling toward him in little macabre stops and starts.

The ball of glowing energy left Traian's hands, hurtling through the chamber to land squarely on the writhing organ. The heart burst into a white-hot flame, burning blue and then purple. Tiny writhing maggots fell onto the ice, burning. The flames leapt from the heart to the outstretched hands of the vampire, racing up his arms to his shoulders. The long strands of dank hair caught fire. The vampire's mouth gaped open, his eyes wide with shock and horror.

The heart incinerated completely, ashes erupting in a blackened volcano, throwing more maggots into the air. The blackened worms lay like drops of black soot staining the ice. The undead shrieked, his cry carrying through the labyrinth of caves, high-pitched and horrible, the sound hurting their ears. Jubal, Gabrielle, and Joie clapped their hands over their ears in an effort to drown out the noise.

Above their heads, great spears of ice shook. Spider-web cracks ran up the walls surrounding them. Jubal caught his sisters by the arm and jerked at them, trying to get them moving out of the chamber as the ominous sound of thousands of years of tons of ice pressing down thundered through the gallery.

Traian sent another ball of fiery energy toward the vampire. Fire engulfed him completely, burning hot and bright. For one ghoulish moment, a blackened skeleton of a man rose up in the smoke, bony fingers reaching for Traian. He stood his ground without flinching and blew on the apparition. A foul stench filled the cavern.

The black smoke vanished, taking with it the stench. The ice settled, all at once quiet, other than the persistent sound of water dripping.

Jubal let out his breath. "Holy shit."

"Okay," Gabrielle said, one hand on her throat, "that's just gross."

"Handy little trick," Joie observed. "You'll have to teach it to me."

Traian managed a boyish grin. "Finally, something impressed you."

A terrible howling, like that of a demon pack, echoed through the subterranean caverns, sending chills down Joie's spine. She swallowed sheer terror and managed a small, wan smile for her sister's sake—sheer bravado. "I think that's our cue to leave."

"Can we climb? How do we know where they are?" Gabrielle asked anxiously.

"Damn it to hell, how many of those things are there?" Jubal demanded.

"It used to be, they hunted alone. Essentially, vampires are very self-centered and vain," Traian answered. "But what I've found here is unprecedented as far as I know. *Three* master vampire—Gallent and Valenteen allowed a third, a much more powerful master to manipulate them and their followers." He reached out and plucked hair from Joie's head. "They are coming for us. We have to get out of here now."

"Ow!" Joie glared at him. "That hurt."

"I need hair from all of you, preferably from the scalp, do not just break it off," Traian instructed, pulling a hair from his own head.

Jubal frowned, but did as Traian asked, handing him his hair. Gabrielle followed suit. Traian pulled a tiny bit of cloth from the wound on his leg, ignoring Gabrielle's hastily covered protest. He wound blood-stained threads around the hair.

"Stay where you are." He rose into the air, moved over the ice to a tunnel leading to the right and gathered more energy. He threw the hair and thread into the chamber and sent a powerful blast of air shooting through the tunnel.

"I'm going to carry you all to the hall you came through and then we're going to run fast. Try to run light. Vampires are creatures with great hearing. We want them to think we went right while we're going left," Traian instructed. "If possible, run single file."

"I'll bring up the rear," Jubal agreed, nodding his head.

Traian caught Joie's hand and tugged, dragging her after him. Joie reached out for Gabrielle.

If we talk telepathically, my brother and sister will hear as well as long as we remain connected like this physically. And we can run in synch, Joie explained as she tried to match Traian's strides, settling her feet where his had been. Her crampons made it easier to run along the ice without slipping, but she feared the scrapes in the ice would alert the vampires.

The vampires will follow the scent of blood and I am masking our noise.

Gabrielle reached for Jubal, who tucked his gun into his belt and ran as lightly as possible in his sister's footsteps.

I don't really understand how you can do that, but you managed to make some kind of fireball and you sort of flew a bit, so I'm convinced, Joie said, careful to use telepathic communication so the sound wouldn't travel through the caves.

A Carpathian needs blood to survive, he explained as they hurried down the hall away from the bloody, blackened chamber. *We do not kill those who give us blood. They are treated with the respect due them. We cannot be out in full sunlight and we sleep beneath the ground.*

He felt it necessary to educate the three humans as quickly as possible. Should they become separated from him, they had to know how to survive. He could feel the stirring interest in all of them. Gabrielle was a scientist, and the information would appeal to her. Jubal would take it as it was meant—to save their lives. And Joie . . . his heart turned over. His lifemate. He hadn't had time to really accept the truth of that.

More, Joie demanded. *If you aren't a vampire, where did they come from?*

We are a species nearly immortal. I say nearly because we can die given the right circumstances. Over time if we do not find our lifemate, the woman holding the other half of our soul—and there is only one—we lose emotion and the ability to see color. The world becomes a dull, unrelenting place.

The tunnel twisted unexpectedly, spilling them out into another great hall. This one had smooth, blue-green walls on three of the four sides, the ice folded in bands. The gallery opened into several hallways. The high ceiling was covered in sharp stalactites hanging down like giant icicle spears. One wall, rather than smooth, was covered in ice balls, many as large as boulders where the water had run down and frozen. The sound of water was louder here, but coming from where, they couldn't tell. The roar seemed to echo through the chamber, making it impossible to tell which direction the underground river was.

Have you been here before? Jubal tested the telepathy link through their joined hands.

I do not know this place. I believe this is a mage cave.

Joie made a single sound in her throat and glanced back at Gabrielle as they paused to take stock of their surroundings and determine the best way back to the surface. *Mage cave? I hate to ask.*

Traian knew he was asking a lot to have these three humans understand his world. They'd been thrown in at the deep end of a very murky pool and were fighting for survival against mythical creatures out of horror films. He wanted to draw Joie into his arms and comfort her, but there was little comfort in a place of such danger.

A roar reverberated through the ice caves, a sound that rose to a high pitch of rage and promise of retribution.

They caught up with the bloody hair. We've got to go. We have to stay to the left. I know the general direction to get out, but we've got to run.

Above their heads, the stalactites rocked, the ominous sound of ice cracking loud, all around them. Traian took off running just as the chamber rocked with loud continuous claps of thunder. Great ice balls hurled out of the walls toward them, big enough and with enough force to kill them should one hit them.

Gabrielle screamed and let go of Joie's hand, sprinting across the ice.

"Stay quiet," Traian hissed. "Stop her," he added to the woman's brother.

Jubal raced after Gabrielle and caught her, throwing her to the floor as a large spear crashed to the floor, shattering, sending shards of ice in all directions. Traian caught up Joie, his arms surrounding her, nearly crushing her against his chest as more ice spears rained down and blocks of ice thundered out of the walls.

"Keep her there," Traian demanded of Jubal.

He ran, dodging spears and boulders of ice with Joie locked in his arms until he made it to Jubal and Gabrielle. He crouched beside them, pushing Joie close to them as he gathered energy. The build-up was so fast and powerful, static electricity sent charges ricocheting off the ice walls and floor.

He covered the group as best he could, building a shield around them so the powerful conical pillars of ice and large ice boulders smashed into the invisible force and broke apart. The ferocity and speed of the weapons flying at them was terrifying to see, as shaking stalactites broke free of the ceiling. They could look up and see the great columns of solid ice coming down right on top of them.

Is this natural? Joie asked. *Because I've never seen anything like it all the years I've been going into caves.* It was a storm of ice, a cavern angry with the intrusion and fighting to drive the trespassers out.

Traian could feel her heart pounding. He pulled her closer, sheltering her with his body. His strength was waning fast. The rags pushed into his wounds were soaked. He needed the healing earth and more blood fast and they were still a distance from the closest exit. He didn't get lost in the sense that he knew direction, but where any tunnel or hall within the cave led, he had no idea.

No. I will get you out. They cannot sustain this attack on us. The moment it lets up, we will make a break for the narrowest hallway to the left.

Gabrielle heard him through the grip her brother had on her. She raised her head to look at the stranger. His face was white and etched with small lines. She nudged Jubal, who glanced over his shoulder at the man.

Can you do this? Jubal asked. *Hold out against this attack?*

There is no other choice, Traian replied. There was no discussion, because there could be no other answer. He did what had to be done. The vampires were throwing a tantrum and doing their best to slow their prey down, but they had no idea exactly where they were yet and they wouldn't use up all their strength when they couldn't see their targets. *We have to stay very quiet. They will find our scent and follow us, but there is no reason to make it easy on them.*

I'm sorry, Gabrielle said. *I'm not usually such a baby, I swear I don't usually lose control and fall apart.*

Joie reached out to comfort her sister, taking her hand and holding it tight. *We'll get out, we always do,* she assured. *You're not being a baby, Gabrielle.*

Traian could hear the love in her voice. He could actually *feel* her love for her sister. The emotion was stark and raw and filled his throat with a lump. It had been too many centuries since he'd experienced such things.

The attack is already waning, Traian assured as he felt the violent energy around him lessen. *A couple of minutes more and then we stay left. There's a tunnel, an ice slide, very narrow but passable, that will take us down and away from them. I can close it after us if we are lucky and then we just have to find our way out.*

His eyes met Jubal's over Joie's head. Her brother was no fool. It wasn't going to be easy finding their way out of the labyrinth. He hadn't explained mages and quite frankly, he didn't want to try. They were dealing with enough trying to get around the knowledge that vampires were real.

The thundering roar died down, leaving only the sound of cracking ice and dripping water. He threw off the shield and jerked the two women up. "We've to go now. They are tracking us and they can move faster than we can."

They ran toward the left hallway.

You could outrun them without us, couldn't you? Joie asked.

That is beside the point. I will not leave you.

You're wounded.

Jubal entered the narrow hallway first. His shoulders scraped along the ice. "It's tight in here," he called back. "It dead-ends into a hole."

"That's the chute. It is a long slide. It was passable the last time I used it and it is the best chance we have." Traian didn't add that it was the only one. What little strength he had left had to get them down that long slide without mishap and then close the way behind them.

The three siblings exchanged a long, shocked look. Jubal studied the entrance, shining his light inside the hole to study what he could see of the narrow tube. "This is too dangerous, Joie. It goes down very sharply. We'd be sliding out of control within minutes."

Joie stepped up next to him and peered inside. She whirled around to face Traian. "Are you crazy? We're not going in there."

"You have no choice," Traian said quietly. "We may be trapped in these caves for a couple of days so whatever you have to do to stay alive, you will need to keep close." He hoped that wasn't so. He didn't want to explain to them what would happen to him when the sun rose above them.

Joie planted herself in front of him, her eyes glittering. "Obviously we aren't like you. We're human. Sliding down an ice chute without checking it out and knowing what we're getting into is just suicide. No way can the three of us go in there."

"Then all of us will die right here. I cannot abandon you

nor will I be able to defeat the vampires in pursuit of us. I am too weak. If you do not take this chance, the only answer is death. And if you must die, you do not want vampires to get their hands on you." Traian spoke as matter-of-factly as possible.

To him there was no other choice. He would stay with this lifemate and defend her brother and sister. In truth, his first reaction was simply to grab her and force her to go with him, but the bond between the three siblings was incredibly strong. Joie wouldn't leave them unless forced and she wouldn't forgive him if he took her. She wasn't looking toward him to protect her, she would only enter the chute if her family agreed with the decision. He had a long way to go to earn her trust. The three of them trusted one another implicitly, knew each other's strengths and weaknesses. He was the outsider.

Jubal closed his eyes briefly, glanced back in the direction they'd come and shook his head. "We have to trust you, but if anything happens to my sisters . . ." He nodded at his sisters.

"I plan to keep you all alive," Traian said.

"Get your crampons off," Joie advised Gabrielle. "You don't want a broken leg. If we're going to do this, we have to take every precaution."

The three hurriedly removed the crampons from their boots.

"I'll go first," Gabrielle announced, her chin up. "If I get stuck, you'll know you won't fit," she added over her shoulder to her brother. Her voice trembled but she was obviously determined.

Jubal caught her arm. "Not a chance, Gabby. I'll be in front. We don't know what's down there."

"The chute may be blocked," Traian explained. "The cave is fighting back and we seem to be tripping mage traps as we go. I will lead the way down the chute and clear it. Once we are clear, I will seal it up behind us so the vampires cannot use that shortcut to follow us. It will not stop them, but it will slow them down. As you go down, shine your light ahead. I'll let you know if the ceiling is low and you have to lie all the way down, but once you do that, you will not be able to see anything ahead of you so once past the obstacle get back into a sitting position as fast as possible."

"Gabby, when you sit down, keep your axe to your side, hold with both hands and dig the point in to act like the brake," Jubal instructed.

Gabrielle swallowed hard. "This sounds more dangerous than I thought."

"We've practiced using the axe as a break," Jubal reminded. "You'll glissade down on your butt. You can do it."

Gabrielle shook her head. "I've done it on skis and we've practiced in soft snow, but not on ice, Jubal. Not like this in a tube. We don't even know where it leads." Even as she protested she leashed her ice axe to her wrist.

"We have no choice, honey," Jubal said. "We'll be fine. Joie will be right in front of you and I'll be close behind."

Gabrielle looked for a moment as if she might cry, but then she squared her shoulders and nodded. "I can do it."

"You may need your axe to self arrest. If I call back, use them fast. I will be clearing the way ahead of us. Hold until I give you the okay to continue." Traian spoke tersely, confidently, needing the three humans to follow him without question.

"You know that doesn't always work, depending on how fast we get going," Joie said. "It's a hit or miss proposition and that chute might be too narrow to flip over."

"It is the best shot we have at living," Traian reiterated, "and if we're going to do it, we need to get moving."

The descent into the ice tube was perilous to say the least. A mage cave was extremely dangerous, filled with all sorts of valuable items and as many or more traps to protect them, each more lethal than the one before. They had stumbled upon a great underground labyrinth, a mage haven beneath the mountain. Few could get past the mage spells pushing dread and fear into the hearts and minds of any trying to make the descent into the deep abyss, making certain to keep everyone away. Traian didn't think the caverns were abandoned. The fact that vampires had entered didn't mean a powerful mage was not at work here. He wanted to get his lifemate and her family out as soon as possible. He didn't understand how they had made it into the caves in the first place, how they had managed to get past mage barriers.

They readied their equipment quickly, and very efficiently, hugging each other briefly before nodding to him that they were ready.

Traian pulled Joie tight against him, ignoring the harness with her rack of climbing gear. "Stay close to me, but try to give yourself room to stop fast if you need to," he said. "It gets narrow in places. We don't want to be crushed in there. We have to get down before they know what we're doing. If there's a problem, call it out and I will do my best to aid you. You will be sliding fast, so pay attention. You will need quick reactions."

"Maybe we should share a rope," Gabrielle suggested.

"It wouldn't be of any use," Jubal said. "Remember to keep your heels up."

"You follow me, Joie. Your sister next." He looked at Jubal over their heads. "You will know in advance that the vampires are close. Insects. A foul smell. A feeling of absolute dread. They are as capable of collapsing the tunnel as I am, but we have to believe they want our blood and they will not. Call out the moment you think they are behind us."

Jubal nodded. "We're ready. Let's do it."

Traian didn't wait, knowing that time was premium now and not wanting any of them to change their minds. He slipped inside the chute and pushed off. The smooth ice looked like a giant slide, but it was so dark the others wouldn't be able to see without angling their heads to point their lamps straight ahead. His shoulders were wide and he touched on both sides. The women wouldn't have much of a problem, but Jubal had good-sized shoulders as well.

"It's snug," he called back and heard Joie relaying the information to her siblings.

Joie took a breath and slipped in after him. It was dark and frightening. She sat on her butt, lifted her heels and placed her ice axe to her side, gripping with both hands, the spike digging into the ice. With the leash of the axe wrapped around her wrist, she breathed through the dread, counting to ten to give Traian a head start and then pushed off into that unknown world.

Are you all right? Traian asked.

A little scared. In all of our conversations, it didn't occur to you to mention a few pertinent facts such as how you're a peculiar sort of man who likes blood and has vampires and other mythical creatures stalking you? You might have mentioned, just once, that you weren't telling me cheery bedtime stories but that you lived this sort of life. Didn't you think that might be important in the grand scheme of things?

Even in his mind, Traian heard the trembling in her voice. She was more than scared and that was all right with him. She had a bravado about her that at times worried him. Vampires were wholly evil. There was no reasoning with them. He didn't want her to ever think defeating them would be easy.

I took into consideration your fear that you had lost your mind. It occurred to me that if I started talking about vampires being real and not fictional, you would have yourself committed.

The ice chute was cold after the unexpected heat Traian had generated in the chamber. Joie slid down into the freezing world of blue ice and crystal, knowing he was right. She would have had herself committed to a hospital for the mentally ill at the mere mention of vampires. The ice sloped alarmingly and she began to pick up speed. Her heart accelerated in direct proportion to how fast she was going.

I still might, she murmured in his mind, trying to stay focused through the unrelenting fear. She was sliding down a narrow chute with no real vision, following a man she didn't know and he wasn't even human. *Having a boyfriend with a neck-biting fetish is definitely not sane.*

Traian heard the underlying note of genuine fear in her voice. Finding him in the ice cave, fighting for their lives against such creatures of evil and knowing he needed blood to survive had shaken her confidence in herself. She had been unknowingly trapped by the connection of lifemates.

Gabrielle is right behind me, she informed him.

He felt the tears in her voice. She definitely felt guilty for bringing her brother and sister into such a dangerous mess. *You had no way of knowing.*

She didn't pretend to misunderstand. *They shouldn't be here. Especially Gabby. Jubal's in the chute. It's difficult to control speed.*

Traian caught sight of the first danger sign. Tiny ice balls clung to the sides of the tube. Overhead little icicles had formed, growing larger as he slid deeper into the abyss.

Instantly he thrust the sight into Joie's mind, knowing she would relay the information to her siblings and they would be trying to slow their descents.

He felt rather than caught the first bump as the ice beneath him had flakes. Cursing to himself, he used more energy trying to smooth the way ahead of them. He could taste fear the other three radiated, especially Joie's sister. She was holding it together by a thread. The intensity of the emotion was amplified by the combination of natural fear, the vampires, and the mage caves. He couldn't waste his strength shielding them from the disturbing broadcast.

He'd slid another ten feet when he saw the large obstacle blocking the path. A ball of ice closed the chute. It was thick and solid. He felt Joie's instant awareness. She was locked in his mind, clinging to the fact that he seemed confident.

On three we self arrest, Joie instructed her siblings.

Gabrielle's sob of alarm echoed through the tube, and Traian's heart stuttered for a moment. If the woman couldn't stop her descent, she'd slam into Joie's head. He had to concentrate on removing the huge block of ice stopping up the slide and there was likely to be more ahead.

One. Two. Three.

He felt the surge of energy as the three climbers slammed the spikes deep into the ice and rolled, their arms taking the shock of the abrupt halt. Joie's wrenching cry was only in her mind, but Traian felt the jolt through his own body. Gabrielle let out a small sob.

I'm slipping, Joie.

We're okay, Joie assured. *Hurry, Traian.*

The three of them had thrown their lot in with him and were trusting in his ability in a situation beyond their comprehension. As he gathered energy he puzzled the best way to dissolve the ice ball. Heat could cause more problems. Blasting it might as well.

Joie. There are handles in this chute, Jubal announced. *This isn't entirely natural.*

It is mage-formed, Traian informed them as he carefully blew a steady blast of heat into the center of the solid ball of ice. He took great care to keep a laser-like projection. He didn't dare allow the sides or ceiling of the tunnel to melt as well.

I can't hold on any longer, Gabrielle informed her siblings, panic edging her voice.

I hear something in the chute. That was Jubal, surprisingly calm.

Traian redoubled his efforts, no longer caring that there might be a small spill. He blew steadily as he approached the blockage. The ice ball melted into a puddle and ran down the slide in advance of him.

Keep coming but really try to control the speed of your descent.

It would take effort for the three to turn over and reposition themselves without falling out of control down the steep slide. He had faith that Jubal could do it. The man was strong. Perhaps Joie, but Gabrielle wasn't experienced enough. He took a breath and sent her strength, knowing he was growing too weak to keep controlling everything around him. He kept the ceiling as smooth as possible as he went down, not wanting any of them injured. Ahead of him, he had to continually clear the chute.

Crickets. Thousands of them, pouring over the top of me.

Again, Traian was astonished at the calm in Jubal's voice. The experience of swarms of insects rushing over one in the dark was eerie and frightening to say the least. He wasn't surprised when Gabrielle burst into tears.

Close your eyes, Jubal advised. *Breath shallow through your nose. They're moving fast. Trying to get out of here like we are. I think they're trying to tell us something.*

Traian knew that last was for him. They were communicating through his strong connection with Joie, but Jubal had to be a strong enough psychic to feel him in Joie's mind.

He knew the moment the crickets reached Joie. Everything in her stilled, rebelled, silently screamed as the bugs poured over her in their effort to get away from the evil following them. The rasping was loud as thousands of legs rushed over the ice and humans, desperate to escape.

Hurry. I am out. Do not worry about how fast you go, I can stop you here at the bottom. I must close the chute behind you before the vampires can enter.

The crickets reached Traian and rushed over him as his feet touched the ground to flee in front of the threat of evil. He leapt out and turned to catch Joie in his arms, whipping her out of the way so he could stop Gabrielle. She was bone white, trembling uncontrollably, but when he set her aside, she swayed, but remained upright. Joie immediately put her arms around her sister and held her as Traian gathered his strength to help Jubal out of the chute.

Be ready. As soon as he is out I will have to close the chute. We will have to run. Stay to left. Always go left. Right goes deeper inside the mountain.

"We won't be separating," Joie said firmly.

Her voice was almost a shock after the intimacy of mind-to-mind contact. He braced himself for Jubal. The man was large, but he also was extremely strong and he'd thankfully managed to control his descent better than the two women. Traian sent a cushion of air to slow him more and as he burst feet first through the chute, he caught the man, using preternatural strength.

Traian waved them back away from the ice tunnel, staggering a little as he reached for another burst of energy. The others could feel the gathering of heat and power. Joie stepped close to him and wrapped her arm around his waist.

"I can help. Draw from me."

"And me," Jubal put his hand on Traian's shoulder.

Gabrielle stepped behind her brother and laid her hand on his shoulder, connecting all of them physically. Joie opened her mind instantly to him, flooding him with her strength and energy, generously sharing everything she had, everything she was. He felt her solidarity with him, that connection that allowed her—without truly knowing him—to trust him when she was always very cautious in close relationships. Through her, her siblings gave just as generously, boosting his power enormously.

A scream of rage and hatred echoed down through the chute, the sound growing in volume until ice shattered above their heads and spider-web cracks appeared along the walls.

Traian began to chant in a soft voice, his hands moving quickly in a pattern the three siblings couldn't quite follow, the movements blurring with his incredible speed, but the ominous sound of ice cracking grew loud enough to be called a clap of thunder. The ice veined in a starburst pattern that spread rapidly outward. At the entrance, the ice began to fall in large chunks, some sliding down the tube toward them.

"Run!" Traian instructed and all of them took off, sprinting for the left entrance.

The sound continued to build behind them, a great roar and a thunderous clap as the tube collapsed in on itself. The earth shook beneath their feet, and the growing rumble emanated from the walls and ceiling surrounding them. Jubal caught Gabrielle's hand as they followed Traian and Joie at a dead run through the narrow hall. Sharp daggers of ice fell from the ceiling as they rushed through the tunnel. Several times, Traian redirected a lethal missile as they raced along the well-worn path.

They ran through the twisting, dark hall with the sound of ice collapsing behind them. Traian stopped so abruptly, Joie ran into him. He caught her to steady her, drawing her close protectively. "I told you not to come here. I am not certain I can get your family out alive. There is something in this cave the vampires are determined to find—and the mages are just as determined to protect."

They were on the edge of a precipice. A very narrow bridge, constructed of ice and stone, was the only way across. It appeared dangerously thin in places and had an obvious hole in one section that dropped into a deep abyss. Jubal and Gabrielle halted just as abruptly, staring in horror at the narrow strip of ice.

"That's no natural bridge," Jubal observed. "Who, or should I ask what, could have carved such a thing? Can we cross it?"

Traian studied it warily. He shook his head. "I fear that bridge is an invitation to death. A trap—a mage trap."

Gabrielle slipped her hand into her sister's. "I'm afraid, Joie. I've got a terrible feeling we're all going to die."

"The vampires are broadcasting terror and images of death to feed your natural fear," Traian explained. "They have been hunting for weeks for something in these caves. The network is very large and, as you can see, not all naturally formed. I stayed to try to find what they are looking for. Vampires do not normally put so much energy into a project. Whatever it is they want, their finding it will not benefit either the Carpathian or the human race."

"They don't need to broadcast fear," Gabrielle pointed out, reminding Traian a bit of Joie's dry humor. "I'm doing quite well on my own."

Jubal nodded toward the raw wounds on Traian's chest. "You've been in a few battles with them."

He nodded. "Yes, and I have noticed changes in their behavior. As a rule, they would have avoided me. Now vampires are running in packs. They used to be out for themselves, or occasionally a master vampire would use the newer ones as fodder for his battles, but lately they seem to have more control and are much better organized. To find two masters serving a third and bringing to him their own followers is unheard of and must be investigated."

Jubal shoved a hand through his hair in agitation. "I feel like I'm losing my mind. Vampires are Hollywood creations, creatures in movies."

"They are shape-shifters. You must be very careful of what and who you trust."

Joie could hear a sound accompanying the drip of the water. A soft clicking, like branches banging together in the wind. It made her edgy. Vampires were one thing, but shape-shifting? She exchanged another look with her siblings, and instantly rejected the idea as they did.

There was no warning. One moment Traian stood in the glare of their headlamps, the next a huge, shaggy black wolf with a mouthful of lethal teeth sat in his place, eyes focused menacingly on Jubal. Gabrielle screamed and stumbled backward. Jubal reached out to catch her, dragging her away from the abyss to comparative safety beside the snarling animal, hastily unzipping his pocket to pull out his gun.

Mouth dry, Joie circled the wolf's neck with a restraining arm. "Totally impressive, but not something I want to take home to Mom." Her heart was pounding so loudly, it sounded like a drum in her ears. She had doubted him and he'd done this to prove how very lethal and cunning the vampires were. Her legs shook, feeling like rubber.

There is no need to fear me. I would never harm you.

"Why would you think I was afraid of you?" Joie demanded. "I'm not in the least afraid. I'm keeping you under control."

It may have something to do with the knife you are holding to my throat. Traian said it casually, a soft amusement in his voice, as if the blade pressed so tightly against him didn't matter in the least.

And that scared her more than the fact he had just shapeshifted into a predator. She looked down at her arm curved around his neck. The fur was thick and luxurious, and her arm was nearly buried in it. But she could feel the handle of the knife in her hand. She let out her breath and slowly eased the blade away from his throat. "I was just making certain you were paying attention," she said as she slipped the blade back into the scabbard.

Traian calmly shifted back into his true form. "Just how many weapons do you carry on you? You seem to be a walking arsenal."

"This is insane," Jubal said. "Cool, but insane."

"I think we're caught in a mass hallucination," Gabrielle suggested. "Can we just get out of here? Joie, find us a way out."

"We're trying, hon," Joie assured. "That clicking noise is driving me crazy. I don't like the rhythm; it's not natural." The dripping of the water was more insistent. She looked anxiously toward Traian. Something was wrong. He knew it. She knew it. She looked at Jubal. He certainly felt it too.

"I will take them across and come back for you," Traian said to Joie. "He can protect your sister while I cross with you." There was no sense in attempting to take his lifemate first. It was clear she would never go without the others, and he didn't want to waste time arguing.

"Not without more blood, you can't," Jubal said. "You're so pale you look nearly transparent." He took a deep breath, shoved his gun back in his pocket and drew his knife. He didn't hesitate, slashing a cut across his wrist and handing Joie the knife. "If he kills me, I expect vengeance." He flashed a wan grin at her as he stepped up and offered the bright blood to Traian. "Get us the hell out of here."

Traian took the offering without hesitation. They would have to most likely fight their way out of the maze of caves and he needed strength. He was grateful Jubal was such a strong man, and large. He was careful not to take too much, but he desperately needed the life-giving substance freely given. He carefully closed the wound with his healing saliva.

"Thank you." Traian acknowledge simply. He held out his hand to Gabrielle. She stared at him in horror, shaking her head, even stepping back. "Hurry. We have to go now."

"Gabrielle," There was warning in Jubal's voice.

She didn't look at him, but rather at her sister. "Do you trust him, Joie?"

Joie looked up at Traian, noting the lines etched in his strong, timeless face. The dark depths of his eyes. Old eyes. Eyes that had seen too much. He was a man who had been alone too long. She was a looking at a warrior. A man of honor. Joie reached out to brush a caress along his jaw with her fingertips. The touch jolted him. Jolted her. Heat flooded her body. Electricity arced between them, lightning flashing in their veins. Instant awareness. They smiled at one another in understanding.

"I would trust him with my life, Gabrielle. More importantly, I would trust him with yours. Please go with him now. I've got that bad feeling I always get when we're in danger."

Gabrielle took Traian's hand, and allowed him to draw her to him. Jubal stepped close so Traian could wrap an arm around him.

Traian leaned close to Joie. "I will be back immediately.

Do not attempt to engage the enemy. They must not get their hands on you." There was an underlying urgency in his voice. Dark eyes stared intently into hers. "Be safe, Joie. I need you to be safe."

He was taking her family to safety for her, when everything in him demanded he take her first. Joie understood his look immediately, recognized how difficult it was for him to do what was important to her rather than to himself. There was a storm of emotion churning inside him, yet his features remained tranquil. Only his eyes burned with intensity. With possession. With promise. With passion.

His mouth fastened on hers, a hard kiss that staked his claim on her. That kiss told her he meant to have her and nothing would stand in his way. She felt his body tremble and tasted his passion, tasted his fear for her. She tasted safety. He would come back for her, brave anything to reach her. Even in the midst of the unknown, in that moment, she felt protected.

He pulled away abruptly, lifting her brother and sister easily, as if they were no more than children, shifting into a creature with wings, half man, half bird, and flying across the abyss into the dark where she could no longer see him.

Joie was left standing alone on the edge of the precipice with the darkness pressing down on her—with the strange rhythmic clicking and the dripping water. Heart pounding and mouth dry, she turned toward the sound, shining her light to see what was behind her.

In the small confines she could see water trickling from the side of the cavern; it was not clear, but a milky yellow, and gathered into a foul-smelling pool. She moved cautiously, positioning herself to keep an eye on what was gathering there. Something evil. Something alive.

The water rippled in response to a dark disturbance below the surface. The pool darkened into an oily substance, revealing two red orbs glaring with terrible malevolence. A chill crept down her spine. The hair on her arms stood up.

Traian. Automatically, without conscious thought, she reached out for him, showed him the pool with its macabre secrets.

Move! Get out of its line of vision, Joie.

Chapter Five

With absolute horror, unable to look away, Joie stared back at the flame-red eyes stalking her from the small dark puddle. The eyes were real, watching her, some terrible apparition set on her destruction. She had never seen so much malice, or so much black hatred pouring from any entity. Her body rebelled, sickened by the evil emanating from the thick slime.

At Traian's warning, she tried to wrench her gaze away, but it was impossible. She was trapped, unable to break eye contact with the red flames. Her airway began to close, choked off by an invisible noose. Instinctively her hands flew up to her throat as if she could pry unseen fingers from around her neck, but there was nothing there. As white stars flashed across a black background, Joie realized dizzily she had only precious seconds to break the invisible hold on her throat. She reached for her knife, following through in one smooth motion with a throw directed by sheer desperation.

The blade sank deep into the fiery left eye. Immediately the water bubbled up in a blackish-red ooze and the hold on her throat loosened, allowing her to breathe. A terrible howl filled the cavern, assaulting her ears. She stumbled away from the poisonous pool, dragging air into her lungs, coughing as her raw throat protested.

The bubbles stacked, one on top of the other, forming a foul-smelling pyramid; the stench of rotten eggs and decaying meat drifted through the chamber, an ugly green vapor that left tendrils floating through the air so that she was afraid of breathing it in. The pyramid grew in height until it was twice the length of the puddle. Slowly, the formation began to tip, the bubbles elongating, forming grotesque fingers. She gasped when she saw the extensions were tiny wiggling parasites, much like maggots, or tiny worms bursting through the ooze.

Joie shuddered and backed a step away from the slime watching the puddle closely, her stomach churning. Something terrible was about to happen. The sounds in the cavern stilled, as if everything waited. The bubbles began to shake grotesquely, and something within the segments moved beneath the surface, desperate to get out. The pyramid tipped toward her and she took another cautious step back. Her heart thundered in the stillness of the cave. Even the water stopped its relentless dripping.

The thick ooze struggled, the bubbles merging into one misshapen blob, whatever was inside, pushing this way and that, distorting the mass of bubbles, as if the glob was giving birth—and she very much feared it was.

Hurry, Traian. Really hurry. There was no way to keep the anxiety out of her voice.

She'd been in desperate situations and never once had she been close to panic, she just wasn't made that way, but this—this *thing*—was definitely lethal and it was coming for her. The thick substance contorted again and broke in one spot, a membrane shielding something inside. Teeth took hold of the covering and ripped a wide tear, allowing the head of the organism to emerge. The creature slithered out of the hole and flopped out of the puddle of ooze onto the ice floor. Tiny worms exploded out of the opening left behind, some falling into the thick primordial soup, and others wiggling violently around the foot-long beast.

She didn't want to touch any of it, even with her equipment. The caterpillar-like being opened its mouth as if snarling at her. Dagger-like teeth seemed to be made of ice, yet those sharp, spiked teeth were very real. Two curved teeth, much like the grim reaper's scythe, dripped yellow venom forming rounded pods of thick amber slime.

Joie backed up another step, giving ground as the thing slithered closer. She considered trying to hop over it, but the pool was continuing to grow and the tiny maggots spread across the ice towards her as well.

Where are you?

I am on my way back.

Even the utter confidence and complete calm in Traian's voice didn't help. He was going to be too late. The organism was almost on her. She had to make a decision fast. Taking a grip on her ice axe, she considered the best place to try to kill it—through the top of the head or behind the neck. She was only going to get one chance.

The head suddenly reared back, the mouth yawning open wide, exposing the dagger-like teeth, curved venomous canines and more yellowish pods inside. For one moment she was staring into a black, fathomless hole, and the next, six snake-like heads rushed out at her, exploding out of the mouth with such speed, Joie stumbled back to avoid the gnashing teeth. The edge of the ice crumbled and she fell into empty space.

She slammed the spike of her axe deep into the ice wall. Her arms took her body weight as she came to an abrupt stop. Letting her breath out slowly, she looked carefully around. She couldn't see below her, the drop off was far too deep. Ice balls clung to the walls of the abyss, a bad sign. She hadn't had time to put her crampons back on her boots, so she couldn't really dig into the ice wall for more stability.

I'm in trouble, Traian.

Above her head, an ominous scratching noise alerted her. She looked up as ice fell. To her horror, ice flakes rained down on her, the small wiggling parasites dropping onto her head and shoulders. She had to force her body under control, refusing to give into the impulse to try to shake them off. The scraping sound continued, growing louder. She risked another look above her. The slug-like creature seemed to have grown even larger with the enormous jaws hanging over the edge and the cold, red eyes glaring at her. The thing opened its mouth wide, displaying teeth and the venomous curved scythes.

Her heart skipped a beat and began to pound. Those hideous snake heads were going to come at her face any moment, no doubt delivering a bite she wouldn't survive. She was going to have to let go of her lifeline with one hand and reach for her knife. If the thing was really fast, she was going to have one very slim chance.

Swallowing hard, never taking her eyes from the monstrous red eyes peering down at her with so much malevolence, she eased her death grip on the ice axe, transferring her weight to one arm. She'd climbed since she was practically a toddler and had the body strength, but it was cold and she was losing strength. She kept her movements slow, not wanting to trigger an attack. Her fingers closed around the hilt of her knife secured in her belt. She eased it out slowly.

Arms caged her against a hard chest and Traian's scent filled her lungs. *I've got you,* he whispered in her mind.

Power snapped and crackled as the energy built around her. Relief made her sag against him. There was no controlling the terrible trembling that started. Flames burst from Traian's hand, a fiery ball that blasted straight down the creature's throat. It screamed, a loud, long, drawn-out piercing cry that shattered icicles. A volcano of parasites burst from it, on fire, falling like ash around them.

Joie buried her face in Traian's chest. "They're in my hair."

"Ssh, I'll get them off of you," he soothed, his voice gentle. "Your helmet prevented them from getting into your scalp."

She felt the soft warm air he used to rid her of the debris that had rained down on her. The thought of the tiny maggots crawling over her skin was worse than the sensations of the thousands of crickets moving over her in the ice chute. She forced air through her lungs and made herself reach out to retrieve her ice axe.

"Are you hurt? Any bites? Did those parasites get under your skin?"

She shook her head, clinging to his strength, not bothering to pretend the encounter hadn't shaken her. He moved quickly through the air, so fast the cold air bit at her face, numbed her arms and tore tears from her eyes. Joie buried her face against his chest again and pushed her body tightly against the unnatural warmth of his, allowing herself a few moments to recover before she faced her siblings.

"You are teaching me the meaning of fear," he said.

"Really? I thought it was the other way around. I don't think your world is the calm environment a woman like me should be in." Her voice shook, embarrassing her. "Frankly, Traian, this is a very terrifying place. And I'm not known for finding environments or situations terrifying. I don't want Gabrielle and Jubal to see me like this. And it's a little humiliating that you are."

"Having courage does not mean being unafraid."

"True, but everyone doesn't have to know I was shaking in my boots. Literally."

"I am not everyone. I am your lifemate, the other half of your soul. We do not hide things from one another. I need to know how you are feeling or if you are injured in any way."

"I have no idea what that means. Nor do I have any idea of this kind of existence. What was that thing?" She shuddered again. "I've been in caves all around the world and I've never encountered anything like we're finding here."

"I have no idea what it was. I have never seen one before either. I was on my way to my homeland when I encountered the packs of vampires. That was unusual enough that I needed to learn more about them. Unfortunately, there were more of them than me and with three master vampires, I ran into Armageddon. Masters are very old and very experienced. They use newer vampires to hunt for them and to weaken prey before they move in for the kill."

"I don't like the sound of the word 'prey.' " Another shudder went through her. "We're going so fast, I would have thought we'd cross over the crevice fast."

"We discovered traps all along the strip leading into a tunnel. I had to take them further into the mountain. We're going to enter it soon and it is very narrow. Getting your brother through it was difficult."

"I'll bet." She took a cautious look around. The bridge appeared more fragile than ever with a deep drop off on either side. The ice appeared solid enough on either side of the bridge, but she could see a hole about five feet in. She drew in her breath. "You tried to set them down there to come after me."

"Yes, your brother went through. I caught his arm and jerked him back. The ice only looks thick. It is an illusion as is much of the ice bridge."

Joie shook her head. "This cave system is one huge death trap."

Traian paused outside the entrance to the tunnel, hovering just above the cap of ice. He touched her face with gentle fingers. "I cannot believe you came to find me. I still have a difficult time believing you are real and not an illusion," he said softly. His lips moved against her cheek, a brush lighter than a butterfly wing, yet she felt it all the way to her toes. That small caress sent blood rushing through her veins, her heart leaping; his touch warmed her as nothing else could.

Joie closed her eyes for a moment, savoring his touch. "I have no idea what's going on between us, but I feel it too. I just having a difficult time believing that any of this is real," she admitted. "And what's up with the wolf? Telepathy, okay, I can accept that. Even your strange little blood fetish, but don't you think changing into animals and flying through the air might be going a little too far?" She knew she was being flippant, but she did think maybe she was bordering on crazy just a little bit. She felt caught in a horror story.

His arms tightened possessively. "You do not enjoy flying?"

"I don't enjoy anything when I'm not in complete control."

His arm was curved around her, pressed against the underside of her breasts. "You will not be in complete control when I make love to you, Joie," he told her softly.

She closed her eyes at the velvet sound of his voice. Danger surrounded them. Her family was close. It didn't seem to matter. She was so aware of him, her body ached with need. With hunger. With absolute longing. She felt edgy and hot; a terrible pressure building inside her.

I feel the same way.

She often spoke with her brother and sister using telepathy, a secret they all shared, but this was different. So much more. An intimacy that whispered of erotic nights and appetites that would never be sated. *Why? Why with you?*

I am your other half. We belong together. I have searched the world for you. Waited lifetimes for you.

Joie tightened her grip on his shirt, burrowed closer to his heart. She was a woman who knew herself well. An adrenaline junkie. A feminist. A believer in justice. She loved her life. Traveling from country to country. One assignment after another taking her into danger. Her recreation time was spent caving, white-water rafting, or skydiving. She was not a woman who wanted or needed a man. She was not a woman who clung to a man and yet already, she couldn't imagine herself without him.

Joie looked up at Traian, the light from her helmet shining on his face. He had changed her very existence for all time. "I'm not altogether certain I approve of you."

Laughter rumbled in his throat. "Fortunately, your approval is not strictly necessary. Lifemates simply are. We have no choice in the matter. We are like two magnets that cannot be torn apart."

"Great. I don't know a thing about you except I can't exactly bring you home to my mother and father. My family is very close, by the way."

"I had not noticed that at all," Traian said with drawling amusement.

He took her into the narrow opening leading to the left. He was staying with his initial plan, choosing to go left to find a way out.

"You can bring me home to your parents." He said it softly, honestly, as he followed Jubal and Gabrielle through a narrow hail. "I would never embarrass you, or frighten them. I want to meet them. Anyone important to you is important to me."

Joie tried to prevent her heart from going crazy. She was no young girl, but a fully grown woman. A man shouldn't have such an effect on her, yet he did. There was honesty in his voice. A simple sincerity that shook her. She knew nothing about him, not even what he really was, yet she knew everything. She knew what kind of man he was. The knowledge was instinctive, the one thing she was certain of.

"Where is your family?" she asked.

"I have only my people. My prince." His eyes were a deep black in the soft glow of the helmet lights. "You are now my family. Your brother and sister have become my family." He arched an eyebrow at her. "And we have only just met. A very strange concept for you, but completely natural to me. Lifemates are two people who meet and need to be together, two halves of the same whole—married in your world—but more. Finding a lifemate is what every Carpathian male dreams of and longs for and fights to keep our world together for, yet few of us ever gain such a treasure. I never thought to experience such an earth-shattering event."

"Are you disappointed that I'm not what you thought I'd be?"

Traian looked down at her. "You do not yet understand the concept of lifemates. I am surprised and even shocked by the idea of a human lifemate, but I could never be disappointed with you. We were made for one another. We complete one another. You are fascinating to me. You always will be."

Joie liked the sound of it. She couldn't imagine ever growing tired of Traian. She needed to climb and find new places to explore. It was as much a part of her as breathing. She needed a man who would welcome challenges. Traian had already proven he was more than up for the task.

The narrow opening widened, spilling into a chamber that clearly widened into another gallery. Jubal and Gabrielle stood close to one another, their faces anxious as they waited for Joie. Traian put her carefully on firm ground. Jubal and Gabrielle rushed to her, flinging their arms around her and hugging her close.

"What the hell happened?" Jubal demanded. "I knew something was wrong when we were trying to find a safe opening. Traian nearly went as ballistic as a man like him can go."

"But he wouldn't say anything," Gabrielle added, sending a look of reprimand at the Carpathian.

Jubal ran his hands over his sister. "Are you hurt?"

Joie shook her head. "There was a very disgusting creature with teeth, venom, and parasitic worms," she looked at her sister, "they looked like maggots, but worse."

Gabrielle looked more intrigued than scared. "Did you get me a sample?"

"I didn't think of it, sorry," Joie said. Now that she was away from the creature, she couldn't believe she hadn't collected a sample of the worm. They all carried containers for just that purpose. Gabrielle came with them for the express purpose of collecting specimens more than because she loved climbing or caving. Joie hated disappointing her after all that had happened. "I should have . . ."

Gabrielle laughed unexpectedly, the sound almost shocking in the cavern. "Don't be silly. I would have run for my life. I'm just glad you're safe."

"We are not safe yet," Traian reminded. They were all shivering and didn't seem to notice, but even with his help and their good ice-climbing clothing, the temperature was getting to them. "We have to keep moving."

Joie immediately sat down to put her crampons on her boots. She wasn't going to take any more chances without them. "Let's find a way out of here," she said, standing.

"Wait, Traian," Jubal objected. "We found something—something really important. You said those vampires were hunting something. You have to take a look at this. We've never seen anything like it."

Traian caught Joie's hand as they followed her siblings through the chamber into the open gallery. She felt a little silly holding hands—she'd never really done it, not even in high school, but there was something warm and comforting, something extraordinary about being close to Traian.

The chamber opened into a high-ceilinged gallery and someone—or something—had carved out rooms and alcoves. Sconces adorned the walls, very high up, and they had no idea how to turn them on, or even if they worked. Joie frowned and looked up at Traian hoping she might find answers to how there could possibly be an ice cave occupied by someone. It had taken time to carve the great columns of ice and all the recesses.

Jubal turned toward a shallow alcove in the wall, directing his headlamp onto the ice. There was a sudden silence as all of them caught their breath. The creature encased in ice was large, an enormous beast with scales covering its body, a wedge-shaped head, a serpentine neck, and a long tail ending in a sharp spike. The wings were folded in close along the body. It had sharp claws for rending and tearing. One eye was wide open and staring at them through the more than ten-feet-thick wall of ice. The ice was so thick, the creature was somewhat distorted.

Joie let her breath out slowly. "That's no dinosaur."

"It has to be," Gabrielle said. "It can't be a dragon. Don't tell me it's a dragon." She looked to Traian for answers. "Please tell me it's possible that the air is bad down here and we're all having a mass hallucination. That there aren't vampires. You can't change your shape, and there aren't dragons."

"I wish I could, Gabrielle," Traian replied gently.

She shook her head and touched the ice with a gloved hand. "It is truly beautiful. No one will ever believe us either."

"Is it real, Traian?" Jubal asked. There was awe, even reverence, in his voice.

"Yes. It is real. I had no idea it was down here." Traian approached the ice wall, his gaze moving over the large dragon. Like Gabrielle, he put his hand on the wall, but there was something much more intimate, more than awe, more than reverence, a kind of loving tribute. "I have not seen a dragon in hundreds of years."

Gabrielle gasped and stepped away from him, moving closer to Jubal as if for protection. They exchanged a long look, but Traian didn't seem to notice. Joie couldn't take her eyes from the rapt look on his face.

"Do you think this is what the vampires are looking for?" Joie asked.

Traian shook his head. "They have no interest in the remains of a dragon. But this is definitely a cave the mages use or used to use. I suspected as much. It could be a gold mine of information for our people. Mages have incredible power and knowledge. They probably are the ones to capture and ultimately kill and preserve this dragon. As a rule, dragon-kind destroyed all evidence of their existence."

"Why would they want to kill such a beautiful creature?" Gabrielle asked.

"Why do humans kill big bats and rhinos? The belief is, certain animals have magical powers. The dragon has long been gone from this earth. Shape-shifters can take the form, but they do not have the wisdom and power of a true dragon—well, there is a lineage in our people—the Dragonseekers—and they have enormous power and some say matching wisdom. Long ago there was a legendary

Dragonseeker, some say, whose lifemate was a shape-shifting dragon. How true that was, no one really knows." He shrugged. "Perhaps it is so."

"If it's true that the mages used dragons for power, wouldn't it be conceivable that vampires would want to do the same?" Gabrielle speculated.

"One would think," Traian acknowledged. "It would be terrifying to think that the vampires might get hold of any of the power the mages wielded. But no, they would not have the ability to use such a resource as a true dragon. One has to have the natural talent—to be mage-born."

"You do incredible things," Joie pointed out.

"I am of the earth and she grants me certain gifts, but the type of thing we are speaking of is entirely different. The power can come from evil just as well as from good."

"Can you get it out of there?" Joie asked.

"Not without possibly bringing tons of ice down on us. It is best to leave this place quickly." Traian turned when Jubal stepped away from the wall to wander across the gallery, drawn by an alcove filled with what looked like ancient, twisted wood.

"Do not touch anything," Traian warned sharply. "We must be very careful in here. The mages used spells and traps to guard what belonged to them."

"That's what you meant when you said the bridge could be a trap. You thought the mages had made it," Jubal said.

"You saw that the bank was a trap. That was not natural, the illusion of a solid wall of ice was too good. They are masters at such things."

Gabrielle held up her hand. "Wow we're talking about things found in fantasy books. Legends. Myths. There has never been evidence of dragons existing. Not even when dinosaurs roamed the Earth. And yet we're standing right in front of one. This is so surreal."

"Surreal or not, we have to get out of here—and carefully," Traian reiterated.

He pulled Joie closer to him. He was well aware of the effect of the cold on their bodies and brains. It sapped strength and being inside the cavern was disorienting. He could feel the subtle influence of power now, working at all of them to drain resources and keep them prisoner.

"I need to seal this area off, slow the vampires down, and get all of you out of this cave," Traian said.

"I'm not so eager to leave," Joie responded, studying the huge body of the dragon. "This is a treasure. There must be other fascinating things down here."

"You are being hunted," Traian said severely. "I am getting you out of here now. I will come back later and find whatever the vampires want so badly."

"When you're alone," Joie guessed.

"When I am alone," Traian confirmed. He urged them toward the narrow hall. "You must not touch anything, no matter how inviting it appears," he added as a precaution.

Jubal glanced at Joie. "It isn't like you to agree to stay behind. Are you certain he doesn't have you under a spell?" He groaned. "That sounds so melodramatic and stupid. I can't believe I said it."

"I'm a professional, Jubal, and I don't need to make a point. This is his area of expertise, not mine."

The hall opened into another huge gallery. Tall columns in a gothic style were carved into the walls. The high cathedral ceiling was impressive. Pillars of ice and crystal formed two rows down the room, each holding several round globes of varying colors. As they walked into the huge ballroom-sized room, lights flickered, flames dancing under man-made glass running up the sides of the thick ice wall.

Traian held up his hand to warn them all to stop moving. "Watch where you step. There has to be a way out through this gallery. A powerful mage has made his home here, at least at some point, and he would have a way to get out fast. Spread out and look, but do not touch anything at all."

Joie was drawn to the aisles of globes as were her siblings. She crossed the ice floor with care, walking along the row of the various-sized spheres, Jubal and Gabrielle close behind her. She peered into one of the largest, a milky blue natural sapphire. As she stared at it, the color deepened, darkened, began to swirl with alarming speed. Mesmerized, she moved closer. The ground beneath her tilted, rippled. She felt a pulling, a drawing as if the swirling sphere called to her.

Traian clapped his hand over her eyes and pulled her away from the globe. "Do not look at them. Gabrielle, come away from there." There was urgency in his normally calm tone. "Jubal, just pull her with you. I can feel the aura of power in all of these objects. Until we know what they are, we need to give them a wide berth."

Joie was stunned that she had been so quickly pulled into the globe's influence. "I thought mages were supposed to be good."

"Absolute power corrupts. It is something one learns when one's life spans hundreds of years." Traian crowded close to Joie, keeping his body between her and the tall pillars.

Joie laughed. "Don't let Jubal or Gabrielle hear you say that. If you tell them you've been alive for a few hundred years, they might change their minds about us."

"I heard it already," Jubal said. He was pacing right behind Gabrielle, pushing her through the long, wide-open room. "I have to say, this is the right up there with the dragon. It's amazing."

There were clear crystal sculptures of mythical creatures. Small blood-red pyramids made of stone were set into chiseled-out archways in the walls. It was difficult not to stare at the gems and strange objects surrounding them, but Traian was obviously fearful of their safety, and they were ever conscious of the deadly creatures following them.

"Jubal," Joie called.

He turned to find her frowning. Gabrielle and Traian were both staring at him as well. "What is it?" he asked.

"Every alcove you walk past, the lights turn on." There was suspicion in Traian's voice.

Jubal shrugged, obviously puzzled. "I must be triggering a hidden switch or something."

"It isn't just the lights, Jubal," Joie said. "The objects on the shelves lean toward you. A few have actually levitated as if trying to reach you." She didn't like the sudden suspicion she heard in Traian's voice or felt in his mind.

Deliberately, Traian moved close to an alcove where weapons lined the racks. No light illuminated the case nearly hidden by the surrounding ice and certainly no weapon moved toward him. He beckoned Jubal over.

Reluctantly, Jubal followed the summons. At once the alcove lit up and the weapons moved as if coming to life. A strange-looking device actually came away from the wall where it had been hung. Star-shaped, it was ringed with curved blades. Obviously a weapon, it floated through the air straight toward him, although there was no seeming threat.

"Hold out your hand," Traian commanded.

"No!" Joie hurried toward her brother to stop him.

Traian caught her as she went to rush past him, his grip impossible to break. "Hold out your hand," he said again, his tone brooking no argument.

Puzzled, Jubal did so. The strange weapon floated easily to him, at the last moment, opening as if hinged in the center to wrap itself around his wrist. It locked with a firm click.

Gabrielle gasped and stepped toward her brother. Traian's arm kept her back. "Who are you?" he demanded. "Only a mage can command such a weapon."

"I'm not mage," Jubal protested.

"We have the same parents," Joie snapped. "He isn't adopted—Mom gave birth to him and Dad is his father. If he's mage, we all are."

"How the hell do I get this thing off?" Jubal demanded. He pushed at it with his fingers. "It's very lightweight. I can barely feel it on me. As for commanding it, Traian, I'd have no idea how to do it."

"He isn't mage," Joie said again. She pulled away from Traian, one hand sliding to the hilt of her knife.

Traian stepped close to Jubal and placed both hands on either side of his head, fingers over his pulse. He allowed his mind to merge with Jubal's through their blood bond. The man was extremely intelligent, brilliant even, but Traian could find no hint of evil, no hint of magic or mage training.

He let out his breath slowly. "You can remove the knife from my balls, Joie." He could easily read his lifemate's mind, just as he could pick up the thoughts of her siblings. Joie loved her brother and sister and would willingly sacrifice her own happiness for them if need be. If he dared to harm her brother, she would have tried to kill him.

"You all right, Jubal?" she asked, sliding the knife carefully away from Traian.

"Yes. I felt Traian moving through my mind, but I didn't feel a threat, only reassurance. Whatever the reason, this place responds to me—and I have no idea why—I don't have a clue about any of the things in this cave."

Gabrielle shook her head. "He would have killed Jubal. Are you certain, Joie? This is your choice? We don't really know him at all."

Joie felt the possession in Traian's touch, felt the brush of his mind in hers. She smiled up at him in reassurance. At the same time, she reached for Gabrielle's hand.

"*I* know him. Deep inside, I know him. The one thing that matters to me is family. I hope I know what I'm doing, Gabrielle. You know I've always relied on my instincts. I feel this is right—*he's* right. I don't understand any of it, but maybe I've been preparing for him all of my life. I fit with him. You're right, I don't know him yet, but I fit with him." She rubbed her face, smearing mud across it. "A one-and-only sort of thing."

Jubal groaned. "Joie, I never thought you'd turn all mushy romantic on us." He slung his arm around Gabrielle's shoulder. "He's solid, honey. Weird, but solid."

Gabrielle exchanged a long look with Jubal and turned to Joie. "Well, I suppose your life with him will always be interesting."

"My sisters have already put gray in my hair," Jubal announced. "I won't survive Traian hanging around, howling at the moon, biting Joie's neck. And, just for the record, stay the hell away from mine, Traian. Having a woman bite my neck might be a turn-on—kinky, maybe, but I could handle it. Having a man bite my neck is out of the question. Doesn't do a thing for me," Jubal said dryly.

"Ouch. That hurts, Jubal," Traian said. "I was really looking forward to a snack later." He leaned down to brush the top of Joie's head with his chin. He had to touch her, keep reminding himself she was real. Even when they were speaking telepathically while he searched the complex of caves for whatever the vampires were frantic to find, he almost believed he had made her up.

Gabrielle managed a grin. "Well, he fits in with our weird family, Joie. I can't wait to see Mom and Dad's reaction."

Jubal touched the weapon on his wrist. "Do you think they can track me with this thing on me?"

"Since we don't know how to get it off other than to chop off your arm," Traian said, "we will just have to chance it."

A deep boom shook the network of caverns. "Go," Traian ordered. "Through that left chamber."

He relied solely on instincts now, rushing them through the narrow hallways that opened into one chamber after another, down a maze of halls into another, larger chamber, again filled with the strange lighting system. They ran from one wall to another, examining each, but they all appeared solid.

"There has to be a way out," Traian said. "Mages are not able to shape-shift or fly. They are nearly as human as you are, only with longer lives and the ability to weave elements together and bend them to their purpose. There must be an opening leading to the surface. Look for something that does not feel right. There will be a hallway leading up to the entrance."

"It's here," Jubal said. "I can feel it."

"Like the rocks outside the cave. The pattern was all wrong," Joie said. "Jubal, you're good at patterns. Find us the opening, and hurry. Jubal's rather infamous in our family for his mathematical mind," she told Traian. "He can see a pattern in just about anything. That's how he makes all his money."

They could hear scratching, a terrible sound amplified by the acoustics of the cavernous room. Great claws scraping at the earth, digging to get at them. They spread out, walked along the wall, carefully examining every surface. All the while they could hear the vampires tunneling furiously through the mud and ice. The sounds grew louder, closer, and Traian dropped back, facing the wall where the creatures were certain to break through.

"I've got it!" Jubal said triumphantly. "We were expecting up, but it's down. The floor. See the pattern on the floor, Joie?"

"Open it," Traian said tersely, not looking, his attention centered completely on the far wall.

Jubal studied the squares, pyramids, and starburst patterns of stone beneath the layers of muddy ice. In the center of each symbol were hieroglyphics, pictures carved into each stone. He stepped on various ones, taking his time, choosing each stone carefully, following the pattern he could see laid out before him.

At last a large stone slid aside to reveal steps carved into the ice. Jubal hesitated. "Are you certain this is the way?"

"It has to be the way," Traian said. "Take your sisters and go."

Jubal was cautious, shining his light down the narrow staircase. The stairs appeared to be a bridge over a dark, fathomless abyss. "It's another bridge, Traian. Do I trust it?"

"You have to. It must have been their way out."

Jubal took a deep breath and stepped onto the first stair, found it solid, and reached back to aid Gabrielle. "Hurry, Joie."

"Come with us, Traian," Joie pleaded.

Water gushed in a dark, muddy stream from the side of the wall. Insects poured into the gallery. The wall to Traian's left collapsed in an oozing pool of dark sludge.

Two hideous creatures flopped onto the floor of the chamber, abominations in the crystal perfection of the room. Gaunt and cadaverous, they were covered in black muck. Baring their jagged, spiked teeth, they stared at Traian from red-rimmed eyes filled with venomous hatred.

Chapter Six

"Gabrielle, run," Joie urged. Fear clawed at her insides, but she dropped back to protect her sister and brother. "Jubal, go, don't look back."

She couldn't leave Traian. She wouldn't leave him—not to face hideous monsters on his own. It didn't matter that he claimed to have hunted vampires all his life, she was incapable of abandoning anyone to face danger alone. And somehow, Traian was connected to her. A part of her blood and bones. Of her heart and soul. She would stand with him.

"Not without you, Joie," Jubal said. "I mean it. Gabrielle, start down that staircase *now*."

"Go with them, Joie," Traian urged. "It will be easier for me to defend myself without having to worry about your safety."

Heart beating hard, Joie hesitated just for a moment and then whirled to run after her brother and sister. Guilt settled hard on her shoulders, but arguing when action was called for was just plain stupid and she refused to be that woman.

Seeing that Joie had committed to following them, Jubal caught Gabrielle's hand and jerked her down the stairs in a race for their lives. Joie took three steps and the chamber shook ominously. Great blocks of ice burst from the walls, shooting across the room from every direction even as the giant icicles hanging on the ceiling rocked, cracking with loud explosive shocks and fell like giant missiles, rocketing toward the floor. Some shattered, so that large chunks and debris fell with the spears of ice.

Traian leapt across the distance to throw Joie down, shielding her with his own body as well as hastily constructing a force around them to deflect the attack from the cave itself. The thick slab of stone slid back into place, cutting them off from the hidden stairway leading out of the chamber. Great chunks of ice fell over the escape hatch, locking Joie in the cavern with Traian and the two furious vampires.

Traian buried his face in her hair for a moment, holding her tightly against him. *We will be all right, Joie. You can do this. Follow my instructions and do not look directly at them. They are masters of illusion.*

Joie had one knife as well as her utility knife, her ice axe, and a few other smaller, less effective weapons and knew Jubal no doubt was inventorying his weapons as well. He would have to protect Gabrielle and find a way out of the elaborate labyrinth while she faced the undead with Traian. Neither seemed a very good position to be in, yet Traian exuded such confidence, in the calmness of his mind and the steadiness of his voice.

Put your brother and sister out of your head. You will need to focus solely on this situation to come out of this alive.

Joie knew Traian was right, but it didn't make it any easier to push her siblings out of her mind. *Be safe Jubal and Gabby. I love you both.*

She took a deep breath and nodded. The warmth of his body infused hers with much needed heat. She flexed her fingers in preparation. *I'll do whatever you need me to do to help.* What else could she do? She had no idea how to fight such evil creatures. You killed them and they just got back up.

Gabrielle cried out as Jubal pushed her in front of him, and then the stairway went completely dark. Jubal caught her shoulders in a firm grip to give her confidence. He turned around, shining his headlamp along the walls of the narrow tunnel they found themselves in.

"Joie didn't make it in, Gabby," he said. "She's on the other side and I think the ceiling came down. I can still feel her—and Traian—so they're alive. We'll have to find our own way out and trust them to find their own way as well."

"He took your blood. Can you talk to him? Can you reach Joie?"

"There's tons of ice between us, Gabby. I tried when the ceiling caved in, but you and I were never as strong as Joie in telepathy. I think it's possible Traian could reach us, but most likely, taking the brunt of the ice fall and vampires hounding them, they have their hands full. We're on our own. We can do this. We've been in caves all of our lives." He spoke confidently, deliberately reminding her of the fact that their parents had belayed them up the sides of cliffs and down into caves when they were toddlers.

Gabrielle nodded. "It's so cold. I think my brain is getting fuzzy. I'm with you, Jubal, I'm not going to panic on you. Let's just find the way out of here."

"I'm going to get out in front of you and I want you to stay close to me, Gabby. I don't know how many of those vampires were in the caves. If we run into one, we have to kill it by going for the heart." He felt her shudder and he squeezed her shoulder. "We can do it. You know we can."

He pushed past her on the narrow stair. The steps were carved of ice and very slippery. There was nothing to hang onto. He proceeded with great caution—examining the walls and each stair before he placed his feet. It was very quiet, almost too quiet. He could hear Gabrielle's labored breathing and every breath she took came out as white vapor.

Jubal slowly became aware that the strange weapon on his wrist emitted heat, somehow infusing his body with warmth, regulating his body temperature. He paused to shine his lamp on the mage object that seemed to have chosen him. Instead of looking like a weapon, the blades had slowly retreated, forming a simple thick band around his wrist. He could make out a pattern etched into the metal, a design he was vaguely familiar with. He'd definitely seen it before.

"What are you doing?" Gabrielle asked curiously and stepped close to him, looking over his shoulder at the band. "What is that?"

"A crest," Jubal answered. There was disbelief in his voice. The design wasn't just any crest—specifically it was the family crest—*his* father's family's crest. The weapon had changed its looks. Could it somehow have "felt" his history through the odd metal? Being made of some kind of metal, the bracelet should have been cold, yet it was warmer than ever.

"This is creepy, Jubal. Maybe you should take it off," Gabrielle suggested.

Jubal felt the weapon's reaction—it gripped his wrist tighter and shuddered. "I don't think so, Gabby. I think this was made for someone in our family to wear. If feels . . ." He paused, searching for the right word: ". . . right."

"That's impossible and you know it, Jubal. Mom comes from South America and Dad . . ." She trailed off.

Jubal nodded. "Exactly. Dad. I'm very much like Dad and he never talks about his side of the family. Never. Mom is a very dominant personality and he's very quiet, but you and I both know we all three are above-average intelligence and we get that part from him. Mom's the one with the athletic abilities and we managed to get that as well. But just suppose Dad's family was somehow part mage?"

Gabrielle drew back. "They're evil."

"An entire species couldn't be wholly evil, Gabby. In any case, we need to find our way out of here. Whatever this thing is—it doesn't feel evil to me and I want to keep it." There was something about the wrist band, a kind of growing attachment, almost affection, he couldn't explain. The thing made no sense, but he was sure, once out of the labyrinth of caves, he could unlock the puzzle.

Jubal turned back to the stairway, hating that Gabrielle shivered continually and yet he was warm. His headlamp revealed that the steep stairway curved around, almost spiraling, taking them down thirty feet or more, and then curved back up. Suppressing the urge to hurry, he kept a steady pace, every once in a while reaching out to make certain Traian and Joie were alive. He couldn't reach either of them telepathically, but he knew they still lived.

Gabrielle didn't say anything at all, but followed him, stumbling every once in a while and catching herself by grasping his shoulder. Jubal knew he had to get her out of the caves and down the mountain—or at least to the tents where he could warm her up. It seemed a lifetime on the winding staircase of ice, with only their headlamps to light the way.

"I think we're close, Gabby," Jubal said encouragingly.

His lamp found the end of the ice stairs. There was a narrow strip of ice that dead-ended abruptly into a thick wall of ice. Gabrielle sank down onto the stair and covered her face with her hands.

"We're trapped, Jubal. I searched the walls as we came down and they're solid."

"There has to be a way out, honey," Jubal said. "Just give me a minute. The entrances and exits seem to be all about patterns and math. You know how my mind works. I practically see in numbers and patterns."

"I'm having a difficult time thinking clearly," she confessed.

Jubal turned to her. She needed to warm up. Her body was protecting her heart and lungs. Soon she wouldn't be able to walk if he didn't find a way to warm her. He glanced down at the thick band of metal circling his wrist. If he could take it off and put it on her . . . the weapon tightened as if reading his thoughts. He put his hands on his sister's shoulders and began to rub her arms up and down through her jacket.

The bracelet brushed against her sleeve. At once he felt the warmth spread through her coat. Immediately he pressed the metal against the back of her neck and when he noticed she stopped shivering, he took both of her hands and cupped them over the weapon. "Are you okay now?" he asked.

Gabrielle nodded. "Much warmer, thank you." She touched the etching on the bracelet, tracing the strange lettering. "You're right, Jubal. I have seen these symbols before, in Dad's study."

He turned back to examine the wall. "Keep your light running over the wall in three foot sections. See if you can spot any differences."

The ice at first seemed to be smooth and very solid and thick. Jubal stepped closer. He moved first to his right and then to his left, examining the wall. When he moved left, the bracelet grew very warm and pulsed with energy. Elation made his heart jump. Oh yeah. He'd found it. He moved his hand carefully over ice and the wall sprang to life, glowing beneath the ice layers to reveal thousands of symbols.

"How is that going to help?" Gabrielle asked. "My God, there's so many."

Jubal walked back and forth, scanning the wall up and down and from left to right and then right to left. The secret was right there. He was certain he would find it. Patiently, he held his wrist up, adding to the light their lamps gave off. Several times the bracelet pulsed in recognition. He knew in the midst of all those symbols was the key to unlocking the door. He cocked his head to one side, eyeing the symbols from every direction. Abruptly he stopped, a slow smile spreading over his face.

"Of course, Gabrielle. It was there the entire time. Do you see it? Do you remember *Draco,* the dragon constellation Dad told us stories about? We had to memorize all the constellations, but *Draco* was his favorite. He would tell us stories about the great dragon in the sky. How the sky was dark, and he was born of fire, a great raging beast with fire in his heart, courage in his soul, and wisdom beyond the ages. Look at this from a right angle. It's a night sky with all the constellations and here, on the northern hemisphere, you can see his head and the way his tail slithers between the Big and Little Dippers."

Gabrielle tilted her head. "You're right. How in the world did you spot that among all the other graffiti on this wall?"

Jubal grinned at her and confidently touched the first point of the Draco constellation. He traced his way along the wedge-shaped great head and down the body to the long tail. The ice began to shimmer with every touch of his hand along the dragon's back. The ice rippled, appeared to flow, going nearly transparent so they could both see through the wall to the other side, to the open mountain.

Gabrielle, eager to get out of the cave, took a step toward the wall.

Gabby, stop! Don't move or make a sound, Jubal cautioned. He held his wrist up for her to see the bracelet was no longer etched metal, but the curved blades had opened like the petals of a flower, unfolding to look lethal and ready for battle. *Something isn't right.*

Gabrielle took a firm grip on her ice axe and nodded. Jubal was grateful she didn't panic. Gabrielle might not be as tough as Joie, but she always could be counted on.

I smell that same foul odor those other vampires put off, Gabrielle told him. *There's got to be one close by, that's why your bracelet turned into a weapon.*

It made sense to both of them. If mages had to protect themselves against vampires, even hundreds of years earlier, they would have had to have weapons to aid them.

It would have been better had it come with an instruction manual, Jubal pointed out.

Gabrielle gave him a wan grin and both turned off their headlamps as he laid his hand over the last star in the dragon constellation. The weapon pulsed and gave off a faint glow, so that both could see the waves rolling in front of him, curving back to form an archway, allowing an escape. The ice glistened and sparkled, the seamless rolls a beautiful entrance—or exit. Instinct told him that the door wouldn't hold long. Jubal stepped in front of his sister. She put her hand on his back and followed him through out into the night.

The curved blades on the weapon around Jubal's wrist began to spin. Cold air blasted them, a wind coming off the mountains as they emerged from the cave. The bracelet on his wrist blazed red, pulsing with energy, the blades spinning so fast, Jubal lifted his arm away from his body to keep from being cut. Behind them, just as smoothly, just as silently, the entrance was gone and they were left in the open with a monstrous vampire staring at them with red eyes.

Jubal barely saw the attack. The apparition had been crouching on the ground and it drove forward at him the moment he emerged. Gabrielle screamed and swung the ice axe at the vampire's head as the spinning blades suddenly leapt from Jubal's wrist, as if alive with a mind of their own. The weapon hummed as it spun through the air, glowing red, giving off a tremendous heat. The whirling blades slammed into the vampire's chest, right over the heart, cutting a perfect circle hole through the chest, burning as it did so.

The spike drove deep into the right temple of the undead. He opened his mouth wide in a scream that had the mountain rumbling ominously. Snow slithered down from above them, the first sign of an avalanche. Jubal shoved Gabrielle back towards the overhang and both watched in a kind of horror as the undead burst into flame and incinerated. The mountain rumbled again and shook itself. The weapon leapt toward Jubal's outstretched arm just as tons of snow blew down the mountain, taking the ashes of the vampire with it.

Gabrielle and Jubal clung to one another there in the shelter of the overhang, waiting for the snow to settle. He stared down at his wrist. The bracelet was once more just that, a thick band of metal with familiar etchings keeping him warm.

Gabrielle lifted her head from his shoulder and gave him a small, wan smile. "If we're going to spend any time around Joie's man, I'm going to have to buy a new ice axe . . . fast."

The two burst out laughing, half relieved, half a little hysterically.

The chamber stopped rumbling and the ice settled around Traian and Joie. Traian was on his feet instantly, facing the threat of the vampires, his hand pulling Joie up with his easy strength. Her heart thundered loudly in her ears and she tasted fear in her mouth.

Let your heart follow the rhythm of mine.

His voice was terribly intimate, a soothing balm that allowed her to keep her breathing even. She moved a distance from Traian, giving him room to fight. She could taste fear in her mouth. She had no gun, and only one knife.

My fourth dan black belt doesn't look too promising considering that those very nasty things have wicked-looking talons and mouths full of shark teeth. We could use a gun or two. Maybe a machine gun.

Stay close to me. I want you where I can protect you. They can move the earth, and rain down missiles from the ceiling. They will not fight in the way you expect.

Traian had never really experienced gut-wrenching, bone-deep fear before. He had never had anything to lose. Now there was everything. A woman whose mind he shared, whose body he didn't yet know intimately.

I'm well aware of that. Joie inched closer to him, trying to appear confident in a situation she'd never encountered and had little idea what to expect.

For some reason her simple words made Traian relax, want to smile. Joie didn't panic easily. She didn't lack for courage and she was committed to fighting with him. She wasn't going to faint because vampires were real and had come with vengeance and death in mind.

Don't count on it, she denied, staying close in his mind, reading his thoughts. *Fainting might be my only option if they get their hands on me, and I'm not above trying it.*

Her wry amusement told him she was a shadow in his mind, looking for strategy on how to defeat the enemy.

Do they have a weakness?

Ego. Vampires are extremely vain.

Joie took a deep breath as the creatures slowly pulled themselves up to their impressive heights. Fire burned in their eyes. A foul stench permeated the cavern, choked off all the cool, clean air and replaced it with a thick putrid substance. The falling ice hadn't come from them, that much was obvious. They had protected themselves just as Traian had done.

Which is the stronger?

Traian noted her calm manner. She accepted that they would have to fight their way clear. Having battled with the same vampires on three occasions, Traian was well aware of their strengths and capabilities.

The one with the incisors over his lower lip—he is extremely powerful. He is called Valenteen and is a master vampire. The other is called Shafe. There might be more, so stay very alert.

Well, darn, and here I was expecting I'd take a nap while you did a little cleanup.

Traian worked at keeping a straight face. Even in their desperate situation, Joie could let him know her feelings.

I was worried you might be a little tired and needing a rest. Can you distract them for a moment?

Joie tapped her foot. "If it isn't the troll brothers. How are you? Just dropped in to be neighborly? I'm so glad you didn't bother to dress formally. It's just a small get-together we're having."

Deliberately she walked across the stone patterns in the floor, keeping their attention centered on her even as she made certain she was just a bit behind Traian. "We're in the midst of redecorating. What do you think? Too many crystal balls?" She indicated the largest, nearly a foot tall, resting on a tall pillar of black obsidian. "They're very valuable. You can see your future in them. This one answers questions and finds objects." She reached out as if to pat the smooth sphere.

Joie was fully aware that Traian was keeping his body between her and the vampires. The two creatures stood in a swirl of steam and mist, coated in black ooze. The moment she mentioned the spheres, greedy eyes stared at the globe.

Surprisingly, Joie felt warmth along her palm as she positioned it above the crystal ball. The crystal leapt to life at the close proximity of her hand. For a timeless moment, she saw her own face swirling in the mists of the globe, and Traian standing behind her, reaching for her, love etched into the lines of his face, hunger and desire burning in the depths of his eyes. She couldn't look away from his face, there in the sphere, from the intensity of his love. He couldn't feel that way about her, could be? He didn't know her. How could two people be so drawn to one another, recognize love so quickly? His look robbed her of breath, of sanity. She wanted to crawl inside the sphere and be with him for eternity.

Get away from that thing.

Joie blinked, and forced herself to look up. White swirls of mist were filling the cavern, consuming Traian. Consuming her. In the tendrils of fog, something moved—something dark and menacing. She caught a glimpse of another shape in the shadows curled protectively around an object, but she couldn't make it out with the white mist and gray shadows merging together.

Traian turned slowly toward those gray shadows, his hands down at his sides and slightly outstretched, palms up as if appeasing something—or someone. Behind him, a darker shadow loomed, one with a hideous skull, skin stretched tight, blood-stained teeth and glowing red eyes.

Watch out!

Joie tackled Traian. Her momentum carried them both away from the vampire and close to the outer wall of the cavern. Traian rolled with her, his arms tight around her, taking her through the dense fog. The drops felt wet on their skin, the blanket muffling sound, but still, something moved inside all that white and gray swirling mist.

Very gently, Traian eased her to her feet. *Stay very still. Perfectly still,* he cautioned.

Joie looked cautiously around her. An array of weapons adorned the nearest alcove. Glittering gems decorated wicked-looking knives and long spears and swords. Here was a virtual treasure trove for Joie. She was drawn to the weapons, yet something held her back, some finely tuned warning system that prompted her to put her hands behind her back and ignore them.

Traian calmly regarded the black shadow that was emerging from the fog in the cavern. "Justice has come, Valenteen," he said to the master vampire. "A shadow warrior has been awakened and he is seeking our deaths. Do we fight each other?"

Valenteen growled harshly, shaking his head, backing away from the large, smoky creature emerging from the shadows.

Joie twisted her fingers in the back of Traian's shirt, peeking around him at the thing Traian had identified as a shadow warrior. It was insubstantial, made of ever-moving black and gray smoke. Its eyes glowed an eerie red, not like the bloodshot eyes of the vampires, but fierce flame burning brightly. There was something very noble in the stern face she occasionally caught sight of, as if the shadow was a warrior of old who had long fought for honor.

I wouldn't mind waking up now. If the vampire is afraid of it, how much trouble are we in?

Traian reached behind him, circling her bare wrist with his fingers. Gently. Barely there. Just a whisper of contact, yet it was enough. They were together. It was all that mattered. He would shield her from the warrior, from the vampires.

Can you get out of here by yourself? It suddenly occurred to her that he could shape-shift, perhaps become as insubstantial as the mist. Maybe even burrow through earth and ice as the vampires had done. He had known she would be a hindrance to him. He'd told her to leave with the others. *Traian? Can you get out of here without me?*

The vampires dissolved, leaving behind a pool of black goo. It bubbled and spat a poisonous brew at the shadow warrior. Joie gasped. There was a strange silence. An icy blast of air cleared the stench from the chamber and pushed the smoky creature away from Traian and Joie.

It matters little if I could. I would never leave you behind. His voice was reassuring. Calm. Steady. Confident.

Joie's mouth went dry. *Jubal and Gabrielle are still in the caves. If the vampires find them . . . my brother and sister can't protect themselves from the vampires.*

Both vampires have remained in this room. They will not leave or move to give away their presence to the warrior. In any case, there is little we can do other than hope they make it out fast. At this moment, both are alive. I would know if your brother perished. You're doing fine. Stay calm. We will get out of this and your brother is a man of great resources.

Joie let her breath out and worked to control the wild beating of her heart. *Why isn't that thing coming at us? Can't he see us?*

The shadow warrior has not attacked because we haven't touched anything. If we draw his attention to us, or take something the mages left behind, he will strike.

Joie frowned. *My brother took the weapon that came to him. It's on his wrist. Why didn't the warrior attack him?*

I believe that is a good question. The shadow warrior would not attack a mage.

Joie didn't like the speculation in his voice or the distrust in his mind. Voices whispered, distracting her. She could hear the continual murmurs filling her mind—filling the chamber with temptation. Before she knew what she was doing, Joie's fingers were nearly curled around a knife with a wicked-looking curved blade. It called to her. Her palm itched to feel the weapon in her hand. She clenched her fist, resisting the temptation. The voices increased in strength. She glanced toward the spheres, saw them all active, the clear colors swirling with life, with deeper hues and sparkling gems.

Traian caught both of her hands in his. *Talk to me. Tell me about yourself. Everything you can think of. Look only at me. Look into my eyes. See me. Only me.*

His hands were much larger than hers, enveloping them. When she obediently tore her gaze from the jeweled daggers and knives, she was caught in the black depths of Traian's gaze. The world narrowed for her.

Around them, smoke and mist drifted upward from the floor, creating a world in the clouds where voices muttered, the words in an ancient tongue, harsh, yet not foul, insistent, yet not commanding. Colors pulsed in the room, bright banners from the spheres, which were alive with heat and energy.

Look only at me, Traian reiterated when she would have turned her head toward the pulsing lights. *This is a trap directed at you, at your love of weapons, at your curiosity. Think of me. Let me tell you who I am, what I am. What I need and want. I want to know everything about you and your family. Talk to me. Tell me who you really are, what you stand for. Tell me everything about yourself.*

His voice was mesmerizing, tugging at her heart when she thought there should be only physical attraction. He was easily the sexiest man she'd ever encountered. They were in mortal danger. Vampires huddled somewhere in the room, awaiting their moment to strike. A warrior come to life out of the shadows that guarded centuries-old treasures in a world of sorcery, yet Joie was fascinated by the man in front of her.

You don't make sense.

I make perfect sense. He smiled, a flash of dazzling white teeth. *We make perfect sense.*

She nearly stopped breathing. *You know I work as a body-guard.*

Joie found it difficult to resist the pull of temptation for those amazing weapons just inches from her fingertips and her gaze strayed to the ornate swords.

Traian tipped her chin up, forcing her gaze to his. *Silly profession, placing your precious body between someone else and danger.*

She laughed softly in her mind, amazed at how, in the middle of danger, he could mesmerize her.

Traian felt the vibration pulse through his body, touch him in places he had long ago forgotten.

You spent several lifetimes chasing vampires. I'm catching very interesting memories in your mind, unless you spent all of your life watching Dracula movies. I think you've placed your precious and very sexy body between danger and people many times. And don't say you're a man and that it makes a difference. That would seriously annoy me.

Growls of hatred mixed with the insidious whispers. The smaller vampire, the one Traian had identified as Shafe, emerged from the black goo, hissing and spitting, dragging himself across the floor on his belly. His gaze firmly fixed on the largest crystal ball, his claws scored the stones as he tried to stop himself from answering the summons.

Even with Traian's mesmerizing eyes and hypnotic voice, it was nearly impossible for Joie to ignore the drama being played out in the swirling mists of the cave. The insistent voices chanted a steady rhythm, drawing the vampire to-ward the glowing crystal. Greed and fear were on the face of the creature as it edged closer and closer. All the while, the dark shadow of the warrior, guardian of the wizard's treasures, watched dispassionately.

Joie shivered. Fear was a living, breathing entity nearly choking her. At times, through the rising mist coming off the stone floor, she could make out a suit of armor on the warrior; at other times it was as insubstantial as the clouds.

Traian pulled Joie into his arms, drawing her tightly against his chest. His movements were deliberately slow, careful, wary of drawing the warrior's attention to them. *We are going to float upward, Joie, just drift toward the ceiling above us. Keep looking at me.*

She was afraid. Battling human adversaries was one thing; facing down vampires and warriors made up of smoke and shadow was something altogether different. She slid her palm up Traian's chest, the solid wall of flesh and blood re-assuring her. Her arm curved around his neck. She locked her fingers there, fitting her body tightly against his. His much more masculine frame was hard like an oak tree. There was little give to the defined muscles beneath his skin. She felt her feet leave the ground and she closed her eyes, sending up a quick prayer.

Traian watched the warrior. Colored lights pulsed through the cavern, lit the mist so that wraith-like creatures appeared to be moving within it—ghosts of the mages, lost so long ago. He tightened his arms around Joie. She fit perfectly to him, her mind comfortable in his, drawing knowledge and studying tactics. He could feel her there inside him, sharing his memories and gathering information on his battles with vampires, fully prepared to join him should there be need.

More than anything else, he wanted her to know him as a man. He wanted time with her. He wanted to hear her laugh, to see warmth and acceptance in her eyes the way he had imagined during their long-distance chats. And he wanted her out of danger. Things could go wrong in an instant and he focused on one thing—getting Joie to safety.

They drifted higher in the cavern, and Traian clouded

their image with more mist, more smoke, so that they seemed part of the haze. He took care that their movements were slow and lazy and as natural as possible, so that nothing would trigger the instincts of the warrior.

The shadow creature was motionless, even while the smoke that made up its body whirled and spun in dark threads. The fierce eyes remained fixed on the vampire crawling toward the temptation of the pulsing crystal orb. Shafe drew closer, closer, reaching out to the visions and promises of wealth and power swirling inside the globe.

Triumphantly the vampire placed his palms around the beckoning crystal. The moment he touched the globe, the shadow warrior threw back its head and roared. For a brief moment the smoke around it cleared. The guardian stood tall and straight, dressed in glittering, multihued scaled armor. And then it was smoke again, rushing across the wide expanse of floor, not quite touching the ground.

Valenteen, the older vampire, oozed from the black pool, shifting into the form of a snake-like creature with a head like a drill. It slithered to the nearest wall and began to burrow through the ice wall. Joie strained to see below her, to see the shadow warrior as he reached the undead cupping the crystal ball.

Your light. Turn it off.

Her heart jumped. *We need the light.*

I see fine in the dark. We want to escape this chamber. I can take us through the air shaft and do not want to chance drawing the warrior's attention.

As she doused the light, Shafe screamed hideously. Colors glowed in the rising mist. A dark blood-red stain slowly began to invade the smoky fog. It spread like a virus. A violent clash of light and sound burst through the chamber as the vampire's voice shrieked and wailed until Joie buried her face in Traian's neck, her body trembling.

His gut knotted. *We are almost out. Do not look. This cave is a trap and we will seal it up so no others can find it.*

You're thinking you'll come back tomorrow night and find out what the vampires were searching for, she guessed.

I have to find out. I have been in these caves several weeks, fighting the vampires on and off. I destroyed more than one, yet they remained. That is highly unusual and it worries me. Worse still is the fact that Valenteen was not the only master. There was another in the group, Gallent. I was able, after several battles, to destroy him, but he was clearly with this group. And I think there is still one more. . . . so much more powerful . . .

Joie sighed and hugged him tighter. *This is not happy news. Sounds like our gang problems. We'd better start looking on the internet for a site called vampires of the world, unite.*

Above her head, he smiled. *It had not occurred to me to check there, but if we find such a thing, are you volunteering for undercover work?*

She made a small growling noise of dissent and bit his shoulder hard.

The air shaft was narrow, but he angled their bodies until they slipped through, taking them to the upper levels. As soon as she felt the ground beneath her feet, she turned on her light, caught his hand, and sprinted through the tunnel toward the entrance.

"Valenteen is not following us. Although he is a master vampire, he will not attempt to fight me alone."

His words stopped her. The idea that a creature as hideous and lethal as a vampire wouldn't fight Traian alone was frightening. What did she know of him, after all? He was a voice speaking to her in the night. A man who drank blood and shifted shapes.

"I am a man of honor. A man who has found the one

woman. The only woman." He put a gentle hand on her shoulder. "I know this happened too fast and you do not altogether trust it."

"If I don't think about it, I trust it, and that scares me, Traian. I'm not particularly a trusting person. All this time I thought I was still in control, after all, I did rescue you. But now you're saying those creatures won't attack you while they're alone and that tells me that they're very afraid of you."

"I am an ancient hunter. I have been tried in battle for more years than I care to remember. I know the ways of the vampire and I am much skilled in what I do." There was no arrogance or bravado in his voice, only acceptance and truth.

"And these vampires?"

"Should not have been together. They should not be here, in the Carpathian Mountains, so close to our prince and many of our males. I was returning to my homeland when I first came across them. I knew they were desperate to find something in that cave. Although it was risky to pit myself against so many, it was my duty to my people to stay and discover what they were looking for. Even after you found me and I recognized who you were, I stayed because the vampires were so frantic to find something. I had no idea this was a cave of mages. And it looks recently occupied."

"And what is the significance of mages to a vampire? I know what it would be to humans. Most of us don't actually believe the fairy tales about wizards and crystal balls—and dragons. That was very cool, by the way."

"You saw the spheres in that room. Ancient spells and power remain in them. We don't want vampires, or anyone, for that matter, to get their hands on things best left alone. Carpathians are of the earth. We have gifts, but we do not wield power in the same way as the mages do."

"You believe that some still live?"

"I would think it likely. At least I would think some of their descendants remain and have retained their knowledge, or at least a portion of it."

Joie sighed. "Lovely thought. Anyone who created that shadow warrior is not going to be counted among my best friends."

"Nor mine." There was an ominous warning to his voice.

She looked up quickly. "I know what you're thinking. You just remembered, if my brother is a mage, than so am I. We are from the same parents and that's an indisputable fact. I can't reach either Gabrielle or Jubal. They're too far away." There was worry in her voice.

Traian took a breath and stopped, seeking his blood bond with Jubal. "They are out of the caves and heading for the inn. They thought to get a rescue team together. I have informed him there is no need, we will join them shortly."

Joie nearly sagged with relief. "You're certain?"

"Absolutely."

Joie followed him through the long hall, already feeling the open air on her body, not looking at the beauty and magnificence of her surroundings as she normally would. She was so relieved that her brother and sister had made it out that she wanted to weep. She searched for a topic to keep from giving in to the intensity of her emotions. "You grew up a long time ago."

He grinned at her, his teeth flashing in the light of her lantern. "Well, yes. I have lived for centuries. I barely remember my parents anymore." His smile slipped away. "The memory of my childhood days has faded. I catch glimpses at times. I do recall the years just before leaving my homeland. The way the prince looked at us all. I saw it in his eyes. His own death, the decline of our people, his dread for all of the warriors he was sending away from home. Our women were so few, even then the numbers were declining. Back then we had alliances with humans. Now we keep to ourselves and just do our best to blend in."

She listened to the sound of his voice and heard the sorrow that ran deep. In his mind she saw the battles, sometimes with childhood friends. She saw his inner demons, the insidious whispers of power, the dark stain that slowly spread over him, calling to him. And he was always alone. In every memory, he was always alone. Joie wanted to comfort him. She caught his hand, tangled her fingers with his. She meant it to be a brief gesture, but he tightened his grip.

"I grew up very differently," she said, ducking her head to avoid a large crystal formation. "My family is very close and very loving. We all talk at the same time and give each other all sorts of unwanted advice. My dad tells outrageous stories. He used to sneak into our bedroom at night with a flashlight shining on his face and tell scary stories until we screamed and laughed and Mom came running in to chastise him. Once, after he read us Stephen King's *Cujo*, he put whipped cream on the muzzle of our huge mutt and shoved him into the bedroom. It's a wonder we all survived his sense of humor."

She laughed at the memory, deliberately sharing with Traian the warmth of her childhood, the love in her family. "We're all a little bit crazy, but it's okay with us."

"Do you think I will fit in?" He brought her hand to his chest and held it against his heart. "I would not mind having a family after all this time."

He was a tall man with wide shoulders and eyes that had seen far too much, yet the lost note in his voice turned her heart over. Joie smiled at him. "I can't wait for you to meet my mother. She does not like men, other than my father, and she can be very intimidating. You're an alpha male and she will definitely have an opinion. We'll see how well you can stand up to her. She ran off every boy who wanted to date my sister or me."

He smiled at her, rather like a wolf smiling at a lamb. "I will have to thank her."

Chapter Seven

The night air was crisp and clean and so fresh, Joie gratefully dragged it deep into her lungs. Fear was dissipating now that she was out in the open and she knew her siblings were safe. She pulled her helmet from her head to allow the wind to comb through her hair. Stretching her arms toward the moon, she laughed softly. "I love the night. I love everything about it. It doesn't matter if it's stormy or not."

She turned her head to look at Traian. His face was beautiful in the moonlight. "Worthy of a Greek god," she murmured, astonished that she *felt* so much for him, that her emotions were so strong and connected with his. His hair fell like black silk around his face to his shoulders. There wasn't so much as a smear of mud on his face. All traces of blood were gone from his chest, leaving only the raw gashes on his flesh.

Joie shook her head, stepping away from him, putting distance between them. She needed space, needed to find balance. "Thanks a lot for leaving me standing filthy and wet all by myself while you're all shined up and looking good. I'm not even going to ask how you did that."

His teeth gleamed at her, more the smile of a wolf than a

man. "I have my little secrets. You are shivering. Hand me your harness and pack and take this jacket." He enfolded her in the warmth of a suit jacket.

Joie decided not to ask him where he found the jacket either, or how he got clean. "How did you find the way out? I couldn't see a thing." She sank down because all at once she was tired and she wanted to feel the ground under her. Traian had changed her entire life in the blink of an eye, and she didn't want to think too much about the bizarre world he lived in.

"There were signs if you knew what to look for. In the old times, Carpathians and mages were not enemies. We lived side by side and enjoyed the benefits of both races. We often used the same glyphs. I saw them as we moved through the halls. Mages and Carpathians actually worked and studied together, were friends and allies. We shared knowledge with one another."

"What happened to change everything?"

Traian sighed. "Mages have great longevity, but they are not immortal. We can be killed, but it is not easy to do. The great mage, Xavier, we all trusted and believed in—he often taught our more gifted children in the arts . . ."

"More gifted than you are?" Joie raised an eyebrow. "You can do just about anything. How much more gifted are your children?"

Instead of smiling he looked sad. "We do not have children any longer. Ours is a dying species. Few women are born, and our children are not surviving. Such treasures are lost to us." He shook his head. "This network of caves could very well have belonged to Xavier at one time and it is possible one of his descendents is using it now—unless he still lives."

"I can hear the distaste and contempt in your voice."

"He betrayed the friendship of our people and began a

war that has been waged for centuries, devastating both of our peoples."

Joie looked up at his face. There was no hatred, only a sorrow that filled him with sadness. To her, Traian was a handsome man, timeless and even elegant in an honorable warrior sort of way. The lines in his face only served to make him more attractive to her. "I'm so sorry, Traian." She couldn't imagine what his life had been like.

Traian crouched down beside her, touched her chin with gentle fingers. "Let me take you back to the inn where you are staying. You are tired and hungry and want a shower. You are also very worried about your brother and sister. You needn't be. I've assured your brother that we are safe and they are waiting at the inn, already warm."

"Thank you, I know you told me they were safe, but it's difficult with everything that's happened not to want to touch them physically to reassure myself. I know they're both experienced climbers and neither panic, but we've never had to face . . ." She broke off and waved her hands. "Vampires and traps." She covered her face for a moment. "That sounds so insane. The world has no idea those things actually exist. It's crazy."

"And they can't know. Every now and then, down through the ages, a society raises the alarm and there is a massive witch hunt. They kill everyone they suspect, human, Carpathian, and just people who they don't like. As far as I know they've never managed to actually kill a vampire."

She shot him a confused look. "You don't want us to say anything."

"We handle it," he said. "Just as we've been doing for centuries."

Joie swept a hand through her hair, pushing it back from her face. "I am tired, Traian. I feel as if I could sleep for a month."

He drew her to her feet, and then simply lifted her into his arms as if she was no more than a child, cradling her against his chest.

Joie burst out laughing. "This is so medieval. Male carries little woman over mountain. Oh, the utter humiliation of it all." She wrapped her arms more tightly around his neck in case he thought to put her down. Joie allowed her head to drop back as she scanned the heavens. "If you ever tell a single soul I let you do this, I'll have to hurt you. I just want to be very clear on this. Not one single word."

Traian looked down into her upturned face. She was trying to be courageous when she was obviously exhausted. He wanted to kiss her. More than anything, it seemed necessary to bend his head and find her mouth with his. Just taste her. Put in his claim. "What is your position on kissing?"

Joie's gaze jumped to his mouth. The wicked, sinful temptation of it. "I'm thinking it over," she conceded. "If I let you kiss me, I'll melt on the spot. That's a given. I already know that, and it's so very humiliating. Worse than being carried around like I'm a fainting, weak bundle of femininity."

"True, but it would be worth it," he pointed out seriously.

She sighed and lifted her hand to his face, her fingertips tracing his sinful mouth. "Yes. But there's another consideration, Traian." Her voice turned very somber. Her gaze went to his. "You're going to be addicting. And then I won't be able to get you out of my system and I'll get all weepy when we have to part, and that's just more than I can bear, crying over some idiot man. Do you see the complications I'm facing here?"

His heart twisted inside his chest. "I do see that might be a problem if we were ever to part, but since we are truly lifemates and have no choice but to be together, I do not really think it is of much importance. In fact, under the circumstance, being addicted to my kisses would be an asset."

He couldn't resist turning his head to capture her finger in the warmth of his mouth.

"The lifemate thing—see? That's part of the problem. I have this overwhelming need to be mistress of my own fate. I don't think I'm cut out to be a lifemate if it entails a *have to* sort of relationship. I'm a *want to* sort of woman. There is a difference."

"That is good, Joie. I do not foresee any problems whatsoever, because it is clear we think so much alike. I am definitely a *want to* sort of man—and I want to kiss you."

There was a devilish smirk on his face, one she couldn't possibly resist. And who wanted to anyway? His mouth descended toward hers, and Joie lifted her face to meet him halfway—because this kiss was her choice, and he needed to know it.

Joie's lips were soft, yielding, welcoming even. After all the long centuries, Traian felt like he had come home. It didn't matter where they were, whose world they were in, she would always be home to him. The Earth stopped spinning, just as he knew it would. Bursts of star fire rained down around them. The embers smoldering deep in his belly burst into flame and raged through his bloodstream. His body knew her almost as intimately as his soul, though he hadn't even really touched her yet.

Joie couldn't think, couldn't breathe, forgot whether it was night or day. It was impossible to get her brain to function. She could only feel. Nothing had prepared her for the unrelenting pressure building so swiftly in her body, the heat rising, flames dancing along her skin, creating an inferno deep inside. Passion coiled tighter and tighter, a spring threatening to explode. Her breasts ached. Her fingers found the silk of his hair, and crushed the thick mass in her palm.

"You shouldn't be able to do this to me," she whispered into his mouth. Into his heart. "I don't let anyone inside."

"I am already inside you." His lips took hers again, over and over, long, drugging kisses that shook them both.

"It has to be the danger factor," she said. "It's the only logical explanation."

"Is there logic? I cannot remember." He couldn't get enough of her. Mud from her face smeared his. Her clothes were wet, soaking his. His wounds burned, but he couldn't feel the discomfort when his body was so heavy and hard with need.

His voice shook her. It was possessive. Husky. Perfect. A seduction in itself. It was Joie who pulled away, framing his face with her hands. She rested her forehead against his. "I need a minute here to come up for air. I can't breathe, or think, or want anything but you."

His mouth curved into a smile. "Is that supposed to stop me?"

Her gray eyes studied every inch of his face. He could see her confusion. "Why do I feel like this? Does this make sense to you, Traian? I don't jump into relationships. All I can think about is having sex with you. Not just sex—wild, uninhibited sex. I'm muddy, exhausted, scared to death and worried about my family, but I want—no need—to feel your body inside mine."

His smile widened. "I think kissing you is the best idea I have ever had."

She couldn't help smiling back. He made her happy in a way she never had been—complete when she hadn't known a part of her was missing. "Why you? You aren't even human." She made a little face at him. "You know you're complicating my life."

"Your entire family has telepathic abilities. Are you certain you are human?"

Laughter spilled over. "Please don't ever ask my father

that. He's outrageous, and he'll tell you some absolutely horrible and untrue tall tale, and we'll all be mortified."

The raw affection in her voice told him her father's outrageous stories never really mortified her and she loved the man very much. "That gives me hope. At least I know you plan on introducing me to your parents, but the list of dos and don'ts is growing. Just out of curiosity, do his outrageous tales ever have to do with dragons and mages?"

"Of course. When we were children, he told us fairy tales all the time, but the mages were wizards in tall hats concocting all sorts of magical spells."

"Good wizards or bad?" he prompted.

"Both, of course. What's a good fairy tale without both?" She turned her face up to his again. "You think I don't know where you're going with this? Every parent tells their children fairy tales. My father is an undisputed genius, tremendously talented, as is Jubal, with numbers and patterns. Gabrielle inherited a lot of that as well. She works as a researcher for hot viruses and she's really done a lot of good, unlocking strands and finding potential ways to combat them. But we're human through and through. We were born in hospitals, go to doctors for regular check-ups, pay taxes, and eat real food."

"I am certain that is the case. It does not, however, prove your father is not mage. We blend into society very well, and mages, far better than Carpathians. They do not sleep in the ground or sustain life on blood."

Joie blinked up at him. "You sleep in the ground?"

"In the soil. It rejuvenates us."

She closed her eyes. "Oh, God. I don't even know what to say to you."

He bent his head to steal another kiss. "Hang on. I am about to take you flying."

She made a noise somewhere between laughter and choking, but her mouth responded, soft and firm and very pliant. He indulged himself for a few more moments, kissing her again and again, finding her mouth a sweet, hot haven he could lose himself in. When he lifted his head, she looked a little dazed.

Traian smiled down at her. "You're being very brave."

"You're cheating. And I'm not being brave. Has it occurred to you I might be afraid of flying?"

"You were engaged in astral projection the first time I laid eyes on you," he pointed out.

"I thought you were drug-induced," she confessed. "I'd been experimenting, but I didn't really believe I was actually accomplishing it. I thought I just sort of hypnotized myself. I would never have been so open with you had I thought you were real." Joie turned her face up to the sky, her head cradled on his shoulder.

"Then I am glad you thought you made me up. I think I will like your family very much, mage or not."

"I wouldn't jump to conclusions until you've met my mother. She's absolutely devoted to us and to our father, but she doesn't welcome others at all. My teachers frankly detested to have her come to school for conferences—especially the male teachers."

"Nevertheless, I intend to win her over. I have not had a family in so many years, the idea of one did not occur to me. Yet now, when I watch you with your brother and sister and feel the love you have for them, it makes me envious."

Her heart turned over at the longing in his voice. Joie had never thought she would feel so intensely about a man. The mere tone he used could make her shiver like the caress of fingers, or wrap around her heart like a fist.

"Did you have siblings? Were you close?"

He rubbed his chin on the top of her head just to feel the

silky strands of her hair against his skin. "Actually yes. I had a sister, Elisabeta. She, of course, was much younger than I was. Carpathian children, as a rule, are born fifty to a hundred years apart, but not always. She was very young when I was sent away from the Carpathian Mountains. I have searched for news of her, but no one seems to know what happened to her. I remember her running barefoot, her long hair streaming out behind her, and it seemed as if every plant turned their head to watch her pass. Our gardens were crazy after she was born. She had a free soul." He closed his eyes, savoring the memory of a little girl, not more than six summers, her laughter making his heart sing when he shouldn't have felt a thing. He had stayed longer than a warrior should, basking in the child's presence.

"Most of the ancient warriors, those that had already lost their emotions and had fought too long and taken too many lives, gravitated toward our home just to be around her. She could make emotions appear when they were long lost. A little miracle really."

He shook his head, blinking down at Joie's upturned face. "I have not thought of her in centuries. Far too long. I accepted that she was lost to our people."

"And to you," Joie said softly. "I'm so sorry, Traian. I don't know what I'd do if I lost my brother and sister. I really don't."

"It was many years ago, Joie, although in truth, I lost my emotions, and sorrows were much easier to bear. They are fresh again with memories returning now that my lifemate has provided a way for me to feel again."

"That's such a difficult concept for me," Joie admitted. "I've never wanted to give myself to anyone, not wholly," she admitted, looking up at him. "Not all of me. I didn't want anyone to see inside me. But you already do, don't you?" Her eyes met his. "You do see me like no one else ever has."

"Yes." Holding her close, protectively, Traian took to the air.

They soared across a night sky so dark it was nearly purple. A blanket of stars sparkled overhead. The few remaining storm clouds drifted rather than spun. Far below them the ground dropped away—mountains and valleys, forests and lakes hiding secrets best kept hidden for all time. The scene below them was a mixture of old world and new.

She could see farms scattered, with great haystacks and patches of gardens struggling for life. Sheep dotted the mountainside along with some cattle and goats. A herder's cabin sat here or there in the remote places higher up on the mountain and more than once she saw stray dogs poking around looking for food along dusty roads.

Old ruins of a castle and a monastery along with numerous churches came into view. The country was beautiful and intriguing. Horse-drawn carts were no more than flatbeds in many cases with rails and car tires. The beauty of the countryside overwhelmed her as well as the simplicity of the villages.

I love it here, she admitted. *You were lucky to grow up in such a beautiful place.*

She looked up at him and her breath caught in her throat. She was half terrified and half fascinated at the shape Traian had assumed. He had the enormous wings of a huge owl, yet human arms held her against the soft, feathered breast. The feathers tickled her skin, and sent a shiver down her spine when she realized it was all too real. She closed her eyes trying to keep her heart rate normal, certain he would notice the difference if she didn't. She was so aware of his every breath and couldn't imagine that it wasn't the same for him.

I have been unable to see beauty in my surroundings for

some time. Traian looked around him. *You are right, it is beautiful. Thank you for giving me such a gift.*

Joie took a cautious peek around her once she had calmed her accelerated heartbeat. She was *flying* through the air with a man who could shift shape. Astral projection was cool, no doubt about it, but this—this was amazing. The sensation of the wind in her face, the way Traian could drop down low and skim the lakes and gorges. Everything, even the leaves on the trees were amazingly clear.

I think you've given me a gift as well. I never thought to experience such a sensation. It's far better than jumping out of an airplane.

She felt his heart leap in his chest.

You jump out of planes?

With a parachute of course. I just don't leap out and pray I'll find a soft landing. Soft laughter bubbled up. Traian flew across the night sky, faced vampires, and shifted into birds, yet he was obviously disapproving of her jumping out of airplanes. How very ludicrous was that?

You are a bit on the medieval side, aren't you?

Perhaps. There was no apology in his voice. *Your need to do dangerous things has got to be curbed, Joie. You have no idea what you have saved me from. I cannot begin to convey to you how necessary it is that you live.*

Joie frowned. He was very somber. She could feel the utter sincerity in him. He was taking a roundabout way to the inn just to allow her the amazing sensation of flying and to really see his homeland. He might be a little on the medieval side, but he was also very kind and thoughtful.

He was turning her inside out and she didn't really have time to consider what was happening to her. She simply let him overpower her with his blatant sexuality, with the intensity of his personality, and the fact that like her, he was a warrior. He was strong enough to stand up to her and she could respect that—and him. She knew she had a strong personality. She automatically took charge in nearly every situation.

Jubal, like her father, was far more laid-back. He would never run in a fight. He was always calm and reasonable and then he got the job done. Gabrielle was fierce in a lab. She was adventurous enough to go with her siblings and parents to high mountaintops and down into deep caves, but she was not aggressive in the same way Joie was.

I'm going to drive you crazy, she confessed to him.

I am well aware of that, Traian replied, amusement filling her mind.

She couldn't help but laugh too. *I'm not certain I want you running around in my brain.* The laughter faded. *You know I nearly committed myself to a hospital because I kept hearing your voice. It was really disturbing when I couldn't stop it.*

Traian frowned. *It was that foreign to you? Even when you are able to speak to your brother and sister telepathically?*

That's entirely different. We've always been able to speak to one another, but not anyone else. We just thought it was a Sanders sort of thing. My mom and dad can do it too.

It could be considered arrogance to think that only your family was capable of telepathic communication.

Joie found herself laughing again. *I suppose you're right. I definitely take it for granted in our family. We've always been that way.*

Both parents?

She tried not to hear the suspicion in his voice, or feel it in her mind. He really had a prejudice toward mages. *Yes, both parents. And we're entirely human. I can show you my birth certificate and all my really bad school photos.*

I would be interested in seeing your bad school photo-

graphs, just because I am interested in everything about you. I cannot imagine you looking bad, especially as a little girl. You have grown into a beautiful woman.

He said it so matter-of-factly, Joie couldn't protest. Like most women, she felt far from beautiful, but it was nice to know he thought she was. She turned her face up to his and smiled. *Thank you. I'm glad you think so.*

Lights from the inn lit the ground below them. Traian dropped to earth some distance from the building, where the shadows were deep. Music spilled out of the two-story building, floating out in all directions. People mingled on the wraparound verandah and on most of the balconies, some dancing, some talking, and others pressed close to one another.

"The festival," Joie said. "I forgot about it. Look at me— I'm a mess."

"You look beautiful to me," Traian objected. "Which room is yours?"

"Second story, third balcony on the left." She grinned at him. "Are we floating?"

"Is the window locked?"

"That wouldn't stop me. I have second-story skills."

His eyebrow shot up. "I am very impressed. I am a hunter and I am certain those skills could come in handy."

She narrowed her gaze, locking her fingers behind his neck. "They come in handy for a bodyguard. I do have a business, and I'm known to be one of the best."

"I'm sure you are." He took her into the sky fast, enjoying the way she clung to him, tightening her arms and gasping as he shot up.

Don't you laugh at me.

I'm not laughing.

I can feel you laughing. You know, it isn't normal to fly through the sky.

It is normal for me.

The balcony floor felt solid beneath her feet. She let go of his neck immediately. "Great, I *would* have to do this with a hundred people around."

"They cannot see you. I have shielded us from their eyes."

She glanced at him over her shoulder. "We're invisible? Sheesh. Is your life easy or what? I wouldn't mind being invisible in my line of work. No wonder vampires are afraid of you."

"They fly, and they can cloak their presence as well."

Joie pushed open the door to her room. "How perfectly charming of them. Where do they come from?"

Traian followed her into the room. She heard his heavy sigh and turned around to face him. He definitely looked troubled, and very reluctant to answer her question.

"I'm not going to like your answer, am I?"

"Vampires are Carpathians who have chosen to give up their souls for a brief moment of power, the thrill of the kill—a rush if you will. Our males lose their emotions and the ability to see in color after the first two hundred years of existence. Some earlier, some later, but all of us eventually lose everything we hold sacred if we do not find a lifemate. Only one woman, the light to our darkness, can return those things to us. For several centuries now, our race has few women and fewer children. We are on the verge of extinction. There is little hope, and more and more of our males are turning."

Joie tried to take in the enormity of what he was saying. "There is only one woman who can restore colors and emotion for every male? *Just one*?"

Traian nodded. "Only one. We can search centuries for her. If we miss one another, or we hunt and kill too long, the need to feel emotions, whatever that is, becomes too tempting and many succumb. Our choices are to turn vampire, or allow the sun to take us."

It was a brutally grim destiny. Joie removed her harness and carefully placed her climbing gear on the floor beside the closet. She removed her crampons and boots, grimacing a little as she saw the mud she'd brought in with her. She needed the time to digest what he was telling her before she managed to meet his gaze. There was compassion in her eyes.

"How terribly sad for all of you. So you and the other hunters are forced to police the vampires. Even if they were once boyhood friends . . . or family."

He nodded, astonished at the wealth of understanding he read in her expression. She clearly saw what others did not: deep below the surface, every destruction of a childhood friend or cousin had cut pieces out of his soul until he feared there was little left. Yet her understanding, the compassion washing over him, changed something. He felt it, felt the first healing touch and the power a lifemate wielded.

She stood there in her filthy clothes with mud smeared all over her face, and she was beautiful to him. A lump the size of his fist rose in his throat, and he turned away from her, afraid of allowing her to see the emotion threatening to choke him. How could she possibly understand what she meant to him?

"I'm sorry, Traian. I know I can't begin to understand what it must have been like, but I feel the weight of it in your mind."

More than that, she felt how alone he had been. The intensity of his pain shook her. His life had been stark. Ugly. Bleak. She caught frightening glimpses of scenes in his past. Terrible battles that lasted for hours. Severe injuries. Death all around him. No one to comfort him. No one to care.

Joie closed her eyes briefly, overwhelmed by longing, by the need to wrap her arms around him and just hold him. Very slowly she removed her outer jacket. Although they hadn't heated the room, after the cold of the mountain, she found it almost too warm indoors. She tossed her gloves on top of her jacket.

"It is almost dawn, Joie. I will need to go to ground. I have lost too much blood and the wounds on my body require healing. There is no other way to do it quickly and the separation from me may be difficult for you. You will need to stay in this room where you will be safe."

"What do you mean, difficult?" Joie couldn't help that her voice was filled with suspicion. Traian didn't just throw things out there for dramatic effect. Clearly he was warning her about something she had yet to experience.

"The pull between lifemates is very strong. You will not be able to reach me telepathically and yet your mind will insist on reaching for mine. You could, if not prepared, believe me to be deceased. My heart will cease to beat and my breath will still in my lungs while the rich soil of my homeland heals my wounds and rejuvenates me. It would be best if you allow yourself to sleep through the day. You are exhausted as are your siblings, who, by the way, are very anxious to reunite with you."

"I don't think I'll have any problem sleeping the day away," Joie assured him. "I'm almost too tired to take a shower, and man, do I need one." Exhaustion had definitely set in.

"I can take care of that."

Joie didn't know what she expected—perhaps for him to throw a bucket of water at her, but she ended up clean with a wave of his hand. It wasn't as satisfying or as soothing as she found a very hot shower was, but she did feel clean. She sank down on the bed and passed her hand over her face.

"Do what you have to do, Traian. I'll survive."

"I will put heavy safeguards on your door and windows. No one will be able to penetrate those safeguards without you opening the door for them," he warned.

"I thought vampires couldn't be in the sun."

"That is true, but do not ever think they work alone. They create puppets of humans, servants to do their bidding. They promise them immortality, but in the end, these puppets go insane and live off the flesh of mortals. They cannot be saved. They are abominations of nature with rotting flesh and brains. They will only do as their masters command. You cannot allow yourself or your siblings to fall into their hands."

Joie considered a smart-ass reply, but pressed her lips together. Traian's world was fraught with more danger than she'd ever faced. It had become a way of life for him. He looked at her as if she was everything to him. While it was exhilarating and a little sexy, it was also very frightening. How could she possibly live up to his expectations?

"If you can put safeguards at my door, can you do the same for Gabrielle and Jubal?"

"Of course." He glanced out the window. "I really cannot stay much longer. I will be here when you awaken. Give me your word that you will remain here waiting for me."

Joie nodded. "If that will give you peace of mind, Traian. I'm tired. I just want to see my brother and sister and know that they're all right."

Traian crossed the room to stand in front of her. He reached down to take her hand and draw her close to him. "I know you are afraid of what is between us. In truth, for me, it makes perfect sense. Lifemates are natural to us, but it is not the same for you. If you wake without me, promise me you will not try to run from this. It is overwhelming for you. I want to be with you and see you through the fears of such a permanent and fast bonding, but I have no choice. I must go to ground before the sun is high."

Joie nodded. "I'm not going anywhere, Traian. I'm pretty good at facing things I'm afraid of. I've got Jubal and Gabrielle with me. We'll be fine."

He cupped her face in his hands and lowered his mouth to hers. His mouth was a hot temptation, masculine and demanding. She felt her body going boneless as everything feminine in her reached for him, responding to his kisses. Joie reached up to circle his neck with one arm, leaning into his strength, still a little shocked that she could respond without inhibition to this man she barely knew.

Sivamet—my love, he whispered. *At long last I have found you.*

When he lifted his head, his dark gaze roaming her face she laughed softly and shook her head. "Technically, I found you."

His smile warmed her. "So you did."

Joie! Jubal's voice was very demanding in her head. *Gabby and I are coming to your room right now.*

Joie's laughter spilled over. "I'm going to have to report all these voices running around in my head. I'll let my brother and sister in and you get out of here. I'll see you when I wake up?" It was definitely more of a question than a statement. Her heart stuttered a little at the thought of him leaving. She wasn't a clinging woman, yet the thought of him going away made her body react physically. She kept her smile firmly in place. She would *not* be a baby and beg him to stay with her. Jubal and Gabrielle would be there any moment.

Traian kissed her again. "No matter what, do not go downstairs without me and know that I will come for you."

Joie swallowed the unexpected protest rising and nodded her head. Her mouth had suddenly gone dry and her heart felt like a stone in her chest. "Be safe," she managed.

Traian glanced out the window toward the dawn streaking across the sky, kissed her again, and slipped outside onto the balcony. He raised his hands and began to weave a pattern, chanting softly, concentration etched into his face.

I will safeguard the rooms of your siblings and then I must go. Your brother and sister are at your door. You will have to allow them in.

She glanced at the door just as someone knocked on it. When she turned back, Traian was gone. Joie took a deep breath and with a trembling hand opened the door to her siblings. Jubal swept her up in his arms and Gabrielle put her arms around both of them. They held one another for some time. Joie remembered to kick the door closed after a few minutes of a long group hug.

She looked over her brother and sister for scrapes and bruises. "You both got out unscathed."

"We fought a vampire," Gabrielle declared, her eyes bright. "Jubal killed it and the darn thing has my ice axe." She gave a delicate shudder. "Not that I want it back after sinking the spike into its head."

"Oh, my God, you *fought* one of those evil things and actually managed to kill it without Traian?" Joie was shocked. "They seem invincible."

Gabrielle sank into a chair, trying to cover a yawn. "It was Jubal's bracelet. It doesn't like vampires."

Jubal held out his arm for Joie's inspection. With him dressed in a tee and jeans, his arms bare, the thick metal just looked like an ordinary bracelet. "This thing bears our family crest, Joie. And it kept me warm in the caves as well as lit the way and also cut out and burned the heart of the vampire. I have no idea how it happened. I didn't direct it, the blades jumped out and began spinning and the metal warmed up as it unlinked from my arm."

Joie studied the innocent-looking bracelet. It would take

a strong man with large arms to wear such a thing well. It looked as if it had been made for Jubal.

"The staircase we went down was long and winding and carved of ice. At the bottom was a wall of symbols and stars," Jubal said. "The secret password to open it was actually the Draco constellation."

Joie's gaze jumped to his. "What are you saying, Jubal?"

"I don't know, Joie, but this is a pretty big coincidence that the bracelet came to me, bears our crest, and that the secret to the way out was the Draco constellation."

Jubal's tone was matter-of-fact. Jubal rarely got upset or too excited. Gabrielle and Joie often joked that he'd never have a heart attack.

"Do you think Dad's family is somehow descendents of mages?" Joie could barely manage to voice the question. Had she not seen vampires and the other extraordinary things she'd witnessed through the long night, the question would have been ludicrous.

"I think there is a possibility," Jubal acknowledged. "We were always drawn to this region and Dad didn't want us coming here. I think he has his secrets and maybe the tales he told us were truer than we ever suspected."

"That's what Traian said. He doesn't trust mages at all and I doubt if others like him do. Maybe we should be really cautious about speculating other than among the three of us," Joie ventured. "At least until we have a chance to talk to Dad."

"Agreed," Gabrielle said. She yawned again. "I'm going to bed."

"We all should," Jubal agreed.

"Stay in your rooms during the day," Joie cautioned. She told them what Traian had said about vampires using human puppets. "We can sort all this out tomorrow night when he's back and figure out what we're going to do."

She hugged them both and shut door after them, locking it and after a couple of moments, pushed the dresser up against it. She was very tired and had no idea if she would wake up if an intruder tried her door.

Chapter Eight

Joie dreamt of a man with the face of an angel and the body of the devil. She could hear the sound of her heart beat drumming like thunder every moment of the dream—whether in fear or in exhilaration—she couldn't tell. One moment she ran for her life, the next she was in his arms, kissing him over and over. Monsters ran through her dream, chasing her, tearing the flesh off of him. In the background her father watched with strange eyes, standing by, doing nothing, holding a glowing sphere in his hands. Beside him a great jungle cat covered in spots watched Traian hungrily and as one of the monsters tore at him, the cat leapt the distance, landing on his back and settling teeth around his head.

Joie rushed across an endless bridge of ice, driving a knife deep into the ribs of the cat in an effort to save Traian. The jaguar turned its head and looked at her. The amber eyes filled with hatred, slowly turned gentle, sorrowful. Joie blinked to bring the face into focus through unaccustomed tears. She gasped and backed away as blood ran down the side of the cat and pooled on the ground beneath it. She was looking directly into the face—the eyes—of her mother.

She fought her way out of the web of her dark dream,

tears running down her face, her chest heavy and her heart beating wildly. She didn't recognize the hotel, only the deep sense of dread and danger surrounding her and the gun in her hand. She was already tracking around the small room, seeking out an enemy.

"Romania," she said aloud in the gathering darkness. "You're in Romania with Jubal and Gabrielle and a man you might have made up."

Traian emerged out of the darkness slowly, hands up, palms facing her. Darkness swirled around him, cloaking him one moment and then revealing his strong features the next. She slipped the gun beneath her pillow and sat up, tasting passion in her mouth. He could very well be a dream, a mere fantasy that her mind tricked her into believing was real.

"You're already here." Her gaze drifted over him slowly, inspecting him for damage. The raw wounds were nearly healed, an amazing feat considering what he'd looked like when he'd left in the early-morning hours. "You're lucky I didn't shoot you." Defensively she put out her hand as if to ward him off.

He smiled at her and kept coming. "You would never make that mistake. You will always recognize me."

Of course it was true. She had known the moment he moved that it was him. He took her breath away. It was so trite. So unlike her, but it was the stark truth. He came right up to the side of her bed, reached down, framed her face with both hands and kissed her. His mouth robbed her of all ability to breathe. She was not a woman to be intimated by a dominating male, nor did she ever feel small or fragile or even beautifully feminine, yet Traian managed to make her feel all those things.

Her reactions to him confused her more than the vampires, secret caves of mages, and his shifting shape. Her fingers curled in the thick silk of his hair. On him the long hair seemed natural, almost elegant, pulled back from his face and captured at the back of his neck with a thin cord. His chest was wide and thick, his arms enormously strong, his hips, encased in black trousers, narrow. She had a difficult time believing a man as attractive as Traian would want to be with her.

He laughed softly and ruffled her thick cap of hair. "I told you, a Carpathian cannot see any woman other than his lifemate—certainly not once he's found her. I have heard there have been one or two throughout the centuries who were not quite right, but you have only to look into my mind to see what you mean to me. Lifemates cannot lie to one another."

"I have morning mouth," Joie said, wiping her hand across her lips, more to prevent more kissing than to cover her breath. More kissing was going to most assuredly lead to other things.

His smile lit his eyes. "It is evening."

"Whatever. Still. I just woke up and unlike you, I have to brush my teeth to have fresh breath."

"As far as I'm concerned, your breath is fresh. You taste like a mixture of honey and mint." He flashed her a reassuring smile.

Traian realized she was very nervous. Joie seemed to be very confident, but he suspected she was confident in action rather than inaction. Deliberately he paced across the room to give her space, and toed a chair around to straddle it, knowing his height and shoulder width made her feel as if he was taking up the room.

"You had a nightmare." He made it a statement.

Her gaze jumped to his face, a little wary. She nodded. "Yes." She shrugged. "It was unsettling but hardly surprising. The things we witnessed last night were a lot to take in.

Who knew there was an entire world of mythical beings living in the same world as us? You said you were traveling back to your homeland. Where have you spent all of your time?"

He knew she was searching for reassurance that they weren't moving too fast, that the pull between them was real and not simply powerful chemistry. She needed a few seconds just to breathe. He refrained from pointing out that all she had to do was access his mind and she'd know everything about him she wanted to know. He would hold nothing back—good or bad, but she needed the breathing space and the humanness of speech.

"Centuries ago, my prince called the ancient hunters together and told us the war was coming and more vampires would roam the earth. It was our duty to rid the world of them. Those of us who agreed to go were sent to far-off places with little or no contact of our kind. I was assigned basically to cover India and outer regions such as Sri Lanka. It was a very extensive territory and not developed much. Wars occurred often among kingdoms trying to seize control."

"Did you participate in the wars?"

Traian shook his head. "Very rarely. If I came across a woman or child being abused, I stepped in, but I had enough to do moving through such a large area trying to keep any vampire from establishing himself."

"It's hard to believe that vampires were in India."

He smiled at her. "Think of the legends and myths you hear in every country around the world. You would be hard put to find a country that didn't have some form of vampire firmly entrenched in the tales and lore recorded. And what of all the strange animals one hears of, the ones even now that have occasionally been captured on film but are always put down to a hoax, whether proved to be so or not. Even in the States there are strange sightings."

Joie leaned toward him. He could see the open speculation in her eyes. She was an unusual woman in that she had
a very open mind to anything others would never consider.

"Are you saying those strange animals are vampires?"

He shook his head. "No, but more than likely they are
among the species still existing that are capable of shifting
shape, and that includes the undead."

Joie shoved a hand through her hair, drawing his attention to the cap of thick, dark strands. She looked a little disheveled, her large gray eyes still sleepy, her skin smooth,
looking petal soft, her hair tousled. Need slammed into him
before he could stop it, ran unchecked through his veins,
the slow heat turning to flames.

"Tell me about India. I haven't been there," Joie admitted, oblivious to his growing hunger.

Traian drank her in. The sight of her, the scent of her
brought him a peace he'd never known. He had risen, appre-
ciating after centuries the richness of his homeland's soil.
He saw beauty in the land around him as if seeing with new
eyes—and maybe he was. Colors were vivid, even scents
seemed more pleasing. *She* was in the world. Joie.

"Tell me," she repeated. "It's important to me to know
what your life has been and the influences on you. You see
my family. But tell me of the early days in India."

He was pleased she wanted to learn about him, but he
had other much more pleasing ways to pass the time before
the evening's demands would be on them. He swallowed a
small sigh and indulged her.

"India was forest and jungle when I first arrived there. I
felt at home very quickly in that environment. I found myself spending quite a bit of time with elephants. Over time
my emotions and memories faded, more so with each hunt
and kill of the undead and for some reason, when I stayed
around the elephants, I could tap into them. For many cen-

turies they were content and peaceful, teaching me an acceptance of life, of the ways of the land shaping the future. They do not fight what they cannot control. Eventually many were harnessed into the service of man, and still, they lived their lives as patiently and as well as they could. Buddhism was very influential and I couldn't help, at times, to compare the teachings, the quiet acceptance of life, the living in the moment, with the way the elephants lived their lives."

He spread his hands out. "I have managed to shift into every animal I have come across and fooled the others of the species into believing I belonged, but not the elephants. They accepted my presence among them and as time went on, I believe they looked forward to my company, but they always knew I was not a true elephant. There is something very special about them."

Joie frowned. "Traian, you've been all over the world and had experiences, watched the world change century after century. I have such a different background. How can someone like me hope to keep a man like you from being bored after a few days or weeks in my company?"

"Is that what worries you?" His voice was tender.

"Among a million other things," she admitted. "Seriously, how could you possibly be happy with someone who has such little experience compared to you living centuries and seeing the world take shape? You've been here when there was barely a population and have lived through wars and plagues and things I can't even imagine."

Joie pushed strands of hair behind her ear and regarded him thoughtfully. "I was raised to be very independent. I think for myself and I'm a woman of action. Compared to the knowledge you have, I'm a child. Being with you, as tempting as it is to throw myself into your arms and just take whatever you're offering to me, I'm afraid eventually I would lose who I am. I like making my own decisions, it's who I am. I need to climb cliffs and find caves no one's been in. I find satisfaction in my job."

She thought herself safe sitting there on the bed, her body covered up by the man's shirt that only managed to make her look sexier than ever. He shook his head. "I cannot believe you are worried you will lose yourself when you are with me. Joie, I want you the way you are, not changed into something else. You are a very intelligent woman. You are a warrior and I respect that, and your need for action. I also know that when you are working with anyone, whether you are climbing or going deep into a cave or protecting someone, if another person has more knowledge than you, your ego would never get into the way. You would listen. I trust you implicitly to do that."

She pressed her lips together tightly.

"Do you think I will not listen to you? I have no knowledge of the way of families. Or friends. Or even the joys of using one's skills in the way you climb a cliff. I want to learn all of those things. I will rely heavily on your expertise so that I fit smoothly into your world. I might know the ways of the vampire and how to shift, I might have seen history, but the things that are important to life—a wife, a child, family—those things I have no knowledge of. I hear your laughter, feel the closeness of your brother and sister and I want to feel that with them as well. I want Jubal to be my brother and Gabrielle to be my sister. I would like for your parents to think of me as a son. Only you can give me those things. Only you can teach me the right way to be part of something I have never had the chance to experience."

Her eyelashes fanned her high cheekbones. Her tongue darted out and touched her lower lip. His heart shifted in his body. She had all the power and didn't even realize it, believing he would grow bored with her.

"I observed history, I didn't feel it. I saw the foreign lands and recognized they could be beautiful, but I saw them in shades of gray, without emotion, without color or feeling. I have facts at my disposal, millions of them, and I know war, but little else. I need you, Joie."

Joie swallowed hard. He was breaking her heart. The stark, raw admission was brutally honest. She could feel his need and hunger beating at her. She had chosen service as her profession because it was inherent in her character to respond to the need of others, to protect them from harm. This man who seemed so completely invincible was exposing his deepest vulnerability to her.

More than that, she felt as if her entire life she'd been apart from others, standing to one side and not quite fitting in. With Traian, a being far removed from her understanding, another species, in his company, she felt as if she belonged. If she did this, if she stepped off the cliff and let herself fall with him, she knew she'd go all the way, heart and soul. There would be no turning back for her. He would be part of her, *inside* so deep she would never be able to get him out, even if he walked away from her.

She took a breath, her gaze moving over his face. Wonder. Magic. The combination was stamped into every angle and plane, the set of his shoulders and the defined muscle of his chest. It wasn't just his physical beauty, the sheer athleticism of him, the power he exuded; the draw was in the single-minded focus he turned on her when he looked at her—as if she was the most beautiful, intriguing woman in the world. The *only* woman. And he needed her desperately.

He just sat across from her looking at her. Waiting. She moistened her lips. She had to get some distance to get some perspective. "I need to take a shower."

"You do not have to. I can make you feel refreshed."

Joie hastily shook her head. "I enjoy my showers. I like the feel of the water on my skin."

"Is that an invitation?"

Was it? Had she chosen a shower because the thought of him naked was firmly entrenched in her mind? She didn't know, but the erotic images playing through her mind faintly shocked her.

Joie stared at him, at the hard angles and planes of his face. At his dark, fathomless eyes. If the attraction between them was merely physical, Joie would have thrown him on the bed and ripped his clothes off right there. But he stirred unfamiliar feelings in her—deep and frightening feelings for a woman in charge of her own destiny. She was terribly susceptible and the plunge was going to be very long, the fall very hard, but it was beginning to look as if she wouldn't be able to break his mesmerizing spell on her. She was certain she should try a little harder but . . .

With indecision written so clearly on Joie's face, Traian felt as if his world was balanced on the point of a needle. He was afraid to move. Afraid to speak. He knew their joining was inevitable. He would have her. She was his. She belonged to him. But he still wanted it to be her decision. He wanted her to want him in the same way he wanted her.

"It's a small shower stall," she said in low, hesitant tone, still giving herself room to run.

"I have never taken a shower. I have never needed to, nor would I have been able to enjoy the sensation of water on my skin. I would very much like to do so with you."

She put both trembling hands behind her back and he knew that she was afraid of the next step, but she took it because she was nothing if not courageous. She lifted her chin and smiled at him in invitation.

He didn't wait for her to come to him; he took the few steps separating them and swept her up into his arms, cradling her close to his chest.

Joie smiled up at him. "This is becoming a habit."

"I like keeping you close to me," he admitted. He carried her through to the small bathroom and set her on her feet.

His hands dropped to the buttons of her shirt, his gaze holding hers captive. She moistened her lips and her heart sped up. He smiled at her in reassurance.

"You are very safe with me, Joie. Just breathe."

He slipped each button out of the tiny hole, allowing her shirt to open all the way before he glanced down at the treasure he'd so carefully unwrapped. His breath caught in his throat. "You are so beautiful, Joie." His hand skimmed down from her breast to her belly, down further to strip the panties from her.

He had no idea he would feel like this, emotion welling up so deep and strong, the intensity shaking him. It took a moment to remove his own clothes and step into the confines of the shower with her.

Steam fogged the clear glass of the shower door, and rose up to curl around the two bodies standing beneath the spray of hot water. Joie allowed the water to pour over her, drenching her hair and skin, washing the sleep from her body. The shower stall was small, forcing her into close contact with Traian. She thought she was completely prepared for the sight of his very masculine body, but found she could barely breathe. He was all defined muscle, his chest wide, his hips narrow. She dared not look below his waist. The man had no modesty when it came to his desires. And he desired her.

"Are you going to keep scooting back every time I get close to you?"

There was a hint of amusement in his voice. His tone was like velvet, sliding over her exposed skin, setting every nerve ending on alert.

Her mouth went dry. "It's the only safe thing to do. Before I actually met you, I thought about having you all to myself, alone and naked and . . ." She trailed off a little desperately.

The erotic fantasies were wonderful when he wasn't standing in front of her, larger than life and still nearly a stranger. "Now I have absolutely no idea what I'm going to do with you."

"I distinctly remember you telling me you had lovers lined up," he said, his hands framing her face, his thumb tilting her chin so that her gaze met his. "What were you planning to do with all of them?"

There was a little bite to his voice and his white teeth came together with a definite snap.

Joie tried not to let the sudden smile blossoming inside her show on her face. "You weren't real. I could say anything." It was impossible to look away from the dark intensity of his eyes, the hunger there. His emotions were as naked as his body. "I keep thinking this is happening too fast. I don't really know you. How did you end up in my room? And how did I end up standing naked in the shower with you? I'm a private person, and not very trusting, yet here you are."

It was all he could do not to kiss her. Traian knew he could easily sweep aside her every objection. The attraction between them was mutual. Electric. All-consuming. She would respond to him with the same fierce need he had for her if he kissed her, but she needed to come to terms with her decision.

"Joie." He whispered her name, an ache in his voice. "If you want to talk about this, I suggest we get out of the shower and put the width of the room between us. We have been in each other's minds for weeks. You know me. You know more about me than most people could learn in a lifetime. You know my character and what I stand for. And you know this is no passing fling. This is forever."

"Forever." She tasted the word. "That's a long time, Traian."

The water poured over her body and steam encircled them as she leaned into him so that the tips of her breasts pressed against his chest. She felt him hard and thick and heavy with a man's need, a temptation and a pleading.

"Forever is quite tedious and endless without you. With you, forever is gone in moments."

"You're asking me to make a decision, the enormity of which I can't possibly comprehend. I love my family, Traian. I really love them and would never be happy without them. I don't really know what you're asking of me, but I think it's far more than I've comprehended."

He bent his head to hers. Close. His mouth was inches from hers. "I know what I am asking of you, and I know you have reservations about your family. I do not want to go back to an existence without you. Spend your life with me, Joie," Traian tempted softly. He feathered kisses down her face, over the corners of her mouth. His teeth tugged at her bottom lip. "Spend several lifetimes with me, an eternity. Be with me. Say you want me that much. Let me be part of your family."

She looked up at him, at the intensity burning in his eyes. His emotion was so strong, so hot, it branded her, seared her all the way to her heart. Joie felt the pull of his need, of his loneliness. He was a dangerous predator, not quite human. Powerful beyond anything she had ever dreamed of. And sexy. Heart-stoppingly sexy. Her arms, of their own volition, were already sliding around his neck, her body molding itself to his.

"Can we be together, Traian? How? Tell me how." Because she had been alone in the midst of a family she loved. Always surrounded by people, friends, family, she was always apart. She never knew why until she heard his voice. Something had been missing from deep inside her, some essential part of her.

Somehow, with Traian, she felt safe and at peace. She didn't know why, she was a very independent and self-reliant person, but something in her kept demanding she search all four corners of the Earth, the highest peaks, the deepest caves, *everywhere*, although she had no idea what she was searching for until she'd found . . . him. Traian. He held the missing piece of her.

"It doesn't make sense when you sleep beneath the ground and I can't."

"You can become as I am. You would still be Joie, still part of your family, but with the gifts and the vulnerabilities of my race. Or I can age as you age. My strength will weaken and I will be more vulnerable to our enemies. It is your happiness that counts, Joie. I want to be in your life always."

Butterfly wings fluttered in the pit of her stomach. She felt she was on the edge of a great precipice. Joie tried to pull back before it was too late. The enormity of what he was offering was both frightening and exhilarating. He swamped her with his loneliness, with the intensity of her own feelings, so completely foreign to her. She tried to take refuge in humor. "I don't even know if you're good in bed."

"I want you to acknowledge to me that you know what I am offering you." His mouth skimmed over her face, tracing her high cheekbones, her chin, moved lower to find the pulse beating frantically in her neck. His warm breath bathed her in heat, a seductive temptation every bit as powerful as the feel of his body heavy with need.

She was in his mind, saw the choices clearly. His teeth sinking deep, making her his, bringing her into his world. Or Traian staying with her as if he were human, aging along with her, his great strength slowly fading, always vulnerable to enemies. Two choices. Two worlds. Only a heartbeat of time to choose.

She knew she needed to answer him not because he demanded it, but because the intensity of her feeling for him was so strong, she needed to settle her future in her own mind. His teeth nipped her skin, his tongue swirled over the tiny ache. She felt the throb in her deepest core, the clenching of muscles aching for relief.

"Joie." He breathed her name again. "I will love you to the end of your days."

The water poured over her, heightening her sensitivity to pleasure. She heard the honesty in his voice. The purity. Joie tilted her head to the side to give him better access, closed her eyes in anticipation. She was certain. She might not understand why it was right, but she had never been surer.

His teeth sank deep. White-hot pain pierced her body, giving way instantly to sheer ecstasy. Lightning flashed in her bloodstream, hot whips of pleasure tormenting her. Heat welled up, and threatened to consume her. She held him to her, closer, moving her body enticingly. It should have frightened her, the way he fed on her, devoured her with a hungry, craving lust more sexual than anything else.

Traian traced every line, and curve, every hollow, etching her body in his memory, wanting the moment to last several lifetimes. The rush hit him hard, a sexual hunger mixed with a dark craving nearly uncontrollable. For centuries his appetite had been insatiable, a terrible hunger that could never be assuaged, but now her blood satisfied his inhuman need. But his intense sensual need remained unappeased. He was hard and hot and heavy with desire. His tongue swept across the pinpricks on her skin. His lips traveled down to her breast. Ancient words beat in his head, words of a ritual imprinted on him before his birth. Once said, there was no going back. Traian and Joie would be bound for eternity.

The small sound escaping from her throat only urged him on. His tongue teased and danced over her taut nipple, caught the droplets of water as they beaded on her skin. "You are my lifemate. I claim you as my lifemate. I belong to you. I offer my life for you." His hands shaped her body, slid up to cup her breasts.

His face was dark, his gaze intent as he looked into her eyes. Joie felt a strange wrenching in the vicinity of her heart. A part of her tasted fear, wanted to cry out for him to stop, but another part embraced his words, understood the importance of each promise uttered. Her hands slipped over his chest, and she leaned forward to taste his skin, her teeth nipping his chest, directly over his heart. She had never been a biter, but something urged her to sink her teeth deep, to connect them together. She swirled her tongue over his heavy muscles.

Joie was killing him with her innocent sensuality. His body hurt, a hard, painful ache; he was desperate for relief. "I give you my protection. I give you my allegiance. I give you my heart." His hands tightened on her waist, holding her so tight he felt her soft body melting around his. "I give you my soul. I give you my body. I take into my keeping the same that is yours. Your life, happiness, and welfare will be cherished and placed above my own for all time. You are my lifemate, bound to me for all eternity and always in my care."

The words spilled out of him, the Carpathian ritual marriage, as old as time. He felt thousands of tiny threads binding them together as they were meant to be joined.

He caught her chin in his hand, lifted her face to his, finding her lips almost blindly, wanting to devour her. She opened her mouth to him, melted into him. Traian caught her up in his arms, kissing her wildly, and carried her to the bed, cradling her in his lap so that his heavy erection pressed tightly against her buttocks. He whispered softly in his language, a strong command, even as his fingernail lengthened and he drew a line over his chest.

Joie kissed his throat, her lips drifting down his neck, unerringly finding his chest and the gash there. A hot flame burst inside him, a firestorm of emotion and sensation. The back of her head fit into his palm as he held her to him, encouraging her to make the exchange. Heat poured through his body. He burned for her, his body hard and painful with need, even as pleasure swept through him. Traian shifted, lowering Joie to the comforter, following her down so as not to break the connection between them. When he was certain she had taken enough for a true exchange, he whispered the command to halt and closed the wound himself. At once his mouth was on hers, stealing her breath, giving her his own.

Joie couldn't remember how she ended up beneath him, his hips wedged between her legs. His hands were everywhere, stroking, caressing, inciting. There wasn't an inch of her skin that he didn't explore. She heard her own strangled cry as his fingers sank deep inside her, felt her muscles clench tightly around him. Ready. Waiting. Desperate for his invasion. Her fingers caught at his hips, pulling him to her in a frantic attempt to find relief. She had never wanted or needed anything more than to feel his body deep inside hers.

Traian, certain she was ready for him, pinned her hips and thrust into her in one long, deep stroke. She gasped with pleasure, arched upward toward him, meeting him thrust for thrust. He cried out, unable to stay silent as he surged into her. She was a silken glide of fire and velvet as her feminine sheath gripped him tightly.

Joie clung to him, unable to do much more than hold on, lifting her body eagerly to meet his as he drove harder and deeper, merging them together in a fiery tango that she wanted to go on forever. They were skin to skin. Their hearts beat with the same wild rhythm. The air crackled with electricity, and sparks leapt from nerve ending to nerve ending.

The pressure built and built until she thought she might have to scream with the joy exploding through her.

He poured into her mind, filling every lonely place with—him. She felt the sensations in his body, the gathering of a great force, much like a volcano. Hot. Thick. An inferno of desire and hunger mixed with intense emotion and pure lust. He filled her with flames and heat, an outpouring of pressure building from his toes to the top of his head. At the same time, he felt her every reaction, the waves of pleasure swamping her, racing to overtake them both, consume them completely.

Joie cried his name, clutched his body tightly as they went over the cliff together, free-falling through space in wild exhilaration. She couldn't catch her breath; her heart was pounding out of control. Little explosions continued, rocking her, so that her body refused to let his go, clamping down hard and holding him to her.

"I think I see fireworks," she whispered into his chest.

He laughed softly. "I think we produced the fireworks." He lay over her, his body pinning hers, locked tightly inside her while he kissed her slowly. Thoroughly. Leisurely. Savoring her. "Thank you for finding me, Joie."

"My pleasure, Traian," she answered. He was moving yet not moving, and each small shift sent ripples of aftershocks through her entire body. "I can hear our hearts beating. Really hear them, like pounding drums. And I can hear the blood moving through your veins. Is that normal? Because if it is, eww, ick, and yuck."

He laughed softly, the sound vibrating through her entire body so that her muscles gripped even more tightly around him. "Think about turning the volume down. Our minds are very powerful. You can control the volume with a thought." His teeth tugged at her lower lip "Think about it and you can hear a pin drop in the next room. But, if you want quiet, you simply turn the volume down."

"I don't feel that much different inside. I thought I would notice changes."

"You haven't gone through a conversion, Joie. It takes three blood exchanges. We have only exchanged one time." He caught her firmly in his arms and rolled, taking her with him, so that she was straddling him.

He filled her completely, still hard and thick so that every movement sent pleasure dancing through her body. His hands cupped her breasts. "I want to look at you. I still have a difficult time believing I actually found you. That I am with you."

Deliberately Joie moved, a long, slow glide up and down. She felt him shudder with pleasure and arched back, pushing her breasts into his hands, getting a better angle to take more of him deep inside her. "Why are you waiting, if we need three exchanges?"

He watched himself disappearing inside of her, slick and wet from her body. "I want to give your body time to adjust to the changes. It is not always easy." He found it was difficult to get the words out, difficult to have a coherent thought when she was gripping him so strongly with her muscles, riding him harder and faster with long, deep strokes. Fire licked at his belly, flames erupted over his skin until the heat rushed to one central spot, collected there, and raged out of control.

He let the sexual ecstasy wash over him, through him, take possession of him, all the while watching the glide of her body, the way her muscles moved beneath her skin, the way her breasts pushed into his palms and her nipples teased and tempted him. The sheer enjoyment on her face. Her thoughts, completely taken up with giving them both pleasure, were enough to send him over the edge. He picked up the rhythm, thrusting upward, driving into her as she came down over him. Each stroke took his breath, took his heart. Her body caressed his—was wet and hot and tight and brought him to the brink, setting up an addiction that would never end. He would always want her again and again. He felt her muscles contract, grip, squeeze, and grip until they both went up in flames together.

Joie lay beside him, unable to move, wanting to laugh with joy. Her fingers found his, tangled, and held on. She believed in living life to the fullest, but she had always thought she would do so alone. For the first time in her life, she felt complete and utter satisfaction. Complete and utter peace.

"I feel exactly the same way," Traian said. "I cannot help wondering—if you had been the Carpathian and I the human with a beloved family, would I have been as trusting as you have been? You cannot know what your faith and trust mean to me."

Joie turned her head, a mischievous grin on her face. "I decided I liked flying and the shape-shifting would be cool. And if you do something so silly as to cheat on me or run off with someone else, I'm very good with a knife."

He raised an eyebrow. "I thought you would be worried about giving up food. It does smell good. I have even sampled some from time to time."

"No one said anything about giving up food." She eyed him with suspicion. "There are certain things women can't do without, Traian. Chocolate at certain times of the month is essential to health. Not necessarily my health, but the health of all males in the vicinity. I'm not giving up chocolate, not even for great sex."

He propped himself up on one elbow, the pad of his finger tracing a circle around her breast. "Chocolate is that important, is it?"

"Essential. Absolutely essential. That's nonnegotiable."

"What kind of chocolate must you have?"

"Dark chocolate, of course. Is there any other kind?" He dipped his head to pull her breast into his mouth, suckling strongly just to feel her reaction. His tongue swirled over her nipple before he kissed her. His kiss was long and slow and thorough. When he lifted his head, he laughed softly at her expression. She stared up at him, bemused, one hand touching her lips in wonder where the taste of dark chocolate melting in her mouth was very real.

"How did you do that?"

"You need and I provide—that is how it works. I believe you wanted to see your brother and sister tonight."

She allowed him to pull her up. "Anytime? You can do that anytime? Wow. I think I'm going to like this lifemate business."

Traian laughed, hardly able to believe the happiness blossoming inside him. Hardly daring to believe Joie was real.

Chapter Nine

Joie stood in the doorway of the lounge, her gaze scanning the crowd as she always did, getting a feel for the throng, picking out the ones most likely to cause trouble and the ones who might be interested in more than they should. She noted a tall, dark-haired man in the corner who looked up when she walked in with Traian. He quickly glanced away from them, taking a sudden interest in his drink, but she could tell he was watching them carefully. A second man drew her interest. He sat in one of the high-backed chairs near the fire, a newspaper in his hands. He was short and slender and wore reading glasses. He was looking over the top of the thick rims at Gabrielle.

Joie glanced up at Traian's inscrutable face. He, too, had assessed the room in one quick glance and she realized he had moved slightly to put himself between her and the tall, dark-haired man pretending interest in his drink.

Who is he?

I do not know, but he is very interested in your family. This is a dangerous place for travelers who may have mage blood running in their veins, he warned. Deliberately he didn't look at Jubal when he sent him a quick command.

*Make certain no one in the bar can see the weapon that
came to you in the caves.*

Jubal turned, very casually and waved to them both.
Gabrielle looked up, gave a glad cry, and jumped up from
the small table she was sharing with her brother near the lit
fireplace to run across the room to them. Behind her, the
flames leapt and danced, glowing orange and gold and red.
The taller man put down his drink and turned his head to
follow Gabrielle's progress.

More predator than man, Traian's instincts sent an
alarm sliding down his back. He reached out very carefully
and touched the man's mind. He liked the look of Gabrielle,
but there was something about her that made him believe
she was far more than she appeared and he was looking
for . . . the undead. It was very obvious to Traian that the
man was attracted to Gabrielle and he justified his interest
by fitting the criteria given to him by others in his secret
society of vampire hunters.

Women were said to be more beautiful, drawing interest
wherever they went. They came out at night looking for men
to seduce to do their bidding. The only women who could
ever be vampires were human women who had no psychic
ability that had been turned by vampires. They were clearly
deranged and no one could ever mistake one. As far as
Traian was concerned, they were pitiful creatures in need of
sympathy and a merciful dispatch to the next realm.

Clearly the man hadn't seen Joie yet, he was too busy
ogling Gabrielle. Traian's blood would enhance Joie's beauty
in a subtle way. He didn't want attention drawn to her family,
especially when Jubal wore the mage's weapon. Before he
stepped away from Joie, he made certain to shield her enough
that she wouldn't appear interesting to the stranger.

Joie prepared herself to be practically bowled over as her

sister embraced her, hugging her with her usual enthusiasm. Looking over Gabrielle's shoulder, she noted the man in the glasses looking past her to Traian. Recognition immediately flickered across his face, and he carefully folded the newspaper and laid it on the small table in front of him.

Traian, Joie warned. *The one in the glasses, with the newspaper. Do you know him? He recognized you.*

Traian sighed. Two members of the vampire hunting society in the small village close to where the prince of the Carpathian people made his home? That was too big of a coincidence for him to swallow. One might be a scout, but two meant they were hunting. The last time there was a hunt, men, women, and children were murdered, both human and Carpathian.

Joie shifted slightly to keep Gabrielle just a little behind her, her posture protective, but the two men were split, one on one side of the room while the other could control his side. Traian let his gaze drift naturally to the slender man with glasses who raised a glass to him the moment their eyes met.

He scanned the man's mind. Clearly human, he recognized that Traian was not. To Traian's amusement, the moment she noticed the stranger's interest in them, Joie again shifted, gliding slightly in front of him, even as she tried to keep an eye on the taller, dark-haired man.

The rush of joy and affection, a lightening of his heart and soul, made Traian tremble. He couldn't remember if anyone in his long lifetime had worried about him or tried to protect him. That small gesture meant the world to him because it revealed her faith in him. She'd made a leap of faith, committing herself to his life, his world.

He is not an enemy, he assured. *Did we forget to discuss the fact that I am not certain I want you guarding bodies?*

Really? She arched an eyebrow at him. *Not even yours? I'm pretty good at it.*

Traian's eyes were on the dark-haired man, but he lifted his hand to hip level, palm down and waved off the man with the glasses just as he'd started to rise. The man immediately sank back into his chair and reached for his newspaper.

He was going to talk to you.

Not yet. I have to deal with someone else first. Visit with your brother and sister for a few minutes. Keep an eye out for trouble.

Don't worry, Traian, I've got my eye on you all the time. She flashed a saucy grin at him.

Traian couldn't help the little glow warming his insides. She believed he wanted her happiness above his own, and she wanted to give him happiness. He had a mad desire to scoop her up and run back to her room, where he could make love to her all over again. He looked at her, allowed the thought to shimmer in his mind, to glow hot in his eyes.

Joie laughed. "Stop that."

Gabrielle looked from her sister to Traian and made a rude noise. "Oh, no. Joie, we leave you alone with him for a few minutes and you seduced him, didn't you?"

Joie shrugged unrepentantly. "You have to admit, he's pretty hot."

Gabrielle's eyes widened and her hand went up to cover her open mouth. "I was *so* joking with you, but you really did. You totally slept with him. I'm telling Mom."

"Well, you tattletale, if you say one word to Mom, I'm going to tell her you were thinking of taking that job researching the Ebola virus. You know what she'll do when she hears that. *And,* for your information, there was no sleeping involved whatsoever."

"You're in such trouble, you hussy, and you wouldn't dare

tell Mom on me," Gabrielle said. She pushed at Joie's shoulder, looking at the man so studiously reading his newspaper, trying unsuccessfully to move her sister aside for a better look. "Now that is a hottie, Joie. There's more to a man than muscle." She grinned at Traian. "No offense or anything."

"None taken," he assured her.

"Your tongue is hanging out, Gabrielle," Joie whispered. "Stop ogling him. For you to be falling at his feet, he must have an IQ of two hundred." She glanced up at Traian. "No man she's ever looked at could carry on a normal conversation. I think she can see straight through to their brains." She nudged her sister. "Your eyes are popping out of your head."

"I was just looking," Gabrielle hissed back. "At least I didn't throw myself at him and show off by doing in underfed trolls fresh out of the grave. *I'm* discreet."

"I was happy she did that," Traian pointed out. "She did rescue me."

"Yes, well, I suppose you would have been happy, under the circumstances," Gabrielle conceded. "But she has a major hickey on her neck. If Mom saw that, there'd be consequences."

Traian bared his strong white teeth at her. "I think I can handle your mother."

Gabrielle and Joie looked at each other and burst out laughing. "It isn't possible, Traian, even for you," Joie said.

He laid his hand very gently on Joie's shoulder. "You will have to excuse me for a few moments. Please stay warm by the fire." He guided both women back to the table where Jubal sat observing the room. "I have a couple of things to do." He maintained eye contact with Jubal who nodded almost imperceptibly. "Do not draw undo attention to yourselves while I am gone."

Joie caught his hand. "Traian, we can help."

"Not with this. Just be safe until I return."

She bit her lip and nodded.

Traian bent his head and brushed her mouth with his before walking over to the bar. He took his time, making his way across the room, shoulders straight, allowing himself to be seen only as slightly intimidating as he approached the man with the dark hair. He leaned onto the bar beside him and lifted one finger toward the innkeeper, who hastened over. He glanced toward the stranger. "What are you drinking?"

The man gave him a tentative smile. "Vodka." He spoke with a slight Hungarian accent.

Traian held out his hand. "Traian, I am visiting my parents, and you?"

The man looked a little relieved. "Gerald Hodkins, just a tourist. I wanted to see this part of the country. I've heard so much about it from various family members."

Traian sent him a friendly smile and ordered two vodkas. The innkeeper, Mirko Ostojic, met his eyes and gave him a brief nod. Traian lifted the glass toward the other man and they drank. Cool water slid down his throat.

"It is beautiful country," he ventured.

Gerald nodded. "Dangerous to travelers who don't know their way around though."

Traian's eyebrow went up. "Not so much anymore. My parents moved to this region about ten years ago. They bought a little farm just up the road, basically to retire, but they like to raise sheep. They told me there was virtually no crime here." He injected a note of worry into his voice. "I work in Sri Lanka, so I do not get to visit often."

Gerald shrugged his shoulder. "This place was cleaned out some time ago, from my understanding, although there might be pockets left."

Traian signaled Mirko over for another round. "Pockets of what?"

Gerald glanced right and left as if someone might be listening. He'd been drinking quite a bit already and he waited until the innkeeper had poured another drink. He raised the glass to his mouth. "Have you heard the rumors of vampires in this region?" He took a healthy swallow and regarded Traian steadily over the rim of the glass.

Traian frowned. "Sure. Everyone has. This is reputed to be vampire country, but everyone knows that's just a myth. I have read that in some of the more remote villages residents still believe that after someone dies, if a member of the family becomes ill, that they have to dig up the body, cut off the head, stuff the mouth with garlic and drive a stake through the heart in order to insure the supposed vampire is dead. That practice has been documented around the world in various countries, but it isn't widespread anymore and these locals certainly don't do such things."

Gerald took another swallow of his drink. "Don't be too sure. It wasn't that long ago that there was a huge purge right around this area."

"I know what you are talking about. I did research into the history of the region when my parents were first considering settling here, but the investigation determined those ritualistic killings were outsiders who murdered a number of people in some sort of misguided belief that vampires exist. It really is safe for tourists and travelers here."

Gerald tossed back the rest of his drink and signaled the innkeeper to refill their glasses. "On my tab," he instructed and then studied Traian over his drink. His face was flushed, his eyes a little bloodshot. "Did you ever consider that there was a cover-up? That maybe those men really had found something?" He turned his back to the bar and surveyed the room. "Maybe all those myths and legends aren't just stories."

"Scary thought," Traian said, allowing interest to creep

into his voice. "History is always interesting because if you read various accounts of anything, the stories change depending on who is telling them."

"*Exactly*," Gerald agreed, slurring the word slightly.

Traian very carefully began to raise the temperature around the man. "There generally is a grain of truth to many of the legends, but most of the time, I have found there is a scientific reason behind unusual occurrences."

Gerald grinned at him as if catching him in a compromising statement. "You half believe the stories about vampires."

Traian looked uncomfortable as he shrugged his shoulders. "No, of course not."

Gerald nodded toward the Sanders family. "Look at that beautiful woman. The one with the long hair. She's the type, you know. She came in early in the morning, slept all day and is up now."

"You mean Gabrielle?" Traian laughed. "She's a researcher for hot viruses on vacation with her sister and brother. They like to climb mountains—mostly during the day." He wiped his forehead. "I think I've had a bit too much to drink. It's getting hot in here."

Gerald took the suggestion. "The innkeeper keeps adding wood to the fire. They never seem to realize the more people are in the building the less they have to heat it." He clapped Traian on the shoulder. "Let's take a little walk outside and get some fresh air."

Obligingly, Traian set his glass on the bar and followed Gerald around the tables, taking one more sweep of the room, tuning in to the various conversations to make certain there was no whisper of conspiracy before he left his lifemate and her family. He stepped out of the inn and allowed the door to swing closed behind him.

Fog slid through the surrounding trees, entering the

village with long fingers, pulling a gray veil over the houses and businesses, draping them in the thick, cool mist. Wind blew gently in from the south, a steady stream that brought with it information of night creatures moving in the deeper woods. Aromas of food cooking drifted to Traian, and he heard the whispers of conversation in buildings he passed as he walked with Gerald along the narrow sidewalk toward the deeper shadows.

"I grew up hearing stories of monsters," Gerald offered. "Of course all of us kids thought our parents were a little crazy because it was obvious they believed in vampires and ghouls. They called them human puppets, flesh-eating fiends who do the bidding of their masters."

"Great bedtime stories," Traian commented, taking Gerald's arm when he stumbled on the uneven ground as they entered the dark space between two buildings. "No wonder you half believe the fairy tales."

"Oh, I believe them all right." Gerald lowered his voice. "There're quite a lot of believers now. But we cleaned them out of this area."

Traian turned, his body blocking the way so that Gerald was forced to halt his staggering progress. Tainted alcoholic blood was never a choice for any Carpathian, but sometimes—like now—it was necessary. He had to be able to monitor Gerald Von Halen's activities. Gerald might have been more resistant to his voice had he not been consuming alcohol, but the amount allowed easy entrance into the man's mind.

Traian bent his head to Gerald's neck and drank, the vampire hunter's mind docile and accepting, following Traian's low, murmured instructions. The hunter probed the society member's mind for information on their next hunt. There was some disagreement, but most seemed to be turning their attention and concentrating efforts to wipe out vampires in South America.

"Leave this place as soon as you can pack. It is urgent that you go," Traian commanded and forced drops of his own blood into the opened mouth. He would always be able to whisper to Gerald, to speak across some distances and ensure he did no harm to any Carpathian. "You will forget the women you saw tonight and remember me only as a drinking buddy you have great affection for."

They were at the entrance to the inn before Traian allowed Gerald to become aware of his surroundings, planting memories of laughter and the slow, vague idea that the society members were taking his dues money and making a fool of him. They patted one another on the back like old friends and Gerald stumbled up the stairs to his room. He waited until Gerald had gone into his room before he returned to Joie's side. He hadn't realized how strong the pull of a lifemate was until he had left her side the morning before. He was anxious to complete the three blood exchanges and bring her fully into his world so he wouldn't have to leave her when the sun rose.

"Is everything all right?" Jubal asked.

Traian toed the chair closest to Joie around and sank into it, his arm sweeping around her shoulders, needing to touch her, to feel her warmth and know she wasn't a fantasy he'd dreamt up there in the cave when the vampires had tortured him.

"Fine. I believe our friend in the glasses is about to join us. Be careful what you say." He directed the comment mainly to Gabrielle. He could tell by her heightened color and the light in her eyes that she found the man very attractive.

The slender man stopped in front of them and held out his hand to Traian. "I'm Gary Jansen. Mikhail Dubrinsky sent me. He asked me to convey his apologies, but unforeseen circumstances prevented him from coming himself. Should there be need, he asked that you put out a call to him and he will send Falcon. Mikhail's brother is in Italy at this time, so I was sent to aid you in any way I can." He chose his words carefully, obviously very aware they were not alone.

Traian gripped Gary's hand firmly. "I am Traian Trigovise. This is my lifemate, Joie Sanders, her sister, Gabrielle and brother Jubal. I trust the prince and his lifemate are well?"

"Raven has been ill," Gary said briefly. His gaze strayed to Gabrielle, but he quickly reined himself in. "If we could go somewhere private, it would be better," he added. "I offer whatever you need freely."

If Traian had any doubts about Gary, that single offer immediately put an end to them. He was offering blood, a way to ensure he could not lie to Traian. The man's mind was without a shield, although when Traian touched it, he knew Gary could have kept him out. A Carpathian had carefully constructed a thick barrier so others could not probe the human mind. Gary had set it aside, in order to gain Traian's trust. He had to be of great value to the Carpathian people for any of them to have protected him with such strength.

Traian nodded. "We do need to speak somewhere quiet. I have news of great importance that must reach our prince as fast as possible."

"My room's just down the hall," Gary offered.

All three of the Sanderses stood. Gary hesitated and looked to Traian for guidance. He nodded and Gary, with a small shrug, led them through the narrow hallway to unlock the door to his room.

"Nice," Jubal commented. "We're on the second story with

small balconies. This is great." He looked out the double doors to the spacious verandah. "Joie, we should have asked for the ground floor."

Gabrielle looked around. "This is a nice room. Our rooms are much smaller." She smiled at Gary.

A dull red swept under Gary's skin as he hastily cleared clothes from a chair. "Sorry about the mess."

Gabrielle's smile widened. "You should see my room. We were in a cave, and our clothes were filthy. All I could think about was taking a hot shower." She blushed, turning away from Gary to study the verandah Jubal seemed so interested in.

Gary nodded toward the Sander siblings. "Forgive me for asking, but are you certain everyone in this room can be trusted?"

"I am more certain of them than I am of you," Traian answered.

Gary smiled, relaxing for the first time. "That's good enough for me. I can give Mikhail your news, although he asked me to have you return home as soon as you are able. He has called in the ancients his father sent out. He needs their knowledge to make informed decisions in the ongoing war with the undead." He glanced at Gabrielle as he added the last.

She shuddered and moved a little closer to her brother. "I never, *ever*, want to meet another one as long as I live."

"You encountered one?" Gary asked, obviously shocked. "And lived through it?"

Gabrielle nodded. "Jubal . . ."

"Perhaps that discussion is best left for another time," Traian interrupted. He didn't know Gary Jansen. He believed him an emissary of the prince, but he needed to protect Joie's family from all possible harm. The last thing he wanted was for the mage weapon to be brought out into the open. "Suffice to say, we escaped and hurried here to give Mikhail the news. Is he well? In danger?"

Gary shook his head. "Raven was pregnant and she lost the baby."

Traian met his eyes. Joie caught the echo of his instant sorrow. Somehow that baby had meant the world to all Carpathians, representing hope.

"That is sad news. I had thought perhaps, with her having been human, and carrying successfully once, she would escape the fate of our women."

"What fate?" Jubal asked, shifting protectively toward Joie.

Traian sighed. He'd hoped to avoid repeating the subject in front of her family, but honor compelled him to answer Jubal's direct question. "Over the last few centuries, fewer and fewer babies survived. Those that did were usually male. It became very rare to have a female child. When our prince found his lifemate in a human psychic, the males had renewed hope. She gave birth to a female child—the first in a very long time. Unfortunately, miscarriage is common and if the child is born, more often than not, they do not survive beyond their first year."

Joie pressed her lips together tightly and looked at her sister. Gabrielle looked as if she might cry.

"How terrible," she whispered.

"I'm doing research," Gary said. "Hoping to find the cause."

"Have you discovered anything that might point you in a direction?" Gabrielle asked, real interest in her voice. "I might be able to help."

Gabrielle, Jubal cautioned. *Slow down. We don't know anything about this man.*

Gabrielle stuck her chin out. *If Traian is discussing important things with him, he obviously trusts him.*

Traian ignored the sibling debate. "I came across a group

of vampires traveling together. Not one master and a puppet, but at least *three* master vampires, each with their own following, even several well-seasoned ones—all traveling and hunting together with an actual battle plan. I have never seen such a thing before. There is definitely something brewing and the conspirators are determined to assassinate the prince. I managed to kill a couple of them, but was wounded, and instead of killed, taken prisoner and used for a food supply, but I had the feeling they wanted to use me for something else. What that could be, I do not know."

"Mikhail wanted me to ask you why you did not simply give him the information when you requested that someone join you here," Gary said.

"Had I used the common telepathic link, the undead would have heard what I had to say," Traian said. "I have never exchanged blood with the prince and do not have a private telepathic link. I believed the news of vampires banding together was far too sensitive for them to know I was passing the information to our prince. I wanted to keep the news as confidential as possible until we had time to assess things."

Gary nodded. "Unfortunately, I fear things are going to get worse before they get better."

"Where is Mikhail's second in command? Why is he not guarding our prince? Our people cannot afford the loss of our prince and his lifemate. I do not like the fact that the undead dare to gather so close to our homeland."

"Gregori is in the United States but will be returning soon. Falcon and Jacques stay close to Mikhail, although he doesn't like it. He says he is quite capable of defending himself."

"Perhaps it is so, but a master vampire is too powerful for any experienced hunter to take on alone and if they are banding together, even the prince and Gregori are in danger. He has not had to deal with so many of them because they spread out to other countries to grow in power and keep from being brought to justice by a hunter," Traian objected, an edge to his voice.

Gary shrugged. "I'm afraid I don't know much about master vampires. I've had a little experience with the undead and have found them difficult to kill. I, of course, go armed at all times and have developed a few weapons more suited to a human defense against them."

"You might share your discoveries with Joie, Gabrielle, and Jubal," Traian suggested. "No doubt they will be exposed again to the undead if they stay in this area long."

His gaze rested on Joie. Had she changed her mind about coming fully into his world? He should have disclosed that the possibility of losing children was very high. He'd discussed Carpathian history with her and had revealed the lack of women and children, but he hadn't actually told her what the reality would be.

Joie sent him a reassuring smile, one fist bunching in the back of his shirt, joining them together. *I'm not going anywhere, Traian. If you and the rest of your people have to face the problem and look for solutions, I can too. And Gabrielle wasn't just talking. She's very good at what she does. She might be able to help Gary if he's really doing what he says.*

Traian turned toward her, unable to help himself, sweeping her under his shoulder. "I was on my way back in answer to the prince's summons when I was attacked by a group of the undead. I killed two of them, but was wounded. They dogged my heels for weeks, nipping at me, wounding me and retreating. Vampires have too big of egos to get along, yet the fight was coordinated. After I killed a couple of them, I expected them to leave, but instead, they redoubled their efforts, attacking and running, but never allowing me to rest. First one master and his followers would attack and then the next. The third, the one I believe pulling the strings, never showed himself to me, but I felt him and he was very powerful."

Worry crossed Gary's face. "You're right. That's very unusual behavior. I've never heard of it either in all the time I've been with Gregori and Mikhail."

Traian was astonished that a human was so trusted that Gregori, guardian to the prince of the Carpathian people, would allow him to get so close. It was obvious, from the familiar way Gary spoke, that he was in the inner circle. Traian had been away from his homeland for centuries and when he'd left, the ruling leader had been Mikhail's father. Traian had yet to swear allegiance to Mikhail, so in some ways, Gary was more trusted by the prince than he would be.

"I went to ground in a network of undiscovered caves in the mountains not far from here," Traian said. "At first I thought the vampires had followed me into the caves, but they were hunting for something there beneath the earth. They were so frantic to find it, instead of avoiding me as would be usual, they engaged me in a series of battles. I was able to kill one master, Gallent, but got no information about the powerful one who was coordinating the fights."

Gary rubbed his jaw. "New behavior in an enemy is always indicative of planning. Someone out there is definitely orchestrating a major battle."

"I believe that to be the case as well. I was severely wounded after one of the battles, and they found my resting place. Instead of killing me, they decided to use my blood and continue searching. Joie, Jubal, and Gabrielle found me. Joie killed one of the vampires."

Gabrielle stirred as if she might give her brother credit as well, but Jubal laid a restraining hand on her arm and she closed her mouth.

"Sort of," Joie corrected when Gary looked at her with

admiration. "The darn thing fried my favorite knife. Traian had to incinerate it before it was really gone." *He knows a lot, don't you think, for someone human?*

Few humans are trusted with the knowledge he has of our people. He must be much respected for Mikhail to send him to me.

"How did you get involved with all of this?" Gabrielle asked Gary curiously.

He looked sheepish. "I'm embarrassed to admit I developed a compound to paralyze the system of Carpathians, thinking, of course, they were vampires. The compound was twisted into a poison and used to torture and dissect whomever the human society of vampire hunters deemed one of the undead. When I tried to expose them and rescue one of their victims, I met Gregori."

"What's he like?" Gabrielle asked curiously. "You must have been shocked."

He shrugged. "I can't describe Gregori or what meeting him was like, but it changed my life. The society would like to see me dead, so as a protection, Gregori brought me here to help with research. I like it here and have developed strong friendships, so I stay."

Who is Gregori? There was so much respect in Gary's voice, Joie was curious.

He is second in command to the prince—his guardian and the one tasked with keeping him alive. He is a great hunter and healer. His lifemate is the daughter of the prince.

Joie looked up at Traian. "I can see the Carpathians have a complex society. Why didn't we know of its existence until now?"

"We take great care to blend in to the human world. It has been our way for centuries and has worked well for us. Unfortunately, our race is on the verge of extinction."

Traian gathered Joie to him. "Without lifemates, we will not survive."

"Lifemates?" Jubal echoed. "You said Joie was your lifemate before, what does that mean?"

"We mate for life. Once a male finds the woman who is his other half, he binds her to him, as you do with a marriage ceremony. If she is a human and does not live fully in our world, it can be very difficult. Lifemates cannot be parted for long periods of time. We have a strong telepathic link and must touch each other's minds frequently or one begins to grieve for the other. As Carpathians cannot walk fully in the human world, it is usually best for the human to walk in our world," Traian explained.

Jubal and Gabrielle exchanged a long, apprehensive look.

"What exactly does that entail?" Jubal asked suspiciously.

"Jubal—" Joie protested.

"No, Joie, I want to know what he's talking about." Jubal didn't look at his sister but rather at Traian. Man to man. Expecting an answer. Demanding one.

"Joie has consented to come fully into my world, Jubal," Traian said, his voice low and without inflection. "I will protect her and watch over her and see to her happiness at all times. The conversion will not take her from your family. She would never be happy apart from you. I hope you and your sister and your parents will be able to accept me into your world, and your family, in the way I know my people will accept Joie into mine."

Jubal swore softly and turned away from them to stare out into the night. "Joie, did you think this through? Do you know what he's asking of you?"

Joie went to her brother, and put her arms around him. "I've never felt as if I truly belonged, Jubal. I accepted that I was different, and yes, I've been happy because I like the work I do and I love my family dearly, but I want more than that. Traian offered me more, and I grabbed the opportunity with both hands."

"Do you hear what he's saying to you? This isn't like a human marriage, Joie, where you can walk away if things don't work out."

Traian stood beside Joie, his fingers laced with hers. "Lifemates not only want to be together, Jubal, they need to be. They find a way to work things out. A male Carpathian knows what makes his lifemate happy and does everything within his power to do it for her. And it works both ways. We always have telepathic communication open to us, so, in a sense, we are used to living in each other's heads. I know that is a big adjustment to make, and I am doing my best to give Joie as much space as she needs. But she is already learning quickly."

"It's what I want, Jubal," Joie said. "Be happy for me."

"I know you, Joie. You aren't going to be satisfied sitting on the sidelines while vampires are hanging around. You're going to go save the world."

Joie couldn't lie to her brother. "Probably. On the other hand, I have no intention of giving up my business. I thought Traian might work with me."

"This is where it is necessary for you to have faith in me, Jubal," Traian said. "I cannot allow anything to happen to Joie."

Jubal laughed without humor. "You don't know Joie if you think you're going to be protecting her. More than likely, it will be the other way around."

"Forgive me for butting in, but I've been around the Carpathian race for some time now," Gary said. "Traian is an ancient Carpathian male. He is far more powerful than you can imagine. They do not allow their women to come to any harm."

"But then you haven't met someone like Joie before," Jubal pointed out. "She's the guardian of the world."

"At least I go after people, not little organisms that you can't see and can't do anything about."

"Hey now," Gabrielle objected, "don't turn the spotlight on me."

A small smile curved Traian's mouth. "I think you are misjudging me because of our first meeting, when I was being held prisoner. I have survived countless battles with the undead, Jubal. A master vampire is every bit as powerful as our greatest hunter."

He turned his attention once more to Gary. "Mikhail must know they are traveling in packs, and that they are planning something big. I also believe it is important to discover whatever it is they are seeking in those caves. Vampires always seek power. They would never waste time working the way they are unless it resulted in more power. That cave now belongs, or once belonged, to a powerful mage," he added in warning. "There are items of great power in the caves, guarded by a shadow warrior."

"I don't know what that is."

"Mikhail and Gregori will know. No one wants to meet a shadow warrior."

Gary nodded. "I'll tell him."

"I'll be returning to the cave just before sundown tomorrow. I hope to surprise them before they rise. In any case, I will do my best to discover what they seek."

"Well, of course I'm going with you," Joie said.

Traian brought her fingertips to his lips, breathed warm air over her hand. "I can travel faster on my own, Joie. And you have not yet learned to prevent them from reading your mind. I would be at risk because of your unguarded thoughts."

Joie's gaze flicked to Gary. The man nodded. "They are adept at reading our thoughts and even controlling us. Traian can go in without their being aware of his presence, but they would know the moment you were near."

Joie frowned. "I don't like the idea of you going in alone. There are several of them, and you've admitted there's more than one master vampire. I might be able to help. Could you block them from reading my thoughts?"

"Probably, but the more tasks I have to perform, the more energy I expend. I have to go in fast and hard and get out the same way."

Jubal immediately stepped to his sister's side. "What if we were nearby, waiting just in case you run into trouble?" he suggested.

Gabrielle nodded. "I think that would be best, Traian. We might be able to slow them down and even incinerate the things for you."

Traian looked at the three of them. Family. Solidarity. Jubal and Gabrielle might not agree with Joie's choice. They might be afraid for her. But when it counted, they stood with her. He bent his head and kissed Joie right in front of them. It was that or humiliate himself with tears shimmering in his eyes. As it was, a lump threatened to choke him.

"Thank you for letting me be a part of your family, Joie. They are wonderful." He looked at Jubal. "I appreciate the offer, but it is safer for me if you are here, a distance away, where the undead cannot perceive a threat to them. Should I have need, I will contact Joie immediately."

He looked at Gary over their heads, and the prince's messenger nodded carefully. He would watch over Traian's lifemate and family. A matter of honor in the Carpathian world.

Chapter Ten

Joie dreamt of a hot, moist mouth pulling strongly at her breast, of hands stroking her body. Of lips traveling down her bare skin to her navel, swirling kisses and teasing bites over her stomach. Hands on her thighs tugging her legs apart. She was already damp with invitation.

She opened her eyes as the waves of sensation burst through her like a gift. The wealth of Traian's silky dark hair slid over her skin, the sight more erotic than she had ever imagined. His fingers moved inside her, found secret ways to shimmer fire through her veins. And then his tongue took the place of his hands, stabbing deep, tasting and teasing and stroking her until she was crying with joy and her body no longer belonged to her. Wave after wave, orgasm after orgasm rippled through her body, so that she bucked and jumped as he held her firmly, his mouth devouring her, claiming her, feeding her sheer pleasure.

She clenched her fists in his hair, holding on while she took the wild ride, while the earth moved and her body shattered into fragments. He took possession of her then, kneeling above her, dragging her hips to him, thrusting deep with powerful strokes while she came over and over in a mind-numbing climax that seemed endless. He was everywhere, in her body, in her mind, their hearts beating in the same rhythm. She could feel the intensity of his emotions, a tidal wave of longing and love, of absolute need and hunger, of caring and loyalty, far more than she could understand, but real all the same.

Traian loved the way Joie clung to him as his body rode out the storm of roiling emotions, each thrust deeper and harder in a fierce, possessive joining. Thunder roared in his ears, lightning sang in his blood, fire raged in his belly until the conflagration merged together at the core of his body. Her feminine sheath was fiery hot, tight and velvet soft, the friction an unbelievable sensation. He tilted her hips, wanting her to take all of him, wanting to crawl inside her body, his home, his sanctuary after several lifetimes of loneliness. He wanted to give her the world, wanted her body to feel the same flames of passion and pleasure that she ignited in him.

He felt her muscles clench around him, the gathering of a great force. He threw back his head, allowed his body to explode with volcanic intensity, thrusting deep, taking her with him, holding her close as they burst into sunlight, the only time he could ever embrace such a thing.

Traian buried his face in her neck and breathed her in. It was early for him to rise, but he had to see her before he went hunting. He had been handed an unexpected miracle and he wasn't about to lose her. "I used to think the word 'forever' was the worst word in any language. And now, I cannot imagine enough time with you."

"I feel the same way," Joie admitted.

His shifted her in his arms, pressed her body to the length of his. "Never go away," he whispered in her ear. "Never leave me to face the endless years alone again."

Joie brushed back the long silk of his hair, framed his face with her hands, and stared up at him—at the lines etched into his beautiful masculine features, put there by battles and years of knowledge of foul things walking the earth. Put there by sheer loneliness. "I want you always, Traian. We'll find our way together."

She shattered his heart so easily with her complete conviction. She had confidence in herself and in him.

"I should have really made you understand about our children and what our women have to go through in trying to have a baby. It has taken a toll on them—one miscarriage after another or carrying the child and loosing it that first year. It is so hard on a mother." He shook his head. "I know I am asking so much of you, Joie, and when I think too much about it, it breaks my heart to think of you going through that same emotional loss."

"I wouldn't be going through the loss of a child alone, Traian. If I get pregnant, I believe you would feel the same sense of loss. We'd be in it together."

"I don't want that kind of pain for you."

She smiled at him. "I can feel that you genuinely don't, but no one can predict what is going to happen in the future, not even an all-powerful Carpathian. Because your prince's wife miscarried, as sad as that is, doesn't mean I will if we are lucky enough to become pregnant."

"I will be more careful in the future to explain details to you, so you know what you are getting into," he promised.

He leaned toward her, kissing her gently, with exquisite tenderness, with the overwhelming love in his heart that he couldn't quite put into words but tried to show by worshiping her with his body. He kissed her over and over, long, slow kisses, his body locked deep inside hers, his hands tunneling in her thick hair. His mouth roamed over her throat, down to her breast, and found her heart unerringly.

Joie felt the swirl of his tongue, and her heart leapt in

anticipation. Her body tightened around his. White-hot pain lanced through her, and then gave way immediately to pleasure. She cradled his head to her while he fed, while his body moved slowly and erotically deep within her. The sensation was unlike anything she'd ever experienced. He was in his body, in her mind, filling every empty space with—him while he took her blood, bringing her ever closer to his world.

She writhed helplessly beneath him, arching her hips up to meet him, her breasts aching and full with need. When his hand cupped the weight of one breast, his thumb sliding over the taut peak of her nipple, she pressed his head closer to her, offering more—offering everything she was to him.

Joie could hear her heart picking up the exact same rhythm of his. Her blood pounded in her veins, rushing toward him, hot and carrying the very scent and taste of her to him, matching the hammering beat of his blood. It should have been frightening, even disgusting, having him take her blood, but for her, the act was sensual.

Traian closed his eyes, savoring the taste of her, the craving for her growing as power and energy rushed through his body, soaking into every cell, sinew, and bone, filling him up with such strength he knew she completed him. She'd given him so much just by being born, being in his world, surrendering herself to save him. The gift was a miracle to him.

He swept his tongue across the pinpricks, tasted the temptation of her breast before finding her mouth to share the taste of their life's essence. He took his time, his tongue thoroughly exploring her mouth, teasing and dancing and mating with hers.

"Come into my world, Joie. Another step closer," he murmured in his dark, mesmerizing voice, a seductive invitation, she couldn't possibly resist—nor did she want to.

This time she was locked in a dreamy haze, aware of his

body's sensations as she moved restlessly, wantonly under him. As her mouth moved against his chest, taking his precious gift, his fingers stroked her throat, her breast, keeping the intimacy between them sensual, as well as helping her to feed. His body thickened inside her, moved with greater force and purpose. She felt the now familiar flames, hot and white and pure, burning in his veins, pulsing through him even as they crackled with life, pulsing through her.

She was overjoyed to be able to bring him such pleasure, so much happiness. She wanted to be fully in his world, with him just like this, so close she couldn't tell where he ended and she began. She moved more aggressively until he was surging into her with strength and power, until she felt the gathering of every nerve ending, every muscle, and the flow of blood, until they soared together higher than ever.

I want more time with you. I want to touch your body and know it the way you know mine. I want to see the things you've seen and make you feel the way you've made me feel, she whispered into his mind.

"We have time," he said. "All the things you fantasize about, all the things that matter to you—we have time for everything." Very gently he stopped her feeding, closing the slash across his chest. He laid her on the bed, his hands gentle, loving, stroking her bare skin while he brought her fully out of the enthrallment.

Joie blinked up at him. "That's twice," she said. "I'm that much closer to being in your world." She touched his face with gentle fingers. "I've fallen pretty hard for you, Traian."

He knew what she was saying. She was fully committed and just that little bit scared that somehow he would change his mind about her. There was no way to adequately explain the concept of lifemates when she lived in a human world where divorce seemed a way of life. It would be absolutely impossible to leave a true lifemate.

"You are not alone, Joie," he assured. "I had no idea emotions could be so intense, but when I look around me, I can see only you. You are truly the light to my darkness."

She sent him a small, tentative smile, rolling onto her side, propping up her head with one hand. "I don't know about that. I doubt if either of my siblings would ever call me light to anyone's darkness."

"I guess they do not see you as I do."

"You guess right."

Traian gave a sigh of regret. "I have to go, Joie. It is almost sunset. I have to find at least one of the master vampire's lairs before he rises."

"Do you have an idea where to look?" She traced first his face, and then his mouth with her fingertips, committing his face to memory with each caressing stroke.

"I hope they did not leave the cave. They were so reluctant to leave it before, but we had not discovered the mage traps. It is a dangerous place to be, even for the undead—maybe especially for the undead."

"Promise me that you'll contact me if you run into any trouble." She looked him straight in the eye, insisting on the truth.

"You are my lifemate, Joie. If I run into trouble, you will know." He bent his head to kiss her. Slowly. Lingering over it. Pouring his heart and soul into it.

Her mouth went dry the moment he stepped away from her. She sat all the way up and reached for a blanket, holding it to comfort her. "Traian, it's difficult to let you go alone."

"I know it is, *sivamet*—my love, and I thank you for your understanding. I know allowing me to hunt alone is against your nature, but truly, you and your brother and sister are in great danger here. It is just as difficult for me to leave you unguarded when I know danger is close. Your scents still linger in the cave and the undead can hunt using scent alone. Do not think for one moment that you are not hunted."

"Here? Surrounded by everyone in the village? Are they really that bold?"

"Vampires are very vengeful creatures. And they use humans to do their bidding. Anyone is a potential enemy."

"I have a lot to learn about vampires," Joie sighed. "All the training I've been through and my experiences on my job don't seem to count for much in dealing with them."

He caught her chin and kissed her again. When he stepped back, he was fully clothed, looked immaculate and a little bit lethal. "I removed the safeguards at your door so your siblings can enter without worry, but those at your windows remain. I will return as soon as possible."

Just that fast, Traian was gone. Joie lay back on the sheets, staring up at the ceiling, her heart pounding in fear for him. He was gone, slipping out through the window, a cloud of vapor streaming into the air. It wasn't yet sunset, but she felt as if the sun had gone down on her world.

Nothing can happen to you, she whispered into his mind. *I would never forgive myself for letting you do this alone.*

I can see I will have to impart my knowledge of hunting the undead as quickly as possible to you. It really is difficult for you to be left behind when there is danger surrounding me. Think of your siblings, Joie. They have great need of you.

Joie pressed her hand to her heart in an attempt to control the wild pounding. She took a deep breath to steady herself. This wasn't just about him going off alone to fight. Dread built fast. Had she not been touching his mind, she knew she would have thought him dead to her. Sorrow lurked just behind the dread.

It is only the effects of our connection. I am with you.

Feel with your mind as a Carpathian must. It takes time to learn our ways, I know, but I cannot have you suffering grief when I am alive and well and able to reach out to you.

Determined to combat her growing sorrow, when there was no real reason for it, Joie sat up. *It is amazing how intense the feeling is. And it is a little frightening to think that emotion is stronger than logic. I know where you are, yet I still have such a need to touch you—to feel you in my mind. It makes no sense.*

The terrible need inside of her *didn't* make sense. Joie considered herself a very logical woman. She didn't like this out-of-control feeling, a dark dread that stole her good sense and her ability to reason. She lifted her chin. There were changes taking place in her body and mind, but that didn't mean she would give in to melancholy.

I'll be perfectly fine, Traian. You worry about yourself. I'll hang with Jubal and Gabrielle while you're gone, she assured him. *I'm strong and can get through this. Don't you worry about me, just take care of yourself.*

Stay close to Gary as well. He knows both the undead and my people.

Joie did the mental equivalent of rolling her eyes. *As if. Traian, you're going to have to get over your outdated attitude toward women. It must be your age. Gary is the one who needs protection. He lives in another world, just like Gabrielle, I can see it in him. He's more at home in a lab than fighting vampires.*

But he knows the ways of the undead and how best to combat them. Stay close to him.

Joie clenched her teeth. She was never going to be the little woman, hiding behind the big brave man. *If that's the kind of woman you want, you started something you never should have.*

She felt a stroking caress along her face—feather-light—the gentle touch of fingers, yet he was no longer close to the inn.

I know exactly who you are, Joie, and what you are capable of. I do not mean to make you feel as if I don't think you can handle yourself. I know you will not panic and that you will fight the undead without hesitation. I am merely saying stay safe and keep the person who has been around Carpathian hunters close while I am gone. That makes sense, does it not?

Of course it made sense. She didn't have to like it, did she? Nor did she want to let go of her irritation, not with the strange grief of separation edging so close to her.

You might have mentioned your archaic attitude and your stubbornness when you were being so blasted charming a few minutes ago.

His soft laughter echoed through her mind. *You might have warned me I was going to be dealing with a modern female who is determined to get herself into dangerous situations.*

The teasing in his tone warmed her—settled her. She took a deep breath and let it out. She knew he had to go without her in his mind. The vampires could detect him through his connection with her.

Just do whatever you have to do and return home safe to me.

Again she felt that feather-light brushing caress along her face. She placed her palm over the invisible mark, holding him close to her as his mind slipped from hers. At once she felt bereft, as though instead of mist streaming through the sky toward the caves, Traian lay beneath the earth dead to her. She was astonished at the strength of emotion pouring into her mind, once he was actually away from her.

Determined not to give in to the strange reaction to their separation, Joie took a long, hot shower. It was nearly impossible to stand beneath the cascading water without thinking of Traian, but she concentrated on pushing him out of her mind enough to figure out how to tell her parents that she was essentially married—and to someone not quite human.

Her father was accepting of everything his children did and was a very tolerant man. Her mother was fiercely protective of her children and loved them very much. Her family was her world. It had been her mother who insisted all of them take self-defense lessons almost from the time they could walk. Her father had been the climber of mountains and delved deep into the caves around the world. He had taught them a love of nature.

Joie sighed. Her mother wasn't going to welcome Traian. She had a major problem with alpha males, bristling the moment they walked into the room—almost as if she had radar. She'd been particularly hard on Jubal as they'd grown up.

She found she could hear conversations whispered in the rooms around her and even as far away as people moving in the sitting room. It took some practicing to turn down the volume, but not before she heard her sister and brother walking down the hall to her door. The cursory knock didn't at all surprise her, but the sound of a tool scratching in the lock did. She tensed and eased one hand out of the shower enough to grip her weapon until she recognized her sister's scent as she stuck her head in the bathroom.

"What are you doing, you crazy woman?" Joie demanded. "Were you hoping to get a peek at my man? That's grounds for shooting you."

"Ha! You wouldn't you know. And hurry up. Jubal and I are getting tired of waiting for you two. And you'd better not be doing anything perverted in that tiny little shower stall." She sounded more hopeful than anything else.

"How did you get into my room, you peeping Tom?" Joie threw a wet washcloth with deadly accuracy. "It was locked."

Gabrielle squealed when the cloth hit her square in the face. "I'm picking up your bad habits and wanted to show off." She sounded a little smug. "You aren't the only one who can pick a lock. In any case, Jubal double-dog dared me. What else could I do?"

"Pretend you're discreet while I'm trying to land a man. Sheesh, Gabby, he's going to think we're all a pack of perverts. You don't have to accept every one of Jubal's juvenile challenges."

"You do," Gabrielle pointed out, not in the least repentant.

"He only does that to make Mom crazy," Joie said.

"Are you in there alone? Because I don't want to see any naked bodies."

Joie let out a little sniff. "Then what are you doing in here, trying to see through the steam. I'm naked, if you want to know, but Traian already went back to the cave."

Gabrielle sighed. "I've already seen you naked and it's nothing to get too excited about, but that man of yours is drop-dead gorgeous. I don't know about this Carpathian business. He likes to be underground so much, he could very well be a troll. What are you going to tell Mom and Dad?" This time there was glee in Gabrielle's voice.

"I've been rehearsing," Joie admitted. She emerged from the stall, wrapped in a bath sheet. "It has occurred to me to lie to them. And I thought you preferred skinny men. I saw you ogling Gary last night."

"I don't ogle," Gabrielle sniffed indignantly. "I never ogle. I just thought he was rather on the cute side. And you weren't looking close enough. He's not skinny, he has plenty of muscle, just not obscenely sticking out everywhere." She sighed heavily, frowning. "I wish I was one of those really beautiful, stick-thin model types all men fall over. Even if I dyed my hair blonde and learned to flip it around, I don't think I'd ever perfect the art of flirting."

Joie glared at her. "You are beautiful, you idiot. You're just crazy. If this man can't see your worth, he isn't as smart as you think he is."

"Yeah, yeah, I'm all about brains and he's going to be madly intrigued with my intellect and dazzled with my cushy body." Gabrielle made a face, trying to laugh, but looking as if she might cry.

"Gabby, what's gotten into you?" Joie asked, stepping closer to her sister, feeling waves of distress pouring off her sister.

"It's just that I blow it every single time I'm actually attracted to a man. It doesn't happen very often. Most of the time, I'm bored out of my mind and can't stay in their company for five minutes. But when someone comes along who makes sense, and can discuss topics I'm really interested in, if I'm physically attracted, I come off looking like an idiot—or next to you and Jubal—the damsel in distress who needs rescuing." She stuck her chin out. "I'm not, you know."

"Of course I know. You forget, Gabrielle, Jubal and I climb with you and go into caves. We've gone down the Amazon and into the rain forest. You never flinch."

"I flinched in the ice cave."

"Yeah, well, here's a news flash for you, sister, so did I. Anyone who doesn't flinch inside that place is plain suicidal and out of their mind."

"Really?" Gabrielle asked. "Neither you or Jubal looked as if you freaked out."

"Of course we did. Bodyguards can't show freak-outs, babe, that's the bottom line and Jubal prides himself on *never* showing a freak-out because we'd tease him unmercifully until the day he died and maybe after as well." Joie shared a grin with her sister. "Is Jubal hanging out in the bedroom? I need my clothes?"

"I'll get you something presentable." Gabrielle disappeared.

Joie heard her giggle. Gabrielle never did anything so undignified as to giggle. Unashamed, Joie listened to the murmured conversation in the next room. Gary had joined her brother and sister in her bedroom and Gabrielle had clearly forgotten her mission to produce clothes for her sister.

Joie stalked to the door. "Hello! I hate to remind you all, but I'm stuck here, naked in the bathroom. Vacate or toss me some clothes."

Jubal groaned and covered his eyes. "You are so sick, Joie. I didn't need that visual. Gary, you ought to try having a couple of sisters bent on tormenting you. They gang up on me like you wouldn't believe."

Gabrielle blew him a kiss. "We keep your life from being extraordinarily dull and boring."

"Don't believe her," Jubal cautioned Gary.

Joie caught the bundle of clothes her sister tossed inside the bathroom. "Thanks for remembering me," she hissed.

"I remembered," Gabrielle replied with a smirk. "Getting your clothes just didn't seem all that important all of a sudden."

You are truly a hussy, Joie said and closed the bathroom door firmly on her sister's teasing laugh. *I know exactly what you were doing. That poor man has no idea you've got your hook out and you're fishing.*

I'm going to dose his drink with a love potion, Gabrielle shot back.

Gabrielle rarely was depressed or upset for long. She was naturally upbeat and had a sunny personality. Joie found herself smiling in spite of the deep dread in the pit of her stomach. Being with her family was exactly what she needed.

She dressed carefully, for war. She didn't want to be unprepared for anything. She had weapons stashed in both the bedroom and her bathroom and she donned as many as she could carry without detection. Her clothes were loose enough to hide the weapons and to move in fast, yet wouldn't get in the way should she need to climb or fight hand to hand.

Gary stood up when Joie entered the room. "Good evening." He bowed slightly, a habit he'd acquired from the Carpathians. "I take it Traian left already? I figured he'd rise as early as possible. There were clouds blocking the sunlight. They sometimes arrange the weather to protect their sensitive eyes." He smiled at Joie. "He wants me to get you to drink some juice this evening."

Joie pressed a hand to her stomach. "I don't think that's going to happen, but I'm sure Gabrielle and Jubal are hungry."

"Starved," Jubal agreed instantly. "I thought Joie was going to sleep forever."

"You'll get used to the different hours they keep," Gary said. "I work in the lab and forget the time myself. If I'm on to something promising, I don't seem to need sleep."

"I'm the same way," Gabrielle said. "Sometimes I look up and it's two days later." She exchanged a long smile of complete understanding with Gary.

Jubal threw his hands into the air. "I'm *starving*. I need to get food and whether you're hungry or not, Joie, we need to stick together. Let's go down to the dining room."

Joie rolled her eyes. "Big surprise that you're starving, Jubal. I swear you were born that way. Are you armed?" Joie dragged on her boots and shoved a knife down into the leather scabbard built in.

Gary raised an eyebrow, but Gabrielle just shrugged, her

grin sheepish. "We're used to Joie. She's nearly always lethal."

"Of course I'm armed." The smile faded from Jubal's face as he turned to Gary with sober eyes. "Are you?"

There was a small silence. Gabrielle pressed her lips together. Joie and Jubal just waited for the answer. If Gary was even remotely interested in their sister, he'd better know how to protect her.

Gary gave them a small smirk, not in the least intimidated. "I carry weapons at all times. Here, working with the Carpathians, I have no choice. They rest during the day and if the undead send human puppets to find their resting places, they have to be protected."

"Great," Gabrielle said. "We don't just have to worry about vampires trying to kill us, but other things as well."

Gary nodded. "Sadly, it's true. And don't ever forget the secret society of humans that hunt and condemn various people to death and torture and kill them. This is a dangerous part of the world to live in, so if you're going to be here, you have to learn as much as you can about protecting yourself at all times. Basically, expect the unexpected."

Jubal pulled open the door. "I won't have to worry about ghouls or crazy vampire hunters if we don't eat soon. Go now!" He glared at his sisters.

Both of them laughed at him, but obediently followed Jubal into the hall and down the stairs.

Gabrielle leaned close to Gary. "Jubal is very grumpy until he eats," she whispered overly loud so her brother could be certain to hear her. "We still call him 'grumpy pants.'"

Jubal groaned. "*Never* have sisters. Just an FYI."

"News flash, Jubal," Joie said, her gaze, like his, on the few people milling around the dining room as they entered. "You adore your sisters and everyone knows it."

"I do make you think that, otherwise you wouldn't do my laundry for me," Jubal pointed out smugly.

Joie noticed Gary was every bit as alert and watchful as Jubal and she were. Food was served buffet style, so they quickly got the dishes they preferred, Jubal taking plenty of healthy helpings while Joie settled for a small glass of juice. They sat down at the table nearest the door for a quick exit.

Joie frowned as her siblings ate with gusto, needing the calories after the ordeal in the ice caves. Her stomach lurched at that thought of food. She felt Gary watching her and she wrapped her fingers around the glass to forestall any attention he might draw to her sister and brother to the fact that she couldn't eat.

"Do you live here permanently, Gary?" she asked.

He nodded. "I'm needed here. The work that I do is very valuable and there's satisfaction in that. This species is too amazing to go extinct. There has to be a way to solve the problem of successfully carrying a baby. Besides, it's heartbreaking to live among them, get to know them and then have one of the few women miscarry or lose her precious child."

"I can't imagine how painful that would be," Gabrielle said, compassion pouring into her voice. "If you wouldn't mind, I'd like to see what you're doing, since I'm here anyway. Maybe I could help."

"Usually Carpathians erase all memories of an encounter with them," Gary said. "I was surprised that Traian hadn't done so."

Jubal looked up, a dark scowl on his face. "Yeah, I don't think so. He can forget that."

Joie kicked him under the table. "He isn't going to do that. I'd shoot him and he knows it. Don't be such a dork." She saw Gary watching her, so she put the glass to her lips and took a small sip. Her stomach cramped almost instantly. She set the glass down with great care. "Do you travel much?"

Gary shrugged, shaking his head. "I've been on a hit list for a while now and it isn't safe. The Carpathians protect me and in all honesty, I'm pretty focused on my work."

"That's the way I am when I get in a lab. Time passes and sometimes I'm there for days without sleep," Gabrielle admitted.

Joie became aware of the exact moment the sun set. She didn't see the orange and red hues, but in the midst of the conversation going on around her she simply knew. She felt the sudden shuddering of the earth as the vampires rose. Her heart leapt in fear.

Traian! She reached out to him. Touched him. Felt his immediate reassurance. He had not discovered the resting places of the vampires. They had not gone to ground in the cave of the mages.

"Joie?" Gabrielle touched her hand. "Are you all right?"

Jubal put down his fork and looked carefully around the room. *The bracelet is heating up again, it's merely warm, but that isn't a good sign.*

A dark shadow passed over the inn, moving fast, so that for a moment silence fell in the dining room and people looked at one another uneasily.

Gary reacted instantly. He caught Gabrielle's wrist, rising so fast his chair fell backward. "Come with me, right now." He tugged Gabrielle to her feet and began to weave his way through the tables, dragging her with him.

Jubal looked at his meal with regret as Joie smacked the back of his head. "It might be your last meal if you don't move it," she cautioned.

"It might be my last meal anyway," he groused. But he was on his feet and rushing after Gary and Gabrielle, covering his wrist with his other hand as the band began to give off a faint light.

Definitely going hot, Jubal told his sisters. *The blades will come out next.*

"Call him back, Joie," Gary ordered over his shoulder. "Call Traian and get him back here. We don't have much time."

Joie didn't hesitate. There was too much urgency in Gary's voice. *Traian. They are here. The undead are here at the inn. Gary says it's urgent that you return as quickly as possible.*

Do as Gary says. He will know what to do until I am able to return. They cannot get their hands on any of you. Go for the heart if you have to defend yourself. They often inject poison into the bloodstream, and they are great deceivers and shape-shifters.

Traian's matter-of-fact voice calmed Joie. *Jubal's bracelet is going hot. The last time that happened, the blades came out. Gary will see them, there's no way to hide it from him.*

We have no choice but to trust him. We do not know your ancestry, but you are my family and under my protection. He will know that. If any Carpathian should threaten you because that mage weapon is seen, you tell them all of you are under my protection. This time there was steel in his voice.

Gary shoved open the door to his room on the first floor. It was faster to get there and provided an excellent escape should they need one. "Quick, get inside and stuff everything you can find in the cracks around the doors and windows." He tossed Gabrielle shirts as he hurried to the door leading to the verandah. "We'll have to hole up in here. They'll try to call us out, using compulsion. Jubal, there's a small CD player on the desk. Pick some obnoxious music from the collection and turn it up loud. Very loud."

Joie locked the door behind her. "The keyhole, Gabrielle—

stuff something in that as well." If vampires could do what she had seen Traian do, stream through tiny spaces as vapor, she didn't see how they were going to keep them out. "So why are they here?"

"Most likely because you are," Gary answered. "The surest way to bring a Carpathian male out into the open is to go after his lifemate. They'll want one of you to invite them in. If you hear a voice talking sweetly, it is a deceiver. Put cotton in your ears, put your hands over your ears. Do anything to keep from listening. If one of you observe another going to the door or even talking, inviting someone into the room, stop him, even if it means knocking him out."

"They're definitely here," Jubal said, pulling back his sleeve. His bracelet spilled light into the room, the wicked curved blades very much in evidence.

Gary stepped back, shook his head, and sighed. "I'm not even going to ask."

Shadows passed across the window, moving back and forth as if searching for something. The wind picked up so that the tree branches scraped against the inn with a sickening screech. Clouds spun and boiled, casting hideous apparitions across the moon. A stain spread across the sky, slowly blotting out the stars, creeping insidiously until nearly all light was extinguished. The wind howled against the windows, slammed into the verandah door, carried with it voices. Soft. Cunning. Sweet and enticing. Pleading voices. Cries for help. A woman called out just beyond the door, begging for entrance, her voice rising on the wind.

"Joie?" Gabrielle looked to her sister for guidance.

Gary was close to her and he put his arm around her protectively. "Traian will be here soon. We can hold out until then."

Jubal cranked up the CD player so that it blared loudly. Something grabbed the door handle and shook it so hard, the door rattled and splintered. Jubal leapt to place his body between the door and sisters. Joie stepped up beside him.

"Gary, get Gabby out of here," Joie said, her heart pounding. Jubal had killed one of these things with his bracelet. Maybe it could happen again. She sent up a silent prayer.

"Believe me, we're safer inside this room than anywhere else right now. And there's less danger if we stick together," Gary said. He took up a position at her side. "Jubal, watch the windows. If you see anything that looks like smoke or fog trying to get in through a crack, you have to stuff in a shirt, the blankets, anything at all to keep it out."

The door was struck again from outside, hard enough to shake the frame. Gabrielle clapped her hand over her mouth to keep from crying out.

"You can't come in," Gary said, not raising his voice. "You have not been invited and you can't gain entrance into this room."

Maniacal laughter greeted Gary's calm words. A great weight thudded against the door and began a steady pushing. The wood began to bulge inward.

Chapter Eleven

In the shape of an owl, Traian streaked across the darkened sky. Joie had no hope of fighting off a master vampire, even with Gary's vast knowledge of the undead and Jubal's weapon. Often it took two and sometimes three very experienced hunters to kill a master vampire. The most the humans could hope for was to delay the vampires until he arrived.

The wind increased in speed so that gusts hurled branches and twigs into the air like missiles. A funnel cloud whirled and spun ominously from ground to sky, a dark, turbulent monster leaping with greedy outspread fingers toward him. He flew into an invisible barrier, hit the obstacle hard and plummeted toward the ground below.

The black mass stretched wide, forming a ghastly head with a gaping mouth and long, bony arms, reaching for the body of the owl as it tumbled toward the ground. Traian shifted into dark droplets of vapor, merging with the black mass, spreading thin to avoid detection. The tornado dropped from the heavens as if it had never been, leaving behind an eerie calm and a clear sky.

A tangle of silver fell from the tree branches, a fine solid blanket of woven strands. Traian was already shifting again, landing in a crouch on the ground. The silver hit his arm but slid off, landing inches from his feet. Pain streaked through his body. Angry red welts rose immediately on his skin where his flesh had come into contact with the glittering silver. Thousands of stinging insects flew at his face, a solid wall of them, programmed to find and attack. Traian dissolved to avoid them, sliding back into the forest to cling to a tree branch in the shape of a frog.

He reached out with his senses, trying to locate his opponent. Master vampires rarely revealed themselves, especially in battle. Traian knew the undead had deliberately drawn him back to the inn with the hope of trapping and destroying him.

I am in a fight for all of our lives. If you can avoid a confrontation, do so. If not, always go for the most dangerous vampire and go for the heart. Nothing else will put them down. Delay. Stall. Try to avoid a battle.

He waited, his heart beating a little too hard, fear eating at his mind until Joie answered. Her voice was calm and steady, even confident, settling the hard knots in his belly.

Don't think about us little mortal people, Traian. We can handle the dead guys. You just don't get a single scratch on you or I'll be upset—and you've never seen me upset.

The relief nearly overwhelmed him. She was unhurt .

You have taught me the real meaning of fear. Always, I have gone into battle with nothing to lose. I do not much care for the feeling.

Well, it's mutual, Traian, so don't go feeling sorry for yourself. I've got the ugly guys at the door, so I'm going to have to let you go.

Joie made him want to laugh. She sounded like she was talking to him on the phone and a neighbor had dropped by to borrow a cup of sugar. *Do not get overconfident.* He couldn't help cautioning her, although he knew it would annoy her.

A walk in the park. You worry about yourself.

He could see the insects scattering, returning, flying through the trees in search of any sign of him. The bugs always returned to swarm around the same rotted trunk of a fallen tree. *I love you, Joie, and I cannot do without you. Keep that in mind when you decide how best to handle the situation. You are deciding for both of us.*

She hissed at him between her teeth. He could hear it clearly, the irritation and annoyance of a woman beyond her limits of patience. His heart did a curious flip, a strange reaction to her feminine exasperation. For some unexplained reason, he felt joy.

The little frog hopped along the tree branch, taking great care to blend in with the leaves and twigs. He was some distance from the fallen tree, and the ground stretching between was covered with debris. Traian glanced skyward at the black, spinning clouds. At his mental command, lightning shot bright sparks into the massive cauldron overhead. The white-hot energy spun into a large ball, breaking away from the clouds and hurtling toward the ground. The air crackled with electricity.

Traian leapt from the branch, shape-shifting into his true form, his hands directing the spinning threads of energy, launching the ball as he melted back into the trees. The sphere slammed into the center of the rotten trunk, carving a blackened hole as it went all the way through to hit the ground, forming a deep crater. White whips sizzled and crackled inside the depression.

Black vapor rose from the trunk of the tree to mix with the dark, spinning clouds. A terrible piercing howl of rage filled the air. High-pitched and obscene, the voice shredded nerves and pierced eardrums. The trees shuddered and shook. Grass and leaves shriveled. The sound bounced from ground to cloud with the force of a clap of thunder. The blast hit Traian in the back and drove him forward, slamming him into a tree. He just managed to whip his head back before he hit.

He inhaled quickly, took in the noxious, foul smell of burnt flesh, and knew he had scored a hit. Fire rained from the sky, red glowing embers igniting the foliage. Hungry flames licked at the grass and leaves, and then raced up the trees with glee. Traian spread out his arms, gave a command, and the clouds burst open, pouring sheets of water on the rising flames. The sky overhead went black with smoke and whirling clouds. It was impossible to tell where the vampire was. The undead was experienced enough not to give away his presence by blank spots in the air. He chose to blend into the chaos of his surroundings, sidestepping further battles now that he was wounded.

Without warning Traian was hit from behind, a thick branch thunking hard across his back, knocking him to his knees. Instantly, a body was on him, teeth tearing at him, missing his neck and hooking into his shoulder. Using tremendous strength, he drove upward and back, slamming his body down hard over the top of the vicious vampire.

Instinctively he knew, this was the master's pawn, sent to slow Traian down, a sacrifice the master hoped would wound him enough to allow the kill. He heard the vampire grunt with pain and he rolled. The undead refused to let go, his teeth clamped hard in Traian's shoulder. As he rolled, he felt flesh and muscle tear. He reached back, gripped the head with both hands and wrenched hard, throwing the body over his shoulder as he leapt to his feet.

The vampire landed with a thud against the same tree Traian had run into. The force of the body hitting it shook the trunk so that branches rocked and leaves and twigs rained down over the thin, stick-like figure. Traian almost didn't recognize that this vampire once had been a childhood friend. The man was every bit as old as he was and the fact that he was a fledgling, commanded by a master, meant he'd only recently turned. He'd held out against the growing darkness as long as he was able and rather than seeking the dawn, he'd succumbed to the whispers for the rush of feeling a kill would bring.

Deliberately, Traian ignored the blood oozing from the bite marks and torn flesh on his shoulder. He bowed slightly toward the vampire.

"Emilian, I scarce recognized you. It has been many long years since last we met."

The fledgling vampire climbed clumsily to his feet. His bloodshot eyes met Traian's and slithered away, unable to see himself in the eyes of a hunter. He dusted his clothes off and made an effort to settle an illusion of who he had once been over his rotting body. His hair changed from all gray to black and gray. His skin, pitted and sunken, filled out to once again look smooth. He pulled himself up to try to look dignified.

"Traian. You have angered the master. Come, join us. He will forgive you if you aid us."

Traian's eyebrow shot up. "I never thought to hear you say you have a master. Carpathians are free. We roam the earth, take to the skies, go below the ground, wherever we choose, with no one commanding us, yet you give up freedom to become a slave to a master. That makes no sense to me, Emilian."

Deliberately he continued to use the vampire's name, distracting him, perhaps even confusing him from his goal. Traian shifted a bit to his right, a barely perceptible movement that took him a few inches closer to the lesser vampire.

"You are slave to the prince," Emilian accused, showing his teeth. Once immaculately white, they were stained brown and beginning to take the shape of serrated spikes.

"The prince of our people does not command us, Emilian, you know that."

"Have you forgotten that he sent us from our homeland, banished us and kept the women for himself and those he favored?" Emilian snarled the words, hatred pouring through his voice.

"Is that what your master has told you?" Traian risked another couple of inches, the glide smooth enough that the agitated vampire failed to notice once again. "Have you forgotten so much? The prince allowed each of us to make our own decision, as is the way of our people. You *chose* to leave our homeland and I did as well. Do not blame your failure to keep your honor on our prince."

Emilian bared his teeth, the bloodshot eyes turning ruby red as his temper flared. "If you chose to cow down before him and crawl like a dog at his bidding, more fool you. I will enjoy power and have the world bowing at my feet."

Traian managed another two inches, within striking distance now. "As you crawl like the dog you have become to your master, whining for a pat on the head as you bow at his feet?"

He moved with blurring speed, streaking across the short distance, slamming his fist deep into the chest of his old friend, fingers burrowing deep for the beating heart. Emilian tore at him with claws and teeth, desperately trying to break free from the hunter's merciless grip.

Black blood burned Traian's skin as he tore the heart free and threw it a distance from him. Emilian faltered, staring at his own heart, crying out and reaching toward it. He went down to his knees and fell face down, stretching his arms pleadingly toward his heart.

Traian took a few steps to get clear of the trees to call down the lightning. The ground spewed dirt and rocks into the air just a foot in front of him, a geyser erupting violently. A rock hit his chest, driving him away from Emilian's heart and back toward the vampire lying on the ground.

Another relatively new vampire sprung at him, leaping on his shoulders, clawing at his eyes. Traian dissolved, or attempted to; Emilian caught his ankle and sank lengthy talons deep to keep him from shifting shape. Gleeful laughter erupted from the sky as the master vampire once more was certain he'd gained the upper hand against the hunter.

Traian turned and ducked forward all in one motion, hurtling the vampire off of him and slamming his fist hard into Emilian's back, breaking the spine with an audible crack. Emilian screamed and released him and Traian leapt into the clearing, calling down the lightning. The sizzling bolt struck the heart with deadly precision. Emilian convulsed, his mouth opening wide, maggots pouring out, attempting to abandon the dying corpse. The bolt of lightning jumped from earth to sky and back, this time incinerating the body, leaving ash to blow away in the wind.

The second lesser vampire attacked with blinding speed, rushing toward Traian and at the last moment, shifting, taking to the air as a giant, winged bird with a wedge-shaped head, wicked curved beak and claws the size of a grizzly's. Traian managed to duck, allowing the bird to skim past him, cutting a razor-thin fiery streak across his back and shoulder as the thing went past.

The ground rolled, tossing Traian off balance, a signal that the master helped his pawn from a distance and he had to gain the upper hand fast or the master would come in to finish the kill. He was losing blood and that was the whole point of these attacks by the lesser pawns—to weaken him. No master vampire would risk his existence unless he had an advantage. They always used the fledglings, unless they had no puppets to control and then, as a rule, they avoided hunters.

Around him, in a large loose circle, the ground shook and rolled and geyser after geyser exploded upward. Out of the raining debris vampire after vampire stepped, fiery eyes glowing red in the dark, staring at him, raising heads to sniff the blood dripping from his wounds, pulling back thin lips to bare blackened, stained teeth.

"Join us," they whispered, hands stretched toward him.

Feet stomped the ground, setting up a peculiar rhythm. The sound echoed through his mind, like the dripping of the water in the cave and the clacking of the branches, a hypnotic, mesmerizing sound evading his mind. The vampires swayed to the beat, blurring images until all he could focus on were the red eyes streaking back and forth as the bodies moved in unison.

"Join us." This time the entreaty was louder, moving through his mind. "Join us. Join us." The refrain became a chant echoing through the forest and reverberating from the roiling clouds to the rolling ground.

Traian shook his head, trying to get the terrible buzzing out of his mind. The ensnaring refrain moved through his mind and his blood seemed to respond, reaching toward those calling to him. Out of the corner of his eye he caught movement and his brain filled in the pieces. This master, strong enough to command another powerful master vampire, had taken his blood. He could reach inside of him through the blood bond, influence his movements, track him at will and push him toward taking that last step to giving up his honor.

He forced a laugh. "You think to trap me as you would one of your pawns? I am a hunter with centuries of experience."

"Join me or die an ugly death and I will strip the very flesh from your lifemate and feed it to my dogs," the voice taunted from the safety of a vantage point close by. There was a hint of anger as the master realized Traian wasn't as far under his spell as he'd hoped. His confidence was a little shaken.

"You have enough dogs to do your bidding and still, as

many times as you have set them upon me, you have failed. Sooner or later they will tire of your continual defeats and see you are all words with no real power."

Traian clapped his hands together hard and thunder boomed in answer. A white-hot whip of lightning streaked across the sky and slammed to the earth in a large circle, striking the master vampire's apparitions with a vicious, well-aimed cut. The illusions burned like paper dolls, dust flying into the air along with ashes from the debris.

He spun to face the lesser vampire coming at him out of the dark, springing like a great jungle cat. Before the creature reached him, Traian shifted as well, taking the heavier form of a tiger, teeth and claws meeting the smaller leopard in midair. The two bodies crashed together, raking at one another's bellies, trying for a throat hold. The force of the larger cat drove the leopard backward and as they fell, the leopard landed on its back.

The two cats rolled together, the growls and roars shaking the ground as they tumbled, each fighting for a hold on the other with vicious teeth. As they rose up a second time on hind feet, Traian gripped the throat with his larger muzzle, driving the teeth deep, puncturing the neck of the other cat. At the same time, he shifted one great paw back to his true form. He drove his fist through the armor of fur, muscle, and sinew to go after the heart of the undead.

The leopard stiffened, arched its back, and tried to shift, but Traian was too fast and brutally strong, ripping the heart from the vampire and tossing it high into the air as the bolt of lightning streaked toward it. The vampire still tried, shifting to the form of a winged bat, great drops of black acid blood trailing behind him, as he tried to reach his heart before the whip of lightning did.

The bat reached the heart just as the white-hot energy struck, incinerating the heart and bat simultaneously. Traian shifted, crouching on the ground, trying to drag air into his lungs and keep a wary eye out for the master.

"I think you are losing your dogs. Perhaps you might want to show a little courage and come after me yourself," he challenged, standing slowly, bathing his arms in the white light to remove the acid burns. He looked as nonchalant as he could with rips and tears all over his body.

A tree branch snapped off just to his left, coming at him like a large spear. Traian moved with blurring speed, shifting to his right and standing tall and dignified.

"Is that your best? You really are losing your power. Come to me and receive the justice of our people."

Malevolent silence answered him.

Traian tried one last tactic, knowing the vampire might disappear for many years, avoiding all contacts with hunters in order to survive. There was one last chance to call him into the open, and Traian used it, risking revealing his position to send a summons into the night. His call was pure and commanding, his voice that of an ancient in full power ordering the vampire to ground.

In his ancient tongue he called to the master vampire, naming him for what he was. *Te kalma, te jama ńiŋ3kval, te apitäsz arwa-arvo*—You are nothing but a walking maggot-infected corpse, without honor. *Muonìak te avoisz te*—I command you to reveal yourself.

Thunder boomed, the sound so loud it shook the ground and trees. Above him, for one brief moment the hideous creature was outlined in the sky, a ghoul as evil and sinister as centuries of deviant behavior and killing for the sake of watching others suffer could make him. He stared down at Traian with hate-filled eyes, his jagged teeth snapping together in defiance. Just the fact that he'd been unable to stop himself from resisting the ancient hunter's command made him furious.

Traian went still. The vampire was changed over the centuries of being undead, but there was something familiar about him. Could it be? Vadim Malinov? A hunter from one of the strongest Carpathian families. It was difficult to tell, but if so, he would make a powerful and dangerous enemy the likes of which they'd never come up against. His family was known for their ability to plan battles. Their fighting skills were legendary.

More than any other, the master vampire loathed the hunter he'd tried for weeks, using a small army, to kill and yet still Traian triumphed. The master vampire threw back his head and howled with sheer rage.

A sound burst in Traian's head, swelling in volume, a counter-command of death and destruction. Every cell in Traian's body reacted. He was a jangle of nerve endings, paralyzed, forced to stand vulnerable out in the open, at the mercy of the vampire.

I am your master. The echo reverberated through Traian's muscles and tissue, through every organ.

No! Joie's whisper was a soft, sensuous counterpoint to the poisonous command. *He took your blood. He's using that as a weapon against you. Shut out his voice. He has no dominion over you, over either of us. I don't care how strong he is, Traian, or what he is. We're stronger. He can track you through your blood, but he cannot command you.*

A part of Traian recognized that she was there with him, in his mind, ferreting out the memories of what this vampire and his pack had done during those days of captivity in the ice cave. The torture, enduring this master vampire feeding from his veins and taunting him every moment they were awake, always a shadowy figure to make him seem all the more dangerous and powerful.

Foolish woman. I own his mind. The master vampire, now that he had used his blood bond to restrain the weakened hunter, wasn't about to lose his advantage. *He is my puppet, and soon all the others will be too. He cannot touch me, but I can find him anywhere. And through him, I can find you and your pitiful family. Join with me. I will one day rule both Carpathians and humans alike. If you do not, you will kneel before me and I will show no mercy to you or yours.*

Joie deliberately laughed, the sound like a breath of fresh air, ripping the dark dread from Traian's heart and clearing his mind. *You are the foolish one. There is only one for me. We will destroy you because you're nothing but a rotten, empty shell. And you're just nasty, if you ask me. The only way you managed, even for one brief moment to ensnare him, was through his wounds. He is far too valiant and strong for the likes of you, which is why he managed to command you to reveal yourself when you can't get him to lie down and die for you. I'd rather be dead than spend a moment with you.*

So be it.

Traian felt the monster's rage, bursting in his head, in his veins, as if his blood boiled, but he was free of the terrible paralysis. He clapped his hands together and spread his fingers wide, arms outstretched toward the vampire, which was already dissolving into vapor. Lightning forked and sizzled, sending multiple bolts across the night sky.

The furious vampire screamed once, and a putrid smell polluted the night air. Clearly one of those white-hot whips of pure energy had struck, inflicting wounds.

Kill her. Kill all of them, the master vampire commanded his followers.

Thunder splintered the sky. The earth rolled and bucked and the storm raged, a wild hurricane slamming into the forest and village as the vampire raged against Traian. Trees toppled and branches fell, some onto the rooftops of homes on the outer ring of the village.

They throw tantrums, Joie said, her breath in her throat. This time there was fear in her voice. She could feel the fury behind the storm, a foul thing bent on the destruction of humans and Carpathians alike.

Traian raced across the night sky toward the inn, doing his best to countermand the killing storm. He was still leaking too much blood, his body weakened by the multiple attacks, a common warfare for vampires against an experienced hunter. Still, he fought back, countering the vicious winds and the onslaught of rain pounding the village.

Valenteen, the vampire at your door, is dangerous beyond belief, Joie, a master vampire long sought after by Carpathian hunters. Whoever this master is, he commands Valenteen, and that is both shocking and terrifying.

I think I really made him angry, Traian, it might not have been such a good idea to tell him I thought he was nasty.

The entire inn shook, the walls swaying as if from the shock of an earthquake. The door to the verandah sagged, splintered again as something struck it with tremendous force.

Hurry, Traian, they're breaking through the door. Joie's heart was pounding so hard she was afraid it would burst through her chest.

Whispers filled the room, soft, insidious whispers made with sweet voices entreating them to open the door and allow entry. The bracelet on Jubal's wrist glowed brightly. A series of curved, wicked looking razor-sharp blades sprang out.

"What is that?" Gary demanded.

"A weapon to kill vampires," Jubal answered tersely. "Get behind me, Gabrielle."

Gabrielle cried out and put her hands over her ears. She took several steps toward the door, nodding her head, her lips beginning to move.

Gary leapt to her side, dragged her back, his hand over

her mouth. He put his lips against her ear. "They're trying to command you to invite them in. You must not listen to them."

They heard something large thump hard in the room above their heads. Someone pounded on the upstairs floor, sending a spider-web of cracks along the ceiling of Gary's room. Pieces of debris fell and the light fixture swayed and then crashed to the floor. Jubal leapt back as the bracelet slipped from his wrist and spun close to him.

"They're breaking through above us," Jubal said. "Gary, keep Gabrielle close to you. If anything happens, get her out and somewhere safe. Joie, I'll take the ones coming through from upstairs, you keep the ones at the door out."

Jubal and Joie each knew the way the other worked, what they were capable of and that each would have the other's back. Gary was an unknown and they preferred to rely on each other despite his expertise.

"I've got it," Joie replied, not certain what she was going to do to prevent vampires from invading the room. "I need a shotgun." She kept her eyes on the door.

"Gary, do you have one? Where is it?" Gabrielle asked.

"Under the bed." Gary indicated his bed with his chin, his eyes remaining on the door.

Gabrielle retrieved the gun and handed it to her sister.

The ceiling shook a second time, and more debris rained down. Wood splintered and cracked, caving in just as the door burst inward, splintering through the middle. A swarm of insects flew straight at Jubal, bringing in the wind and the wild rain. Above their heads, a creature with glowing red eyes and stained teeth glared triumphantly down at them. The whirling blades of Jubal's bracelet rose swiftly into the air, spinning, giving off a low hum as the metal grew hotter and began to glow red.

A second dense cloud of stinging bugs swarmed through the hole in the door, attacking exposed flesh, biting viciously. Gabrielle screamed as she fought them off, slapping at them as they clung to skin and hair. Gary threw a blanket over Gabrielle's head, wrapping her face and arms to protect her from the worst of the bites.

Jubal cursed and beat at his face and neck in a frantic attempt to keep the insects off of him; at the same time, he refused to take his eyes from the widening hole in the ceiling. The vampire beat at the wood and ripped the beams away. He reached down through the hole toward Jubal's head, claws lengthening.

Gary dragged Gabrielle away from the danger of the swinging claw. He met the eyes of the vampire. "You cannot enter this room, foul thing. You are not welcome here."

The arm smoked. Little flames licked up the rotting flesh. The vampire screamed and jerked his arm away, thrashing around on the floor of the bedroom above them before thrusting his head just outside the widening hole and spitting venom at them. The spinning blades rose into the air and smashed into the exposed head, tearing through the face, burning and cutting as it went. The vampire screamed horribly and fell back out of sight.

Jubal closed his eyes, shutting out everything but the bracelet, forming an image in his head of the spinning weapon targeting the vampire's heart. He was oblivious to the insects swarming over him, Gabrielle's cries, or Gary's chanting. The only thing, in that moment that was real for him, was the mage weapon and the vampire.

The scent of burned flesh and hideous screams that cut off abruptly were his only confirmation that he'd been successful. He called the bracelet back to him. It came through the door with the master vampire's retaliation—hordes of bats. The bats covered his body, driving him to the ground with their weight, teeth biting into his flesh with the intention of devouring him.

Gary shoved Gabrielle behind him, toward the bathroom. "Get in there, cover every crack," he ordered and turned back to try to clear the bats from Jubal, knocking them to the floor and to incinerate them with a small torch he took from atop his dresser, ignoring the ones using their wings as feet and walking menacingly across the floor toward him.

A vampire appeared in the hole and Joie shot him with the shotgun, blowing him backward. Immediately the gun grew too hot to hold and she dropped it hastily, inhaling sharply when she saw what she faced. The vampire was back, the bloody hole blown through the body spewing maggots, but he was still standing as though unfazed.

Through the door, Joie could see that this was the real enemy. She stood stoically facing the monster outside in the hall. His smile was a terrible parody, as was his bow. He looked smug as he watched the black horde of insects biting the occupants of the room and the bats covering the body of her brother like a living blanket. Joie knew she was staring at something far more foul than the creature she had knifed in the cave. He beckoned to her with his clawlike fingers, and she felt a tremendous pull. It was only the pain from the vicious bites of the insects that kept her from stepping out of the room and into the hallway. She had no doubt that this vampire would kill her—that he would kill all of them.

She struggled to keep her mind her own, rather than allow his soft voice to intrude and command. "You are Valenteen," she named him. "A master vampire without equal. Tell me why you do the bidding of the other, the one who hides behind your strength."

The only weapon she had was to flatter the vampire's ego—stall him in the hope that Traian would come before

Valenteen could entice her out to him. "It's clear you're much more powerful. Why would you serve such a creature?" She forced interest and admiration into her voice. "I find it hard to believe that a man like you needs someone like him."

Valenteen's lip curled, exposing blackened gums. "I allow him to think he commands me. It suits me to fall in with his plans. We both seek the same thing. If he finds it, I will take it from him."

Joie was being compelled forward, one slow step at a time. She struggled to stay grounded, flinging her hand out to Jubal. Her brother crawled to her in spite of the weight of the bats, clawing his way across the floor, pushing with elbows and toes until his fingers grasped hers while Gary continued to throw the bats off his back and legs. Jubal gripped her hand without hesitation.

"Of course you'll take whatever it is the two of you seek. He's a fool to think he can treat you with so little respect. I've been all over the world and have never encountered a man as powerful as you." Joie tried to interject a flirty note in her voice, but her acting skills didn't stretch that far. "You should lead them all. Everyone would benefit from your knowledge."

In spite of Jubal's restraining hand, she was jerked another step forward. Joie felt like a puppet on a string. She couldn't stop her body from going toward the beckoning hand, even with Jubal trying to hold her back.

Gary flung up his hands to stop her. "Leave this place," he commanded.

Valenteen sent a thrust of foul air toward Gary's face. Gary stumbled, grasping his throat and going down to one knee. At once the bats began to climb his legs, biting with vicious teeth.

Ignoring the others in the room as though nothing had

happened and his conversation with Joie hadn't been interrupted, Valenteen nodded his head. "It is true that I have much experience in leadership. Perhaps killing you is not the best answer. Perhaps bringing you to my side would serve us both better."

Jubal let go of her hand and caught her around the waist, lifting her away from the threshold. At the same time, he tried to send the mage weapon spinning toward the master vampire. At once the vampire closed his hand, staring at Jubal's throat. Joie's brother went down hard, choking, coughing, fighting for air. The insects instantly swarmed over him, clogging his throat, attacking his exposed face. The weapon retreated toward Jubal, obviously trying to protect him from the insects and bats without the guidance of his thoughts.

Gary made a valiant effort to stagger to his feet, still fighting the bats, making a grab for Joie, but she shook her head and deliberately stepped into the hall.

"Help Jubal," she ordered. She kept her gaze on the vampire, trying to appear fascinated. Traian was close. He was with her, moving in her mind, giving her strength. The vampire believed he was still compelling her to do his bidding, but with Traian's aid, she moved on her own. She didn't look behind her to see if Gary was able to clear out the bats, she had to trust that he would. Intuitively she knew it was better for all of them to keep the vampire's attention centered on her.

Her stomach lurched at the prospect of being close to such an evil creature. She could see him clearly now, without the illusion the undead often used on their victims. Flesh hung from his bones. Tufts of hair clung to his scalp. His long, thick fingernails were in the shape of hooked claws, sharp and twisted and black. His eyes appeared red, streaked with yellow. The hole she'd put in him showed the rot in his insides. The black insects and wiggling white worms spilled from inside of him. Malevolence clung to him, sickening her and fouling the air around him. Instead of trying to stop herself from moving toward him, now Joie had to force her shaking legs to take a step.

Impatience crossed his face and he showed his teeth.

Her heart jumped, accelerated in spite of the need to stay calm. "Joining with a man so powerful and knowing he's certain to rule those around him sounds like a good idea. I've always admired strength." She tried to appease him even when it was obvious her reluctance showed.

Inches from his outstretched hand, Joie purposely tripped on a piece of the splintered door and stumbled. She protected herself with a palm to the ground, her body slightly turned, giving herself precious seconds to slide her other hand along her leg to grab the knife in her boot, the blade hidden flat against her wrist.

Valenteen leaned over her, spittle drooling from his mouth as he caught her by her hair and wrenched her to her feet. He dragged her against his body, jerking her head back to expose her neck, and sank his teeth deep, gulping as he drank.

Joie registered the fiery pain of an acid burn as he tore a gaping wound in her neck. Her vision blurred, and the ground lurched as her legs went rubbery. She could hear the sound of his heart, although she couldn't feel it beating. She made no sound of protest, made no struggle, giving herself up willingly. Some of the tension slipped from the undead's body. With every ounce of strength she possessed, everything she was, Joie plunged the knife deep into his chest, driving straight for his heart.

Lifting his head, Valenteen screamed horribly, the sound shattering glass from windows. Gripping her hair, he dragged her backward as his body fought to stay up in spite of the knife in his heart. With his other hand he grabbed her chin with every intention of breaking her neck.

Blood gushed from the wound in her neck so that his hand slipped off. Joie clamped both hands on the back of the fist clutching her hair to hold his hand to her head. Dropping low, she spun around and stood up fast, snapping bones in his hand. He howled as he let her go, raking at her with poison-tipped talons.

Traian emerged from the darkness, his eyes flaming red, dragging the vampire off of her, wrenching his head around hard. The knife handle dropped uselessly to the floor of the verandah, the blade completely eaten away by acid in the blood of the undead. Traian's fist shot out, plunging deep, following the trail of the knife. Valenteen matched the move, driving his good hand into the wall of Traian's chest, through the muscle and tissue, seeking his heart.

Valenteen and Traian stood eye to eye, toe to toe, both driving toward one another's heart. Traian ignored the pain of a claw tearing through muscle and tissue, ripping his flesh. He had one purpose. He *had* to reach that heart and kill the vampire, even if Valenteen managed to kill him. His lifemate and her siblings had no chance without him succeeding. His fingers burrowed deep. Acid blood poured over his arm, burning through to his bones. The vampire raked at him with his other arm and bent forward to try to tear his neck open with his teeth stained with Joie's blood.

Staring into the vampire's eyes, Traian ripped the shriveled, blackened organ out and tossed it aside. "You lose, Valenteen. You are dead."

"Not yet," Valenteen's teeth snapped around Traian's neck.

Chapter Twelve

Traian felt stabbing pain as teeth sank into his neck and the fist continued burrowing through his chest toward his heart. No master vampire would go down so easily. Already the rotten heart rocked to the summons of its growling, snarling master and began to slither across the floor to its host. Traian staggered under the weight of the heavy body trying to bring him to the ground. Insects abandoned the room to rush to the aid of their master. Bats darkened the hallway, rushing from the bedroom abandoning the two men they were trying to drain of blood, to serve Valenteen.

Gary and Jubal both stumbled to their feet, half blind with blood dripping from hundreds of bites, bodies swelling from insect bites, both trying to make their way to aid Traian. Gabrielle burst from the bathroom, sweeping up the shotgun as she ran, turning it as she would a baseball bat and as Valenteen lifted his head to spit blood in Traian's face, she slammed the butt of the shotgun full force into the vampire's face, driving him back and away from Traian.

"Get off of him!" She followed the vampire, hitting him a second time just as hard, with just as much adrenaline as the first strike. She stepped in Joie's blood and slipped. Instantly she dropped to her knees beside her sister, hands clamping around her torn neck in an effort to slow down the bleeding. "Jubal! Help me."

The hand groping for Traian's heart fell free as Valenteen fell backward. Traian went to his knees as the bats went into a frenzy, eager for the hunter's blood. Jubal tore handfuls of bats from Traian. Gary did the same. At Gabrielle's cry, Jubal turned to see his youngest sister lying in an alarmingly large pool of blood.

Traian, still kneeling, covered in insects and biting bats, a hole torn in his chest, ignored all of it, blocking out pain and weakness from blood loss. He lifted his hands toward the hole in the ceiling of the bedroom. In answer, the clouds roiled with energy, silver streaks edging each of the spinning, dark fountains. Lightning forked in the sky, spun until it was a bright white sphere, hurtling down from the heavens like a streaking comet.

Valenteen shrieked and threw himself toward his heart, grasping at it with his outstretched hand. Gary slammed his booted foot down on his wrist to prevent him from reaching it as the spinning white-hot ball of lightning struck the heart, incinerating it. Valenteen grasped Gary's ankle in his talons, driving them deep, digging through flesh to try to get to bone in an effort to force him to move.

"Get away from him," Traian ordered, his voice hoarse. "If I destroy his body, his servants will leave as well, but you have to get back."

Gary jerked a long-bladed knife from inside his loose jacket, took a breath and slammed the blade as hard as he could across the wrist of the vampire, the edge going through skin and bone. The hand fell away from the arm and he leapt back. Valenteen shrieked and the bats and insects renewed their frenzied biting, swarming over Traian, trying to drive him to the ground.

With a tremendous effort, Traian reached for the lightning once more, commanding a single bolt through the hole in the above bedroom floor to strike the body of the master vampire. Valenteen's body began to incinerate, exploding outward with wiggling white parasites, spewing ash and cinder. His mouth gaped wide, teeth bared, fiery eyes promising retaliation and then that too was gone. Only the hand remained, the talons digging long lines in the floor as it tried, with one last effort of pure malevolence, to get to the Carpathian hunter. The lightning forked, jumping to the hand to incinerate it as well.

The moment the last remnant of Valenteen had been reduced to ashes, the bats and insects fell away from Traian to flit aimlessly through the halls as if, without the direction of their master, they had no idea what to do.

Traian bathed his hands and arms in the energy, removing the acid burning his flesh before he attempted to stagger over to Joie. Joie lay on the floor in the hallway, watching him with a kind of awe. She couldn't talk because of the wound in her neck and loss of blood. She was barely conscious but seemed to know they were all there. Her fingers moved a little against Gabrielle's thigh as if to reassure her.

"Your wound must be attended first," Gary told Traian. "She'll need to be brought over and you cannot do that without strength. Jubal, we'll need soil. There's a bag in my closet. Get it as fast as you can."

Jubal nodded and forced his body, covered in bites and throbbing in pain, to move. He tore open the door to the closet to find the bag of rich Carpathian soil.

"I don't understand how they could get in from above us," Gabrielle sobbed, pressing harder on Joie's wound. "Do something, Traian. I can't stop the bleeding."

"Whoever had the room above mine must have allowed the vampire in," Gary explained. He very casually sliced a long line in his wrist and held the welling blood out to

Traian. "Drink now. You'll need more later. You know what you have to do here, if she's going to survive."

"What?" Gabrielle demanded. She took a breath and looked from one man to the other. "Tell me what we have to do. Don't let her die, Traian."

"Pour a handful of soil into that bowl and bring it here," Gary instructed Jubal.

Traian drank from the man's wrist, his eyes on Joie, his mind in hers. *Stay with me, sivamet*—my love. *You must give yourself into my keeping.*

Joie tried to smile at him in reassurance. She was cold, very cold, but she didn't hurt anymore. She knew she was drifting away from all of them. Gabrielle, her beloved sister, trying so frantically to close the wound, Jubal, hell-bent on action to save her, and Traian . . . Traian. She didn't remember if she'd told him she loved him. She'd never thought it ever possible that she would find a man to love. She regretted that she hadn't had time with him.

You will stay with me. This time it was a command.

Traian closed the wound on Gary's wrist with a small nod of his head in thanks. He buried his face against Joie's torn throat, using his own healing saliva to close the wound. She needed blood and soil, but more, she needed strength to get through the conversion and they had very little time.

"Carpathian soil," Gary said, taking the bowl from Jubal's hand. "We'll need your saliva to mix this. I have to plug that hole in your chest."

Traian glanced down at the mess of his chest. He had scarcely been aware of his wounds, blocking all pain until he could ensure Joie's safety. He obliged Gary, mixing his healing saliva with the mineral rich soil of his homeland. Gary hastily made a paste, noting Gabrielle watched his every movement carefully.

"You'll have to sit up for me," Gary said. "I'll put this in your chest and then on her neck. You'll need to go inside her to heal from the inside out to stop her losing any more blood before you convert her." He spoke the obvious to the Carpathian so that Joie's siblings would understand what was about to take place.

Traian nodded tersely. "Hurry. Her spirit is moving away from me."

Gary packed the wad of mud tight into the hole in Traian's chest under Gabrielle's watchful gaze.

"He has a healing agent in his saliva," Gary informed her as he worked. "Teeth can inject the anticoagulant needed to keep the blood flowing and saliva can heal it. Combined with their natural soil, it is a better healing agent than anything we've got for them."

"Joie isn't Carpathian," Gabrielle said. "The risk for her to get an infection could be very high." There was more question than statement in her observation.

"Traian will have to bring her across to his world. She's more than halfway there," Gary said as he packed Joie's wound. "He's holding her to us through sheer will, which is why I'm explaining all this to you, not him. He can't expend energy talking."

He looked around him. They were in the hall with a good part of the inn damaged and people milling around in shock. Mirko Ostojic rushed down the hall toward them, a shotgun in his hands. Behind him, Slavica, his wife, and their daughter Angelina herded the guests away from the area.

"Tell us what to do to help," Mirko said.

Gary answered him. "Tell your guests that the storm damaged this part of the inn and the noise was thunder and lightning hitting the roof and going through to the first story. You have to keep them away from here, Mirko. The bats living in the eaves in this area came in, frightened by the lightning."

The innkeeper nodded and indicated Jubal and Joie. "Should I send for a doctor?"

Gary shook his head. "We've got this under control." He turned his attention back to the Carpathian hunter as the innkeeper went back down the hall. "I'll protect your body while you do your best to heal her wounds, Traian," he said. "Mikhail is sending Falcon."

"No," Traian shook his head adamantly. "Tell Falcon to stay with the prince. There is another master close by, looking for a chance to kill Mikhail. Above all else, Falcon must protect him. We must do this ourselves."

Gary sighed. "So be it. Jubal, get on the other side of the hall and keep everyone away from us. No more than twenty feet in."

Traian blocked out all sound. Gary had shown remarkable knowledge of their ways and he had no other choice but to trust him. Still . . . *Jubal, I will be out of my body. I do not know this man enough to put Joie's life in his hands. Keep watch.*

Will do. Just save her. Jubal glanced at his sister. "Gabrielle, come here by me."

"I want to see what he's doing," Gabrielle said. "I'm a doctor."

"I need you here," Jubal reiterated firmly.

Gabrielle squeezed her sister's cold hand. "Save her, Traian," she whispered and reluctantly climbed to her feet to go to her brother.

Jubal touched her shoulder gently in reassurance. *Tell me if anyone comes toward us. I'm going to keep an eye on Gary, just in case. I don't know what's about to happen, but Traian will be in some danger and he wants my protection.*

Gabrielle gave him the briefest of nods. It was obvious

she didn't want to take her eyes from her sister, but Jubal made sense. She liked Gary, but she didn't know him. They had thrown their lot in with Traian and only he appeared to be able to save Joie's life.

Traian blocked out everything, the wreckage of the room, the few remaining insects buzzing around, the bat clinging to the ceiling and the three humans surrounding him. There was only Joie and her cold body, her life slipping away. He had to repair the damage done in order to give her the strength needed for the conversion. He left his own body, a mere shell, damaged and bleeding, behind, to become pure spirit. His body was unprotected. He had no choice but to rely on Joie's brother, Jubal.

He entered Joie's body as white healing energy, reaching for her spirit to lock her to him so she had no chance to slip away before he completed the complicated task of healing her from the inside out.

Her neck was the worst, the artery needing to be sealed before anything else. It took time, precious time he didn't have. It was more difficult than he had thought to keep from being in the present, aware of time ticking away and her spirit sliding further from him as he worked.

She will die. You think you won, but I have killed you both. The voice of the third master vampire slipped into his mind. The undead had taken his blood in the cave and could reach him when he chose. The voice, after seeing him, nearly convinced Traian the unknown master could be one of the Malinov brothers. He didn't have the strength to fight the vampire and save Joie at the same time.

Unexpectedly, it was Jubal who placed himself as a shield between Traian's mind and the vampire. *You're a coward, hiding behind insects, those supposedly less powerful than you and a few bats. You didn't capture the Carpathian hunter, your little army wore him down, but in the end he defeated them and drove you away. You can't do a thing to him and you know it. All you have is your empty threats.*

Behind the shield Jubal gave him, Traian worked quickly. The vampire sent waves of doubt and distrust, trying to build a wall between the Carpathian and the human. When he realized it wasn't working he studied the human.

Mage-blood. He spat the accusation. *You have gotten a hold in his mind. How very clever of you. You are nowhere near as strong as I am. I have only to get a hold of you and he and all who are under his protection will be mine.*

Jubal laughed. *I don't really believe in you. You're a maggot, nothing more. It's a little difficult to take you seriously when you're nothing but a voice threatening mayhem, but never really doing anything.*

"You're playing a very dangerous game," Gary cautioned. "If you're doing what I think you're doing, Jubal." He could feel the energy building around Jubal and read the concentration on his face.

Jubal didn't glance at him. He kept his eyes fixed on Traian. The Carpathian grew pale before his eyes. He could actually feel the energy draining from the hunter and was determined that the vampire didn't feel it. He kept disdain uppermost in his mind. It wasn't that difficult. If this was the master vampire commanding all the others, he didn't have the courage to fight his own battles. He thought himself the brains and sent his army, but in defeat, he retreated, running away because he wouldn't fight unless he had a distinct advantage.

I will face you, the vampire offered. *Come out into the night alone without your friends. We shall see who survives our meeting.*

Jubal laughed softly. *And leave you the ability to worm your way into the hunter's mind when he is far too busy to bother with your endless empty threats?*

Black rage was thrust into Traian's mind, battering at Jubal. Jubal kept his eyes on the Carpathian. If the man got any whiter he was going to be translucent. Jubal wanted to follow the path of Traian's mind to see what he was doing to Joie, but the vampire was strong and all he had to defend Traian was sarcasm, keeping the undead's attention on him rather than pursuing his attack on Traian.

I will kill you and everyone you love. You are nothing.

Jubal gave the mental equivalent of a sigh. *I think you're actually beginning to repeat yourself. You need a few new lines. You do know this is not the only hunter in the area, don't you? I believe they are spreading out looking for you. Sooner or later, one is bound to cross your path and then they'll band together and track you down.*

You will notice that it will take more than one.

Jubal gave a sniff of disdain. *It matters little to them. You are simply a duty to them. They remove all rotting corpses from the earth when they come across them. They have nothing to prove to you or anyone else.*

Traian blinked and became aware of the world around him as he slipped back into his own body. Weak, he nearly collapsed over the top of Joie.

"We do not have much time. We need to get her out of this hallway and back into the bedroom where I can convert her. I will need blood," he instructed.

He became aware of Jubal shielding his mind, and realized the vampire had tried to prevent him from healing Joie's worst wound.

"You can step aside," he said quietly. "I thank you for what you did."

This does not end here. I will find you again, the vampire promised both of them—and then he was gone.

Tangling with a master vampire was never a good idea. They were vengeful creatures with long memories, and this one—and Traian was afraid he knew who the master was now—would not forget Jubal as long as he was alive. He would hate him with every breath he took and he would never stop plotting revenge. A vampire could live a long time and while the memory for Jubal would fade away, it never would for the undead.

With a small sigh, Traian lifted Joie into his arms and carried her into the wrecked bedroom. "Gary, have Mikhail send a couple of our people to repair the damage here when we know the master vampire has left our region." He laid Joie carefully on the bed and slipped to the floor beside her, weak, his body swaying.

Gabrielle swallowed hard and stepped close to him. "You'll have to use my blood."

Traian glanced at her pale, set face. She looked determined but very frightened. He half smiled. It was all he could do to give her reassurance. "Gary or Jubal can give blood."

She stuck her chin out. "They both have done so already and they're wounded. Use mine." She stuck out her wrist and closed her eyes. "I can't cut myself, so just do it fast."

For the first time Traian was uncertain of what to do. He needed the blood. Time was slipping away for Joie, but this was her sister, sacred to her.

"Do it," Gabrielle hissed without opening her eyes.

He raised his eyes to Jubal. The man nodded. Traian took the extended wrist gently and murmuring softly to enthrall Gabrielle so she would not feel any sensation, he took what she offered, drawing vital sustenance in order to provide enough blood to Joie for the conversion. All the while, he kept Joie's spirit locked to his, preventing her from slipping away. She was no longer losing blood, but her human body was giving up the fight for survival.

Very gently he closed the two wounds on Gabrielle's

wrist and woke her from the enthrallment. Gary swept his arm around her shoulders and stepped back, taking Gabrielle with him. "Only Traian can help her now."

Gabrielle swallowed hard. "What can you do?"

"I will bring her fully into my world. She had consented to be Carpathian," Traian said.

Jubal met the Carpathian's gaze squarely. "Do it. Whatever you have to do. Just don't let her die."

Traian looked at their faces, swollen and red from the bites of the insects. Joie's siblings were brave, but watching their sister go through such a difficult process might be too much for even them. "Should anything go wrong, I will follow her and care for her, but you must know, Jubal, that the chances of any hunter killing the one who got away are very slim and he will come after you. Never forget him and how he felt in your mind." Traian glanced up at Gary. "I will need candles, herbs, soil. Everything to help her through this, and quickly."

Gary tugged at Gabrielle. "Come with me. Mirko will have most of the herbs and candles. I'll need you."

They rushed from the room.

Jubal watched every movement as Traian laid his hands on Joie's wounds and bites from the insects. Once again, Traian left his own body and entered Joie's. Jubal remained vigilant in case the vampire returned, ready to place himself as a shield between the Carpathian and the undead. He could see the lines deepen in the hunter's face, his color paling visibly as if his strength was slowly being drawn from him.

This time was much shorter. He swayed a little, his face lined with exhaustion, but he gathered Joie into his arms, cradling her now, close to his chest.

Gary and Gabrielle hurried back into the room. Gary set a bowl of rich, dark soil on the floor beside the bed, and Gabrielle dumped various herbs into a second bowl.

Gary handed candles to Jubal. "Spread these around the room and light them. We don't want any artificial lights on, just the candles. Gabrielle, mix the herbs together in the bowl. We need the scents to blend."

Traian rocked Joie gently, holding her close, murmuring softly to her in his mind. He had done his best to heal her body enough to get her through the conversion. This was their moment. The conversion could easily kill her if she was too weak.

Gary put his hand on Traian's shoulder as if reading his thoughts. "She is strong. Her will is strong. Joie was a surprise to Valenteen. She was wonderful, unbelievable. She didn't even hesitate. It never occurred to a vampire that a woman would stand between others and danger. And he certainly never thought she would be willing to plunge a knife into his heart."

"She used my memories," Traian explained as he mixed healing saliva into the soil and packed the wounds in Joie's throat with fresh soil. "She flattered him and stalled him, hoping I would get there in time. And when I didn't, she did what she always does, she courageously put herself in harm's way in order to get close enough to make certain she destroyed him."

Gary took handfuls of the mixture and packed more into Traian's chest. "Even with all I know, the draw to go to him was so powerful, I doubt that we would have survived."

"He was a master vampire and he ran with another much more powerful master." Traian lifted his head to look at Gary. "I never saw the other one clearly. He took my blood in the cave, yet he stayed in the shadows. I saw him for one moment earlier and if it is the warrior I remember from long ago, he is extremely dangerous. Keep Jubal away from him. Protect Joie's siblings. I cannot go near our prince. You will have to relay to him all information. Until the vampire is found, and I very much doubt that he will remain in this country now, I will stay away from Mikhail. We cannot take a chance with his life."

"He won't see it the same way," Gary pointed out.

"You know I am right. He should not chance his life by entering into battles in the way that he does. His purpose is to serve and lead our people, not hunt the vampire. We have many hunters and only one leader. His brother is strong and powerful, but he has been damaged by the torture he endured. He cannot lead. If the vampire or humans managed to kill Mikhail, I fear our race would be mortally wounded."

Traian smoothed his hand over Joie's hair. He was reluctant to bring her over when she was so close to death. If he failed . . .

"You have no choice," Gary said. "She will die either way."

"Explain it to them. They shouldn't be here," Traian said.

Traian didn't look up at Gary to see if he agreed or not. He gathered Joie into his arms. *You must accept my blood, Joie. This will convert you to my race, and it is not a pleasant experience to go through.*

He felt her touch, gentle, tender, on his face, yet she lay motionless in his arms. A faint smile appeared in his mind as if she found his warning amusing.

"He will take her blood and then give her his own," Gary said. "Her human body will die and if this works, she will become fully Carpathian. The process can be brutal on the body. Once he starts, there is no turning back," he added gently to Gabrielle. "It is best if you leave. This will be painful for you to watch."

"We stay," Jubal said. "The vampire may try to attack him again and in any case, if Joie goes through this, we stay to protect her."

Gabrielle nodded. "We won't interfere."

Traian turned his body slightly, not wanting to drain his

strength further by masking what he was doing from her siblings. If they chose to stay, they would see how very difficult the transition was regardless.

The soothing aroma from the herbs and candles mixed through the room, driving out the foul stench of the vampire. Gary began to softly chant in the ancient language of the Carpathian people. The sounds of chanting filled Traian's mind as other voices, far away, joined on the common communication path in the age-old healing chant.

I offer life, Joie. Traian bent his head and sank his teeth above her breast, right where her pulse beat, shallow and slow.

Her blood flowed into him, mixing with his ancient Carpathian blood. *Come to me. Give yourself to me.* Her spirit was weak, but she didn't try to fight him. Instead, that bright light, fading slowly, moved weakly toward him.

He felt her trust surround him. Warmth. Traian closed his eyes, savoring the feeling, sending up a silent prayer that she would survive the transition.

Very gently he closed the small wound when he was certain he'd taken enough for a final exchange. *You must take my blood for the third exchange. Your neck is torn and you are weak, but I will help you.*

He opened his wrist. She would not be able to take the blood herself. He would have to press it to her mouth and stroke her throat, forcing her to accept the gift of a life. At first Joie didn't respond, and a few drops trickled from the corner of her mouth.

"Joie, please," Gabrielle said. "Please." She suppressed a small sob and hid her face against Gary's shirt.

For our children. For me. For your family. You can do this, Traian encouraged. *Try for me, Joie.*

It wasn't about acceptance. Joie had already given her life

into Traian's keeping. It was finding the strength for that last effort.

You are a fighter, Joie, and so am I. I will fight to keep you with me, but no matter what happens here, I will go with you.

Joie's mouth moved feebly against his wrist. Traian stroked long fingers over her throat. She accepted his blood just the way she did everything else where he was concerned, with complete faith. It humbled him that she did so.

Sivamet—my love—that's right. That's what you have to do. Take more. You need a fair amount to make the exchange. Hold close to me. Do not let your spirit drift.

Gabrielle clutched Gary's arm tightly. "Can he save her?"

Gary put his arm around her. "If it's possible, he'll do it. Lifemates are completely devoted to each other. If she doesn't make it, he'll follow her."

"I don't know what that means."

"Basically, he'll suicide. One can't live without the other. The ritual binding words the male says to the female ties them together in some way we can't possibly understand. Literally, one is a shadow without the other. He's said he'll follow her and he means it. Their belief is, that they go from one life to another—that they will go together to the next life."

Gabrielle looked to her brother for reassurance. Jubal had a strange expression on his face and held up his hand for silence. His gaze remained fixed on Traian.

What is it? Gabrielle asked.

He's here—the master vampire. Lurking in the back of Traian's mind. He's waiting to strike. I can feel him. Traian's too far into Joie. I need to be watchful, Gabby.

Traian concentrated on holding Joie's spirit tight. She was drifting now, slipping into a semi-conscious state. He hoped that he'd given her sufficient blood because it was nearly impossible for her to take any more. He closed the wound on his chest and laid her gently on the comforter, blinking a little as he looked around the room.

"Perhaps you all should leave the room. She would not want you to see her this way. This will get . . . brutal."

"You need blood and care yourself," Gary pointed out. "You're weaker than you think, Traian. Take my blood and let me help the two of you through this. I know what to expect. Gabrielle and Jubal can wait in their rooms."

"We'll stay," Jubal said decisively. "She's our sister. And Traian," he hesitated, unsure whether to tell the hunter and risk the vampire knowing he was aware of his presence.

Their eyes met. Traian's nod was barely perceptible. "I will count on you."

Jubal let out his breath. "You can."

"I know."

Traian took a deep breath. He had done as much as he could to make certain Joie could undergo the transition from human life to Carpathian life. The rest was up to her. All he could do was watch and be ready to send her to sleep the moment the transition was complete. He would have insisted her brother and sister leave, but they were not faint of heart. They'd stood with him in the caves and again here at the inn, fighting a master vampire. It seemed impossible that they'd delayed Valenteen and helped him to defeat the undead.

Gary stepped close to Traian. "You must feed."

"You are already weak," Traian said.

"Then I'll get Mirko, he's helped us many times," Gary said and hurried away, preventing argument.

"Is it done?" Gabrielle asked anxiously as Gary left the room. "You gave her your blood. She's still barely breathing."

Traian laid his head back against the wall. All at once, his body seemed like lead, drained of all energy. "I wish I could say that was all there is to it, but her body essentially dies before she is reborn as one of us. This will get messy."

"If it's messy, Traian, Joie would want me here to see to her needs. She's very meticulous about certain things." Gabrielle lifted her chin, prepared to fight for her right to stay. "In any case, I'm a doctor. I've seen messy."

"It might be different when it is someone you love," Traian said, but he didn't argue with her. He was coming to know Joie's family. They stood for one another, and they were determined to stand for him as well.

Mirko entered with Gary, going to Traian's side without hesitation and extending his wrist. "I offer freely," he said without hesitation.

"I am sorry for the trouble," Traian said. "We will send help."

"Everything will be fine," Mirko assured. "Take what you need." He frowned down at Traian, really observing him as he fed. "Your wound is deep, hunter. You need to go to ground. Even with my blood, you don't have strength enough to heal that gash. He nearly tore out your heart."

Gabrielle watched Traian feeding from Mirko. It should have repulsed her, but instead she was fascinated. It seemed such a noble moment to her, one being reaching out to aid another. Mirko, like Gary, seemed completely unafraid and matter-of-fact about giving blood, as if it were an everyday occasion. There was no enthrallment with these men as the Carpathian had done with Gabrielle.

Traian closed the wound on Mirko's wrist and nodded. "I will go to ground when my lifemate is able. Again, thank you. I owe you."

Mirko shook his head. "Mikhail is a friend. We'll keep

everyone from this side of the inn." When he went out, he hung a blanket across the ruined door so there was no chance of anyone seeing inside the room.

Traian kept his eyes on Joie. The first ripple of pain crossed her face and sent a shudder through her body. Traian felt the pain take her, a fire burning with the force of a torch in the center of her body, blossoming outward like an explosion.

Jubal gasped as pain burst through his brain.

"Stay out," Traian said.

"He's watching. Waiting. You take care of Joie. I can do this," Jubal said.

Traian couldn't protect both of them. Jubal had to make his own choices. He merged with Joie, trying to take the brunt of the pain, determined to make her initiation into his world as easy as possible.

Joie's body arched, convulsed, and she turned her head, violently sick. He caught her shoulders to steady her and seized her spirit a little tighter to shoulder more of the pain. Instantly the vampire struck, waiting for that perfect moment when Traian would be at his weakest, striking at Joie's unprotected mind through his blood-bond with the hunter.

Go to your death! The master vampire commanded, pushing the compulsion as deep as possible.

Jubal's spirit leapt in front of the compulsion, a wall of absolute resolve. The compulsion hit him hard, filling his head with the need to reach for the gun lying on the floor. He fought back, refusing to move, filling his mind with love of his sister and his implacable will that she live.

You will not harm either of them.

Thunder rocked the inn. Furious, the vampire sent another deluge of rain pouring into the room, but he slipped out of Traian's mind, unable to take the pain consuming all of them as Joie's body fought to rid itself of toxins and her organs reshaped.

Jubal slumped against the wall and slid down it, wiping sweat from his face. He had fought a mental battle and stood his ground, finding it far more exhausting than a physical battle. He couldn't imagine how difficult Traian's battle to save Joie's life was. The hunter's wounds should have killed him and he'd healed Joie's body as best he could, given her blood and was fighting to hold her spirit to his while shouldering most of that brutal pain. Jubal shook his head and covered his face with his hands for a brief moment.

Gabrielle handed him a glass of water. "Drink this, and then we have to help."

Traian was amazed at Joie's siblings, certain they would be horrified and afraid as the convulsions started, when Joie was violently sick and it was impossible to control the waves of unrelenting pain. Her brother and sister worked together as a team, seeming to understand that he couldn't talk or direct them. His full attention was on blocking as much pain as possible and helping Joie through the conversion.

Gary kept the room clean and smelling of the soothing aromas from the herbs and candles. All of them picked up the words to the ancient healing chant. Gabrielle wiped beads of blood from Traian's brow and then Joie's. He managed a faint smile of acknowledgment, but his focus remained on his lifemate, working to keep the pain bearable and waiting for the moment her body had completely accepted the conversion.

The moment he sensed that her body had undergone the transformation and he could safely do it, he sent her to sleep. Exhausted, he looked up at her family, grateful the sun was about to rise and the master vampire would have to go to ground. Traian doubted he had much battle left in him. He needed the healing, rejuvenating sleep of his kind, deep beneath the earth.

"I have to take her away for a few days. We will be unable to get in touch with you, but she is alive and she will heal quickly." He avoided all references to the ground. Joie's family had been through enough without knowing the specifics of where he would take her and how she would spend her days.

Gabrielle leaned over and brushed a kiss on the top of Traian's head. "You take care of her. We're depending on you. I'm not sorry she found you, not after watching the way you've cared for her."

Traian could see she was blinking back tears. "Thank you, Gabrielle. As soon as possible, I'll bring her to you."

"I'll stay here with them," Gary offered.

Traian shook his head. "Warn Mikhail. I don't want to send the information to him on the chance that the one who took my blood could find a way to use me to harm him. Let him know there is something in that cave of value to the vampires and that there are numerous traps. He'll understand when you tell him it is a cave the mages used." He frowned, for the first time unsure. If he named the master as a Malinov and he was wrong, it would be a terrible blow to the Malinov reputation. He needed more time to think on it.

Gary nodded. "Jubal and Gabrielle may come with me, if they choose."

Traian rose, Joie in his arms. "Go then, go tonight. The rules that have always applied to vampires seem to be changing rapidly." He met Jubal's eyes. "You will be safer under Mikhail's protection. Stay with them until Joie and I are recovered."

He slipped out onto the balcony, into the night where he belonged—where he was comfortable. The wind blew into his face, ruffled his hair, brought him information from creatures around him.

He took to the skies, the sleeping Joie in his arms, and

headed for a small cave he remembered from his younger days, a cave of healing with hot springs and glacier-water pools. Far below, his homeland stretched out before him, a place he had not seen in many years. The sight brought back memories of his parents and his childhood friends. He was home and he held his lifemate in his arms.

She will never be safe. You will always be linked to me. I spared your life, but I can take it whenever I choose. And I will take hers. The hate-filled voice of the master vampire invaded his mind.

Traian didn't hesitate. He sent a clap of deafening thunder back along the mental path the vampire had initiated, a bolt of lightning streaking through the sky like a spear homing in on prey. Just as quickly, he moved his own position, fully prepared for a war in the sky.

An explosion of pain burst in Traian's head in angry retaliation. He rode it out, certain he'd scored a hit.

You will pay for that.

I am an ancient warrior. I do not fear you or any other of your kind. If you wish to pursue me or mine, I welcome the opportunity to carry out your death sentence.

You and your kind will never find me. I will disappear until you and yours forget me and then I will return to kill all of you, everyone you have ever loved, the vampire vowed.

Traian moved again, certain of reprisal. He had not displayed fear or awe, or even respect, and the vampire was used to his minions admiring him.

A shower of hot stones poured from the sky. Traian protected Joie, covering her body with his like a blanket. The stones fell harmlessly around them, but the attack was a halfhearted attempt. The vampire was fleeing and simply wanted to instill fear in Traian. He hugged Joie closer to him.

"I have been a warrior so long, I barely recall any other existence. Even a master vampire cannot change my chosen path. If he should come to find us, Joie, I will not turn away. He will not take you from me, nor will he take me from you." He made the promise to her aloud beneath the stars. And then he took her deep beneath the surface to the healing caverns.

Chapter Thirteen

Joie awoke quickly. One moment she knew nothing, and the next she was fully conscious. She heard the steady fall of water, the thrum of life beating in the earth. She felt different, completely alive, yet her body ached and her neck felt torn. She turned her head to look at the man holding her.

Traian lay beside her, his arms around her, one hand on her bare stomach, his fingers splayed wide. His long hair fell like a dark waterfall around his face. His eyes were dark, wide open, framed with long lashes, so beautiful she wanted to fall into the deep well of love she saw there.

They were lying in a deep hole in the damp soil of a cave. Overhead the ceiling sparkled with crystals, and water shimmered in a pool not far from them. She knew it, saw it, yet it should have been impossible, buried in the soil as they were.

"Open the ground above us," she ordered, trying not to let her pounding heart get so out of control she had a heart attack.

"Carpathians do not have heart attacks," he said, a smile in his voice, but he obligingly opened the earth above them so she could see the gems on the ceiling of the cave they occupied.

"I was seeing what you've seen," she guessed. Her voice

was different, husky, not at all the way she'd sounded before. "The gems. The pool."

"Yes." His teeth nipped her shoulder. "We're in a cave I used to swim in as a young man."

Joie looked around her, reached out, and touched the damp soil. "It's a darned good thing I don't have a cleanliness fetish. Aren't beds appropriate when you're injured?" She was trying very hard to keep the nerves out of her voice, resorting, as usual when she was uncertain, to humor.

"The soil heals us." He kissed her neck, swirled his tongue over the wounds on her neck. "We can remove all traces of dirt easily. Our wounds were packed earlier with soil but are very clean now. I will repack them before we go to sleep again."

"How lovely for us. Are there worms in this particular little bed of soil? And did I happen to mention worms in any of our talks?"

"I do not believe you did."

"There was a reason for that." Her fingers tangled with his. His hand on her stomach was soothing her in some way she didn't understand. Her insides ached. "Did someone take a baseball bat to me?"

"No. The conversion is difficult."

She didn't want to remember the horror of that seemingly endless pain. The complete loss of control. The helpless feeling she had or the look in his eyes. Especially the look in his eyes. Begging forgiveness. He'd looked guilty, terrified of losing her. She recalled the blood-red tears that had fallen on her face. "Yes, it was difficult." She touched his face with gentle fingers and gave him a faint smile. "For both of us."

Traian caught her fingers and pulled them into the heat of his mouth. "You scared me. I will admit that to you now." He nuzzled the top of her head with his chin. "Watching you have to go through such pain was almost more than I could bear. You saved everyone there at the inn with your sacrifice, you know that, don't you?"

"We all worked together," Joie said. "I knew you would come. I just had to buy us some time."

"All of you were more than lucky. Any vampire is difficult to defeat, but master vampires have lived for century upon century, growing in strength and power. They use others as minions and puppets and keep themselves from dangerous battles. They sacrifice lesser pawns and slide away when hunters are in the area. They only fight when they are assured of victory. Valenteen had a reputation as a fierce hunter. It helped that mage blood ran in your veins. He had more trouble getting past the barriers in your minds and controlling you. Gary is protected by Gregori, so he wasn't as susceptible as most humans would be."

"Do you really think we're descendents of a mage?" Joie asked, once again stroking her fingers over his lips.

"I do not think there is much doubt. The genetics are quite strong in your brother and since you claim he is a full blood brother, the mage is in all of you. I believe that is what allowed you to resist Valenteen the way you did."

"I can't really recall much after I landed on the floor. Jubal and Gabrielle are all right, aren't they? I vaguely remember Gabrielle's hand holding mine and once I felt my brother very close. Tell me they're both okay. They had to have been terrified when that nasty vampire ripped my neck open."

Traian felt the tremor run through her and pressed his body closer. "They were incredible." He still had trouble believing that neither of them looked at him with blame. And Gabrielle had been so generous in her parting words to him. "They are both fine. Gary took them to our prince. They are with Mikhail and his lifemate, under their protection. I like your brother and sister very much."

Joie covered the hand pressed into her stomach. "You sound a little surprised. Haven't you liked many humans?"

"I never really thought about it before. We live in the world with humans and protect them, but to keep our race safe, we have always remained apart. This has been my first close contact with humans where they actually know who and what I am. I found your family to be accepting and tolerant of me and my people, even with all the danger I brought with me. I feel genuine affection and admiration for Jubal and Gabrielle, which is somewhat of a surprise to me."

"And Gary? Is he all right?"

"He is fine, Joie. Gary is an extraordinary man and obviously trusted by our prince." Traian rubbed her nose with the pad of his finger, and then traced her mouth.

Joie smiled and nibbled gently at his hand. He touched her continually, as if seeking the reassurance of physical contact.

"You'd better have a deep affection for my brother and sister," she cautioned with a wry smile. "It's the only safe thing to do with those two. And with my parents also, I might add. They're going to drive you crazy, so you have to love them, otherwise you'd do them in. I can't wait for you to meet my mom and dad." She burst out laughing at the thought.

"Why do you do that?" Traian asked suspiciously. "You have a wicked way of laughing every time you mention introducing me to your parents."

"Don't worry, I'll protect you from them. Jubal, Gabrielle, and I always go home for visits together. If we team up, we have a chance."

"I am Carpathian," he pointed out.

"Like that's going to matter. But you keep thinking it will." Her hand fluttered to her neck, still raw and sore from the attack. "How come I didn't wake up gorgeous and perfect?" Joie glared at him. "I had visions of a makeover."

"You are gorgeous and perfect." He sounded puzzled. "I

woke you early to give you more blood, but you'll be going back to the ground until you are fully healed." He touched his chest. "We both will."

She turned her head to look more fully at him, and her breath caught in her throat. "Oh, Traian, let me see." She rose up onto her knees in spite of his restraining hands. "You're really hurt."

Her eyes held worry, concern. Her hands moved over his chest with anxious, caressing strokes. Traian held his breath, shocked at the tidal wave of emotion sweeping through him. "It is of no consequence, but thank you for worrying."

"It's of great consequence," she contradicted him. "How do you do that healing thing? Can I do it to you? Would it work?"

He smiled at her, wrapping her up in his arms. "You are Carpathian. Whatever I can do, you can do. Probably more, but if you really want to try it, let's clean off."

"*Not* your way. I love the water on my skin. Is that hot spring there too hot to bathe in?" Joie indicated the pool, although it wasn't in her sight, but she knew exactly where it was positioned by the map in his head.

"If you want to bathe in a pool, *sivamet*—my love, we will bathe in a hot pool." He wrapped his arms around her and floated to the surface. "We may have to sleep during daylight hours, but in truth, few of us long for the day. We were born for the night and for us, it is beautiful. The things we can do make up for our vulnerabilities during daylight hours."

He kept his arm around her to steady her as he put her feet in the heated pool. Joie had no idea how weak she truly was. He had gone out early to feed before he woke her, needing to supply her with more blood. He could feel her hunger beating at him, although she steadfastly refused to acknowledge it. She needed to cling to her human ways just a little longer, to slowly accept a new, completely different way of life.

Joie was far too courageous and if her family and Gary were true examples of human bravery then he had been missing out on knowing many good people. It made him a little ashamed to think he hadn't even tried to get to know those humans around him. He hadn't trusted any of them, and yet when he'd needed help, four generous people had come to his aid. Joie had been so trusting of him, and he honestly didn't know if he could say had it been the other way around, that he would have been so trusting of her.

He rubbed his chin along the top of her hair, enjoying the feeling of the thick, silky strands against his jaw. Very gently he began to wash her body, his hands moving down the line of her back and smoothing over the curve of her hips. Her breath caught in her throat and her hands began to move over him, tentatively at first, but washing the lacerations and bite marks the insects and bats had made clean, pressing her mouth against the terrible, raw, barely healing wound Valenteen had made in his chest.

The touch of her lips moving against his skin so close to his heart moved him unexpectedly—shook him. His body reacted with a hard, painful ache, shocking in its intensity. He closed his eyes for a moment, savoring her touch. Blood rushed hotly in his veins, his teeth lengthened, and need pounded through his head.

Joie lifted her head, her eyes meeting his. "Yes," she whispered. A siren calling to him. "Always *yes*."

He had to stop before he lost his head. They were both clean of the soil packs and all traces of the rich loam needed to provided healing and rejuvenation for his people. He swept her up in his arms and floated them back to their earth bed. In concession to her humanity, he pressed a simple sheet over the earth as he took her down to their bed. He could remove it later, after he'd fed her and sent her to sleep.

"Not yet," she whispered. "I promised myself the first thing I'd learn as a Carpathian was how to heal my husband's . . . my lifemate's wounds," she corrected.

Before he could stop her, she was already leaning over him, her tongue swirling around the edges of his mangled skin.

Traian closed his eyes. He should stop her, just give her blood and send her back to sleep, but the seduction of her mouth was far too enticing. Her tongue was soothing, a gentle caress that took him by surprise. She was attempting the healing chant in her head, the words soft and hesitant, but she got them right. His eyes burned, his throat clogged, and even his chest felt tight. It had not occurred to him that she would try to take care of his wounds—not first—not before anything else. Another woman would have chosen so many other things.

"Silly man," she whispered. "Of course I'm going to take care of you. I *need* to take care of you."

He didn't open his eyes, afraid she might see tears there. "I thought you were a *want* kind of woman."

"True, but women get to change their minds all the time. Right now I need to do this." She laughed, and her breath was warm against his skin. "You might be surprised at the things I need to do." Her mouth began to move dangerously lower.

"Oh no, you don't," he objected. "You need to heal first, Joie. I am going to give you blood and put you back to sleep."

She laughed again, blew warm air over the head of his erection. "Really?" Her tongue licked him as if he were an ice cream cone and then swirled and danced and did outrageous things. "I'm back to the 'I'm a *want to* kind of woman.' I want a lot of things right now. And I want you wanting me enough to stop worrying about whether or not I can make love in my delicate condition. And I want your body inside mine. Only you will do, Traian. I've fallen desperately in love with you, so, darn it, you have a few responsibilities."

His breath caught in his lungs as she engulfed his thick shaft, taking him into the heat of her mouth persuasively. He grit his teeth. "Responsibilities? I believe my main responsibility is to see to your health."

She licked him again, sat up and straddled his hips. "I would be far healthier if you'd take care of a little business. I'm burning up here. Every cell in my body wants yours. I'll sleep after. I promise."

She positioned her body over his. There was no denying her, not with that seductive, sexy look of passion on her face. He caught her hips, lifting her into a better angle, and slowly allowed her body to drop over his so that he impaled her, driving through those exquisite, fiery, oh-so-tight petals that reluctantly unfurled from him as he pushed deep inside of her.

Her breath left her lungs in a little rush. His breathing matched hers. She reached out with her hands and he caught them, threading his fingers through hers while she began a slow, sensuous ride, her eyes on his. Her breasts swayed invitingly with every movement while the scorching heat surrounded him.

"You are so beautiful to me," he whispered. And she was. She filled his heart with her beauty, with her courage, with her complete giving of herself to him.

Traian swept his hand through her hair as he bent his head toward the pulse beating just above her breast. Fire swept through his veins, rushed to his very core as her body sheathed his again and again, those long slow glides that just pushed his hunger higher. He slid his hands up her waist to her breasts, the soft firm flesh drawing his attention. He lingered there for a moment, lavishing attention on first one then the other before he sank his teeth into that beckoning pulse.

Joie threw her head back as the pleasure/pain burst through her like a firestorm. Her feminine sheath clamped down tight, nearly strangling him, as he dragged steely flesh over her sensitive bundle of nerve endings, feeding from her body in the age-old ritual between lifemates. She cried out, a soft broken gasp of startled pleasure, her hands cradling his head to her as she rode him, slowing just a little to better absorb the sensations he created deep in her body.

His tongue slid over the small strawberry he'd left on the swell of her breast and he lifted his gaze to hers. "I need you now, Joie." His hand wrapped around the nape of her neck, drawing her down over his body toward his chest.

The action pushed his thick shaft hard against her most sensitive bud and she shivered, but she didn't resist or take her eyes from his as she brought her head toward him. His body shuddered in anticipation.

"Feel your teeth," he instructed in a low, husky voice. "Can you feel the need pulsing through your body, throbbing in your veins? That dark hunger spreading like a wildfire?"

She nodded.

"Show me. I want to see."

She opened her mouth to reveal the lengthened teeth. His thick erection jerked with excitement—in anticipation.

"I have waited centuries for this moment," he whispered, his fingers threading through her cap of dark, silky hair and bunching the strands inside his tightly closed fist.

Joie licked at his broad chest, right over the pounding beat. She felt the answer in her veins. That dark need that throbbed and burned. So much hunger. She couldn't tell the difference between her sexual appetite and her need to connect them together through his pure, ancient blood. All that mattered was the lust rising in his eyes. The way his body surged into hers, connecting them. The way his mind moved so erotically in hers and that deep well of hunger inflaming her every nerve ending.

She sank her teeth deep. His body arched. His hips slammed deep and hard sending shock waves of sheer pleasure rushing through her. Little whips of lightning sizzled through her veins and rushed to her core. She felt his essence flow into her, filling her the way his mind and body filled her. She would never be alone, always connected to him. She didn't think she'd ever get enough of him, not his mind, not his blood and certainly not his body. She drank as though starved, embracing the life he'd given her.

Enough, use your tongue to close the wound.

The moment she did as he instructed, Traian trapped her in his arms and rolled over, pinning her underneath him, dragging her legs up over his shoulders, almost in one smooth motion, hands sliding to her hips, taking control. He surged into her over and over, driving her up further and further until she was gasping his name.

He felt her sheath clamp down hard, a fiery sensation that milked and gripped until he couldn't hold back any longer, emptying himself into her, giving her everything he was. She cried out as the waves of pleasure crashed over and through her. The aftershocks continued as they lay together, holding one another close. Traian spent a good amount of time kissing her before he reluctantly left her body.

"You really need to go to sleep, Joie. I am being far too selfish."

She laughed softly. "I started it."

Traian wrapped his body around hers protectively, her

head on his shoulder, his breath warm on her neck. "I must say I am glad you did."

"We only managed to kill two of the master vampires, Traian," Joie said, nuzzling his shoulder drowsily. "There were three of them, and the other one took your blood. Is that going to be a major problem? Should we go after him?"

"He is long gone, Joie. Perhaps we will not see him for another century, let us hope not. I fear if he returns, his hatred of your brother will outweigh his hatred of the prince."

"Then we'll have to stick close to Jubal, although he can never know that's what we're doing," she said, her eyelashes drifting down.

He wrapped his arm around her. "The three of you are so close, I can't imagine that being a problem, although because the master vampire took my blood, he could conceivably try to use me to spy on my people. I intend to stay away from the prince just to be on the safe side."

"Perhaps visiting my parents will make tracking down the master vampire who got away much more of an interesting proposition."

He laughed softly, kissing the top of her head. "I am looking forward to the visit home."

"Mom won't be happy I'm not having an elaborate wedding."

"We will have to give her five or six little grandchildren to make up for it then." He held his breath.

She turned her head to look at him. "Is that possible?"

"We can only try. If you are willing."

A slow smile lit her eyes. She leaned into him for a kiss before she settled down again, ready for sleep. "I think it will be the only possible way to appease my mother. I'm all for it."

"Go to sleep, *avio päläfertiilam*—my lifemate," Traian

whispered, love rising to overwhelm him. Joie had courage and she would face whatever their future held right beside him. "I am a lucky man." He gave the command to send her to the deep sleep of their people to allow both of them to heal properly.

For My Readers

Be sure to go to www.christinefeehan.com/members/ to sign up for her PRIVATE book announcement list and download the FREE e-book of *Dark Desserts*, a collection of recipes sent by readers all over the world. Join her community and get firsthand news, enter the book discussions, ask your questions and chat with Christine. Please feel free to e-mail her at Christine@christinefeehan.com. She would love to hear from you. Join her for a fun-filled time at her FAN convention. Visit www.fanconvention.net for more information.

Read on for a
bonus Carpathian story

DARK DREAM

Prologue

The night was black, the moon and stars blotted out by ominous swirling clouds gathering overhead. Threads of shiny black obsidian spun and whirled in a kind of fury, yet the wind was still. Small animals huddled in their dens, beneath rocks and fallen logs, scenting the mood of the land.

Mists floated eerily out of the forest, clinging to the tree trunks so that they seemed to rise up out the fog. Long, wide bands of shimmering white. Swirling prisms of glittering opaque colors. Gliding across the sky, weaving in and out of the overhead canopy, a large owl circled the great stone house built into the high cliffs. A second owl, then a third appeared, silently making lazy circles above the branches and the rambling house. A lone wolf, quite large, with a shaggy black coat and glittering eyes, loped out of the trees into the clearing.

Out of the darkness, on the balcony of the rock house, a figure glided forward, looking out into the night. He opened his arms wide in a welcoming gesture. At once the wind began to move, a soft, gentle breeze. Insects took up their nightly chorus. Branches swayed and danced. The mist thickened and shimmered, forming many figures in the eerie night. The owls settled, one on the ground, two on the balcony railing, shape-shifting as they did, the feathers melting into skin, wings expanding into arms. The wolf was contorting even as it leaped onto the porch, shifting easily on the run so that a man landed, solid and whole.

"Welcome." The voice was beautiful, melodious, a sorcerer's weapon. Vladimir Dubrinsky, Prince of the Carpathian people, watched in sorrow as his loyal kindred materialized from the mist, from the raptors and wolves, into strong, handsome warriors. Fighters every one. Loyal men. True. Selfless. These were his volunteers. These were the men he was sending to their death. He was sentencing each of them to centuries of unbearable loneliness, of unrelenting bleakness. They would live out their long lives until each moment was beyond endurance. They would be far from home, far from their kin, far from the soothing, healing soil of their homeland. They would know no hope, have nothing but their honor to aid them in the coming centuries.

His heart was so heavy, Vladimir thought it would break in two. Warmth seeped into the cold of his body, and he felt her stirring in his mind. Sarantha. His lifemate. Of course she would share this moment, his darkest hour, as he sent these young men to their horrendous fate.

They gathered around him, silent, their faces serious— good faces, handsome, sensual, strong. The unblinking, steady eyes of confident men, men who were tried and true, men who had seen hundreds of battles. So many of his best. The wrenching in Vladimir's body was physical, a fierce burning in his heart and soul. Deep. Pitiless. These men deserved so much more than the ugly life he must give them. He took a breath, let it out slowly. He had the great and terrible gift of precognition. He saw the desperate plight of his people. He had no real choice and could only trust in God to be merciful as he could not afford to be.

"I thank all of you. You have not been commanded but

have come voluntarily, the guardians of our people. Each of you has made the choice to give up your chance at life to ensure that our people are safe, that other species in the world are safe. You humble me with your generosity, and I am honored to call you my brethren, my kin."

There was complete silence. The Prince's sorrow weighed like a stone in his heart, and, sharing his mind, the warriors caught a glimpse of the enormity of his pain. The wind moved gently through the crowd, ruffled hair with the touch of a father's hand, gently, lovingly, brushed a shoulder, an arm.

His voice, when it came again, was achingly beautiful. "I have seen the fall of our people. Our women grow fewer. We do not know why female children are not born to our couples, but fewer are conceived than ever before, and even fewer live. It is becoming much more difficult to keep our children alive, male or female. The scarcity of our women has grown to crisis point. Our males are turning vampire, and the evil is spreading across the land faster than our hunters can keep up. Before, in lands far from us, the lycanthroscope and the Jaguar race were strong enough to keep these monsters under control, but their numbers have dwindled and they cannot stem the tide. Our world is changing, and we must meet the new problems head on."

He stopped, once again looking over their faces. Loyalty and honor ran deep in their blood. He knew each of them by name, knew each of their strengths and weaknesses. They should have been the future of his species, but he was sending them to walk a solitary path of unrelenting hardship.

"All of you must know these things I am about to tell you. Each of you weigh your decision one last time before you are assigned a land to guard. Where you are going there are none of our women. Your lives will consist of hunting and destroying the vampire in the lands where I send you. There will be none of your countrymen to aid you, to be companions, other than those I send with you. There will be no healing Carpathian soil to offer comfort when you are wounded in your battles. Each kill will bring you closer to the edge of the worst possible fate. The demon within will rage and fight you for control. You will be obliged to hang on as long as you are able, and then, before it is too late, before the demon finds and claims you, you must terminate your life. Plagues and hardships will sweep these lands, wars are inevitable, and I have seen my own death and the death of our women and children. The death of mortals and immortals alike."

That brought the first stirring among the men, a protest unspoken but rather of the mind, a collective objection that swept through their linked minds. Vladimir held up his hand. "There will be much sorrow before our time is finished. Those coming after us will be without hope, without the knowledge, even, of what our world has been and what a lifemate is to us. Theirs will be a much more difficult existence. We must do all that we can to ensure that mortals and immortals alike are as safe as possible." His eyes moved over their faces, settled on two that looked alike.

Lucian and Gabriel. Twins. Children of his own second in command. Already they were working tirelessly to remove all that was evil from their world. "I knew that you would volunteer. The danger to our homeland and our people is as great as the danger to the outside world. I must ask that you stay here where the fight will be brother against brother and friend against friend. Without you to guard our people, we will fall. You must stay here, in these lands, and guard our soil until such time as you perceive you are needed elsewhere."

Neither twin attempted to argue with the Prince. His word was law, and it was a measure of his people's respect and love that they obeyed him without question. Lucian and Gabriel exchanged one long look. If they spoke on their private mental path, they didn't share their thoughts with any other. They simply nodded their heads in unison, in agreement with their Prince's decision.

The Prince turned, his black eyes piercing, probing, searching the hearts and minds of his warriors. "In the jungles and forests of far-off lands the great Jaguar have begun to decline. The Jaguar are a powerful people with many gifts, great psychic talents, but they are solitary creatures. The men find and mate with the women then leave them and the young to fend for themselves. The Jaguar men are secretive, refusing to come out of the jungles and mingle with humans. They prefer that the superstitious revere them as deities. The women have naturally turned to those who would love them and care for them, see them as the treasures they are. They have, for some time, been mating with human men and living as humans. Their bloodlines have been weakened; fewer and fewer exist in their true form. Within a hundred years, perhaps two hundred, this race will cease to exist. They lose their women because they know not what is precious and important. We have lost ours through nature itself." The black eyes moved over a tall, handsome warrior, one whose father had fought beside the Prince for centuries and had died at the hands of a master vampire.

The warrior was tall and straight with wide shoulders and flowing black hair. A true and relentless hunter, one of so many he would be sentencing to an ugly existence this night. This fighter had been proven many times over in battle, was loyal and unswerving in his duties. He would be one of the few sent out alone, while the others would go in groups or pairs to aid one another. Vlad sighed heavily and forced himself to give the orders. He leaned respectfully toward the warrior he was addressing, but spoke loudly enough for all to hear.

"You will go to this land and rid the world of the monsters

our males have chosen to become. You must avoid all confrontation with the Jaguar. Their species, as ours must, will either find a way to join the world or become extinct like so many others before us. You will not engage them in battle. Leave them to their own devices. Avoid the werewolf as best you can. They are, like us, struggling to survive in a changing world. I give you my blessing, the love and thanks of our people, and may God go with you into the night, into your new land. You must embrace this land, make it your own, make it your home.

"After I have gone, my son will take my place. He will be young and inexperienced, and he will find it difficult to rule our people in troubled times. I will not tell him of those I have sent out into the world as guardians. He cannot rely on those much older than he. He must have complete faith in his ability to guide our people on his own. Remember who you are and what you are: guardians of our people. You stand, the last line of defense to keep innocent blood from being spilled."

Vladimir looked directly into the gaze of the young warrior. "Do you take this task of your own free will? You must decide. None will think the less of any who wish to remain. The war here will also be long and difficult."

The warrior's eyes were steady on the Prince. Slowly he nodded acceptance of his fate. In that moment his life was changed for all time. He would live in a foreign land without the hope of love or family. Without emotion or color, without light to illuminate the unrelenting darkness. He would never know a lifemate, but would spend his entire existence hunting and destroying the undead.

Chapter One

The streets were filthy and smelled of decay and waste. The dreary drizzle of rain could not possibly dispel the offensive odor. Trash littered the entrances to rundown, crumbling buildings. Ragged shelters of cardboard and tin were stacked in every alleyway, every conceivable place, tiny cubicles for bodies with nowhere else to go. Rats scurried through the garbage cans and gutters, prowled through the basements and walls. Falcon moved through the shadows silently, watchful, aware of the seething life in the underbelly of the city. This was where the dregs of humanity lived, the homeless, the drunks, the predators who preyed on the helpless and unwary. He knew that eyes were watching him as he made his way along the streets, slipping from shadow to shadow. They couldn't make him out, his body fluid, blending, a part of the night. It was a scene that had been played out a thousand times, in a thousand places. He was weary of the predictability of human nature.

Falcon was making his way back to his homeland. For far too many centuries he had been utterly alone. He had grown in power, had grown in strength. The beast within him had grown in strength and power also, roaring for release continually, demanding blood. Demanding the kill. Demanding just once, for one moment, to *feel*. He wanted to go home, to feel the soil soak into his pores, to look upon the Prince of his people and know he had fulfilled his word of honor. Know that the sacrifices he had made had counted for something. He had heard the rumors of a new hope for his people.

Falcon accepted that it was too late for him, but he wanted to know, before his life was over, that there was hope for other males, that his life had counted for something. He wanted to see with his own eyes the Prince's lifemate, a human woman who had been successfully converted. He had seen too much death, too much evil. Before ending his existence, he needed to look upon something pure and good and see the reason he had battled for so many long centuries.

His eyes glittered with a strange red flame, shining in the night as he moved silently through the filthy streets. Falcon was uncertain whether he would make it back to his homeland, but he was determined to try. He had waited far too long, was already bordering on madness. He had little time left, for the darkness had nearly consumed his soul. He could feel the danger with every step he took. Not emanating from the dirty streets and shadowed buildings, but from deep within his own body.

He heard a sound, like the soft shuffle of feet. Falcon continued walking, praying as he did so for the salvation of his own soul. He had need of sustenance and he was at his most vulnerable. The beast was roaring with eagerness, claws barely sheathed. Within his mouth his fangs began to lengthen in anticipation. He was careful now to hunt among the guilty, not wanting innocent blood should he be unable to turn away from the dark call to his soul. The sound alerted him again, this time many soft feet, many whispering voices. A conspiracy of children. They came running toward him from the three-story hulk of a building, a swarm of them, rushing toward him like a plague of bees. They called out for food, for money.

The children surrounded him, a half dozen of them, all sizes, their tiny hands slipping under his cloak and cleverly into his pockets as they patted him, their voices pleading and begging. The young ones. Children. His species rarely could keep their sons and daughters alive beyond the first year. So few made it, and yet these children, as precious as they were, had no one to cherish them. Three were female with enormous, sad eyes. They wore torn, ragged clothing and had dirt smeared across bruised little faces. He could hear the fear in their pounding hearts as they begged for food, for money, for any little scrap. Each expected blows and rebuffs from him and was ready to dodge away at the first sign of aggression.

Falcon patted a head gently and murmured a soft word of regret. He had no need of the wealth he had acquired during his long lifetime. This would have been the place for it, yet he had brought nothing with him. He slept in the ground and hunted live prey. He had no need of money where he was going. The children all seemed to be talking at once, an assault on his ears, when a low whistle stopped them abruptly. There was instant silence. The children whirled around and simply melted into the shadows, into the recesses of the dilapidated and condemned buildings as if they had never been.

The whistle was very low, very soft, yet he heard it clearly through the rain and darkness. It carried on the wind straight to his ears. The sound was intriguing. The tone seemed to be pitched just for him. A warning, perhaps, for the children, but for him it was a temptation, a seduction of his senses. It threw him, that soft little whistle. It intrigued him. It drew his attention as nothing had in the past several hundred years. He could almost see the notes dancing in the rain-wet air.

The sound slipped past his guard and found its way into his body, like an arrow aimed straight for his heart.

Another noise intruded. This time it was the tread of boots. He knew what was coming now, the thugs of the street. The bullies who believed they owned the turf, and anyone who dared to walk in their territory had to pay a price. They were looking at the cut of his clothes, the fit of his silk shirt beneath the richly lined cape, and they were drawn into his trap just as he'd known they would be. It was always the same. In every land. Every city. Every decade. There were always the packs who ran together bent on destruction or wanting the right to take what did not belong to them. The incisors in his mouth once more began to lengthen.

His heart was beating faster than normal, a phenomenon that intrigued him. His heart was always the same, rock steady. He controlled it casually, easily, as he controlled every aspect of his body, but the racing of his heart now was unusual, and anything different was welcome. These men, taking their places to surround him, would not die at his hands this night. They would escape from the ultimate predator and his soul would remain intact because of two things: that soft whistle and his accelerated heartbeat.

An odd, misshapen figure emerged from a doorway straight in front of him. "Run for it, mister." The voice was low, husky, the warning clear. The strange, lumpy shape immediately melted back and blended into some hidden cranny.

Falcon stopped walking. Everything in him went completely, utterly still. He had not seen color in nearly two thousand years, yet he was staring at an appalling shade of red paint peeling from the remnants of a building. It was impossible, not real. Perhaps he was losing his mind as well as his soul. No one had told him that a preliminary to losing his soul was to see in color. The undead would have bragged of such a feat. He took a step toward the building where the owner of that voice had disappeared.

It was too late. The robbers were spreading out in a loose semicircle around him. They were large, many of them displaying weapons to intimidate. He saw the gleam of a knife, a long-handled club. They wanted him scared and ready to hand over his wallet. It wouldn't end there. He had witnessed this same scenario too many times not to know what to expect. Any other time he would have been a beast whirling in their midst, feeding on them until the aching hunger was assuaged. Tonight was different. It was nearly disorienting. Instead of seeing bland gray, Falcon could see them in vivid color, blue and purple shirts, one an atrocious orange.

Everything seemed vivid. His hearing was even more acute than usual. The dazzling raindrops were threads of glittering silver. Falcon inhaled the night, taking in the scents, separating each until he found the one he was looking for. That slight misshapen figure was not a male, but a female. And that woman had already changed his life for all time.

The men were close now, the leader calling out to him, "Throw me your wallet." There was no pretending, no preliminary. They were going to get straight down to the business of robbing, of murdering. Falcon raised his head slowly until his fiery gaze met the leader's cocky stare. The man's smile faltered, then died. He could see the demon rising, the red flames flickering deep in the depths of Falcon's eyes.

Without warning, the misshapen figure was in front of Falcon, reaching for his hand, dragging at him. "Run, you idiot, run now." She was tugging at his hand, attempting to drag him closer to the darkened buildings. Urgency. Fear. The fear was for him, for his safety. His heart turned over.

The voice was melodic, pitched to wrap itself around his heart. Need slammed into his body, into his soul. Deep and hard and urgent. It roared through his bloodstream with the force of a freight train. He couldn't see her face or her body, he had no idea what she looked like, or even her age, but his soul was crying out for hers.

"You again." The leader of the street gang turned his attention away from the stranger and toward the woman. "I told you to stay outta here!" His voice was harsh and filled with threat. He took a menacing step toward her.

The last thing Falcon expected was for the woman to attack. "Run," she hissed again and launched herself at the leader. She went in low and mean, sweeping his legs out from under him so that the man landed on his backside. She kicked him hard, using the edge of her foot to get rid of his knife. The man howled in pain when she connected with his wrist, and the knife went spinning out of his hand. She kicked the knife again, sending it skittering over the sidewalk into the gutter.

Then she was gone, running swiftly into the darkened alleyway, melting into the shadows. Her footfalls were light, almost inaudible even to Falcon's acute hearing. He didn't want to lose sight of her, but the rest of the men were closing in. The leader was swearing loudly, vowing to tear out the woman's heart, screaming at his friends to kill the tourist.

Falcon waited silently for them to approach, swinging bats and lead pipes at him from several directions. He moved with preternatural speed, his hand catching a lead pipe, ripping it out of astonished hands, and deliberately bending it into a circle. It took no effort on his part and no more than a second. He draped it around the pipe wielder's head like a necklace. He shoved the man with casual strength, sent him flying against the wall of a building some ten feet away. The circle of attackers was more wary now, afraid to close in on him. Even the leader had gone silent, still clutching his injured hand.

Falcon was distracted, his mind on the mysterious woman who had risked her life to rescue him. He had no time for battle, and his hunger was gnawing at him. He let it find him, consume him, the beast rising so that the red haze was in his mind and the flames flickered hungrily in the depths of his eyes. He turned his head slowly and smiled, his fangs showing as he sprang. He heard the frenzied screams as if from a distance, felt the flailing of arms as he grabbed the first of his prey. It was almost too much trouble to wave his hand and command silence, to keep the group under control. Hearts were pounding out a frantic rhythm, beating so loudly the threat of heart attack was very real, yet he couldn't find the mercy in him to take the time to shield their minds.

He bent his head and drank deeply. The rush was fast and addictive, the adrenaline-laced blood giving him a kind of false high. He sensed he was in danger, that the darkness was enveloping him, but he couldn't seem to find the discipline to stop himself.

It was a small sound that alerted him, and that alone told him just how far gone he really was. He should have sensed her presence immediately. She had come back for him, come back to aid him. He looked at her, his black eyes moving over her face hungrily. Blazing with urgent need. Red flames flickering. Possession stamped there.

"What are you?" The woman's soft voice brought him back to the reality of what he was doing. She gasped in shock. She stood only feet from him, staring at him with large, haunted eyes. "What are you?" She asked it again, and this time the note of fear registered deep in his heart.

Falcon lifted his head, and a trickle of blood seeped down

his prey's neck. He saw himself through her eyes. Fangs, wild hair, only red flames in his otherwise empty eyes. He looked a beast, a monster to her. He held out his hand, needing to touch her, to reassure her, to thank her for stopping him before it was too late.

Sara Marten stepped backward, shaking her head, her eyes on the blood running down Nordov's neck to stain his absurdly orange shirt. Then she whirled around and ran for her life. Ran as if a demon were hunting her. And he was. She knew it. The knowledge was locked deep within her soul. It wasn't the first time she had seen such a monster. Before, she had managed to elude the creature, but this time was very different. She had been inexplicably drawn to this one. She had gone back to be sure he got away from the night gang. She *needed* to see that he was safe. Something inside her demanded that she save him.

Sara raced through the darkened entryway into the abandoned apartment building. The walls were crumbling, the roof caving in. She knew every bolt hole, every escape hatch. She would need them all. Those black eyes had been empty, devoid of all feeling until the . . . thing . . . had looked at her. She recognized possession when she saw it. Desire. His eyes had leaped to life. Burning with an intensity she had never seen before. Burning for her as if he had marked her for himself. As his prey.

The children would be safe now, deep in the bowels of the sewer. Sara had to save herself if she was going to continue to be of any assistance to them. She jumped over a pile of rubble and ducked through a narrow opening that took her to a stairwell. She took the stairs two at a time, going up to the next story. There was a hole in the wall that enabled her to take a shortcut through two apartments, push through a broken door and out onto a balcony where she caught the lowest rung of the ladder and dragged it down.

Sara went up the rungs with the ease of much practice. She had scoped out a hundred escape routes before she had ever started working in the streets, knowing it would be an essential part of her life. Practicing running each route, shaving off seconds, a minute, finding shortcuts through the buildings and alleyways, Sara had learned the secret passageways of the underworld. Now she was up on the roof, running swiftly, not even pausing before launching herself onto the roof of the next building. She moved across that one and skirted around a pile of decaying matter to jump to a third roof.

She landed on her feet, already running for the stairs. She didn't bother with the ladder, but slid down the poles to the first story and ducked inside a broken window. A man lolling on a broken-down couch looked up from his drug-induced fog and stared at her. Sara waved as she hopped over his outstretched legs. She was forced to avoid two other bodies sprawled on the floor. Scrambling over them, she was out the door and running across the hall to the opposite apartment. The door was hanging on its hinges. She went through it fast, avoiding the occupants as she crossed the floor to the window.

Sara had to slow down to climb through the broken glass. The splintered remains caught at her clothes, so that she struggled a moment, her heart pounding and her lungs screaming for air. She was forced to use precious seconds to drag her jacket free. The splinters scraped across her hand, shearing off skin, but she thrust her way outside into the open air and the drizzling rain. She took a deep, calming breath, allowing the rain to run down her face, to cleanse the tiny beads of sweat from her skin.

Suddenly she went very still, every muscle locked, frozen. A terrible shiver went down her spine. He was on the move. Tracking her. She *felt* him moving, fast and unrelenting. She had left no trail through the buildings, she was fast and quiet, yet he wasn't even slowed down by the twists and turns. He was tracking her unerringly. She knew it. Somehow despite the unfamiliar terrain, the crumbling complex of shattered buildings, the small holes and shortcuts, he was on her trail. Unswerving, undeterred, and absolutely certain he would find her.

Sara tasted fear in her mouth. She had always managed to escape. This was no different. She had brains, skills; she knew the area and he didn't. She wiped her forehead grimly with the sleeve of her jacket, suddenly wondering if he could smell her in the midst of the decay and ruin. The thought was horrifying. She had seen what his kind could do. She had seen the broken, drained bodies, white and still, wearing a mask of horror.

Sara pushed the memories away, determined not to give in to fear and panic. That way lay disaster. She set off again, moving quickly, working harder at keeping her footfalls light, her breathing soft and controlled. She ran fast through a narrow corridor between two buildings, ducked around the corner, and slipped through a tear in the chain-link fence. Her jacket was bulky, and it took precious seconds to force her way through the small opening. Her pursuer was large. He'd never be able to make it through that space; he would have to go around the entire complex.

She ran into the street, racing now with long, open strides, arms pumping, heart beating loudly, wildly. Aching. She didn't understand why she should feel such grief welling up, but it was there all the same.

The narrow, ugly streets widened until she was on the fringes of normal society. She was still in the older part of the city. She didn't slow down, but cut through parking lots, ducked around stores, and made her way unerringly uptown. Modern buildings loomed large, stretching into the night sky. Her lungs were burning, forcing her to slow to a jog. She was safe now. The lights of the city were beginning to appear, bright and welcoming. There was more traffic as she neared the residential areas. She continued jogging on her path.

The terrible tension was beginning to leave her body now, so that she could think, could go over the details of what she had seen. Not his face; it had been in the shadows. Everything about him had seemed shadowed and vague. Except his eyes. Those black, flame-filled eyes. He was very dangerous, and he had looked at her. Marked her. Desired her in some way. She could hear her own footsteps beating out a rhythm to match the pounding of her heart as she hurried through the streets, fear beating at her. From somewhere came the impression of a call, a wild yearning, an aching promise, turbulent and primitive so that it seemed to match the frantic drumbeat of her heart. It came, not from outside herself but rather from within; not even from inside her head but welling up from her very soul.

Sara forced her body to continue forward, moving through the streets and parking lots, through the twists and turns of familiar neighborhoods until she reached her own house. It was a small cottage, nestled back away from the rest of the homes, shrouded with large bushes and trees that gave her a semblance of privacy in the populous city. Sara opened her door with shaking hands and staggered inside.

She dropped her soggy jacket on the entryway floor. She had sewn several bulky pillows into the overlarge jacket so that it would be impossible to tell what she looked like. Her hair was pressed tight on her head, hidden beneath her misshapen hat. She flung the hairpins carelessly onto the countertop as she hurried to her bathroom. She was shaking uncontrollably; her legs were nearly unable to hold her up.

Sara tore off her wet, sweaty clothes and turned on the

hot water full blast. She sat in the shower stall, hugging herself, trying to wipe away the memories she had blocked from her mind for so many years. She had been a teenager when she had first encountered the monster. She had looked at him, and he had seen her. She had been the one to draw that beast to her family. She was responsible, and she would never be able to absolve herself of the terrible weight of her guilt.

Sara could feel the tears on her face, mingling with the water pouring over her body. It was wrong to cower in the shower like a child. She knew it did no good. Someone had to face the monsters of the world and do something about them. It was a luxury to sit and cry, to wallow in her own self-pity and fear. She owed her family more than that, much more. Back then, she had hidden like the child she was, listening to the screams, the pleas, seeing the blood seeping under the door, and still she hadn't gone out to face the monster. She had hidden herself, pressing her hands to her ears, but she could never block out the sounds. She would hear them for eternity.

Slowly she forced her muscles under control, forced them to work once again, to support her weight as she drew herself reluctantly to her feet. She washed the fear from her body along with the sweat from running. It felt as if she had been running most of her life. She lived in the shadows, knew the darkness well. Sara shampooed her thick hair, running her fingers through the strands in an attempt to untangle them. The hot water was helping her overcome her weakness. She waited until she could breathe again before she stepped out of the stall to wrap a thick towel around herself.

She stared at herself in the mirror. She was all enormous eyes. So dark a blue they were violet as if two vivid pansies had been pressed into her face. Her hand was throbbing, and she looked at it with surprise. The skin was shredded from the top of her hand to her wrist; just looking at it made it sting. She wrapped it in a towel and padded barefoot into her bedroom. Dragging on drawstring pants and a tank top, she made her way to the kitchen and prepared a cup of tea.

The age-old ritual allowed a semblance of peace to seep into her world again and make it right. She was alive. She was breathing. There were still the children who needed her desperately, and the plans she had been making for so long. She was almost through the red tape, almost able to realize her dream. Monsters were everywhere, in every country, every city, every walk of life. She lived among the rich, and she found the monsters there. She walked among the poor, and they were there. She knew that now. She could live with the knowledge, but she was determined to save the ones she could.

Sara raked a hand through her cap of thick chestnut hair, spiking the ends, wanting it to dry. With her teacup in hand, she wandered back outside onto her tiny porch, to sit in the swing, a luxury she couldn't pass up. The sound of the rain was reassuring, the breeze on her face welcome. She sipped the tea cautiously, allowing the stillness in her to overcome the pounding fear, to retake each of her memories, solidly closing the doors on them one by one. She had learned there were some things best left alone, memories that need never be looked at again.

She stared absently out into the dazzling rain. The drops fell softly, melodically onto the leaves of the bushes and shimmered silver in the night air. The sound of water had always been soothing to her. She loved the ocean, lakes, rivers, anywhere there was a body of water. The rain softened the noises of the streets, lessened the harsh sounds of traffic, creating the illusion of being far away from the heart of the city. Illusions like that kept her sane.

Sara sighed and set her teacup on the edge of the porch,

rising to pace across its small confines. She would never sleep this night; she knew she would sit in her swing, wrapped in a blanket, and watch the night fade to dawn. Her family was too close, despite the careful closing off of her memories. They were ghosts, haunting her world. She would give them this night and allow them to fade.

Sara stared out into the night, into the darker shadows of the trees. The images captured in those gray spaces always intrigued her. When the shadows merged, what was there? She stared at the wavering shadows and suddenly stiffened. There was someone—no, *something* in those shadows, gray, like the darkness, watching her. Motionless. Completely still. She saw the eyes then. Unblinking. Relentless. Black with bright red flames. Those eyes were fixed on her, marking her.

Sara whirled around, springing for the door, her heart nearly stopping. The thing moved with incredible speed, landing on the porch before she could even touch the door. The distance separating them had been nearly forty feet, but he was that fast, managing to seize her with his strong hands. Sara felt the breath slam out of her as her body impacted with his. Without hesitating, she brought her fist up into his throat, jabbing hard as she stepped back to kick his kneecap. Only she didn't connect. Her fist went harmlessly by his head, and he dragged her against him, easily pinning both of her wrists in one large hand. He smelled wild, dangerous, and his body was as hard as a tree trunk.

Her attacker thrust open the door to her home, her sanctuary, and dragged her inside, kicking the door closed to prevent discovery. Sara fought wildly, kicking and bucking, despite the fact that he held her nearly helpless. He was stronger than anyone she had ever encountered. She had the hopeless feeling that he was barely aware of her struggles. She was losing her strength fast, her breath coming in sobs. It was painful to fight him; her body felt battered and bruised. He made a sound of impatience and simply took her to the floor. His body trapped hers beneath it, holding her still with enormous strength, so that she was left staring up into the face of a devil . . . or an angel.

Chapter Two

Sara went perfectly still beneath him, staring up into that face. For one long moment time stopped. The terror receded slowly, to be replaced by haunted wonder. "I know you," she whispered in amazement.

She twisted her wrist almost absently, gently, asking for release. Falcon allowed her hands to slip free of his grip. She touched his face tentatively with two fingertips. An artist's careful stroke. She moved her fingers over his face as if she were blind and the memory of him was etched into her soul rather than in her sight.

There were tears swimming in her eyes, tangling on her long lashes. Her breath caught in her throat. Her trembling hands went to his hair, tunneled through the dark thickness, lovingly, tenderly. She held the silken strands in her fists, bunching the heavy fall of hair in her hands. "I know you. I do." Her voice was a soft measure of complete wonder.

She did know him, every angle and plane of his features. Those black, haunting eyes, the wealth of blue-black hair falling to his shoulders. He had been her only companion since she was fifteen. Every night she slept with him, every day she carried him with her. His face, his words. She knew his soul as intimately as she knew her own. *She knew him.*

Dark angel. Her dark dream. She knew his beautiful, haunting words, which revealed a soul naked and vulnerable, and so achingly alone.

Falcon was completely enthralled, caught by the love in her eyes, the sheer intensity of it. She glowed with happiness she didn't even try to hide from him. Her body had gone from wild struggling to complete stillness. But now there was a subtle difference. She was wholly feminine, soft and inviting. Each stroke of her fingertips over his face sent curling heat straight to his soul.

Just as quickly her expression changed to confusion, to fright. To guilt. Along with sheer terror he could sense determination. Falcon felt the buildup of aggression in her body and caught her hands before she could hurt herself. He leaned close to her, capturing her gaze with his own. "Be calm; we will sort this out. I know I frightened you, and for that I apologize." Deliberately he lowered his voice so that it was a soft, rich tapestry of notes designed to soothe, to lull, to ensnare. "You cannot win a battle of strength between us, so do not waste your energy." His head lowered further so that he rested, for one brief moment, his brow against hers. "Listen to the sound of my heart beating. Let your heart follow the lead of mine."

His voice was one of unparalleled beauty. She found she *wanted* to succumb to his dark power. His grip was extraordinarily gentle, tender even; he held her with exquisite care. Her awareness of his enormous strength, combined with his gentleness, sent strange flames licking along her skin. She was trapped for all time in the fathomless depths of his eyes. There was no end there, just a free fall she couldn't pull out of. Her heart did follow his, slowing until it was beating with the exact same rhythm.

Sara had a will of iron, honed in the fires of trauma, and yet she couldn't pull free of that dark, hypnotic gaze, even though a part of her recognized she was under an unnatural black-magic spell. Her body trembled slightly as he lifted his head, as he brought her hand to his eye level to inspect the shredded skin. "Allow me to heal this for you," he said softly. His accent gave his voice a sensual twist she seemed to feel right down to her toes. "I knew you had injured yourself in your flight." He had smelled the scent of her blood in the night air. It had called to him, beckoned him through the darkness like the brightest of beacons.

His black eyes burning into hers, Falcon slowly brought Sara's hand to the warmth of his mouth. At the first touch of his breath on her skin, Sara's eyes widened in shock. Warmth. Heat. It was sensual intimacy beyond her experience, and all he had done was breathe on her. His tongue stroked a healing, soothing caress along the back of her hand. Black velvet, moist and sensual. Her entire body clenched, went liquid beneath him. Her breath caught in her throat. To her utter astonishment, the stinging disappeared as rough velvet trailed along each laceration to leave a tingling awareness behind. The black eyes drifted over her face, intense, burning. *Intimate.* "Better?" he asked softly.

Sara stared at him helplessly for an eternity, lost in his eyes. She forced air through her lungs and nodded her head slowly. "Please let me up."

Falcon shifted his body almost reluctantly, easing his weight from hers, retaining possession of her wrist so he could pull her to her feet in one smooth, effortless tug as he rose fluidly. Sara had planned out each move in her head, clearly and concisely. Her free hand swept up the knife hidden in the pocket of her sodden jacket, which lay beside her. As he lifted her, she jack-knifed, catching his legs between hers in a scissors motion, rolling to bring him down and beneath her. He continued the roll, once more on top. She tried to plunge the knife straight through his heart, but every cell in her body was shrieking a protest and her muscles refused to obey. Sara determinedly closed her eyes. She could not look at his beloved face when she destroyed him. But she would destroy him.

His hand gripped hers, prevented all movement. They were frozen together, his leg carelessly pinning her thighs to the floor. Sara was in a far more precarious position than before, this time with the knife between them. "Open your eyes," he commanded softly.

His voice melted her body so it was soft and yielding like honey. She wanted to cry out a protest. His voice matched his angel face, hiding the demon in him. Stubbornly she shook her head. "I won't see you like that."

"How do you see me?" He asked it curiously. "How do you know my face?" He knew her. Her heart. Her soul. He had known nothing of her face or her body. Not even her mind. He had done her the courtesy of not invading her thoughts, but if she persisted in trying to kill him, he would have no choice.

"You're a monster without equal. I've seen your kind, and I won't be fooled by the face you've chosen to wear. It's an illusion like everything else about you." She kept her eyes squeezed tight. She couldn't bear to be lost in his black gaze again. She couldn't bear to look upon the face she had loved for so long. "If you are going to kill me, just do it; get it over with." There was resignation in her voice.

"Why do you think I would want to harm you?" His fingers moved gently around her hand. "Let go of the knife, *piccola*. I cannot have you hurting yourself in any way. You cannot fight me; there is no way to do so. What is between us is inevitable. Let go of the weapon, be calm, and let us sort this out."

Sara slowly allowed her fingers to open. She didn't want the knife anyway. She already knew she could never plunge it into his heart. Her mind might have been willing but her heart would never allow such an atrocity. Her unwillingness made no sense. She had so carefully prepared for just such a moment, *but the monster wore the face of her dark angel*. How could she *ever* have prepared for such an unlikely event?

"What is your name?" Falcon removed the knife from her trembling fingers, snapped the blade easily with pressure from his thumb, and tossed it across the room. His palm slid over her hand with a gentle stroke to ease the tension from her.

"Sara. Sara Marten." She steeled herself to look into his beautiful face. The face of a man perfectly sculpted by time and honor and integrity. A mask unsurpassed in artistic beauty.

"I am called Falcon."

Her eyes flew open at his revelation. She recognized his name. *I am Falcon and I will never know you, but I have left this gift behind for you, a gift of the heart.* She shook her head in agitation. "That can't be." Her eyes searched his face, tears glittering in them again. "That can't be," she repeated. "Am I losing my mind?" It was possible, perhaps even inevitable. She hadn't considered such a possibility.

His hands framed her face. "You believe me to be the undead. The vampire. You have seen such a creature." He made it a statement, a raw fact. Of course she had. She would never have attacked him otherwise. He felt the sudden thud of his heart, fear rising to terror. In all his centuries of existence, he had never known such an emotion before. She had been alone, unprotected, and she had met the most evil of all creatures, *nosferatu*.

She nodded slowly, watching him carefully. "I have escaped him many times. I nearly managed to kill him once."

Sara felt his great body tremble at her words. "You tried

such a thing? The vampire is one of the most dangerous creatures on the face of this earth." There was a wealth of reprimand in his voice. "Perhaps you should tell me the entire story."

Sara blinked at him. "I want to get up." She felt very vulnerable lying pinned to the floor beneath him, at a great disadvantage looking up into his beloved face.

He sighed softly. "Sara." Just the way he said her name curled her toes. He breathed the syllables. Whispered it between exasperated indulgence and purring warning. Made it sound silky and scented and sexy. Everything that she was not. "I do not want to have to restrain you again. It frightens you, and I do not wish to continue to see such fear in your beautiful eyes when you look upon me." He wanted to see that loving, tender look, that helpless wonder spilling from her bright gaze as it had when she first recognized his face.

"Please, I want to know what's going on. I'm not going to do anything." Sara wished she didn't sound so apologetic. She was lying on the floor of her home with a perfect stranger pinning her down, a stranger she had seen drinking the blood of a human being. A rotten human being, but still . . . *drinking blood*. She had seen the evidence with her own eyes. How could he explain that away?

Falcon stood up, his body poetry in motion. Sara had to admire the smooth, easy way he moved, a casual rippling of muscles. Once again she was standing, her body in the shadow of his, close, so that she could feel his body heat. The air vibrated with his power. His fingers were wrapped loosely, like a bracelet, around her wrist, giving her no opportunity to escape.

Sara moved delicately away from him, needing a small space to herself. To think. To breathe. To be Sara and not part of a Dark Dream. Her Dark Dream.

"Tell me how you met the vampire." He said the words

calmly, but the menace in his voice sent a shiver down her spine.

Sara did not want to face those memories. "I don't know if I can tell you," she said truthfully and tilted her head to look into his eyes.

At once his gaze locked with hers, and she felt that curious falling sensation again. Comfort. Security. Protection from the howling ghosts of her past.

His fingers tightened around her wrist, gently, almost a caress, his thumb sliding tenderly over her sensitive skin. He tugged her back to him with the same gentleness that often seemed to accompany his movements. He moved slowly, as if afraid to frighten her. As if he knew her reluctance, and what he was asking of her. "I do not wish to intrude, but if it will be easier, I can read the memories in your mind without your having to speak of them aloud."

There was only the sound of the rain on the roof. The tears in her mind. The screams of her mother and father and brother echoing in her ears. Sara stood rigid, in shock, her face white and still. Her eyes were larger than ever, two shimmering violet jewels, wide and frightened. She swallowed twice and resolutely pulled her gaze from his to look at his broad chest. "My parents were professors at the university. In the summer, they would always go to some exotic, fantastically named place, to a dig. I was fifteen; it sounded very romantic." Her voice was low, a complete monotone. "I begged to go, and they took my brother Robert and me with them." Guilt. Grief. It swamped her.

She was silent a long time, so long he thought she might not be able to continue. Sara didn't take her gaze from his chest. She recited the words as if she'd memorized them from a textbook, a classic horror story. "I loved it, of course. It was everything I expected it to be and more. My brother and I could explore to our hearts' content and we went everywhere. Even down into the tunnels our parents had forbidden to us. We were determined to find our own treasure." Robert had dreamed of golden chalices. But something else had called to Sara. Called and beckoned, thudded in her heart until she was obsessed.

Falcon felt the fine tremor that ran through her body and instinctively drew her closer to him, so that the heat of his body seeped into the cold of hers. His hand went to the nape of her neck, his fingers soothing the tension in her muscles. "You do not have to continue, Sara. This is too distressing for you."

She shook her head. "I found the box, you see. I knew it was there. A beautiful, hand-carved box wrapped in carefully cured skins. Inside was a diary." She lifted her face then, to lock her eyes with his. To judge his reaction.

His black eyes drifted possessively over her face. Devoured her. *Lifemate.* The word swirled in the air between them. From his mind to hers. It was burned into their minds for all eternity.

"It was yours, wasn't it?" She made it a soft accusation. She continued to stare at him until faint color crept up her neck and flushed her cheeks. "But it can't be. That box, that diary, is at least fifteen hundred years old. More. It was checked out and authenticated. If that was yours, if you wrote the diary, than you would have to be . . ." She trailed off, shaking her head. "It can't be." She rubbed at her throbbing temples. "It can't be," she whispered again.

"Listen to my heartbeat, Sara. Listen to the breath going in and out of my lungs. Your body recognizes mine. You are my true lifemate."

For my beloved lifemate, my heart and my soul. This is my gift to you. She closed her eyes for a moment. How many times had she read those words?

She wouldn't faint. She stood swaying in front of him, his

fingers, a bracelet around her wrist, holding them together. "You are telling me you wrote the diary."

He drew her even closer until her body rested against his. She didn't seem to notice he was holding her up. "Tell me about the vampire."

She shook her head, yet she obeyed. "He was there one night after I found the box. I was translating the diary, the scrolls and scrolls of letters, and I felt him there. I couldn't see anything, but it was there, a presence. Wholly evil. I thought it was the curse. The workmen had been muttering about curses and how so many men died digging up what was best left alone. They had found a man dead in the tunnel the night before, drained of blood. I heard the workers tell my father it had been so for many years. When things were taken from the digs, it would come. In the night. And that night, I knew it was there. I ran into my father's room, but the room was empty, so I went to the tunnels to find him, to warn him. I saw it then. It was killing another worker. And it looked up and saw me."

Sara choked back a sob and pressed her fingertips harder into her temples. "I felt him in my head, telling me to come to him. His voice was terrible, gravelly, and I knew he would hunt me. I didn't know why, but I knew it wasn't over. I ran. I was lucky; workmen began pouring into the tunnels, and I escaped in all the confusion. My father took us into the city. We stayed there for two days before it found us. It came at night. I was in the laundry closet, still trying to translate the diary with a flashlight. I felt him. I felt him and knew he had come for me. I hid. Instead of warning my father, I hid there in a pile of blankets. Then I heard my parents and brother screaming, and I hid with my hands pressed over my ears. He was whispering to me to come to him. I thought if I went he might not kill them. But I couldn't move. I couldn't move, not even when blood ran under the door. It was black in the night, not red."

Falcon's arms folded her close, held her tightly. He could feel the grief radiating from her, a guilt too terrible to be borne. Tears locked forever in her heart and mind. A child witnessing the brutal killing of her family by a monster unsurpassed in evil. His lips brushed a single caress onto her thick cap of sable hair. "I am not vampire, Sara. I am a hunter, a destroyer of the undead. I have spent several lifetimes far from my homeland and my people, seeking just such creatures. I am not the vampire who destroyed your family."

"How do I know what you are or aren't? I saw you take that man's blood." She pulled away from him in a quick, restless movement, wholly feminine.

"I did not kill him," he answered simply. "The vampire kills his prey. I do not."

Sara raked a trembling hand through the short spikes of her silky hair. She felt completely drained. She paced restlessly across the room to her small kitchen and poured herself another cup of tea. Falcon filled her home with his presence. It was difficult to keep from staring at him. She watched him move through her home, touching her things with reverent fingers. He glided silently, almost as if he floated inches above the floor. She knew the moment he discovered it. She padded into the bedroom to lean her hip against the doorway, just watching him as she sipped her tea. It warmed her insides and helped to stop her shivering.

"Do you like it?" There was a sudden shyness in her voice.

Falcon stared at the small table beside the bed where a beautifully sculpted bust of his own face stared at him. Every detail. Every line. His dark, hooded eyes, the long fall of his hair. His strong jaw and patrician nose. It was more than the fact that she had gotten every single detail perfect, it was *how* she saw him. Noble. Old World. Through the eyes of love. "You did this?" He could barely manage to get the words past the strange lump blocking his throat. *My Dark Angel, lifemate to Sara.* The inscription was in fine calligraphy, each letter a stroke of art, a caress of love, every bit as beautiful as the bust.

"Yes." She continued to watch him closely, pleased with his reaction. "I did it from memory. When I touch things, old things in particular, I can sometimes connect with events or things from the past that linger in the object. It sounds weird." She shrugged her shoulders. "I can't explain how it happens, it just does. When I touched the diary, I knew it was meant for me. Not just anyone, not any other woman. It was written for me. When I translated the words from an ancient language, I could see a face. There was a desk, a small wooden one, and a man sat there and wrote. He turned and looked at me with such loneliness in his eyes, I knew I had to find him. His pain could hardly be borne, that terrible black emptiness. I see that same loneliness in your eyes. It is your face I saw. Your eyes. I understand emptiness."

"Then you know you are my other half." The words were spoken in a low voice, made husky by Falcon's attempt to keep unfamiliar emotions under control. His eyes met hers across the room. One of his hands rested on the top of the bust, his fingers finding the exact groove in a wave of the hair that she had caressed thousands of times.

Once again, Sara had the curious sensation of falling into the depths of his eyes. There was such an intimacy about his touching her familiar things. It had been nearly fifteen years since she had really been close to another person. She was hunted, and she never forgot it for a single moment. Anyone close to her would be in danger. She lived alone, changed her address often, traveled frequently, and continually changed her patterns of behavior. But the monster had followed her. Twice, when she had read of a serial killer stalking a city she was in, she had actively hunted the beast, determined to rid herself of her enemy, but she had never managed to find his lair.

She could talk to no one of her encounter; no one would believe her. It was widely believed that a madman had murdered her family. And the local workers had been convinced it was the curse. Sara had inherited her parents' estate, a considerable fortune, so she had been lucky enough to travel extensively, always staying one step ahead of her pursuer.

"Sara." Falcon said her name softly, bringing her back to him.

The rain pounded on the roof now. The wind slammed into the windows, whistling loudly as if in warning. Sara raised the teacup to her lips and drank, her eyes still locked with his. Carefully she placed the cup in the saucer and set it on a table. "How is it you can exist for so long a time?"

Falcon noticed she was keeping a certain distance from him, noticed her pale skin and trembling mouth. She had a beautiful mouth, but she was at the breaking point and he didn't dare think about her mouth, or the lush curves of her body. She needed him desperately, and he was determined to push aside the clawing, roaring beast and provide her with solace and peace. With protection.

"Our species have existed since the beginning of time, although we grow close to extinction. We have great gifts. We are able to control storms, to shape-shift, to soar as great winged owls and run with our brethren, the wolves. Our longevity is both gift and curse. It is not easy to watch the passing of mortals, of ages. It is a terrible thing to live without hope, in a black endless void."

Sara heard the words and did her best to comprehend what he was saying. Soar as great winged owls. She would love to fly high above the earth and be free of the weight of her guilt. She rubbed her temple again, frowning in concentration. "Why do you take blood if you are not a vampire?"

"You have a headache." He said it as if it were his most important concern. "Allow me to help you."

Sara blinked and he was standing close to her, his body heat immediately sweeping over her cold skin. She could feel the arc of electricity jumping from his body to hers. The chemistry between them was so strong it terrified her. She thought of moving away, but he was already reaching for her. His hands framed her face, his fingers caressing, gentle. Her heart turned over, a funny somersault that left her breathless. His fingertips moved to her temples.

His touch was soothing, yet sent heat curling low and wicked, making butterfly wings flutter in the pit of her stomach. She felt his stillness, his breath moving through his body, through her body. She waited in an agony of suspense, waited while his hands moved over her face, his thumb caressing her full lower lip. She felt him then, his presence in her mind, sharing her brain, her thoughts, the horror of her memories, her guilt. . . . Sara gave a small cry of protest, jerked away from him, not wanting him to see the stains forever blotting her soul.

"Sara, no." He said it softly, his hands refusing to relinquish her. "I am the darkness and you are the light. You did nothing wrong. You could not have saved your family; he would have murdered them in front of you."

"I should have died with them instead of cowering in a closet." She blurted out her confession, the truth of her terrible sin.

"He would not have killed you." He said the words very softly, his voice pitched low so that it moved over her skin like a velvet caress. "Remain quiet for just a moment and allow me to take away your headache."

She stayed very still, curious as to what would happen, afraid for her sanity. She had seen him drink blood, his fangs in the neck of a man, the flames of hell burning in the depths of his eyes, yet when he touched her, she felt as if she belonged to him. She *wanted* to belong to him. Every cell in her body cried out for him. Needed him. *Beloved Dark Angel.* Was he the angel of death coming to claim her? She was ready to go with him, she would go, but she wanted to complete her plans. Leave something good behind, something decent and right.

She heard words, an ancient tongue chanting far away in her mind. Beautiful, lilting words as old as time. Words of power and peace. Inside her head, not from outside herself. His voice was soft and misty like the early morning, and somehow the healing chant made her headache float away on a passing cloud.

Sara reached up to touch his face, his beloved familiar face. "I'm so afraid you aren't real," she confessed. *Falcon. Lifemate to Sara.*

Falcon's heart turned over, melted completely. He pulled her close to his body, gently so as not to frighten her. He trembled with his need of her, as he framed her face with his hands, holding her still while he slowly bent his dark head toward hers. She was lost in the fathomless depths of his eyes. The burning desire. The intensity of need. The aching loneliness.

Sara closed her eyes right before his mouth took possession of hers. And the earth moved beneath her feet. Her heart thudded out a rhythm of fear. She was lost for eternity in that dark embrace.

Chapter Three

Falcon pulled her closer still, until every muscle of his body was imprinted on the softness of hers. His mouth moved over hers, hot silk, while molten lava flowed through her bloodstream. The entire universe shifted and moved, and Sara gave herself up completely to his seeking kiss. Her body melted, soft and pliant, instantly belonging to him.

His mouth was addictive. Sara made her own demands, her arms creeping up around his neck to cradle him close. She wanted to feel him, his body strong and hard pressed tightly to hers. Real, not an elusive dream. She couldn't get enough of his mouth, hot and needy and so hungry for her. Sara didn't think of herself as being a sensual person, but with him she had no inhibitions. She moved her body restlessly against his, wanting him to touch her, *needing* him to touch her.

There was a strange roaring in her ears. She knew no thoughts, only the feel of his hard body against hers, only the sheer pleasure of his mouth taking possession of her so urgently. She gave herself up completely to the sensations of heat and flame. The rush of liquid fire running in her veins, pooling low in her body.

He shifted her closer, his mouth retaining possession, his tongue dueling with hers as his hand cupped her breast, his thumb stroking her nipple through the thin material of her shirt. Sara gasped at the exquisite pleasure. She hadn't expected company and she wore nothing beneath the little tank top. His thumb nudged a strap from her shoulder, a simple thing, but wickedly sexy.

His mouth left hers to blaze a path of fire along her neck. His tongue swirled over her pulse. She heard her own soft cry of need mingle with his groan of pleasure. Teeth scraped gently, erotically, over her pulse, back and forth while her body went up in flames and every cell cried out for his possession. His teeth nipped, his tongue eased the ache. His arms were hard bands, trapping her close so that she could feel the heavy thickness of him, an urgent demand, tight against her.

A shudder shook Falcon's body. Something dark and dangerous raised its head. His needs were swamping him, edging out his implacable control. The beast roared and demanded its lifemate. The scent of her washed away every semblance of civilization so that for one moment he was pure animal, every instinct alive and darkly primitive.

Sara sensed the change in him instantly, sensed the danger as his teeth touched her skin. The sensation was erotic, the need in her nearly as great as the need in him. *Fraternizing with the enemy.* The words came out of nowhere. With a low cry of self-recrimination, Sara dragged herself out of his arms. She had *seen* him take blood, his fangs buried deep in a human neck. It didn't matter how familiar he looked; he wasn't human, and he was very, very dangerous.

Falcon allowed her to move away from him. He watched her carefully as he struggled for control. His fangs receded in his mouth, but his body was a hard, unrelenting ache. "If

I planned on harming you, Sara, why would I wait? You are the safest human being on the face of this planet, because you are the one I would give my life to protect."

I am Falcon and I will never know you, but I have left this gift behind for you, a gift of the heart.

Sara closed her eyes tightly, pressed a hand to her trembling mouth. She could taste him, feel him; she *wanted* him. How could she be such a traitor to her family? The ghosts in her mind wailed loudly, condemning her. Their condemnation didn't stop her body from throbbing with need, or stop the heat moving through her blood like molten lava.

"I felt you," she accused, the tremors running through her body a result of his lethal kiss more than fear of his lethal fangs. She had almost wanted him to pierce her. For one moment her heart had been still as if it had waited all eternity for something only he could give her. "You were so close to taking my blood."

"But I am not human, Sara," he replied softly, gently, his dark eyes holding a thousand secrets. His head was unbowed, unshamed by his dark cravings. He was a strong, powerful being, a man of honor. "Taking blood is natural to me, and you are my other half. I am sorry I frightened you. You would have found it erotic, not distasteful, and you would not have come to any harm."

She hadn't been afraid of him. She had been afraid of herself. Afraid she would want him so much the wails of her family would fade from her mind and she would never find a way to bring their killer to justice. Afraid the monster would find a way to destroy Falcon if she gave in to her own desires. Afraid to reach for something she had no real knowledge of. Afraid it would be sinfully and wonderfully erotic.

For my beloved lifemate, my heart and my soul. This is my gift to you. It was his beautiful words that had captured her heart for all time. Her soul did cry out for his. It didn't matter that she had seen those red flames of madness in his eyes. In spite of the danger, his words bound them together with thousands of tiny threads.

"How is it you came to be here in Romania? You are American, are you not?" She was very nervous, and Falcon wanted to find a safe subject, something that would ease the sexual tension between them. He needed a respite from the urgent demands of his body every bit as much as Sara needed her space. He was touching her mind lightly, could hear the echoes of her family demanding justice.

Sara could have listened to his voice forever. In awe, she touched her mouth, which was still tingling from the pressure of his. He had such a perfect mouth and such a killer kiss. She closed her eyes briefly and savored the taste of him still on her tongue. She knew what he was doing, distracting her from the overwhelming sexual tension, from her own very justified fears. But she was grateful to him for it. "I'm American," she admitted. "I was born in San Francisco, but we moved around a lot. I spent a great deal of time in Boston. Have you ever been there?" Her breath was still fighting to find its way into her lungs and she dragged in air, only to take the scent of him deep within her body.

"I have never traveled to the United States but I hope that we will do so in the future. We can travel to my homeland together and see my Prince and his lifemate before we travel to your country." Falcon deliberately slowed his heart and lungs, taking the lead to get their bodies, both raging for release, back under control.

"A Prince? You want me to go with you to meet your Prince?" In spite of everything, Sara found herself smiling. She couldn't imagine herself meeting a Prince. The entire evening seemed something out of a fantasy, a dark dream she was caught in.

"Mikhail Dubrinsky is our Prince. I knew his father, Vladimir, before him, but I have not had the privilege of meeting Mikhail in many years." Not for over a thousand years. "Tell me how you came to be here, Sara," he prompted softly. The Prince was not entirely a safe subject. If Sara began thinking too much about what he was, she would immediately leap to the correct conclusion that Mikhail, the Prince of his people, was also of Falcon's species. Human, yet not human. It was the last thing he wanted her to dwell on.

"I saw a television special about children in Romania being left in orphanages. It was heartrending. I have a huge trust fund, far more money than I'll ever use. I knew I had to come here and help them if I could. I couldn't get the picture of those poor babies out of my mind. It took great planning to get over to this country and to establish myself here. I was able to find this house and start making connections."

She traced the paths of the raindrops on the window with her fingertip. Something in the way she did it made his body tighten to the point of pain. She was intensely provocative without knowing it. Her voice was soft in the night, a melancholy melody accompanied by the sounds of the storm outside. Every word that emerged from her beautiful mouth, the way her body moved, the way her fingertips traced the raindrops entranced him until he could think of nothing else. Until his body ached and his soul cried out and the demon in him struggled for supremacy.

"I worked for a while in the orphanages, and it seemed an endless task—not enough medical supplies, not enough people to care for and comfort the babies. Some were so sick it was impossible to help them. I thought there was little hope of really helping. I was trying to establish connections to move adoption proceedings along quicker when I met a woman, someone who, like me, had seen the television special and had come here to help. She introduced me to a man who showed me the sewer children." Sara pushed at her gleaming sable hair until it tumbled in spiky curls and waves all over her head. The light glinted off each strand, making Falcon long to touch the silky whorls. There was a terrible pounding in his head, a relentless hammering in his body.

"The children you whistled a warning to tonight." He tried not to think about how enticing she looked when she was disheveled. It was all he could do not to tunnel his hands deep in the thick softness and find her mouth again with his. She paced restlessly across the room, her lush curves drawing his dark gaze like a magnet. The thin tank top was ivory, and her nipples were dark and inviting beneath the sheath of silk. The breath seemed to leave his body all at once, and he was hard and hot and uncomfortable with a need bordering on desperation.

"Well, of course those were only a few of them. They are excellent little pickpockets." Sara flashed a grin at him before turning to stare once again out the window into the pouring rain. "I tried to get them to turn in earlier, before dark, because it's even more dangerous on the street at night, but if they don't bring back a certain amount, they can be in terrible trouble." She sighed softly. "They have a minicity underground. It's a dangerous life; the older ones rule the younger and they have to band together to stay safe. It isn't easy winning their confidence or even helping them. Anything you give them could easily get them killed. Someone might murder them for a decent shirt." She turned to look over her shoulder at him. "I can't stay in one place too long, so I knew I could never really help the children the way they needed."

There was a sense of sadness clinging to her, yet she was not looking for pity. Sara accepted her life with quiet dignity. She made her choices and lived with them. She stood there with the window behind her, the rain falling softly, framing her like a picture. Falcon wanted to enfold her in his arms and hold her for eternity.

"Tell me about the children." He glided silently to the narrow table where she kept a row of fragrant candles. He could see clearly in the darkness, but Sara needed the artificial light of her lamps. If they needed lights, he preferred the glow of candlelight. Candlelight had a way of blurring the edges of shadows, blending light into dark. He would be able to talk of necessary things to Sara in the muted light, to talk of their future and what it would mean to each of them.

"I found seven children who have interesting talents. It isn't easy or comfortable to be different, and I realized it was my difference that drew that horrible monster to me. I knew when I touched those children that they would also draw him to them. I know I can't save all the orphans, but I'm determined to save those seven. I've been setting up a system to get money to the woman aiding the children in the sewers, but I want a home for my seven. I know I won't be able to be with them always, at least not until I find a way to get rid of the monster hunting me, but at least I can establish them in a home with money and education and someone trustworthy to see to their needs."

"The vampire will only be interested in the female children with psychic talents. The boys will be expendable; in fact, he will view them as rivals. It will be best to move them as quickly as possible to safety. We can go to the mountains of my homeland and establish a home for the children there. They will be cherished and protected by many of our people." Falcon spoke softly, matter-of-factly, wanting her to accept the things he told her without delving too deeply into them yet. He was astonished that she already knew about vampires, and that she could be so calm about what was happening between them. Falcon didn't feel calm. His entire being was in a meltdown.

Her heart pounded out a rhythm of fear at the casual way he acknowledged that her conclusions were correct. The vampire would go after her children, and she had inadvertently placed them directly in his path.

She watched curiously as Falcon stared at the candles. The fingers of his right hand swirled slightly and the entire row of candles leaped to life. Sara laughed softly. "Magic. You really are magic, aren't you?" Her beloved sorcerer, her dark angel of dreams.

He turned to look at her, his black eyes drifting over her face. He moved then, unable to keep from touching her, his hands framing her face. "You are the one who is magic, Sara," he said, his voice a whisper of seduction in the night. "Everything about you is pure magic." Her courage, her compassion. Her sheer determination. Her unexpected laughter in the face of what she was up against. *Monster without equal.* And worse, Falcon was beginning to suspect that her enemy was one of the most feared of the vampires, a true ancient.

"I've told you about me. Tell me about you, about how you can be as old as you are, how you came to write the diary." More than anything else, she wanted the story of the diary. Her book. The words he had written for her, the words that had poured out of his soul into hers and filled her with love and longing and need. She wanted to forget reality and lean into him, taking possession of his perfect mouth.

Sara needed to know how his words could have crossed the barrier of time to find her. Why had she been drawn into the darkness of those ancient tunnels? How had she known precisely where to find the hand-carved box? What was there about Sara Marten that drew creatures like him to her? *What had drawn one of them to her family?*

"Sara." He breathed her name into the room, a whisper of velvet, of temptation. The rain was soft on the rooftop, and his lifemate was only a scant few inches from him, tempting him with her lush curves and beautiful mouth and enormous violet eyes.

Reluctantly he allowed his hands to fall away from her face. He forced his gaze from her mouth when he needed the feel of it again so desperately. "We are very close to the Carpathian Mountains. It is wild still, where we will go, but your plan to establish a house for the children will be best realized there. Few vampires dare to defy the Prince of our people on our own lands." He wanted her to accept his words. To know he meant to be with her and help her with whatever she needed to make her happy. If she wanted a house filled with orphans, he would be at her side and he would love and protect the children with her.

Sara took several steps backward. Afraid. Not so much of the man exuding danger and power, filling her home with his presence, filling her soul with peace and her mind with confusion. She was afraid of herself. Of her reaction to him. Afraid of her terrible aching need of him. He was offering her a life and hope. She had not envisioned either for herself. Not once in the last fifteen years. She pressed her body close to the wall, almost paralyzed with fear.

Falcon remained motionless, recognizing she was fighting her own attraction to him, the fierce chemistry that existed between them. The call of their souls to one another. The beast in him was strong, a hideous thing he was struggling to control. He needed his anchor, his lifemate. He must, for both of their sakes, complete the ritual. She was a strong woman who needed to find her own way to him. He wanted to allow her that freedom, yet they had so little time. He knew the beast was growing stronger, and his new, overwhelming emotions only added to his burden of control.

Sara smiled suddenly, an unexpected humor in her eyes.

"We have this strange thing between us. I can't explain it. I feel your struggle. You need to tell me something but you are very reluctant to do so. The funny thing about it is that there is no real expression on your face and I can't read your body language, either. I just know there's something important you aren't telling me and you're very worried about it. I'm not a shrinking violet. I believe in vampires, for lack of a better word to call such creatures. I don't know what you are, but I believe you aren't human. I haven't made up my mind whether you are one of them; I'm afraid I'm blinded by some fantasy I've woven about you."

Falcon's dark eyes went black with hunger. For a moment he could only stare at her, his desire so strong he couldn't think clearly. It roared through him with the force of a freight train, shaking the foundations of his control.

"I am very close to turning. The males of our race are predators. With the passing of the years, we lose all ability to feel, even to see in color. We have no emotions. We have only our honor and the memories of what we felt to hold us through the long centuries. Those of us who must hunt the vampire and bring him to justice are taking lives. That adds to the burden of our existence. Each kill spreads the darkness on our souls until we are consumed. I have existed for nearly two thousand years, and my time has long since past. I was making my way home to end my existence before I could become the very thing I have hunted so relentlessly." He told her the truth starkly, without embellishment.

Sara touched her mouth, her eyes never leaving his face. "You feel. You could never fake that kiss." There was a wealth of awe in her voice.

Falcon felt his body relax, the tension draining from him at her tone. "When we find a lifemate, she restores our ability to feel emotion. You are my lifemate, Sara. I feel everything.

I see in color. My body needs yours, and my soul needs you desperately. You are my anchor, the one being, the only being who can keep the darkness in me leashed."

She had read his diary; the things he was telling her were not new concepts. She was light to his darkness. His other half. It had been a beautiful fantasy, a dream. Now she was facing the reality, and it was overwhelming. This man standing so vulnerable in front of her was a powerful predator, close to becoming the very thing he hunted.

Sara believed him. She felt the darkness clinging to him. She felt the predator in him with unsheathed claws and waiting fangs. She had glimpsed the fires of hell in his eyes. Her violet eyes met his without flinching.

"Well, Sara." He said it very softly. "Are you going to save me?"

The rain poured onto the roof of her home, the sound a sensual rhythm that beat through her body in time to the drumming of her heart. She couldn't pull her gaze away from his. "Tell me how to save you, Falcon." Because every word he'd spoken was truth. She felt it, *knew* it instinctively.

"Without binding us with the ritual words, I am without hope. Once I speak them to my true lifemate, we are bound together for all eternity. It is much like the human marriage ceremony, yet more."

She knew the ancient words. He had said them to her, had *whispered* them to her a thousand times in the middle of the night. Beautiful words. *I claim you as my lifemate. I belong to you. I offer my life for you. I give to you my protection, my allegiance, my heart, my soul, and my body. I take into my keeping the same that is yours. Your life, happiness, and welfare will be cherished and placed above my own for all time. You are my lifemate, bound to me for all eternity and always in my care.*

She had stumbled over the translation for a long time,

wanting each word perfect in its beauty, with the exact meaning he had intended. The words that had gone from his heart to hers. "And we would be considered married?"

"You are my lifemate; there will never be another. We would be bound, Sara, truly bound. We would need the touch of our minds, the coming together of our bodies often. I could not be without you, nor you without me."

She recognized that there was no compulsion in his voice. He was not trying to influence her, yet she felt the impact of his words deep inside her. Sara lifted her chin, trying to see into his soul. "Without binding us, you would really become like that monster who killed my family?"

"I struggle with the darkness every moment of my existence," he admitted softly. A jagged bolt of lightning lit the night sky and for one moment threw his face into harsh relief. She could see his struggle etched plainly there, a certain cruelty about his sensual mouth, the lines and planes and angles of his face, the black emptiness of his eyes. Then once again the darkness descended, muted by the glow of the candles. Once again he was beautiful, the exact face in her dreams. Her own dark angel. "I have no other choice but to end my life. That was my intention as I made my way to my homeland. I was already dead, but you breathed life back into my shattered soul. Now you are here, a miracle, standing in front of me, and I ask you again: Are you willing to save my life, my soul, Sara? Because once the words are said between us, there is no going back, they cannot be unsaid. You need to know that. I cannot unsay them. And I would not let you go. I know I am not that strong. Are you strong enough to share your life with me?"

She wanted to say no, she didn't know him, a stranger who came to her straight from taking a man's blood. But she did know him. She knew his innermost thoughts. She had read every word of his diary. He was so alone, so completely, utterly alone, and she knew, more than most, what it was like to be alone. She could never walk away from him. He had been there for her all those long, empty nights. All those long, endless nights when the ghosts of her family had wailed for vengeance, for justice. He had been there with her. His words. His face.

Sara put her hand on his arm, her fingers curling around his forearm. "You have to know I will not abandon the children. And there is my enemy. He will come. He always finds me. I never stay in one place too long."

"I am a hunter of the undead, Sara," he reminded, but the words meant little to him. He was only aware of her touch, the scent of her, the way she was looking at him. Her *consent*. He was waiting. His entire being was waiting. Even the wind and rain seemed to hesitate. "Sara." He said it softly, the aching need, the terrible hunger, evident in his voice.

Closing her eyes, wanting the dream, she heard her own voice in the stillness of the room. "Yes."

Falcon felt a surge of elation. He drew her against him, buried his face in the softness of her neck. His body trembled from the sheer relief of her commitment to him. He could hardly believe the enormity of his find, of being united with his lifemate in the last days of his existence. He kissed her soft, trembling mouth, lifted his head to look into her eyes. "I claim you as my lifemate." The words broke out of him, soared from his soul. "I belong to you. I offer my life for you. I give to you my protection, my allegiance, my heart, my soul, and my body. I take into my keeping the same that is yours. Your life, happiness, and welfare will be cherished and placed above my own for all time. You are my lifemate, bound to me for all eternity and always in my care." He buried his face once more against her soft skin, breathed in her scent. Beneath his mouth her pulse beckoned, her life force calling to him, tempting. So very tempting.

She felt the difference at once, a strange wrenching in her body. Her aching heart and soul, so empty before, were suddenly whole, complete. The feeling filled her with elation; it terrified her at the same time. It couldn't be her imagination. She *knew* there was a difference.

Before she could be afraid of the consequences of her commitment, Sara felt his lips, velvet soft, move over her skin. His touch drove out all thought, and she gave herself willingly into his keeping. His arms held her closer still to his heart, within the shelter of his body. His teeth scraped lightly, an erotic touch that sent a shiver down her spine. His tongue swirled lazily, a tiny point of flame she felt raging through her bloodstream. Of their own volition, her arms reached up to cradle his head. She was no young girl afraid of her own sexuality; she was a grown woman who had waited long for her lover. She wanted the feel of his mouth and hands. She wanted everything he was willing to give her.

His hands moved over her, pushing aside the thin barrier of her top to take in her skin. She was softer than anything he had ever imagined. He whispered a powerful command; his teeth sank deep, and whips of lightning lashed through his body to hers. White-hot heat. Blue fire. She was sweet and spicy, a taste of heaven. He wanted her, every inch of her. He needed to bury his body deep within her, to find his safe haven, his refuge. He had fed well, and it was a good thing, or he never would have found the will to curb his strength. It took every ounce of control to stop himself from indulging wildly. He took only enough for an exchange. He would be able to touch her mind, to reassure her. That would be absolutely necessary for their comfort and safety.

He slashed his own chest, pressed her mouth to his ancient, powerful blood, and softly commanded her obedience. She moved sensuously against him, driving him closer and closer to the edge of his control. He wanted her, needed her, and the moment he knew she had taken enough for the exchange, he whispered his command to stop feeding. He closed the wound carefully and took possession of her mouth, sweeping his tongue along hers, dueling and dancing, so that, as she emerged from the enthrallment, there was only the strength of his arms, the heat of his body, and the seduction of his mouth.

Without warning, the storm increased in intensity, battering at the windowsills. Bolts of lightning slammed into the ground with such force, the ground shook. Sara's little cottage trembled, the walls shaking ominously. Thunder roared so that it filled the spaces in the house, a deafening sound. Sara tore herself out of his arms, clapped her hands over her ears, and stared in horror out into the fury of the squall. She gasped as another bolt of lightning sizzled across the sky in writhing ropes of energy. Thunder crashed directly overhead, wrenching a soft, frightened cry from her throat.

Chapter Four

Before another sound could escape from Sara, Falcon's hand covered her mouth gently in warning. Sara didn't need his caution; she already knew. Her enemy had found her once again. "You have to get out of here," she hissed softly against his palm.

Falcon bent his head so that his mouth was touching her ear. "I am a hunter of the undead, Sara. I do not run from them." The taste of her was still in his mouth, in his mind. She was a part of him, inseparable now.

She tipped her head back to stare up at him, wincing as the wind howled and shrieked with enough force to cause small tornadoes in the street and yard, throwing loose paper, leaves, and twigs into the air in a rush of anger. "Are you any good at killing these things?" She asked it with a hint of disbelief. There was a challenge in her voice. "I need to know the truth."

For the first time that he could remember, Falcon felt like smiling. It was unexpected in the midst of the vampire's arrival, but the doubt in her voice made him want to laugh. "He is sending out his threat ahead of him. You have angered him. You have a built-in shield, a rare thing. He cannot find you when he scans, so he is looking for an awareness, a surge of fear that will tell him you know who he is. That is how he tracks you. I will send my answer to him so he is aware that you are under my protection."

"No!" She caught his arm with suddenly tense fingers. "This is it, our chance. If he doesn't know about you, then he will come for me. We can lay a trap for him."

"I do not need to use you as bait." His voice was very mild, but there was a hint of some unnamed emotion that made her shiver. Falcon was unfailingly gentle with her, his tone always soft and low, his touch tender. But there was something deep inside him that was terribly dangerous and very dark.

Sara found herself shivering, but she tightened her hold on him, afraid that if he went into the raging storm he would be lost to her. "It's the best way. He'll come for me; he always comes for me." Already her bond with Falcon was so strong, she couldn't bear the thought of something happening to him. She must protect him from the terrible thing that had destroyed her family.

"Not tonight. Tonight I'll go after him." Falcon put her from him gently. He could clearly see her fears and her fierce need to be sure that he was safe. She had no concept of what he was, of the thousands of battles he had fought with these very monsters: Carpathian males who had waited too long, or who had chosen to give up their souls for the fleeting momentary pleasure of the kill. His brethren.

Sara caught his arm. "No, don't go out there." There was a catch in her voice. "I don't want to be alone tonight. I know he's here, and for the first time, I'm not alone."

He leaned down to capture her soft mouth with his. At once there was that melting sensation, the promise of silken heat and ecstasy he had never dared to dream about. "You are worried about my safety and seek ways to keep me with you." He said the words softly against her lips. "I dwell within you now; we are able to share thoughts with one another. This is my life, Sara; this is what I do. I have no choice but to go. I am a male Carpathian sent by the Prince of my people into the world to protect others from these creatures. I am a hunter. It is the only honor I have left."

There was that aching loneliness in his voice. She had been alone for fifteen years. She couldn't imagine what it would be like to be alone for as long as he had been. Watching endless time go by, the changes in the world, without hope or refuge. Sentenced to destroying his own kind, perhaps even friends. *Honor.* That word had been used often in his diary. She saw the implacable resolve in him, the intensity that swirled dangerously close to the surface of his calm. Nothing she could say would stop him.

Sara sighed softly and nodded. "I think there is much more in you to honor than just your abilities as a hunter, but I understand. There are things I must do that I don't always want to, but I know I couldn't live with myself if I didn't do them." She slipped her arms around his neck and pressed her body close to his. For one moment she was no longer alone in the world. He was solid and safe. "Don't let him harm you. He's managed to destroy everyone I care about."

Falcon held her, his arms cradling her body, every cell needing her. It was madness to hunt when he was so close to turning and the ritual had not been completed, but he had no choice. The wind beat at the window, the branches of trees sweeping against the house in a kind of fury. "I will be back soon, Sara," he assured her softly.

"Let me go with you," she said suddenly. "I've faced him before."

Falcon smiled. His soul smiled. She was beautiful to him, nearly unbelievable. Ready to face the monster right beside him. He bent once more and found her mouth with his. A promise. He made it that. A promise of life and happiness.

And then he was gone, wrenching open the door while he still could, while his honor was strong enough to overcome the needs of his body. He simply dissolved into mist, mixing with the rain for camouflage, and streamed through the night air, away from the shelter and temptation of her body and heart.

Sara stepped out onto the porch after him, still blinking, unsure where he had gone, it had happened so quickly. "Falcon!" His name was a cry wrenched from her soul. The wind whipped her hair into a frenzy. The rain doused her clothes until the silk was nearly transparent. She was utterly alone again.

You will never be alone again, Sara. I dwell within you as you are within me. Speak to me; use your mind, and I will hear you.

She held her breath. It was impossible. She felt a flood of relief and sagged against the column of her porch for support. She didn't question how his voice could be in her mind, clear and perfect and sexy. She accepted it because she needed it so desperately. She jammed her fist in her mouth to stop herself from calling him back to her, forgetting for a moment that he must be reading her thoughts.

Falcon laughed softly, his voice a drawling caress. *You are an amazing woman, Sara. Even to be able to translate my letters to you. I wrote them in several languages. Greek, Hebrew. The ancient tongue. How did you accomplish such a feat?* He was traveling swiftly across the night sky, scanning carefully, looking for disturbances that would signal the arrival of the undead. Sometimes blank spaces revealed the vampire's lair. Other times it would be a surge of power or an unexpected exodus of bats from a cave. The smallest detail could provide clues to one who knew where to look.

Sara was silent a moment, turning the question over in her mind. She had been obsessed with translating the strange documents wrapped so carefully in oilskin. Perseverance. She had *needed* to translate those words. Sacred words. She remembered the feeling she had each time she touched those scrolled pages. Her heart had beat faster, her body had come to life, her fingers had smoothed over the fibers more times than she wanted to count. She had known that those words were meant for her. And she had seen his face. His eyes, the shape of his jaw, the long flow of his hair. The aching loneliness in him. She had known that only she would find the right translation.

My parents taught me Greek and Hebrew and most of the ancient languages, but I had never seen some of the letters and symbols before. I went to several museums and all the universities, but I didn't want to show the diary to anyone else. I believed it was meant for me. She had known that the words were intimate, meant only for her eyes. There had been poetry in those words before she had ever translated them. Sara felt tears gathering in her eyes. Falcon. She knew his name now, had looked into his eyes, and she knew he needed her. No one else. Just Sara. *I studied the diary for several months, translated what I could, but I knew it wasn't right, word for word. And then it just came to me. I felt when it was right. I can't explain how, but I knew the moment I hit on the key.*

Falcon felt the curious wrenching in his heart. She could make his soul flood with warmth, overwhelming him with such intense feeling that he was no longer the powerful predator but a man willing to do anything for his lifemate. She humbled him with her generosity and her acceptance of what he was. He had written those words, expressing emotions he could no longer feel. Writing the diary was a compulsion he couldn't ignore. He had never expected anyone to read it, yet he had never destroyed it, unable to do so.

Dawn was a couple of hours away and the vampire would

still be lethal. More than likely he was searching for lairs, escape routes, gathering information. Falcon had hunted and successfully battled the vampire for centuries, yet he was growing distinctly uneasy. He should have picked up a trail, yet there were none of the usual signs to indicate the undead had passed over the city. Few of the creatures could achieve such a feat; only a very powerful ancient enemy would have such skills.

You are my heart and soul, Sara. The words I left for you are truth, and only my lifemate would know how to find the key to unlock the code to translate the ancient language. His tone held admiration and an intensity of love that wrapped her in warmth. *I must concentrate on the hunt. This one is no fledgling vampire, but one of power and strength. It requires my full attention. Should you have need of me, reach with your mind and I will hear you.*

Sara crossed her arms across her breasts, moving back onto her porch, watching the sheets of rain falling in silvery threads. She felt Falcon's uneasiness more than heard it in his tone. *If you need me, I will come to you.* She meant it. Meant it with every cell in her body. It felt wrong to have Falcon going alone to fight her battles.

Falcon's heart lightened. She would rush to his aid if he called her. Their tie was already strong, and growing with each passing moment. Sara represented the miracle granted to his species. *Lifemate.*

He was cautious as he moved across the sky, using the storm as his cover. He was adept, able to shield his presence easily. He began surveying the areas most likely to harbor the undead. Within the city, it would be the deserted older buildings with basements. Outside of the city, it would be any cave, any hole in the ground the ancient vampire could protect.

Falcon found no traces of the enemy, but the uneasiness

in him began to grow. The vampire would have already attacked Sara if he had known for certain where she was.
Obviously, he had vented his rage because he *hadn't* found
her, and he had hoped to frighten her into betraying her
presence. That left one other avenue open to Falcon. He
would have to find the vampire's kill and trace him from
there. It would be a painstakingly slow process and he would
have to leave Sara alone for some time. He reached for her.
*If you feel uneasy, call for me at once. Anything at all, Sara,
call for me.*

He felt her smile. *I have been aware of this enemy for
half my life. I know when he is close, and I have managed
to escape him time after time. You take care of yourself,
Falcon, and don't worry about me.* Sara had been alone a
long time and was an independent, self-sufficient woman.
She was far more worried about Falcon than she was about
herself.

The rain was still pouring down, the wind blowing the
droplets into dismal heavy sheets. Falcon felt no cold in
the form he had taken. Had he been in his natural body, he
would have regulated his body temperature with ease. The
storm was a deterrent to seeking his enemy by using scent,
but he knew the ways of the vampire. He found the kill unerringly.

The body was in an alleyway, not far from where Sara's
sewer children had rushed Falcon. His uneasiness grew. The
vampire obviously had become adept at finding Sara. There
was a pattern to her behavior, and the undead capitalized on
it. Once he found the country and the city she had settled
in, the vampire would go to the places where Sara would
eventually go. The refuges of the lost, the homeless, the
unwanted children and battered women. Sara would work in
those areas to accomplish what she could before she moved
on. Money meant little to her; it was only a means to keep

moving and to do what she could to help. She lived frugally and spent little on herself. Just as Falcon had studied vampires to learn their ways, this vampire had studied Sara. Yet she had continued to elude him. Most vampires were not known for their patience, yet this one had followed Sara relentlessly for fifteen years.

It was a miracle that she had managed to avoid capture, a tribute to her courageous and resourceful nature. Falcon's frame shimmered and solidified in the dreary rain beside the dead man. The vampire's victim had died hard. Falcon studied the corpse, careful not to touch anything. He wanted the scent of the undead, the feel of him. The victim was young, a street punk. There was a knife on the ground with blood on the blade. Falcon could see the blade was already corroding. The man had been tortured, most likely for information about Sara. The vampire would want to know if she had been seen in the area. The echoes of violence were all around Falcon.

He couldn't allow the evidence to remain for the police. He sighed softly and began to summon the energy in the sky above him. Bolts of lightning danced brightly, throwing the alley into sharp relief. The whips sizzled and crackled, white-hot. He directed the energy to the body and the knife. It incinerated the victim to fine ashes and cleansed the blade before melting it.

The flare of power was all around him as the lightning burned like an orange flame from the ground back up to the dark, ominous clouds, where it veined out in radiant points of blue-white heat. Falcon suddenly raised his head and looked around him, realizing that the power vibrating in the air was not his alone. He leaped back, away from the ashes as the blackened ruins came to life. An apparition of horror rose up with a misshapen head and pitiless holes for eyes.

Falcon whirled, a fraction of a second too late, to meet

the real attack. A claw missed his eye and raked his temple. Razor-sharp tips dug four long furrows into his chest. The pain was excruciating. Hot, fetid breath exploded in his face and he smelled rotting flesh, but the creature was a blur, disappearing as Falcon struck instinctively toward the heart.

His fist brushed thick fur and then empty air. At once, the beast within Falcon rose up, hot and powerful. The strength of it shook him. There was a red haze in front of his eyes, chaos reigning in his mind. Falcon spun around as he took to the sky, barely avoiding slamming bolts of energy that blackened the alley and took out the sides of the already crumbling building. The sound was deafening. The beast welcomed the violence, embraced it. Falcon was fighting himself as well as the vampire, battling the hunger that could never be assuaged.

Falcon? Her voice was a breath of fresh air, pushing aside the call of the kill. *Tell me where you are. I feel danger to you.* It was the naked concern in her voice that allowed him to control the raging demon, to push it aside despite the desire for violence.

Falcon struck fast and hard, a calculated risk, flying toward the bizarre figure made of ash, his fist outstretched before him. The ashes scattered in a whirlwind, rising high like a tower of grotesque charcoal. For an instant a form shimmered in the air as the vampire attempted to throw a barrier between them. Falcon drove through the flimsy structure, again feeling the brush, this time of flesh, but the creature had managed to dissolve again. The vampire was gone, vanishing as swiftly as it had appeared.

There was no trace of the monster, not even the inevitable blankness. Falcon searched the area carefully, thoroughly, looking for the smallest clue. The longer he searched, the more he was certain that Sara was hunted by a true ancient, a master vampire who had managed to elude all hunters throughout the centuries.

Falcon moved through the sky warily. The vampire would not strike at him again now. Falcon had been tested, and the ancient had lost the advantage of surprise. The enemy now knew he was up against an experienced hunter well versed in battle. He would go to ground, avoid contact in the hopes that Falcon would pass him by.

A clap of thunder echoed across the sky. A warning. A dark promise. The vampire was staking his claim, despite the fact that he knew a hunter was in the area. He would not give Sara up. She was his prey.

Sara was waiting for Falcon on the small porch, reaching for him with eager arms. Her gaze moved over him fearfully, assessing him for damage. Falcon wanted to gather her into his arms and hold her against his heart. No one had ever welcomed him, worried about him, had that look on her face. Anxious. Loving. She was even more beautiful than he remembered. Her clothes were soaked with rainwater, her short hair spiky and disheveled, her eyes enormous. He could drown in her eyes. He could melt in the heat of her welcome.

"Come into the house," Sara said, touching his temple with gentle fingers, running her hands over him, needing to feel him. She drew him into her home, out of the night air, out of the rain. "Tell me," she urged.

Falcon looked around him at the neat little room. It was soothing and homey. Comforting. The stark contrast between his ugly, barren existence and this moment was so extreme, it was almost shocking. Sara's smile, her touch, the worry in her eyes—he wouldn't trade those things for any treasure he had ever come across in his centuries on earth.

"What happened to you, Falcon? And I don't mean your

wounds." The fear for him she felt deep within her soul had been overwhelming in those moments before their communication.

Falcon shoved a hand through his long hair. He had to tell her the truth. The demon in him was stronger than ever. He had waited too long, been in too many battles, made too many kills. "Sara," he said softly. "We have a few choices, but we must make them swiftly. We do not have the time to wait until you fully understand what is happening. I want you to remain quiet and listen to what I have to say, and then we will have to make our decisions."

Sara nodded gravely, her eyes on his face. He was struggling, she could see that clearly. She knew he feared for her safety. She wanted to smooth the lines etched so deeply into his face. There was blood smeared on his temple, a thin trail that only accented the deep weariness around his mouth. His shirt was tattered and bloody, with four distinct rips. Every cell in her body cried out to hold him, to comfort him, yet she sat very still, waiting for what was to come.

"I have tied us together in life or death. If something were to happen to me, you would find it very difficult to continue without me. We must get to the Carpathian Mountains and my people. This enemy is an ancient and very powerful. He is determined that you are his, and nothing will deter him from hunting you. I believe you are in danger during both the hours of sunlight and darkness."

Sara nodded. She wasn't about to argue with him. The vampire had been relentless in his pursuit of her. She had been lucky in her escapes, willing to run at the smallest sign that he was near. Had the vampire stalked her silently, he would have had her, she was certain, but he didn't seem to credit her ability to ignore his summons. "He's used creatures during the day before." She looked down at her hands.

"I burned one of them." She admitted it in a low voice, ashamed of herself.

Falcon, feeling her guilt like a blow, took her hands, turned them over, and placed a kiss in the center of each palm. "The vampire's ghouls are already dead. They are soulless creatures, living on flesh and the tainted blood of the vampire. You were lucky to escape them. Killing them is a mercy. Believe me, Sara, they cannot be saved."

"Tell me our choices, Falcon. It is nearly morning and I'm feeling very anxious for you. Your wounds are serious. You need to be looked after." She could hardly bear the sight of him. He was smeared with blood and so weary he was drooping. Her fingers smoothed back stray strands of his long black hair.

"My wounds truly are not serious." He shrugged them off with a casual ripple of his shoulders. "When I go to ground, the soil will aid in healing me. While I am locked within the earth, you will be alone and vulnerable. During certain hours of the day I am at my weakest and cannot come to your aid. At least not physically. I would prefer that you remain by my side at all times to know you are safe."

Her eyes widened. "You want me to go beneath the earth with you? How would that be possible?" There were things left undone, things she needed to do in the daylight hours. Business hours. The world didn't accommodate Falcon's people so readily.

"You would have to become fully like me." He said it softly, starkly. "You would have all the gifts of my people, and also the weaknesses. You would be vulnerable during daylight hours, and you would require blood to sustain your life."

She was silent for a moment, turning his words over in her mind. "I presume that if I were like you, that would not be so abhorrent to me. I would crave blood?"

He shrugged. "It is a fact of our lives. We do not kill; we keep our prey calm and unknowing. I would provide for you, and it would not be in such a way that you would find it uncomfortable."

Sara nodded her acceptance of that even as her mind turned over his use of the word *prey*. She had lived in the shadows of the Carpathian world for fifteen years. His words weren't a shock to her. She drew Falcon toward the small bathroom where she had a first aid kit. He went with her because he could feel her need to take care of him. And he liked the feel of her hands on him.

"I can't possibly make a decision like this in one night, Falcon," she said as she ran hot water onto a clean cloth. "I have things I have to finish and I'll need to think about this." She didn't need to think too long or too hard. She wanted him with every fiber of her being. She had already learned in the short time while he was off chasing her enemy what it would be like to be without him.

Sara leaned into him and kissed his throat. "What else?" Her full breasts brushed against his arm, warm, inviting. Very gently she dabbed at the lacerations on his temple, wiping away the blood. The wounds on his chest were deeper. It looked as if an animal had raked claws over his chest, ripping his shirt and scoring four long furrows in the skin.

"I came very close to losing my control this night. I need to complete the ritual so we are one and you are my anchor, Sara. You felt it; you sensed the danger to me and called me back to you. Once the ritual is complete, that danger would no longer exist." He made the confession in a low voice, his overwhelming need evident in his husky tone. He couldn't think straight when she was so close to him, the roar in his head drowning out everything but the needs of his body.

Sara caught his face in her hands. "That's it? That's the big confession?" Her smile was slow and beautiful, lighting her eyes to a deep violet. "I want you more than anything on this earth." She bent her head and took possession of his mouth, pressing her body close to his, her rain-wet silken tank top nearly nonexistent, her breasts thrusting against him, aching with need. A temptation. An enticement. There was hunger in her kiss, acceptance, excitement. Her mouth was hot with her own desire, meeting the demands of his. Raw. Earthy. Real.

She lifted her head, her gaze burning into his. "I have been yours for the last fifteen years. If you want me, Falcon, I'm not afraid. I've never really been afraid of you." Her hands pushed aside his torn shirt, exposing his chest and the four long wounds.

"You have to understand what kind of commitment you are making, Sara," he cautioned. He needed her. Wanted her. *Hungered* for her. But he would not lose his honor with the most important person in his life. "Once the ritual is complete, if you are not with me below the ground while I sleep, you will fight a terrible battle for your sanity. I do not wish this for you."

Chapter Five

Sara blinked, drawing attention to her long lashes. Her gaze was steady. "Neither do I, Falcon"—her voice was a seductive invitation—"but I'd much rather fight my battles briefly than lose you. I'm strong. Believe in me." She bent her head, pressed a kiss into his shoulder, his throat. "You aren't taking anything I'm not willing to give."

How could she tell him, explain to him that he had been her only salvation all those long, endless nights when she'd hated herself, hated that she was alive and her family dead? How could she tell him he had saved her sanity, not once, but over and over? All those long years of holding his words close to her, locked in her heart, her soul. She knew she belonged with Falcon. She knew it in spite of what he was. She didn't care that he was different, that his way of surviving was different. She only cared that he was real, alive, standing in front of her with his soul in his eyes. Sara smiled at him, a sweet, provocative invitation, and simply drew her tank top over her head so that he could see her body, the full, lush curves, the darker peaks. Sara dropped the sodden tank top in a little heap on top of his shirt. She tilted her chin, trying to be brave, but he could see the slight trembling of her body. She had never done such an outrageous thing in her life.

Falcon found the nape of her neck, his fingers curling possessively as he dragged her close to him. His wounds were forgotten, his weariness. In that moment everything was forgotten but that Sara was offering herself to him. Pledging to give her life and her body into his keeping. Generously. Unconditionally.

Falcon thought she was the sexiest thing he had ever seen in all his years of existence. She was looking at him with enormous eyes so vulnerable his insides turned to mush. His breath slammed right out of his lungs. His body was so hot, so hard, so tight, he was afraid he might shatter if he moved. Yet he couldn't stop himself. His hand of its own volition drifted down her throat to cup her breast. Her skin was incredibly soft, softer even than it looked. It was shocking the way he felt about her, the sheer intensity of it. Where he had never wanted or needed, where no one had mattered, now there was Sara to fill every emptiness in him. His fingertips brushed over the curve of her breast, an artist's touch, explored the line of her ribs, the tuck of her waist, returned to cup her lush offering.

His black gaze burned over her possessively, scorching her skin, sending flames licking along the tips of her breasts, her throat, her hips, between her legs. And then he bent his head and drew her breast into the hot, moist cavern of his mouth.

Sara cried out, clutched his head, her fingers tangling in the thick silk of his hair, her body shuddering with pleasure. She felt the strong, erotic pull of his mouth in the very core of her body. Her body clenched tightly, aching, coiled with edgy need.

Falcon skimmed his hand down the sleek line of her back. *Are you certain, Sara? Are you certain you want the complete intimacy of our binding ritual?* He sent her the picture in his head: his mouth on her neck, over her pulse, the intensity of his physical need of her. He was already pulling her closer, devouring her skin, the lush curves so different from the hard planes and angles of his own body.

If Sara had wanted to pull back, it was already far too late. She was lost in the arcing electricity, the dazzling lightning dancing in her bloodstream. The images and the sheer pleasure in his mind, darkly erotic, only added to the firestorm building in her body. She had never experienced anything so elemental, so completely right, so completely primitive. She needed to be closer to him, skin to skin. The need was all-consuming, as hot as the sun itself, a firestorm raging, crowning, until there was nothing else, only Falcon. Only feeling. Only his fierce possession. She cradled his head to her breast, arcing deeper into his mouth while her body went liquid hot.

She wrapped one leg around his hips, pushing her heated center against the hard column of his thigh, a hard friction, moving restlessly, seeking relief. Her hands were tugging at his clothes, trying to get them off him while his mouth left flames on her neck, her breasts, even her ribs. His hands skimmed the curve of her hips, taking the silken pajamas down her thighs so the material pooled on the floor in a heap. He caught her leg and once more wrapped it around his hips so that she was open to him, pressed, hot and wet, tight against him.

Falcon's mouth found hers in a series of long kisses, each inflaming her more than the last. His hands were possessive on her breasts, her belly, sliding to her bottom, the inside of her thigh.

She was hot and wet with her need of him, her scent calling to him. Falcon's body was going up in flames. Sara had no inhibitions about letting him know she wanted him, and it was a powerful aphrodisiac. Her body moved against his, rubbing tightly, open to his exploration. She was pushing at his clothes, trying to get closer, her mouth on his chest, her tongue swirling to taste his skin. He removed the barrier of his clothing in the easy manner of his people, using his mind so that her hands could find him, thick and hard and full and throbbing with need. The moment her fingers stroked him, little firebombs seemed to explode in his bloodstream.

She knew him intimately, his thoughts, his dreams. She knew his mind, what he liked, what he needed and wanted. And he knew her. Every way to please her. They came together in heat and fire, yet for all his enormous strength, his desperate need, his touch was tender, exploring her body with a reverence that nearly brought tears to her eyes. His mouth was everywhere, hot and wild, teasing, enticing, promising things she couldn't conceive of.

Sara clung to him, wrapped her arms around his head, tears glistening like diamonds in her eyes, on her lashes. "I've been so alone, Falcon. Never go away. I don't know if you're real or not. How could anything as beautiful as you be real?"

He lifted his head, his black eyes drifting over her face. "You are my soul, Sara, my existence. I know what being alone is. I have lived centuries without home or family. Without being complete, the best part of me gone. I never wish to be apart from you." He caught her face between his hands. "Look at me, Sara. You are my world. I would not choose to be in this world without you. Believe in me." He bent his head to fasten his mouth to hers, rocking the earth for both of them.

Sara had no idea how they ended up in the bedroom. She was vaguely aware of being pressed against the wall, a wild tango of drugging kisses, of hot skin and exploring hands, of moving through space until the comforter was pressed against her bare body, her skin so sensitive she was gasping with the urgency of her own needs.

His mouth left hers to trace a path over her body, the swell of her breasts, her belly, his tongue trailing fire in its wake. His hands parted her thighs, held her tight as her body exploded, fragmented at the first stroking caress of his tongue.

Sara cried out, her hands fisting in his wealth of thick, long hair. She writhed under him, her body rippling with aftershocks. "Falcon." His name came out a breathy whispered plea.

"I want you ready for me, Sara," he said, his breath warming her, his tongue tasting her again and again, stroking, caressing, teasing until she was crying out again and again, her hips arcing helplessly into him.

His body blanketed hers, skin to skin, his heavier muscles pressed tightly against her softer body so that they fit perfectly. Falcon was careful with her despite the wildness rising within him. He watched her face as he began to push inside her body. She was hot, velvet soft, a tight sheath welcoming him home. The sensation was nothing like he had ever imagined, pure pleasure taking over every cell, every nerve. In the state of heightened awareness that he was in, his body was sensitive to every ripple of hers, every clench of her muscles, every touch of her fingers. Her breath—just her breath gave him pleasure.

He thrust deeper until her breath came in gasps. Until her body coiled tightly around his. Until her nails dug into his back. She was so soft and welcoming. He began to move, surging forward, watching her face, watching the loss of control, feeling the wildness growing in him, reveling in his ability to please her. He thrust harder, deeper, over and over, watching her rise to meet him, stroke for stroke. Her breasts took on a faint sheen, tempting, enticing, a lush invitation.

Falcon bent his head to her, his dark hair sliding over her skin so that she shuddered with pleasure, so that she cried out with unexpected shock at another orgasm, fast and furious.

Sara knew the moment his mouth touched her skin. Scorched her skin. She knew what he would do, and her body tightened in anticipation. She wanted him wild and out of control. His tongue found her nipple, lapped gently. His mouth was hot and greedy, and she heard herself gasp out his name. She held him to her, arcing her body to offer him her breast, her hips moving in perfect rhythm with his.

His mouth moved to the swell of her breast, just over her heart, his teeth scraping gently, nipping, his tongue swirling. Sara thought she might explode into a million fragments. Her body was so hot and tight and aching. "Falcon . . ." She breathed his name, a plea, needing to fulfill his every desire.

His hands tightened on her hips, and he buried himself deep inside her body and inside her mind, his teeth sinking into her skin so that white-hot lightning lashed through her, through him, until she was consumed by fire. Devoured by it. She cradled his head, but her body was rippling with pleasure, again and again until she thought she might die from it. Endless. On and on, again and again.

His tongue swirled lightly over the small telltale pin-pricks. He was trembling, his mind a haze of passion and need. He whispered softly to her, a command as he lifted her head to the temptation of his chest. Falcon felt Sara's mouth move against his skin. His body tightened, a pain-edged pleasure nearly beyond endurance. With Sara firmly caught in his enthrallment, he indulged himself, coaxing her to take enough blood for a true exchange. His body was hard and hot and aching with the need for relief, the need for the ecstasy of total fulfillment. He closed the wound in his chest and took possession of her mouth as he awakened her from the compulsion.

And then he was surging into her, wild and out of control, taking them closer and closer to the edge of a great preci-pice. Sara clung to him, her softer body rising to meet his with a wild welcome. Falcon lifted his head to look at her, wanting to see the love in her eyes, the welcome, the intense need for him. Only him. No other. It was there, just as when she had first recognized him. It was deep within her soul, shining through her eyes for him to see. Sara belonged to him. And he belonged to her.

Fire rushed through him, through her. A fine sheen of sweat coated their skin. His hands found hers and they moved together, fast and hard and incredibly tender. She felt him swell within her, saw his eyes glaze, and her own body tightened, muscles clenching and rippling with life. His name caught in her throat, his breath left his lungs as they rushed over the edge together.

They lay for a long while, holding one another, their bodies tangled together, skin to skin, his thigh over hers, in between hers, his mouth and hands still exploring. Sara cradled him to her, tears in her eyes, unbelieving that he was in her arms, in her body, one being. She would never be alone. He filled her heart and her mind the way he filled her body.

"We fit," he murmured softly. "A perfect fit."

"Did you know it would be like this? So wonderful?"

He moved then, rising from the bed and bringing her up with him, taking her to the shower. As the water streamed off them, he licked the water from her throat, followed the path of several beads along her ribs. Sara retaliated by tasting his skin, sipping the water beads as they ran low along his flat, hard belly. Her mouth was hot and tight, so that he had to have her again. And again. He took her there in the shower. They made it as far as the small dresser, where he found the sight of her bottom too perfect to ignore. She was receptive, as hot and as needy as Falcon, never wanting the night to end.

The early morning light filtered through the closed curtains. They lay together on the bed, talking together, holding each other, hands and mouths stroking caresses in between words. Sara couldn't remember laughing so much; Falcon hadn't thought he knew how to laugh. Finally, reluctantly, he leaned over to kiss her.

"You must go if you are going to do this, Sara. I want you high in the Carpathian Mountains before nightfall. I will rise and come straight to you."

Sara slid from the bed to stand beside the bust she had made so many years earlier. She didn't want to leave him. She wanted to remain curled up beside him for the rest of her life.

Falcon didn't need to read her mind to know her thoughts; they were plain on her transparent face. For some reason, her misgivings made it easier for him to allow her to carry out her plans. He stood up, his body crowding close to hers. He needed sleep; he needed to go to ground and fully heal. Mostly he needed to be with Sara.

"I'm afraid that if I leave, I might never get the children. The officials are disturbed because I'm asking for all seven of them and there are no records." Sara's fingers twisted together in agitation.

"Mikhail will be able to get rid of the red tape for us. He has many businesses in this area and is well known." Falcon brought her fingers to the warmth of his mouth to calm her. "I have not been to my homeland in many years, but I am well aware of everything that is happening. He will be able to assist us."

"How do you know so much if you've been away?" Sara wasn't ready to trust a complete stranger with something so important as the children.

He smiled and tangled his fingers in her hair. "The Carpathian people speak on a common mental pathway. I hear when hunters have gone through the land or some trauma has taken place. I heard when our Prince nearly lost his lifemate. Not once, but on two occasions. I heard when he lost his brother and then his brother returned to him. Mikhail will assist you. When you reach the area, he will find you in the evening and you will be under his protection. I will rise as soon as possible and come straight to you. He will assist us in finding a good location for our home. It will be near him and within the protection of all Carpathians. I have marked the trails for you in the mountains." Falcon bent his head to the temptation of her breast, his tongue lapping at the tight, rosy peak. His hair skimmed over her skin like so much silk. "You must be very careful, Sara. You cannot think you are safe because it is daylight. The undead are locked within the earth, but they are able to control their minions. This vampire is an ancient and very powerful."

Her body caught fire, just like that, liquid flames rushing through her bloodstream. "I will be more than careful, Falcon. I've seen what he does. I'm not going to doing anything silly. You don't have to worry. After I contact my friends and get a call through to my lawyer, I'll be going straight to the mountains. I'll find your people," she assured. Her heart was beating a little too fast at that thought, and she knew he heard it. Her own hearing was far more acute than it had been, and the thought of food made her feel slightly sick. Already she was changing, and the idea of being separated from Falcon was frightening. Sara lifted her chin determinedly and flashed him a reassuring smile. "Once I set everything up, I'll get on the road." Her fingers were continually sliding over the bust of Falcon's head, lovingly following the grooves marking the waves in his hair.

Watching her, knowing that statue had been her solace in years past, Falcon felt his heart turn over. He gathered her close to him, his touch possessive, tender, as loving as he could make it. "You will not be alone, Sara. I will heed your call, even in my most vulnerable hour. Should your mind start to play tricks on you, telling you I am dead to you, call me and I will answer."

Sara molded her body against his, clinging to him, holding him close so that he felt real and strong and very solid. "Sometimes I think maybe I dreamed of you for so long I'm hallucinating, that I made you up and any minute you'll disappear," she confessed softly.

His arms tightened until he was nearly crushing her against him, yet there was great tenderness in the way he held her. "I never dared to dream, even to hope. I had accepted my barren existence. It was the only way to survive and do my duty with honor. I am not ever going to leave you, Sara." He didn't tell her he was terrified at the thought of going to ground while she faced danger on the surface. She was a strong woman, and she had survived a long, deadly duel with the vampire completely on her own. He couldn't find it in him to insist she do things his way simply for his comfort.

Sara was touching his mind, could read his thoughts, the intensity of his fear for her safety. A wave of love swept through her. She turned her face up to his, hungrily seeking his mouth, wanting to prolong her time with him. His mouth was hot and dominant, as hungry as hers. As demanding. A fierce claim on her. He kissed her chin, her throat, found her mouth again, devouring her as if he could never get enough. There was an edginess to his kiss now, an ache. A need.

Sara's leg slid up his leg to wrap around his waist. She pressed against the hard column of his thigh, grinding against him, so that he felt her invitation, her own demand, hot and wet and pulsing with urgency.

Falcon simply lifted her in his arms, and she wrapped both legs around his waist. With her hands on his shoulders, her head thrown back, she lowered her body to the thick hardness of his. He pressed against her moist entrance, making her gasp, cry out as he slowly, inch by inch, filled her completely. Sara threw back her head, closed her eyes as she began to ride him, losing herself completely in Falcon's dark passion. They took their time, a long, slow tango of fiery heat that went on and on as long as they dared. They were in perfect unison, reading each other's minds, moving, adjusting, giving themselves completely, one to the other. When they were spent, they leaned against the wall and held one another, their hearts beating the same rhythm, tears in their eyes. Sara's head was on his shoulder and Falcon's head rested on hers.

"You cannot allow anything to happen to yourself, Sara," he cautioned. "I have to go now. I cannot wait much longer. You know I cannot be without you. You will remember everything I have said to you?"

"Everything." Sara tightened her hold on him. "I know it's crazy, Falcon, but I love you. I really do. You've always been with me when I needed you. I love you."

He kissed her, long and tender. Incredibly tender. "You are my love, my life." He whispered it softly and then he was gone. Sara remained leaning against the wall, her fingers pressed against her mouth for a few moments. Then she sprang into action.

She worked quickly, packing a few clothes and tossing them in her backpack, making several calls to ask friends to keep an eye on the children until she could return. She had every intention of coming back for them as soon as she sorted out the extensive paperwork and set up a home for them. She was on the road heading toward the Carpathian Mountains within an hour.

She needed the darkness of sunglasses, although the day was a dreary gray with ominous clouds overhead. Her skin prickled with unease as rays of sunlight pushed through the thick cloud covering to touch her arm as she drove. She tried not to think about Falcon locked deep within the ground. Her body was wonderfully sore. She could feel his touch on her, his possession, and just the thought of him made her hot with renewed desire. She couldn't prevent her mind from continually seeking his. Each time she touched on the void, her heart would contract painfully, and it would take tremendous effort to control her wild grief. Every cell in her body demanded that she go back, find him, make certain he was safe.

Sara tilted her chin and kept driving, hour after hour, leaving the cities for smaller villages until she was finally in a sparsely populated area. She stopped twice to rest and stretch her cramped legs, but continued steadily, always driving up toward the region Falcon had so carefully marked for her. She was concentrating so hard on finding the trail leading into wild territory that she was nearly hit by another vehicle as it overtook her and roared by. It shot past her at breakneck speed, a larger, much heavier truck with a camper. She was forced to veer off the narrow track to keep from being shoved off the trail. The vehicle went by her so quickly she nearly missed seeing the little faces peering out at her from the window of the camper shell. She nearly missed the sounds of screams fading into the forest.

Sara froze, her mind numb with shock, her body nearly paralyzed. The children. Her little ones, the children she had promised safety and a home. They were in the hands of a puppet, a ghoul. The walking dead. The vampire had taken a human, enslaved him, and programmed the creature to take her children as bait. She should have known, should have guessed he would discover them. She gave chase, hurtling along the narrow, rutted trail, clinging to the steering wheel as her truck threatened to break apart.

Two hours later, she was completely and hopelessly lost. The ghoul was obviously aware that she was following and it simply drove where no vehicle should have been able to go, racing dangerously through hairpin turns and smashing his way through vegetation. Sara attempted to follow, driving at breakneck speed through the series of turns, wheels bouncing over the rough pits in the roads. Once a tree was down directly across her path and she had to take her truck deeper into the forest to get around it. She was certain the ghoul had shoved the tree there to block her pursuit, to delay her. The trees were so close together, they scraped the paint from the sides of her truck. She couldn't believe she could possibly have lost the other vehicle; there weren't that many roads to turn onto. She tried twice to look at the map on the seat beside her, but with the terrible jouncing, it was impossible to focus. Branches scraped the windshield; twigs snapped off with an ominous sound.

With her arms aching and her heart pounding, Sara managed to maneuver her truck back onto a faint trail that might pass for a road. It was very narrow and ran along a deep, rocky ravine that looked like a great crack in the earth. In places, the boulders were black and scarred as if a war had taken place. The branches slapped at her truck as it rushed through the trees along the winding road. She would have to pull over and consult the map Falcon had given her.

His name immediately brought a welling of grief, of fear that he was lost to her, but Sara attempted to push the false emotion aside, grateful that he had prepared her for such a possibility. A sob welled up, choking her; tears blurred her vision but she wiped them away, wrenching at the wheel determinedly when her truck nearly bounced off the road from a particularly deep rut.

This couldn't be happening. The children, *her* children in the hands of the vampire's evil puppet. A flesh-eating ghoul. Sara wanted to continue driving as fast as she could, terrified that if she stopped she would never be able to catch them.

She was well aware that it was late afternoon and once the ghoul delivered the children to the vampire, she had little hope of saving them.

Sara sighed softly and slowed the truck with great reluctance, pulling to the side of the trail. A steep cliff rose up sharply on her left. It took tremendous discipline to force herself to stop her vehicle and spread the map out in front of her. She needed to look for places where she could have gotten off the track, where the ghoul could have gotten away from her. She found she was nearly choking with grief. She shoved the door open and, leaving the vehicle running, jumped out where she could breathe the cool, crisp, fresh air.

Falcon. She breathed his name. Wanted him. Dashing the tears away, Sara grabbed the map from the seat and stared down at the clearly marked trail. Where had the ghoul turned off? How had she missed it? She had been driving as fast as she dared, yet she had still lost sight of the children.

A terrible sense of failure assailed her. She spread the map out on the hood of the truck and glared at the markings, waiting for inspiration, for some tiny clue. Her fingernails beat out a little tattoo of frustration on the metal hood. All around her was the sound of the wind whipping through the trees and out over the cliffs into empty space. But some sixth sense warned her she was not alone.

Sara turned her head. The creature was lumbering toward her, his blank expression a hideous reminder that he was no longer human. There would be no reasoning with him, no pleading with him. He had been programmed by a master of cunning and evil. She let out her breath slowly, carefully, centering herself for the attack. Sara crouched lower on the balls of her feet, her mind clear and calm as the thing neared her. Its eyes were fixed on her, its fingers clenching and unclenching as it shuffled forward. She didn't dare allow it to get its hands on her. Her world narrowed to the thing approaching her, her mind clear, as she knew it would have to be.

She waited until the creature was nearly on top of her before she moved. She used her speed, whirling in a spin, generating power as her leg lashed out, the edge of her foot catching the ghoul's kneecap in an explosion of violence. She sprang away, out of reach of those clawed hands. The creature howled loudly, spittle spraying into the air, a thick drool oozing from the side of its mouth. The eyes remained dead and fixed on her as its leg buckled with an audible crack. Unbelievably, it lurched toward her, dragging its useless leg but coming at her steadily.

Sara knew its kneecap was broken, yet it continued toward her relentlessly. Sara had faced such a thing before, and she knew it would keep coming even if it had to drag itself on the ground. She angled sideways, circling to the ghoul's left in an attempt to slide past it. It bothered her that she couldn't hear the children, that none of them were crying or yelling for help. With her hearing so acute, Sara was certain she would have been able to hear whimpers coming from the ghoul's truck, but there was an ominous silence.

She stood her ground, shaking her arms to keep them loose. The ghoul swiped at her with its long arm, its huge, hamlike fist missing her face as she ducked and slammed her foot into its groin, then straight up beneath its chin. It howled, the sound loud and hideous, its body jerking under the assault, but it only rocked backward, jolted for a moment. Sara had no choice but to slip out of its reach.

It was a lesson in sheer frustration. No matter how many times she managed to score a kick or hit, the creature refused to go down. It howled, spittle exploding from its mouth, but its eyes were always the same, flat and empty and fixed on her. It was like a relentless machine that never stopped. As a last resort, Sara tried luring it near to the edge of the ravine in the hope that she could push it over, but it stood for a moment, breathing heavily, and then turned unexpectedly and lumbered away from her into heavier brush and trees.

Sara hastily scrambled to her truck, her heart pounding heavily. A thunderous crash made her swing her head around. To her horror, the ghoul's heavier vehicle was mowing down brush and even small trees, roaring out of the forest like a charging elephant, aimed straight at the side of her truck. More out of reflex than rational thought, her foot slammed down hard on the accelerator.

Her truck slewed sideways, fishtailed, the tires spinning in the dirt. Sara's heart nearly stopped as the larger vehicle continued straight at her. She could see the driver's face as it loomed closer. It was masklike, the eyes dead and flat. The ghoul appeared to be drooling. She could hear the screams of the children, frightened and alone in the madness of a world they couldn't hope to understand. At least they were alive. She had been afraid that their former silence meant the ghoul had murdered them.

The truck hit the side of hers, buckling the door in on her and shoving her vehicle closer to the edge of the steep ravine. Sara knew she was going to go over the crumbling cliff. Her small truck slid, metal grinding, children screaming, the noise an assault on her sensitive ears. A strange calmness invaded her, a sense of the inevitable. Her fingers wouldn't let go of the steering wheel, yet she couldn't steer, couldn't prevent the truck from sliding inch by inch, foot by foot toward the edge of the cliff.

Two wheels went over the edge, the truck tilted crazily, and then she was falling, tumbling through the air, slamming into the ravine, sliding and rolling. The seatbelt tightened, a hard jolt, biting into her flesh, adding to the mind-numbing pain. *Falcon.* His name was a soft sigh of regret in her mind. A plea for forgiveness.

Falcon was wrenched from his slumber, his heart pounding, his chest nearly crushed in suffocation. He was far from Sara, unable yet to aid her. He would build a monstrous storm to help protect his eyes so he could rise early, but he still would not reach her in time. *Sara*. His life. His heart and soul. Terror filled him. Took him like a crushing weight. *Sara*. His Sara, with her courage and her capacity for love.

She was already in the Carpathian Mountains, caught in the trap the vampire had laid for her. He had no choice. Everyone of Carpathian blood would hear, and that included the undead. It was a risk, a gamble. Falcon was an ancient presumed dead. He had never declared his allegiance to the new Prince and he might not be believed, but it was Sara's only chance.

Falcon summoned his strength and sent out his call. *Hear me, brethren. My lifemate is under attack in the mountains near you. You must go to her aid swiftly as I am far from her. She is hunted by an ancient enemy and he has sent his puppets to acquire her. Rise and go to her. I warn all within my hearing, I am Falcon, a Carpathian of ancient blood, and I will be watching to protect her.*

Chapter Six

There was a swirling fear in Sara's mind, in his. Falcon burst through the soil and into the sky. Light assailed his sensitive eyes and burned his skin, but it didn't matter. Nothing mattered except that Sara was in danger. One moment he was merged mind to mind with Sara; in the next microsecond of time, there was a blank void. He had an eternity to feel the helpless terror roiling in his gut, the fist clamping his heart like a vise, the emptiness that had been his world, now unbearable, unthinkable, a blasphemy after knowing Sara. Falcon forced his mind to work, reaching relentlessly into that blank void for his very soul. For his life. For love.

Sara. Sara, answer me. Wake now. You must wake. I am on my way to you, but you must awaken. Open your eyes for me. He kept his voice calm, but the compulsion was strong, the need in him raw. *Sara, you must wake.*

The voice was far away, coming from within her throbbing head. Sara heard her own groan, a foreign sound. She was raw and hurting everywhere. She didn't want to obey the soft command, but there was a note she couldn't resist. The voice brought with it awareness, and with awareness came pain. Her heart began to pound in terror.

She had no idea how long she had been unconscious in the wreckage of the truck, but she could feel the metal pressing on her legs and glass cutting her body. She was trapped in the twisted metal, shattered glass all around her, blood running down her face. She didn't want to move, not when she heard movement close to her. She squeezed her eyes shut and willed herself to slip back into oblivion.

Relief washed over Falcon, through him, shook him. For a moment he went perfectly still, nearly falling from the sky, nearly unable to hold the image he needed to stay aloft. His mind was fully merged with Sara's, buried within hers, worshiping, examining, nearly numb with happiness. She was alive. She was still alive! Falcon worked at controlling his body's reaction to the sheer terror of losing her, the unbelievable relief of knowing she was alive. It took discipline to lower his heart rate, to steady his terrible trembling. She was alive, but she was trapped and hurt.

Sara, piccola, *do as I ask, open your eyes.* Keeping his voice gentle, Falcon gave her no choice, burying a compulsion within the purity of his tone. He felt pain sweeping through her body, a sense of claustrophobia. She was disoriented; her head was pounding. Now his fear was back again in full force, although he kept it hidden from her. Instead, it was trapped in his heart, in his deepest soul, a terror such as he had never known before. He was moving fast, streaking across the sky as quickly as possible, uncaring of the disturbance of power, uncaring that all ancients in the area would know he was racing toward the mountains. She was alone, hurt, trapped, and hunted.

Sara's eyes obeyed his soft command. She looked around her at the crushed glass, the twisted wreckage, and the sheered-off top of her truck. Sara wasn't certain she was still actually inside the vehicle. She couldn't recognize it as a truck any longer. It looked as if she were trapped in a smashed accordion. The sun was falling in the mountains, a shadow spreading across the rocky terrain.

She heard a noise, the scrape of something against what was left of her truck, and then she was looking into the face of a woman. Sara's vision was blurry, and it took a few moments of blinking rapidly to bring the woman into focus. Sara remembered how she had gotten in her predicament, and it frightened her to think of how much time might have passed, how close the ghoul might be. She tried to move, to look past the woman. When she moved, her body screamed in protest and a shower of safety glass fell around her. Her dark glasses were missing, and her eyes burned so that they wept continually.

"Lie quietly," the woman said, her voice soothing and gentle. "I am a doctor and I must assess the severity of your injuries." The stranger frowned as she lightly took Sara's wrist.

Sara felt very disoriented, and she could taste blood in her mouth. It was far too much of an effort to lift her head. "You can't stay here. Something was chasing me. Really, leave me here; I'll be fine. I've got a few bruises, nothing else, but you aren't safe." Her tongue felt thick and heavy and her tone shocked her, thin and weak, as if her voice came from far away. "You aren't safe," she repeated, determined to be heard.

The woman was watching her carefully, almost as if she knew what Sara was thinking. She smiled reassuringly. "My name is Shea, Shea Dubrinsky. Whatever is chasing you can be dealt with. My husband is close by and will aid us if necessary. I'm going to run my hands over you and check you for injuries. If you could see your truck, you would know what a miracle it is that you survived."

Sara was feeling desperate. Shea Dubrinsky was a beautiful woman, with pale skin and wine-red hair. She looked very Irish. She was serene despite the circumstances. It was only then that the name registered. "Dubrinsky? Is your husband Mikhail? I've come looking for Mikhail Dubrinsky."

Something flickered in Shea Dubrinsky's eyes behind her smoky sunglasses. There was compassion, but something else, too, something that made Sara shiver. The doctor's hands moved over her impersonally, but thoroughly and gently. Sara knew that this woman, this doctor, was one of *them. The others.* Right now Shea Dubrinsky was communicating with someone else in the same manner Sara did with Falcon. It frightened Sara nearly as much as the encounter with the ghoul. She couldn't tell the difference between friend and foe.

Falcon. She reached for him. Needed him. Wanted him with her. The accident had shaken her so that it was difficult to think clearly. Her head ached appallingly and her body was shaky, trembling beyond her ability to control it. It was humiliating for someone of Sara's strong nature. *She is one of them.*

I am here. Do not fear. No one can harm you. Look directly at her, and I will observe what you see. There was complete confidence in Falcon's voice and he swamped her with waves of reassurance, the feel of strong arms stealing around her, gathering her close, holding her to him. The feeling was very real and gave her confidence.

She speaks to another. She says her name is Dubrinsky and her husband is close. I know she speaks to him. She has called him to us. Sara said it with complete conviction. The woman looked calm and professional, but Sara felt what was happening, knew that Shea Dubrinsky was communicating with some other even though Sara could not see anyone else.

Sara gasped as the woman's hands touched sore places.

She tried to smile at the other woman. "I'm really okay, the seat belt saved me, although I hurt like crazy. You have to get away from here." She was feeling a bit desperate searching for signs of the ghoul. Sara tried to move and groaned as every muscle in her body protested. Her head pounded so that even her teeth hurt.

"Stay very quiet for just a moment," Shea said softly, persuasively, and Sara recognized a slight "push" toward obedience. Falcon was there with her, sharing her mind, so she wasn't as afraid as she might have been. She believed in him. She knew he would come, that nothing would stop him from reaching her side. "Mikhail Dubrinsky is my husband's brother. Why are you seeking him?" Shea spoke casually, as if the answer didn't matter, but once again, there was that "push" toward truth.

Sara made an attempt to raise her hand, wanting to remove the broken glass from her hair. Her head was aching so much it made her feel sick. "For some reason, compulsion doesn't work very well on me. If you are going to use it, you have to use it with much more strength." She was struggling to keep her eyes open.

Sara! Focus on her. Stay focused! Falcon's command was sharp. *I sent a call ahead to my people to alert them to find you. Mikhail did have brothers, but you must remain alert. I must see through your eyes. You must stay awake.*

Shea was grinning at her a little ruefully. "You are familiar with us." She said it softly. "If that is the case, I want you to hold very still while I aid you. The sun is falling fast. If you are hunted by a puppet of the undead, the vampire will be close by and waiting for the sun to sink. Please remain very quiet while I do this." Shea was watching Sara's face for a reaction.

There was a movement behind Shea and she turned her head with a loving smile. "Jacques, we have found the one we were seeking. She has a lifemate. He is watching us through her eyes. She is one of us, yet not." Out of courtesy she spoke aloud. There was a wealth of love in her voice, an intimacy that whispered of total commitment. She turned back to Sara. "I will attempt to make you more comfortable, and Jacques will get you out of the truck so we may leave this place and get to safety." There was complete confidence in her gentle tones.

Sara wanted the terrible pounding in her head to go away. She couldn't shift her legs; the wreckage was entombing her as surely as a casket. Falcon's presence in her mind was the only thing that kept her from sliding back into the welcoming black void. She struggled to stay alert, watching Shea's every move. The unknown Jacques had not come into her line of vision, but she felt no immediate threat.

Shea Dubrinsky was graceful and sure. There were no rough edges to her, and she seemed completely professional despite the bizarre way she was healing Sara. Sara actually felt the other woman inside her, a warmth, an energy flowing through her body to soothe the terrible aches, to repair from the inside out. She was amazed that the terrible pounding in her head actually lessened. The nausea disappeared.

Shea leaned over to unfasten the seat belt that was biting into Sara's chest. "Your body has suffered a trauma," she said. "There will be extensive bruising, but you're very lucky. Once we are safe, I can make you much more comfortable." She moved out of the way to allow her lifemate access to the wreckage.

Sara found herself staring up at a man with a singularly beautiful face. His eyes, as he took off his sunglasses, were as old as time, as if he had seen far too much. Suffered far too much. He pushed the glasses onto Sara's face, bringing a measure of relief to her burning eyes. Shea brushed Jacques's hand with hers, the lightest of gestures, but it was more intimate than anything Sara had ever witnessed. She could feel the stillness in Falcon, could feel him gathering his strength should there be need.

"Hold very still," Jacques cautioned softly. His voice held the familiar purity that seemed to be a part of the Carpathian species.

"He has the children. Go after him. If you're like Falcon, you have to go after him and get the children back. He's taking them to the vampire." *Falcon, I'm all right. You must find the children and keep them from the vampire.* She was beginning to panic, thinking much more clearly now that the pain was receding.

Jacques grasped the steering column and gave a wrench, exerting strength so that it bent away from her, giving her more room to breathe. "The ghoul will not reach the vampire. Mikhail has risen and he will stop the puppet from reaching his master." There was complete confidence in Jacques's soft voice. "Your lifemate must be on his way, perhaps already close to us. All heard his warning, although he is not known to us." It was a statement, but Sara heard the question in his words.

She watched his hands push the crumbling wreckage from around her legs so that she could move. The relief was so tremendous she could feel tears gathering in her eyes. Sara turned her head away from the probing gaze of the stranger. At once warmth flooded her mind.

I am with you, Sara. I feel your injuries and your fear for the children, but this man would not lie to you. He is the brother of the Prince. I have heard of him, a man who has endured much pain and hardship, who was buried alive by fanatics. Mikhail will not fail to rescue the children.

You go; don't worry about me. You make certain the children are safe!

She didn't know the Prince. She knew Falcon and she

trusted him. If the children could be snatched away from the vampire, he would be the one to do it. And he was closer now, she was certain of it. His presence was much stronger and it took little effort to communicate with him.

"I am going to help you out of there," Jacques warned.

Sara had desperately wanted to be free of the wreckage of her truck, but now, faced with the prospect of actually moving, it didn't seem the best of ideas. "I think I'll just sit here for the rest of my life, if you don't mind," she said.

To her shock, Jacques smiled at her, a flash of white teeth that lit his ravaged eyes. It was the last thing she'd expected of him, and she found herself smiling back. "You do not frighten very easily, do you?" he asked softly. He gave no sign that the light of day hurt his eyes, but she could see they were red and streaming. He endured it stoically.

Sara lifted a trembling hand to eye level and watched it shake. They both laughed softly together. "I'm Sara Marten. Thanks for coming to my rescue."

"We could do no other, with your lifemate filling the skies with his declaration." The white teeth flashed again, this time reminding her of a wolf. "I am Jacques Dubrinsky; Shea is my lifemate."

Sara knew he was watching her closely to see what effect his words had on her. She knew Falcon was watching Jacques through her eyes, catching every nuance, sizing up the other man. And Jacques Dubrinsky was well aware of it, too.

"I am going to lift you out of there, Sara," he said gently. "Let me do the work. I have never dropped Shea, so you do not need to worry," he teased.

Sara turned her head to look at the other woman. She lifted an eyebrow. "I don't think that's much of a reassurance. She's much smaller than I am."

Shea grinned at her, a quick, engaging smile that lit her entire face. "Oh, I think he's up to the task, Sara."

Jacques didn't give her any more time to think about it. He lifted her out of the wreckage and carried her easily to a flat spot in the high grass, where his lifemate bent over her solicitously. The movement took Sara's breath away, sent pain slicing through her body. Shea carefully brushed glass from Sara's hair and clothing. "You have to expect to be a bit shaky. Tell your lifemate we are going to take you to Mikhail's house. You will be safe there, and Raven and I can look after you while Jacques joins the men in the hunt for these lost children."

I want the male to stay near you while I am away.

Sara heard the underlying irony in Falcon's voice and she laughed softly. The thought of any male near Sara was disconcerting to him, but he needed to know she was safe.

Sara's relief that Falcon was close and was searching for the children was enormous. She could breathe again, yet, inexplicably, she wanted to cry.

Shea knelt beside her, took her hand, and looked into her eyes. "It's a natural reaction, Sara," she said softly. "It's all right now, everything is going to be all right." Unashamedly she used her voice as a tool to soothe the other woman. "You are not alone; we really can help."

"Falcon says the vampire is ancient and very powerful," Sara said in warning. She was struggling to appear calm and to control the trembling of her body. It was humiliating to be so weak in front of strangers.

Jacques swung his head around alertly, his eyes black and glittering, his entire demeanor changed. All at once he looked menacing. "Is she able to travel, Shea?"

Shea was straightening slowly, a wary look on her beautiful face. A flutter of nerves in Sara's stomach blossomed into full-scale fear. "He's here, isn't he? The ghoul?" She bit her lip and made a supreme effort to get to her feet. "If he's close to us, then so are the children. He can't have handed them off to the vampire." To her horror, she only managed to get a knee under her before blackness began swirling alarmingly close.

"The ghoul is making his way quickly to his master," Jacques corrected. "The vampire probably has summoned the ghoul to him. The undead is sending his warning, a challenge to any who dare to interfere with his plans."

Shea slipped her arm around Sara to keep her from falling. "Do not try to move yet, Sara. You are not ready to stand." The woman turned to her lifemate. "We can move her, Jacques. I think it best to hurry."

They know something I don't. Sara rubbed her pounding head, frustrated that she was unable to see or hear the things heralding danger. *Something is wrong.*

At once she could feel Falcon's reassurance, his strong arms, warmth flooding her, though he was many miles away. *The vampire is locked within his lair, but he is sending his minions across the land searching for you. The male wishes to take you to safety.*

Do you really want me to go with him? I feel so helpless, Falcon. I don't think I could fight my way out of a paper bag.

Yes, Sara, it is best. I will be with you every moment.

The sky was becoming dark, not because the sun was setting but because the winds had picked up, whirling faster and faster, gathering dust, dirt, and debris together, drawing it into a towering mass. Swarms of insects assembled, masses of them, the noise of their wings rivaling the wind. *The children will be so afraid.* Sara reached out for assurance.

Falcon wanted to gather her close, hold her to him, shelter her from the battles that would surely take place. He sent her warmth, love. *I will find them, Sara. You must stay alert so I can guard you while we are apart.*

For some reason, Falcon's words humbled her. She wanted to be at his side. She needed to be at his side.

Jacques Dubrinsky leaned down to Sara. "I understand how you feel. I dislike to be away from Shea. She is a researcher, very important to our people." He looked at his lifemate as he gathered Sara easily into his arms. His expression was tender, mixed with pride and respect. "She is very single-minded, focused on what she is doing. I find it somewhat uncomfortable." He grinned ruefully, sharing his confession candidly.

"Wait!" Sara knew she sounded panic-stricken. "There's a backpack in the truck, I can't leave it. I can't." Falcon's diary was in the wooden box. She carried it everywhere with her. She was not about to leave it.

Shea hesitated as if she might argue, but obligingly rummaged around in the wreckage until she triumphantly came up with the backpack. Sara had her arms outstretched and Shea handed it to her.

Jacques lifted an eyebrow. "Are you ready now? Close your eyes if traveling swiftly bothers you."

Before she could protest, he was whisking her through space, moving so fast that everything around her blurred into streaks. Sara was happy to be away from the wreckage of her truck, from the fierce wind and the swarms of insects blackening the sky. She should have been afraid, but there was something reassuring about Jacques and Shea Dubrinsky. Solid. Reliable.

She had the impression of a large, rambling house with columns and wraparound balconies. She had no time to get more than a quick look before Jacques was striding inside. The interior was rich with burnished wood and wide open spaces. It all blended together—art, vases, exquisite tapestries, and beautiful furniture. Sara found herself in a large sitting room, pressed into one of the plush couches. The heavy drapes were pulled, blotting out all light so only soft candles lit the room, a relief to eyes sensitive to the sun.

Sara removed Jacques's sunglasses with a shaky hand. "Thank you. It was thoughtful of you to lend them to me."

He grinned at her, his teeth gleaming white, his dark eyes warm. "I am a very thoughtful kind of man."

Shea groaned and rolled her eyes. "He thinks he's charming, too."

Another woman, short with long black hair, glided into the room, her slender arm circling Jacques's waist with an easy, affectionate manner. "You must be Sara. Shea and Jacques alerted me ahead of time that they were bringing you to my home. Welcome. I've made you some tea. It's herbal. Shea thinks your stomach will tolerate it." She indicated the beautiful teacup sitting in a saucer on the end table. "I'm Raven, Mikhail's lifemate. Shea said you were searching for Mikhail."

Sara glanced at the tea, leaned back into the cushions, and closed her eyes. Her head was throbbing painfully and she felt sick again. She wanted to curl up and go to sleep. Tea and conversation sounded overwhelming.

Sara! Falcon's voice was stronger than ever. *You must stay focused until I am at your side to protect you. I do not know these strangers. I believe they do not intend you harm, but I cannot protect you if there be need, unless you stay alert.*

Sara made an effort to concentrate. "I have had a vampire hunting me for fifteen years. He killed my entire family and he's stolen children he knows matter a great deal to me. All of you are in great danger."

Jacques's eyebrows shot up. "You eluded a vampire for fifteen years?" There was a wealth of skepticism in his voice.

Sara turned her head to look at Shea. "He isn't nearly as charming when you've been around him a while, is he?"

Shea and Raven dissolved into laughter. "He grows on you, Sara," Shea assured.

"What?" Jacques managed to look innocent. "It is quite a feat for anyone to escape a vampire for fifteen years, let alone a human. It is perfectly reasonable to think there has been a mistake. And I am charming."

Raven shook her head at him. "Don't count too heavily on it, Jacques. I have it on good authority that the inclination to kick you comes often. And humans are quite capable of extraordinary things." She picked several pieces of glass from Sara's clothes. "It must have been terrifying for you."

"At first," Sara agreed tiredly, "but then it was a way of life. Running, always staying ahead of him. I didn't know why he was so fixated on me."

Shea and Raven were lighting aromatic candles, releasing a soothing scent that seeped into Sara's skin, made its way into her lungs, her body, and lessened the aches. "Sara," Shea said softly, "you have a concussion and a couple of broken ribs. I aligned the ribs earlier, but I need to do some work to ensure that you heal rapidly."

Sara sighed softly. She just wanted to sleep. "The vampire will come if he finds out I'm here, and you'll all be in danger. It's much safer if I keep moving."

"Mikhail will find the vampire," Jacques said with complete confidence.

Allow the woman to heal you, Sara. I have heard rumors of her. She was a human doctor before Jacques claimed her.

Sara frowned as she looked at Shea. "Falcon has heard of you. He says you were a doctor."

"I still am a doctor," Shea reassured gently. "Thank you for your warning and your concern for us. It does you credit, but I can assure you, the vampire will not be allowed to harm us here. Allow me to take care of you until your lifemate arrives." Her hands were very gentle as they moved over Sara, leaving behind a tingling warmth. "Healing you as a Carpathian rather than a human doctor is not really all that different. It is faster, because I heal from the inside out. It won't hurt, but it feels warm."

Raven continued to remove glass from Sara's clothing. "How did you meet Falcon? He is unknown to us." She was using a soft, friendly voice, wanting to calm Sara, to reassure her that she would be safe in their home. She also wanted any information available to be transferred to her own lifemate.

Sara leaned into the cushions, her fingers tight around the strap of her backpack. She could hear the wind, the relentless, hideous wind as it howled and moaned, screamed and whispered. There was a voice in the wind. She couldn't make out the words, but she knew the sound. Rain lashed at the windows and the roof, pounded at the walls as if demanding entrance. Dark shadows moved outside the window—dark enough, evil enough to disturb the heavy draperies. The material could not prevent the shadows from reaching into the room. Sparks arced and crackled, striking something they couldn't see. The howls and moans increased, an assault on their ears.

"Jacques." Shea said the name like a talisman. She slipped her hand into her lifemate's larger one, looking up at him with stark love shining in her eyes.

The man pulled his lifemate closer, gently kissed her palm. "The safeguards will hold." He shifted his stance, gliding to place his body between the window and the plush couch where Sara was sitting. The movement was subtle, but Sara was very aware of it.

The sound of the rain changed, became a hail of something heavier hitting the windows and pelting the structure. Raven swung around to face the large rock fireplace. Hundreds of shiny black bodies rained down from the chimney, landing with ugly plops on the hearth, where bright flames leaped to life, burning the insects as they touched the stones. A noxious odor rose with the black smoke. One particularly large insect rushed straight toward Sara, its round eyes fixed malevolently on her.

Chapter Seven

Falcon, in the form of an owl, peered at the ground far below him. He could see the ghoul's truck through the thick vegetation. It was tilted at an angle, one tire dangling precariously over a precipice. A second owl slipped silently out of the clouds, unconcerned with the wicked wind or lashing rain. Falcon felt a stillness in his mind, then a burst of pleasure, of triumph, a glowing pride in his people. He knew that lazy, confident glide, remembered it well. Mikhail, Vladimir Dubrinsky's son, had his father's flair.

Falcon climbed higher to circle toward the other owl. It had been long since he had spoken to another Carpathian. The joy he felt, even with a battle looming, was indescribable. He shared it with Sara, his lifemate, his other half. She deserved to know what she had done for him; it was she who had enabled him to feel emotion. Falcon went to earth, landing as he shifted into his own form.

Mikhail looked much as his father had before him. The same power clung to him. Falcon bowed low, elegantly. He reached out, clasping Mikhail's forearms in the manner of the old warriors. "I give you my allegiance, Prince. I would have known you anywhere. You are much like your father."

Mikhail's piercing black eyes warmed. "You are familiar

to me. I was young then. You were lost to us suddenly, as were so many of our greatest warriors. You are Falcon, and your line was thought to have been lost when you disappeared. How is it you are alive and yet we had no knowledge of you?" His grip was strong as he returned the age-old greeting between warriors of their species. His voice was warm, mellow even, yet the subtle reprimand was not lost on Falcon.

"Your father foresaw much in those days, a dark shadowing of the future of our people." Falcon turned toward the truck teetering so precariously. He began to stride toward the vehicle, with Mikhail in perfect synchronization. They moved together almost like dancers, fluid and graceful, full of power and coordination. "He called us together one night, many of us, and asked for volunteers to go to foreign lands. Vlad did not order us to go, but he was very much respected, and those of us who chose to do as he asked never thought of refusing. He knew you were to be Prince. He knew that you would face the extinction of our species. It was necessary for you to believe in your own abilities, and for *all* our people to believe in you and not rely on those of us who were older. We could not afford a divided people." Falcon's voice was gentle, matter-of-fact.

Mikhail's black eyes moved over Falcon's granite-honed face, the broad shoulders, the easy way he carried himself. "Perhaps advice would have been welcomed."

A faint smile touched Falcon's sculpted mouth, hinted at warmth in the depths of his eyes. "Perhaps our people needed a fresh, new perspective without the clutter of what once was."

"Perhaps," Mikhail murmured softly.

The ghoul had climbed from the truck and moved around the vehicle as if examining it. It didn't look up at the two Carpathian males, or acknowledge their presence in any way. Suddenly it placed its back against the truck, dug its feet into the rocky soil, and began to strain.

The sky erupted with black insects, so many the air seemed to groan with the numbers, raining from the sky with a fury equal to a tempest. From inside the truck, the children began to scream as the metal shrieked. The vehicle was being inched slowly but inevitably over the edge of the cliff.

Falcon put on a burst of preternatural speed, catching the ghoul by the shoulder and whirling it away from the truck. He trusted Mikhail to stop the children from going over. The insects were striking at him, stinging, biting, hitting his body, thousands of them, going for his eyes and nose and ears. Falcon was forced to dissolve into vapor, throwing up a quick barricade around himself as he reappeared behind the ghoul.

The creature swung around awkwardly, dragging one leg as it attempted to turn to face Falcon. Its eyes glowed a demonic red. It was making strange noises, somewhere between growling and snarling. It swiped at Falcon with razor-sharp nails, missed by inches. Falcon stayed just out of reach, watching closely. The ghoul was a mindless puppet to be used by its master. The vampire must have known that Falcon was an ancient, easily able to destroy such a creation, so it made little sense that the creature would attempt to fight him, yet that was exactly what the ghoul did. The macabre puppet grasped Falcon, fumbling to get its hands locked around Falcon's neck.

Falcon easily broke the grip, shattering the thick bones and wrenching the ghoul's head. The crack was audible despite the intensity of the wind and the loud clacking of the insects as they hit the ground. The ghoul seemed to glow for a moment, the eyes lighting an eerie orange in the darkness, the skin sloughing off as if the creature were a snake rather than a man.

"Get those children out of here," Falcon called out gravely, backing away from the creature. The light coming from inside the ghoul was becoming brighter, giving off a peculiar luminescence. "It is a trap."

Mikhail was tossing the children to safer ground. Three little girls and four boys. He leaped out of the way as the truck teetered precariously and then tumbled over the edge. He had shielded the children's minds, knowing they had been terror-stricken for most of the day. The oldest child, a boy, couldn't have been more than eight. Mikhail sensed that each of them was special in some way, each had psychic ability.

Insects were raining from the sky, dropping around them to form thick, grotesque piles of squirming bodies. Although Mikhail had erected a barrier over them and had shielded their minds, the children were staring in wide-eyed horror at the bugs. Mikhail heard Falcon's soft warning, glanced at the ghoul, and immediately shifted his shape, becoming a long, winged creature, the fabled dragon. Using his mind to control the children, he forced them to climb onto his back. They clung to him, their bodies trembling, but they accepted what was happening without real comprehension. Mikhail took to the air, laying down a long red-orange flame, incinerating all of the hideous beetles and locusts within his range.

I will transport the children to safety.

Go now! Falcon was alarmed for the Prince, alarmed for the children. The ghoul was spinning, creating a peculiar whirlwind motion reminiscent of a minitornado. The winds were furious, blowing the insects in all directions, even sucking them up into the sky. The glow was bright enough to hurt Falcon's sensitive eyes. *In all my long centuries of battles with the undead and their minions, this is a new phenomenon.*

New to me also. Mikhail was winging quickly through

the waning light in the sky, battling the ferocity of the wind and the thick masses of insects attacking from all directions. *The undead is indeed powerful to create this havoc while he still lies within his lair. He is without doubt an ancient.*

I sent word to your brother to wait to fight him, as I am certain this one is as old and as experienced as I am. I hope he listens to Sara.

Mikhail, in the body of the dragon, sighed. He hoped so, too. Immediately he touched Jacques's mind, relayed what had transpired and their conclusions.

Falcon moved carefully away from the ghoul, attempting to put distance between them. *The undead baited a trap, drew us away from Sara using the children and the ghoul. He will go after her.* Each direction Falcon chose, the grotesque creature turned with him in perfect rhythm, matching his flowing motions as if they were dance partners. *Get out of here now, Mikhail. Do not wait for me. This thing has attached itself to me like a shadow. A lethal and difficult spell to break. He is a bomb. Get to Sara.*

I will not be happy if such a despicable creature harms you. There was an edge of humor to Mikhail's soft voice. An edge of worry.

I am an ancient. This one will not defeat me. I am concerned only with the safety of you and the children. And with the delay in reaching Sara. It was the truth. Falcon might not have seen such a thing before, but he had supreme confidence in his own abilities. Already he was working at removing the binding attachment from his cells. It was a deep shadowing, as though the ghoul had managed to embed its molecules into Falcon's. Falcon tried various methods but could not find where the binding was impressed into his body. The ghoul was white-hot, blossoming like a mushroom and emitting a strange low hum. Time was running out.

Falcon ran his hands down his arms, across his chest. At once he felt the strange warmth emanating from his chest. Of course. The four long furrows the vampire had carved into his chest! The undead had left the spell in Falcon's chest, spoor for the ghoul to recognize, to adhere itself to. Falcon transmitted the information immediately to the Prince as he hastily began to detach himself from the monstrous time bomb.

The humming was louder, pitched much higher as the insects clacked with more intensity. The bugs were in a kind of frenzy, flying in all directions, swarming, attempting to scratch their way through the barrier Falcon had erected around himself. He had no time to think about poisonous insects; he had to turn his full attention to removing the hidden shadowing on his body. The vampire's fingerprints were etched deep beneath Falcon's skin.

Falcon glided quickly toward the ravine, drawing the ghoul away from the forest. As he twisted this way and that, taking the vampire's puppet with him at every step, he was examining his body from the inside out. He had missed those tiny prints marring his skin, pressed deeply into the lacerations he had already healed. So small, so lethal. He concentrated on scraping the nearly invisible marks from under his skin. It took tremendous discipline to work as he moved, using only his mind, leading the macabre ghoul right over the edge of the cliff. He was floating over empty space, enticing the unholy creature to take the last step that would send it plummeting to the rocks below. The explosion, when it came, could be contained deep within the ravine. Falcon worked rapidly, knowing that if the ghoul was attached to him, even by such tiny and invisible threads, the explosion would kill him.

The ghoul was in the air with him now, and Falcon began the descent slowly, taking the hideous thing where it could do no harm, even as he continued to find each print in the furrows on his chest. The whirling hot light suddenly shuddered, slipped, as if hanging by only a few precarious threads. The humming was now at fever-pitch, a merciless, unrelenting screaming in his head that made it difficult to think.

Falcon shut out the noise, increasing his speed, knowing he was close to throwing off the ghoul, knowing it was close to the end of its run. The vampire was waiting for sunset, holding Falcon away from Sara as surely as if he had imprisoned him. The ghoul pulsed with red-orange light through the white-hot glow just as Falcon sloughed off the last of the vampire's marks. The puppet began to fall, dropping away as Falcon rose swiftly toward the roiling clouds.

Falcon dissolved into mist as he rushed away from the screeching bomb. The explosion was monumental, a force that blew insect parts in all directions, carved a crater into the side of the ravine, and set the brush on fire. Falcon immediately doused the flames with rain, directing the heavy clouds over the steep ravine as he turned toward Mikhail's home, picking the directions out of the Prince's mind.

When Falcon made contact with Mikhail, he found him engaged in conversation with a human male, cautioning the man to protect the children. He knew he need not worry about the children; Mikhail would never place them in a dangerous situation. *Sara, I am some distance away but I will reach you soon.*

Falcon! Sara pushed herself upright despite her dizziness, staring in horror at the hideous beetle scurrying across the floor toward her. It was staring directly at her, watching her, marking her. And she knew what it was. Just as Falcon could use her eyes to see what was happening around her, the vampire was using the beetle's. The hard shell was on fire, the smell atrocious, but it was moving unerringly toward her, the eyes fixed on her. *He knows where I am. He'll kill all these people.* She was terrified, but Sara couldn't live with more guilt. If this monster wanted her so badly, perhaps the solution was simply to walk out the door and find him.

No! Falcon's voice was strong, commanding. *You will do as I say. Warn the male that this enemy is an ancient, most likely one of the warriors sent out by Mikhail's father who turned vampire. The sun has not yet set, we have a few minutes. The male must use delaying tactics until we arrive to aid him.*

Jacques simply stepped on the large insect, flames and all, crushing the thing beneath his foot, smothering the flames. Sara cleared her throat and looked at Jacques with sorrow in her eyes. "I'm so sorry. I didn't mean to bring this enemy to you. He's an ancient, Falcon says, most likely one of the warriors Mikhail's father sent out."

Raven smoothed back Sara's hair with gentle fingers. Jacques hunkered down so he was level with Sara. His expression was as calm as ever. "Tell me what you know, Sara. It will aid me in battle."

Sara shook her head, had to suppress a groan as her head throbbed and pulsed with pain. "Falcon says to delay the battle, to wait for him, and for Mikhail."

"Heal her, Shea," Jacques ordered gently. "The sun has not set and the vampire is locked deep within the earth. He knows where she is and will come to us, but the safeguards will slow him. We have time. Mikhail will make his way here, and her lifemate will come also. This ancient enemy is a powerful one."

The children, Falcon. What of the children? Sara was finding it difficult to think, with the grotesque remains of the insect on the immaculate shining wood floor.

The children are safe, Sara. Do not worry about them. Mikhail has taken them to a safe house. A man, a human, known to him and our people, is there to watch over them. They will be safe while we are hunting your enemy.

Sara inhaled sharply. Hadn't the others seen what she had? The vampire had penetrated the safeguards and had found her, had watched her through the eyes of its servant. Now the children she wanted to adopt were being taken to a perfect stranger. *Who is this man? How do you know of him, Falcon? Maybe you should go there yourself. They must be so afraid.*

Mikhail trusts this man. His name is Gary Jansen, a friend to our people. He will look after the children until we have destroyed the vampire. We cannot afford to draw the undead to them a second time. Mikhail will not leave them frightened. He is capable of helping them to accept this human and their new situation.

Sara lifted her chin, trying to ignore the terrible pounding in her head. "Do you know someone called Gary? Mikhail is taking the children to him." She knew she sounded anxious but she couldn't help it.

Shea laughed softly. "Gary is a genius, a man very much involved with his work. He flew out here from the States to help me with an important project I'm working on." As she spoke she silently signaled her lifemate to lift Sara and transport her to one of the underground chambers below the house. "I wish I'd been there to see the expression on his face when Mikhail showed up at the inn with several frightened children. Gary is a good man and very dedicated to helping us discover why our children are not surviving, why there are so few female children born, but I can't imagine him attempting to take care of little ones all by himself."

"You are enjoying the thought way too much." Jacques's

laughter was low, a pleasant sound in contrast with the loud, frightening noises outside the home. "I cannot wait to tell the human you are pleased with his new role."

"But he *will* take care of them." Sara sought reassurance even as Jacques lifted her high into his arms.

Raven nodded emphatically. "Oh, yes, there's no need to worry. Gary would never abandon the children, and all Carpathians are bound to protect him should he have need. Your children will be very safe, Sara." As they moved through the house, she indicated a framed picture on the wall. "That is my daughter, Savannah. Gary saved her life."

Sara peered at the picture as they went by. The young woman was beautiful, but she looked the same age as Raven. And she looked vaguely familiar. "She's your daughter? She looks your age."

"Savannah has a lifemate." Raven touched the frame in a loving gesture. "When they are small, our children look very young, but their bodies grow at about the same rate as a human child for the first few years. It is only when our people reach sexual maturity that our growth rate slows. That is one reason we have trouble reproducing. It is rare for our women to be able to ovulate for a good hundred years after having a baby. It has happened, but it is rare. Shea believes it is a form of population control, just as most other species have built-in controls. Because Carpathians live so long, nature, or God, if you prefer, built in a safeguard. Savannah will be returning home quite soon. They would have returned immediately upon their union, but Gregori, her lifemate, has received word of his lost family and wishes to meet with them first." Raven's voice held an edge of excitement. "Gregori is needed here. He is Mikhail's second in command, a very powerful man. And, of course, I've missed Savannah."

Sara was suddenly aware that they were going swiftly through a passageway. Raven's chatter had distracted her from her headache and from the danger, but mostly from the fact that they were moving steadily downward, beneath the earth. She felt the leap of her heart and instantly reached out for Falcon. Mind to mind. Heart to heart. *We can only have a child once every hundred years.* She said the first thing she thought of, then was embarrassed that she had whispered a secret dream, now a regret. She longed for a house filled with children. With love and laughter. With all the things she had lost. All the things she had long ago accepted she would never have.

We have seven children, Sara, seven abandoned, half-starved, very frightened children. They will need us to sort out their problems, love them, and aid them with their unexpected gifts. The three girls may or may not be lifemates for Carpathians in sore need, but all will need guidance. We will have many children to love in the coming years. Whatever your dream, it is mine. We will have a home and we will fill it with children and laughter and love.

He was closer, he was on his way to her. Sara wrapped herself in his warmth, in his words. *This is my gift to you.* A dark dream she would embrace. Reach for.

"Where are you taking me?" Sara's anxiety was embarrassing, but she couldn't seem to hold it in check. Falcon had to be able to find her.

She heard the reassurance of his soft laughter. *There is no place they could take you where I could not find you. I am in you as you are in me, Sara.*

"What you are feeling is normal, Sara," Raven said softly. "Lifemates cannot be apart from one another comfortably."

"And you have a concussion," Shea reminded. "We're taking you where you will be safe," she assured again, calmly, patiently.

The passageway wound deep within the earth. Jacques took Sara through what seemed like a door in the solid rock to a large, beautiful chamber. To Sara's grateful surprise, it looked like a bedroom. The bed was large and inviting. She curled up on it the moment Jacques put her down, closing her eyes and wanting just to go to sleep. She felt that even a few minutes' rest would make her feel better. The comforter was thick and soothing, the designs unusual. Sara found herself tracing the symbols over and over.

The candles leaped to life, flickering and dancing, casting shadows on the walls and filling the room with a wonderful aroma. Sara was barely aware of Shea's healing touch with all the precision of a surgeon. Sara could only think of Falcon. Could only wait for him deep beneath the earth, hoping they would all be safe until he arrived.

Chapter Eight

The attack came immediately after sunset. The sky rained fire, streaks of red and orange dropping straight down toward the house and grounds. Long furrows in the ground appeared, moving quickly, darting toward the estate, tentacles erupting near the massive gates and columns surrounding the property. Bulbs burst through the earth, spewing acid at the wrought-iron fence. Insects fell from the clouds, oozed from the trees. Rats rushed the fence, an army of them, round beady eyes gleaming. There were so many bodies the ground was black with them.

Beneath the earth Jacques lifted his head alertly. His lifemate was performing her healing art. His eyes met Raven's over Sara's head. "The ancient one has sent his army ahead of his arrival. The house is under attack."

"Will the safeguards hold?" Raven asked with her usual calm. She was already reaching out to Mikhail. They were still separated by many miles, yet his warmth flooded her immediately.

"Against his servants, the safeguards will certainly hold. The ancient one is attempting to weaken the safeguards so that he can more easily penetrate our defenses. He knows that Mikhail and Sara's lifemate are on their way.

He thinks to have, a quick and easy victory before their arrival." Jacques was calm, his black eyes flat and cold. He was banishing all emotion in preparation for battle. His arms were around Shea's waist, his body pressed close, protectively toward her. He bent his head to kiss her neck, a light, brief caress before moving away.

Raven caught his arm, preventing him from leaving the chamber. "Mikhail and Falcon say this one is dangerous, a true ancient, Jacques. Wait for them, please."

He looked down at her hand. "They are all dangerous, little sister. I will do what is necessary to protect the three of you." Very gently he removed her hand from his wrist, gave her an awkward, reassuring pat, a gesture at odds with his elegance.

Raven smiled at him. "I love you, Jacques. So does Mikhail. We don't tell you nearly enough."

"It is not necessary to say the words, Raven. Shea has taught me much over the years. The bond between us is very strong. I have much to live for, much to look forward to. I have finally convinced my lifemate that a child is worth the risks."

Raven's face lit up, her eyes shiny with tears. "Shea didn't say a word to me. I know she's always wanted to have a baby. I'm happy for you both, I really am."

Shea returned to her body, swaying from the intense effort of healing Sara. She staggered toward Jacques. He caught her to him, drew her gently into his arms, buried his face in the mass of wine-red hair. "Is Sara going to be all right?" he asked softly. There was a wealth of pride in his voice, a deep respect for his lifemate.

Shea leaned into him, turned up her face to be kissed. "Sara will be fine. She just needs her lifemate." She stared into Jacques's eyes. "As I do."

"Neither you nor Raven seems to have much faith in my

abilities. I'm shocked!" Jacques's chagrined look had both women laughing despite the seriousness of the situation. "I have my brother attempting to pull his Prince routine on me, giving me orders not to engage the enemy until His Majesty returns. My own lifemate, brilliant as she is, does not seem to realize I am a warrior without equal. And my lovely sister-kin is deliberately delaying me. What do you think about that, Sara?" He arced one eyebrow at her.

Sara sat up slowly, pushed her hand through her tousled, spiky hair. Her head was no longer pounding and her ribs felt just fine. Even the aches from the bruises were gone. "I don't know about your status as a warrior without equal, but your lifemate is a miracle worker." She had the feeling that Raven and Shea spent a great deal of time laughing when they were together. Neither seemed in the least intimidated by Jacques, despite the gravity of his appearance.

"I cannot argue with you there," Jacques agreed.

Shea grinned at Sara, her face pale. "He has to say that. It is always best to compliment one's lifemate."

"And that is why you and Raven are casting aspersions upon my battle capabilities." Once more Jacques kissed his lifemate. With his acute hearing, he could hear the assault upon the estate.

Sara could hear it, too. She twisted her fingers together anxiously. "He's coming. I know he is."

"Do not fear him, Sara," Shea hastened to assure her. "My lifemate has battled many of the undead and will do so long after this one is gone." She turned her gaze on her husband. "Raven will provide for me while you delay this monster. You will return to me unharmed."

"I hear you, little red hair, and I can do no other than obey." His voice was soft, an intimate caress. He simply dissolved into vapor and streamed from the chamber.

Sara made an effort to close her mouth and not gape in

total shock. Raven, one arm wrapped around Shea's waist, laughed softly. "Carpathians take a little getting used to. I ought to know."

"I must feed," Shea said, her gaze steady on Sara's. "Will it alarm you?"

"I don't know," Sara said honestly. For no reason at all, the spot along the swell of her breast began to throb. She found herself blushing. "I suppose I should get used to it. Falcon and I were waiting until I had settled the red tape with the children before we"—she sought the right word— "finalized things." She lifted her chin. "I'm very committed to him." It seemed a pale way of explaining the intensity of her emotions.

"I am amazed he allowed you the time. He must be extraordinarily certain of his abilities to protect you," Raven said. "Feed, Shea. I offer freely that you may be at full strength once again." She casually extended her wrist to Shea. "Carpathian males usually have a difficult time at the first return of their emotions. They have to contend with jealousy and fear, the overwhelming need to protect their lifemate and the terror of losing her. They become domineering and possessive and generally are a pain in the neck." Raven laughed softly, obviously sharing the conversation with her lifemate.

Sara could feel her heart racing as she watched in horrified fascination while Shea accepted nourishment from Raven. Although it was bizarre, she could see no blood. She was almost comforted by the completely unselfish act between the two women. Sara was humbled by Shea's gift of healing. She was humbled by the way she was accepted so completely into their circle, a close family willing immediately to aid her, to place their lives directly in the path of danger for her.

"Are you really planning to have a child?" Raven asked

as Shea closed the tiny pinpricks in her wrist with a sweep of her tongue. "Jacques said he has finally convinced you." There was a slight hesitation in Raven's voice.

Sara watched shadows chase across Shea's delicate features. Sara had always wanted children, and she sensed that Shea's answer would be important to her dreams, also.

Shea took a deep breath, let it out slowly. "Jacques wants a child desperately, Raven. I have tried to think like a doctor, because the risks are so high, but it is difficult when everything in me wants a child and when my lifemate feels the same. It was a miracle Savannah survived; you know that, you know how difficult it was. It took both Gregori and me that first year of fighting for her life, along with Mikhail and you. I have improved the formula for infants, since we cannot feed them what was once the perfect nourishment. I do not know why nature has turned on our species, but we are fighting to save every child born to us. Still, knowing all this does not stop me from wanting children. I know now that if something happened to me, Jacques would fulfill my wish and raise our child until he or she has a family. I will choose a time soon and hope we are successful with the pregnancy and keeping the child alive afterward."

Sara stood up carefully, a little gingerly, a frown on her face. She could hear the sizzle of fire meeting water, of insects and other frightening things she had no knowledge of. She could hear clearly, even envision the battle outside, the army of evil seeking to break through the safeguards protecting those within the walls of the house. Yet she felt safe. Deep below the earth, she felt a kinship with the two women. And she knew Falcon was on his way. He would come to her. For her. Nothing would stop him.

It seemed crazy, yet perfectly natural, to be in this chamber talking intimately with Raven and Shea while, just above them, the ancient vampire was seeking entrance. "Will I have problems having a child once I become fully like Falcon?" Sara asked. It had not occurred to her that she would not be able to have a child once she was a Carpathian.

Shea and Raven both held out their hands to her. A gesture of camaraderie, of compassion, of solidarity. "We are working very hard to find the answers. Savannah survived and two male children, but no other females. We have much more research to do, and I have developed several theories. Gary has flown out from the United States to aid me, and Oregon will follow in a few weeks. I believe we can find a way to keep the babies alive. I even believe I'm close to finding the reason why we give birth to so few females, but I am not certain that, even once I know the cause, I can remedy the situation. I do believe that every female who was human at one time has a good chance of having a female child. And that is a priceless gift to our dying race."

Sara paced the length of the room, suddenly needing Falcon. The longer she was away from him, the worse it seemed to be. Need. It crawled through her, twisted her stomach into knots, took her breath away. She accepted it, had known the need long before she had known the reality of Falcon. She had carried his journal everywhere with her, his words imprinted on her mind and in her heart. She had needed him then; now it was as if a part of her were dead without him.

"Touch his mind with yours," Raven advised softly. "He is always there for you. Don't worry, Sara, we will be here for you, too. Our life is wonderful, filled with love and amazing abilities. A lifemate is worth giving up what you had."

Sara pushed a hand through her hair, tousling it further. "I didn't have much of a life. Falcon has allowed me to dare to dream again. Of a family. Of a home. Of belonging with someone. I'm not afraid." She suddenly laughed. "Well . . . maybe I'm nervous. A little nervous."

"Falcon must be an incredible man," Shea said.

Not that incredible. Jacques never quite relinquished his touch on Shea. Over the years he had managed to relearn many things that had once been wiped from his mind, but he needed his lifemate anchoring him at all times. Before, he would have been jealous and edgy; now there was a teasing quality to his voice.

Shea laughed at him. Softly. Intimately. Sent him her touch, erotic pictures of twining her body around his. It was enough. She was his lifemate. His world.

Sara watched the expressions chase across Shea's delicate features, knowing exactly what was transpiring between Shea and her lifemate. It made Sara feel as if she really were a part of something, part of a family again. And Raven was right, the moment she reached for Falcon, he was there, in her mind, enfolding her in love and warmth, in reassurance. She wrapped her arms around herself to hold him close to her, felt him in her mind, heard him, the soft whispers, the promises, his supreme confidence in his abilities. It was all there in an instant.

"Sara." Raven brought Sara's attention back to the women, determined to keep it centered on them rather than on the coming battle. "Whose children are these that the vampire went to so much trouble to acquire?"

Sara suddenly smiled, her face lighting up. "I guess they are mine now. I found them living in the sewers. They had banded together because of their difference from most. All of them have psychic abilities. Three little girls and four boys. Not all of their talents are the same, but they still knew, as young as they are, that they needed one another. I had great empathy with them because I grew up feeling different, too. I wanted to give them a home where they could feel normal."

"Three little girls?" Shea and Raven exchanged a long, gleeful grin. Shea shook her head in astonishment. "You are truly a treasure. You've brought us an ancient warrior. We may learn much from him. You have seven little ones with psychic talent, and you are a lifemate. Tell me how it is that you accept our world so readily."

Sara shrugged. "Because of the vampire. I saw him killing in the tunnels of a dig my parents were on. Two days later he killed my whole family." She lifted her chin a little as if in preparation for condemnation, but both women only looked sad, their gazes compassionate. "He chased me for years. I always kept moving to stay ahead of him. Vampires have been part of my life for a long time. I just didn't understand the difference between vampires and Carpathians."

"And Falcon?" Raven prompted.

Sara heard a sudden hush outside the house, as if the wind were holding its breath. The night creatures stilled. She shivered, her body trembling. The sun had set. The vampire had risen and was hurtling through space to reach the estate before Falcon and Mikhail had a chance to return.

Sara was positive that both women were aware of the vampire's rising, but they remained calm, although they linked hands. She took a deep breath, wanting to follow their examples of tranquillity. "Falcon has been my salvation for fifteen years. I just didn't know he was real. I found something that belonged to him." *This is my gift to you. Sara, lifemate to Falcon.* She held his words tightly to her. "I saw him clearly, his face, his hair, his every expression. I felt as if I could see into his heart. I knew I belonged with him, yet he was from long ago and I was born too late."

Falcon, winging his way strongly through the falling night felt her sorrow. He reached out to her, flooding her mind with the sheer intensity of his love for her. *You were not born too late, my love. Accept what is and what has been given to us. A great gift, a priceless treasure. I am with you now and for all time.*

I love you with all my heart, with every breath.

Then believe that I will not allow this monster to tear us apart. I have endured centuries of loneliness, a barren existence without your presence. He will not take you from me. I am of ancient lineage and much skilled. Our enemy is indeed powerful, but he will be defeated.

Sara's heart began to ease its frantic racing, slowing to match the steady beat of Falcon's heart. Deliberately he breathed for her, for them, a shadow in her head as much for his own peace of mind as for hers. He was well aware of the vampire moving swiftly toward the house to find Sara. The foul stench was riding on the night wind. The creatures of the evening whispered to him, scurried for cover to avoid the danger. Falcon had no way of communicating with Mikhail and Jacques without the vampire hearing. He could use the standard path of telepathy used by their people, but the vampire would certainly hear. Mikhail and Jacques shared a blood tie and had their own private path of communication the undead could not share. It would make the planning of a battle against an ancient vampire much easier.

Falcon felt heat sizzling through the air as the first real attack was launched by the vampire. The vibrations of violence sent shock waves through the sky, bouncing off the mountain peaks so that wicked veins of lightning rocked the black, roiling clouds. The avian form he was using could not withstand such force. He tumbled through the sky, falling toward earth. Falcon abandoned that form and shifted into vapor. The wind changed abruptly, a gale force, blowing the droplets of water in the opposite direction from where he wished to go. Falcon took the only avenue safely open to him; he dropped to earth, landing in the form of a wolf, running flat out on four legs toward his lifemate and the Prince's estate.

Despite the miles separating them, Mikhail ran into the

same problem. It was no longer safe or expedient to travel through the air. He took to the ground, a large, shaggy wolf running at top speed, easily clearing logs in his path.

Jacques surveyed the sky thick with locusts and beetles, the arrows of flame and the spinning black clouds veined with forks of lightning. Tentacles erupted along the inside of the gates, a small inconvenience announcing the first break in the safeguards. He was calm as he withered the tentacles and protected the structure from the fire and insects. He began to throw barriers up, small, flimsy ones that took little time to build yet would cost the vampire time to destroy. Minutes counted now. Every moment that he managed to delay the ancient vampire gave Mikhail and Falcon a chance to reach them.

I have been in many battles, yet this is the first time I have encountered a vampire so determined to break through obvious safeguards. Jacques sent the information to his brother. *He knows this is the home of the Prince, that the women are protected by more than one male, yet he is persistent. I think we should send the women deep within the earth and you should stay away until this enemy is defeated.*

What of the human woman? The advice didn't slow Mikhail down. The wolf was running flat out, not breathing hard, nature's perfect machine.

I will protect her until her lifemate arrives. We will defeat this vampire together. Mikhail, you have a duty to your people. If Gregori were here—

Gregori is not here, Mikhail interrupted wryly. *He is off with my daughter neglecting his duty to protect the Prince.* There was a hint of laughter in his voice.

Jacques was exasperated. *The undead is unlike anything we have faced. He has not flinched at anything I have thrown at him. His attack has never faltered.*

It seems that this ancient enemy is very sure of his abilities. Mikhail's voice was a soft menace, a weapon of destruction if he cared to use it. There was a note of finality that Jacques recognized immediately. Mikhail was racing through the forest, so quickly his paws barely brushed the ground. He felt the presence of a second wolf close by. Smelted the wild pungent odor of the wolf male. A large animal burst through the heavy brush, rushing at him on a diagonal to cut him off.

Mikhail was forced to check his speed to avoid a collision. The heavier wolf contorted, wavered, took the shape of a man. Mikhail did so also.

Falcon watched the Prince through thoughtful, wary eyes. "I believe it would be prudent on our part to exchange blood. The ability to communicate privately may come in handy in the coming battle."

Mikhail nodded his agreement, took the wrist that Falcon offered as a gesture of commitment to the Prince. Mikhail would always know where Falcon was, what he was doing if he so desired. He took enough for an exchange and calmly offered his own arm in return.

Falcon had not touched the blood of an ancient in many centuries, and it rushed through his system like a fireball, a rush of power and strength. Courteously he closed the pinpricks and surveyed Vladimir's son. "You know you should not place yourself in harm's way. It has occurred to me that you could be the primary target. If you were to be killed by such a creature, our people would be left in chaos. The vampire would have a chance of gaining a stranglehold on the world. It is best if you go to ground as our last line of defense. Your brother and I will destroy the undead."

Mikhail sighed. "I have had this conversation with Jacques and do not care to repeat it. I have fought countless battles and my lifemate is at risk, as well as the villagers, who are my friends and under my protection." His shape was already wavering.

"Then you leave me no choice but to offer my protection since your second is not present." There was an edge to Falcon's voice. His body contorted, erupted with hair, bent as feet and hands clawed.

"Gregori is in the United States collecting his lifemate." It was enough, a reprimand and a warning.

Falcon wasn't intimidated. He was an ancient, his lineage old and sacred, his loyalties and sense of duty ingrained in him. His duty was to his Prince; honor demanded that he protect the man from all harm no matter what the cost.

They were running again, fast and fluid, leaping over obstacles, rushing through the underbrush, silent and deadly while the skies rained insects and the mist thickened into a fogbank that lay low and ugly along the ground. The wolves relied on their acute sense of smell when it became nearly impossible to see.

They burst into the clearing on the edge of the forest. The ground erupted with masses of tentacles. The writhing appendages reached for them, squirming along the ground seeking prey. The two wolves leaped nearly straight into the air to avoid the grasping tentacles, danced around walls of thorns, and skidded to a halt near the tall, double, wrought-iron gates.

Falcon angled in close to Mikhail, inserting his body between the Prince and a tall, elegant man who appeared before them, his head contorting into a wedge shape with red eyes and scales. The mouth yawned wide, revealing rows of dagger-sharp teeth. The creature roared, expelling a fiery flame that cut through the thick fog straight at them.

Jacques exploded from the house, leaping the distance to

the gate, then jumping over to land on the spot where the undead had been. The vampire used its preternatural speed, spinning out of reach. He hissed into the night air, a foul, poisonous blend of sound and venom. Vapor whirled around his solid form, green and then black. A noxious odor was carried on the blast. The vapor simply dissolved into thousands of droplets of water, spreading on the wind, an airborne cloud of depravity.

The hunters pressed forward into the thick muck. Falcon murmured softly, his hands following an intricate pattern. At once the air was filled with a strange phosphorescent milky whiteness. The trail left by the undead was easily seen as dark splotches staining the glowing white. Falcon took to the clouds, a difficult task with the air so thick and noxious. The splotches scattered across the heavens, tiny stains that seemed to spread and grow in all directions, streaking like dark comets across the night sky.

The vampire could only go in one direction, yet the stains were scattering far and wide, east and south, north and west, toward the village, high over the forest, along the mountain ridge, straight up, blowing like a foul tower and falling to earth as dark acid rain.

On the ground the rats and insects retreated, the walls of thorn wavered and fell, the tentacles retreated beneath the earth. Near the corner of the gate, a large rat stared malevolently at the house for several moments. Teeth bared, the rodent spat on the gate before it whirled around and scurried away. The wrought iron sizzled and smoked, the saliva corroding the metal and leaving behind a small blackened hole.

Mikhail sent out a call to all Carpathians in the area to watch over the villagers. They would attempt to cut off the vampire's source of sustenance. With the entire region on alert, he hoped to find the vampire's lair quickly. He signaled the other two hunters to return to the house. Chasing the vampire when there was no clear trail was a fool's errand. They would regroup and form a plan of attack.

"This one is indeed an ancient," Jacques said as they took back their true forms at the veranda of the Prince's home. "He is more powerful than any other I have come across."

"Your father sent out many warriors. Some are still alive, some have chosen the dawn, and a few have turned vampire," Falcon agreed. "And there is no doubt that this one has learned much over the years. But he had fifteen years to find Sara, yet she escaped. A human, a child. He can and will be defeated." He glanced toward the gate. "He left behind his poisonous mark. I spotted it as we came in. And, Jacques, thank you for finding Sara so quickly and getting her to safety. I am in your debt."

"We have much to learn of one another," Mikhail said, "and the unpleasant duty of destroying the evil one, but Sara must be able to go to ground. She is beneath the earth in one of the chambers. For her protection, it is best that you convert her immediately."

Falcon's dark eyes met his Prince's. "And you know this can be safely done? In my time such a thing was never tried by any but the undead. The results were frightening."

Mikhail nodded. "If she is your true lifemate, she must have psychic abilities. She can be converted without danger, but it is not without pain. You will know instinctively what to do for her. You will need to supply her with blood. You must use mine, as you have no time to go out hunting prey."

"And mine," Jacques volunteered generously. "We will have need of the connection in the coming battle."

Chapter Nine

Sara was waiting for Falcon in the large, beautiful chamber. Candles were everywhere, flames flickering so that the glowing lights cast shadows on the wall. She was alone, sitting on the edge of the bed. The other women had been summoned by their lifemates. Sara jumped up when Falcon walked in. She wore only a man's silken shirt, the tails reaching nearly to her knees. A single button held the edges together over her generous breasts. She was the most beautiful thing he had ever seen in all his centuries of existence. He closed the door quietly and leaned against it, just drinking her in. She was alive. And she was real.

Sara stared up at him, her heart in her eyes. "It seems like forever."

Her voice was soft but it washed over him with the strength of a hurricane, making his pulse pound and his senses reel. She was there waiting for him with that same welcome on her face. Real. It was real, and it was just for him.

Falcon held out his hand to her, needing to touch her, to see that she was alive and well, that the healer had worked her miracle. "I never want to experience such terror again. Locked within the earth, I felt helpless to aid you."

Sara crossed to his side without hesitation. She touched

his face with trembling fingertips, traced every beloved line—the curve of his mouth, his dark eyebrows—and rubbed a caress along his shadowed jaw. "But you did come to my aid. You sent the others to me, and you were always with me. I wasn't alone. More than that, I knew you would save the children." There was a wealth of love in her voice that stole his heart.

He bent his head to take possession of her tempting mouth. She was soft satin and a dark dream of the future. He took his time, kissing her again and again, savoring the way she melted into him, the way she was so much a part of him. *Are you ready to be as I am? To be Carpathian and walk beside me for all time?* He couldn't say it aloud but whispered it intimately in her mind while his heart stood still and his breath caught in his lungs. Waiting. Just waiting for her answer.

You are my world. I don't think I could bear to be without you. She answered him in the way of his people, wanting to reassure him.

"Is this what you want, Sara? Am I what you want? Be certain of this—it is no easy thing. Conversion is painful." Falcon tightened his hold on her possessively, but he had to tell her the truth.

"Being without you is more painful." Her arms crept around his neck. She leaned her body against his, her soft breasts pushing against his chest, her body molding to his. "I want this, Falcon. I have no reservations. I may be nervous, but I am unafraid. I want a life with you." Her mouth found his, tiny kisses teasing the corners of his smile, her teeth nibbling at his lower lip. Her body was hot and restless and aching for his. Her kiss was fire and passion, hot and filled with promises. She gave herself into his keeping without reservation.

He melted inside. It was an instant and complete meltdown, his insides going soft and his body growing hard. She tore him up inside as nothing had ever done. No one had ever penetrated the armor surrounding his heart. It had been cold. Dead. Now it was wildly alive. His heart pounded madly at the love in her eyes, the touch of her fingertips, the generous welcome of her body, the total trust she gave him when her life had been one of such mistrust.

His kiss was possessive, demanding. Hot and urgent, the way his body felt. His hands went to her waist in a soft caress, slid upward to cup the weight of her breasts in his hands. But his mouth was pure fire, wild and hot even when his hands were so tender. He slipped the single button open, his breath catching in his throat, and he stepped back to view the lush temptation of her breasts. "You are so beautiful, Sara. Everything about you. I love you more than anything. I hope you know that. I hope you are reading my mind and you know that you are my life." His finger trailed slowly down the valley between her breasts to her navel. His body reacted, that painful ache of urgent demand. And he let it happen.

Sara watched his eyes change, watched the way his body changed, and she smiled, unafraid of the wildness she glimpsed in him. Wanting it. Wanting him crazy for her. She unbuttoned his shirt, slipped it from his shoulders. Leaning forward, she pressed a row of kisses along his muscles, her tongue sliding around his nipple. She smiled up at him as she rubbed her hand over the bulging material of his trousers, her fingers deftly freeing him from the tight confines. Her hand wrapped around the thick length of him, simply held him for a moment, enjoying the freedom of being able to explore. Then she hooked her thumbs into the waistband of the trousers to remove them. "I think you're beautiful, Falcon," she admitted. "And I know that I love you."

He wrapped his arm around her waist, dragged her to

him, his mouth fusing with hers, all at once aggressive, demanding, a little primitive. Sara met him kiss for kiss. His hands were everywhere; so were hers. He slid his palm over her stomach, wanting to feel a child, his child, growing there, wanting everything at once—her, a child, a family, everything he had never had. Everything he'd believed he never could have. His fingers dipped lower into the thatch of tight curls, cupped her welcoming heat even as his mouth devoured hers. "I know I should slow down," he managed to get out.

"There's no need," she answered, feeling the exact same sense of wild urgency. She needed him. Wanted him. Every inch of him buried deep within her merging their two halves into one whole.

Shadows danced on the wall from the flickering candlelight, threw a soft glow over Sara's face. He lifted his head as he slowly, carefully, pushed two fingers deep inside her. He wanted to watch the pleasure in her eyes. She held nothing back from him, not her thoughts, her desires, or her passion. She gasped, her body tightening, clamping around his fingers, hot and needy. She moved against his hand, a slow, sexy ride, her head thrown back to expose her throat, her breasts a gleaming enticement in the candlelight.

He pushed deeper into her, felt the instant answering wash of hot moisture. Very slowly he bent his head to her throat. His tongue swirled lazily. His teeth nipped. He hid nothing from her, his mind thrusting into hers, sharing the perfect ecstasy of the moment with her, his body's reaction and the frenzy of heated passion. His fingers penetrated deep into her feminine channel as he buried his teeth in her throat. The lightning lanced both of them, hot and white, a pain that gave way to an erotic fire. She was hot and sweet and just as wild as he was. Falcon was careful to keep his appetite under control, taking only enough blood for an exchange. His mouth left her throat with a soothing swirl of his tongue; he lifted her with only one arm wrapped around her waist and took her to the bed. All the time, his fingers were sliding in and out of her, his mouth was fused to hers, the pleasure blossoming and spreading like wildfire through both of them.

She expected to find the taking of her blood disgusting, but it was erotic and dreamy, almost as if he had drawn a veil over her mind, ensnaring her in his dark passion. Yet she shared his mind and knew he had not. She also shared the intensity of his pleasure in the act, and it gave her courage.

"It isn't enough, Falcon. I want more, I want you in my body, I want us together." Her voice was breathless against his lips, her hands sliding over him eagerly, tracing each defined muscle, urging his hips toward hers.

He kissed her throat, her breasts, swirling his tongue over her nipples, along her ribs, around her belly button. Then she was gasping, rising up off the bed, her hands clutching fist-fuls of his hair as he tasted her. She was shattering with the sheer intensity of her pleasure. Falcon could transport her to other worlds, places of beauty, emotion, and physical rapture.

He rose above her, a dark, handsome man with long, wild hair and black, mesmerizing eyes. There was a heartbeat while he was poised there, and then he surged forward, lock-ing them together as they were meant to be, penetrating deeply, sweeping her away with him. He began to move, each stroke taking him deeper, filling her with a rush of heat and fire. She rose to meet him, craving the contact, wanting him deep inside, all the time her body winding tighter and tighter, rushing toward that elusive perfection.

Sara gasped as he thrust deeper still, the fiery friction clenching every muscle in her body, flooding every cell with a wild ecstasy. Then he was merging their minds, thrusting deep as his body took hers. She felt his pleasure, he felt hers, body and mind and heart, a timeless dance of joy and love. They soared together, exploding, fragmenting, waves of release rocking the earth so that they clung together with hearts pounding and shared smiles.

Falcon held her tightly, buried his face in her neck, whispered soft words of love, of encouragement before reluctantly untangling their bodies.

They lay on the bed together . . . waiting. Her heart was pounding, her breath coming too fast, but she tried valiantly to pretend that everything was perfectly normal. That her entire world was not about to be changed for all eternity.

Falcon held her in his strong arms, wanting to reassure her, needing the closeness as much as she did. "Do you know why I wrote the journal?" He kissed her temple, breathed in her scent. "A thousand years ago, the words welled up inside me when I could feel nothing, see nothing but gray images. The emotions and words were burned into my soul. I felt I needed to write them down so I would always remember the intensity of my feelings for my lifemate. For you, Sara, because even then, a thousand years before you were born, more even, I felt your presence in my soul. A tiny flicker and I needed to light the way." He kissed her gently, tenderly. "I guess that doesn't make much sense. But I felt you inside of me and I had to tell you how much you mattered."

"Those words saved my life, Falcon. I wouldn't have survived without your journal." She leaned into him. She would survive this, as well. She was strong and she would see it through.

"I shudder to think what trouble the children are giving this poor stranger who has been called into service," Falcon teased, wanting to see her smile.

Sara nibbled at his throat. "How long will it take us to get the children in a real home? Our home?"

"I think that can be arranged very fast," Falcon assured, his fingers sliding through her thick, silken hair, loving the feel of the sable strands. "The one wonderful thing about our people is that they are very willing to share what they have. I have jewels and gold stashed away. I was going to turn it over to Mikhail to aid our people in any way possible, but we can ask for a house."

"A large house. Seven children require a large house."

"And a large staff. We will have to find someone we trust to watch over the children during the day," Falcon pointed out. "I am certain Raven and Shea will know the best person to contact. The children have very special needs. We will have to aid them . . ."

She turned her head, frowning at him. "You mean manipulate them."

He shrugged his powerful shoulders, unperturbed by her irritation. "It is our way of life in this world. We must shield those who provide sustenance for us, or they would live in terror. Officials who do not want to hand us these children are easily persuaded otherwise. To keep the children from being afraid and allow them to become more used to their environment and more accepting of a new lifestyle, it will be necessary. It is a useful gift, Sara, and one we depend on to keep our species from discovery."

"The children want to live with me. We have discussed it on many occasions. I would have taken them to my home immediately but I knew that eventually the vampire would come. I was attempting to set up a safe house for them, a refuge where I could see them without endangering them. But the officials continually put roadblocks in my way, mostly to charge more money. But the children knew I was trying. They believed in me, and they won't be afraid of a new life."

"You will not be with them during the day, Sara. We must ensure that they trust the humans we will have to rely on to guard them during those hours."

Just then a ripple of fire moved through Sara's body. She put her hand over her stomach and turned her head, meeting his shadowed gaze. He put his hand over hers.

He bent to kiss her, a kiss of sorrow, of apology. "I would spare you this pain if I could." He whispered it against her skin. His body trembled against hers.

She caught his hand, twining their fingers together. Her insides were burning alarmingly. "It's all right, Falcon. We knew it was going to be like this." She wanted to reassure him even though every muscle was cramping and her body was shuddering with pain. "I can do this. I want to do this." She allowed nothing else to enter her mind. Not fear. Not growing terror. It had no place, only her complete belief in him, in them. In her decision. A convulsion lifted her body, slammed it back down. Sara tried to crawl away from him, wanting to spare him.

Falcon caught at her, his mind firmly entrenched in hers. *Together,* piccola. *We are in this together.* He could feel the pain ripping through her body and he breathed deeply, evenly, determined to breathe for both of them, protecting her as best he could. He wanted, *needed,* to take the pain from her, but even with his great strength and all of his powers, he could not alleviate the terrible burning as her organs were reshaped. He could only shoulder part of the terrible pain and share her suffering. He held her as her body rid itself of toxins. Never once did he detect a single moment when she blamed him or wavered in her choice to join him.

For Falcon, time inched by slowly, an eternity, but he forced serenity into his mind, determined to be as accepting as Sara. Determined to be everything she needed, even if all he could do was believe that everything would turn out perfectly. In the centuries of his existence, he had mingled with humans and had seen extraordinary moments of bravery, but her steadfast courage astounded him. He shared his admiration of her, his belief in her ability to ride above the waves of pain and the convulsions possessing her body. She took each moment separately, seeking to reassure him when each wave ebbed, leaving her spent and exhausted.

Once, she smiled and whispered to him. He couldn't hear her, even with his phenomenal hearing. *Having a baby is going to be a piece of cake after this.* There was a wry humor in her soft voice brushing at the walls of his mind. Falcon turned his head away to keep her from seeing the tears in his eyes at the evidence of her deep commitment to him.

The moment he knew it was safe to send her to sleep, Falcon commanded it, opening the earth to allow the healing properties to aid her. Carpathian soil, more than any other, rejuvenated and healed its people, yet they could use whatever was available, as he had been doing for centuries. He had forgotten the soothing richness of his homeland. Falcon carefully cleaned the bedchamber, removing every trace of illness and evidence of Sara's conversion. He took his time, relying on the other two Carpathian males to hold a watchful vigil against further assaults by the ancient vampire. It had been far too long since he had been home, since he had known the comfort of being with his own people, the luxury of being able to depend on others.

Falcon took the sustenance offered to him by Jacques, again grateful for the powerful blood supplied by an ancient of great lineage. He rested for an hour, deep within the earth, his arms wrapped tightly around Sara.

When Falcon was certain that Sara was completely healed, he brought her to the surface, laying her carefully on the bed, her naked body stretched out, clean and fresh, the lit candles releasing a soothing, healing fragrance. His heart was pounding, his mouth dry. *Sara. My life. My heart and soul. Awake and come to me.* He bent his head to capture her first breath as a Carpathian. His other half.

Sara woke to a different world. The vivid details, the smells and sounds, were almost too much to take in. She clung to Falcon, fitting her body trustingly into his. They both could hear her heart pounding loudly, frantically.

He kissed the top of her head, rubbed his chin over the silken strands of her hair. "Ssh, my love, it is done now. Breathe with me. Let your heart follow the rhythm of mine."

Sara could hear everything. *Everything.* Insects. The murmur of voices in the night. The soft, hushed flight of an owl. The rustle of rodents in nearby brush. Yet she was far beneath the earth in a chamber constructed of thick walls and rock. If she could hear everything, so could all people of this species.

Falcon smiled, his teeth immaculately white. "It is true, Sara," he agreed, easily monitoring her thoughts. "We learn discretion at a very young age. We learn to tune out what is not our business. It becomes second nature. You and I have been alone far too long; we are now a part of something again. The adjustment will take some time, but life is an exciting journey now, with you by my side."

Against his shoulder she laughed softly. "Even before I ever underwent conversion, I could read you like a book. Stop being afraid for me. I am strong, Falcon. I made the decision fifteen years ago that you were my life. My everything. You were with me in my dreams, my dark lover, my friend and confidant. You were with me in my darkest hours when everything was bleak and hopeless and I had no one. All my days, all my nights, you were in my heart and mind. I know you. I lived only because of your words. I would never have survived without your journal. Really, Falcon.

You know my mind, you know I am telling the truth. I am not afraid of my life with you. I want it. I want to be with you."

He felt humbled by her tremendous generosity, her gift to him. He answered her the only way he could, his kiss tender and loving, expressing with his body the deep emotion that could not be described by words. "I still cannot believe I found you," he whispered softly.

Her arms circled his neck, her soft breasts pressed tightly against his chest. She shifted her legs in invitation, wanting his body buried deep in hers. Wanting the safe anchor of his strength. "I still can't believe you're real and not my fantasy, the dream lover I made up from a vision."

Falcon knew what she needed. He needed the same reassurance. Sara. His Sara. Never afraid of appearing vulnerable to him. Never afraid of showing her desires. His mouth found hers, shifting the heavens for both of them. Her body was warm and welcoming, his haven, a refuge, a place of intimacy and ecstasy. The world fell away from them. There was only the flickering candlelight and the silk sheets. Only their bodies and long, leisurely explorations. There was gasping pleasure as they indulged their every fantasy.

Much, much later, Falcon lay across the bed, his head in her lap, enjoying the feel of the cool air on his body, the way her fingers played through his hair. "I cannot move."

She laughed softly. "You don't have to move. I like where you are." Her breath tightened, caught in her throat as he blew warm air gently, teasingly, across her thighs. Her entire body clenched in reaction, so sensitized by their continual lovemaking that Sara didn't think she would ever recover.

"Ahh, but I do, my love. I have our enemy to hunt. No doubt he is close and very anxious to finish his work and leave these mountains. He cannot afford to bide his time here." Falcon sighed. "There are too many hunters in this area. He will want to leave as soon as possible. As long as he is alive, the children and you will never be safe." He turned his head slightly to swirl a small caress along her inner thigh with his tongue. His hair slid over her skin so that she throbbed and burned in reaction.

"Stop trying to distract me," she said. His arm was around her, his palm cupping her buttocks, massaging gently, insistently. It was very distracting, rendering her nearly incapable of rational thought.

"And all this time I thought you were distracting me." His voice was melodic with amusement. Deliberately he slid his finger along her moist core. "You are incredibly hot, Sara. Did you stay in my mind while we made love? Did you feel how tightly you wrapped around me? The way your body feels to me when I'm surrounded by your heat? Your fire?" He pushed two fingers into her, a long, slow stroke. "The way your muscles clamp around me?" He let out his breath slowly. "Yes. Just like this. There is nothing else like it in this world. I love everything about your body. The way you look." He withdrew his fingers, brought them to his mouth. "The way you taste."

Her body rippled to life as she watched him insert his fingers into his mouth as if he were devouring her all over again. He smiled, knowing exactly what he was doing to her. Sara laughed softly, happily, the sound carefree. "If we make love again, I'm certain I'll shatter into a million pieces. And you, crazy man, will not be in any shape to go chasing after vampires if you touch me one more time. So if you're determined to do this, behave yourself."

He kissed the inside of her thigh. "I thought I was behaving just fine."

She caught a fistful of his hair. "What I think is that you need me to bag the vampire. To bring him right to you."

He sat up, his black gaze wary all at once. "You just stay right here where I know you are perfectly safe."

"I'm not the safe type, Falcon, I thought you knew that by now. I expect a partnership and I'm not willing to settle for less," she said firmly.

He studied her face for a long moment, reached out to trace the shape of her breast, sending a shiver through her body at his feather-light touch. "I would not want less than a partnership, Sara," he answered honestly. "But you do not fully comprehend what would happen if something should harm you."

She laughed at him, her eyes suddenly sparkling like jewels. "I don't think you fully comprehend what would happen if something should harm *you*."

"I am a hunter, Sara. Please trust my judgment in this."

"More than anything I do trust your judgment, but it is very biased at the moment, isn't it? It makes no sense not to use the one person he would come out into the open to find. You know that if he chased me for fifteen years, he isn't going to stop. Falcon"—she placed a hand on his chest, leaned forward to kiss his chin—"he will show himself if he thinks he has a serious chance of getting to me. If you don't use me as bait, everyone will continue to be in danger. Our children are frightened and in the care of a total stranger. These people have been good to us; we don't want to bring them and the surrounding villagers trouble." She pushed a hand through her short sable hair. "I know I can bring him out into the open. I have to try. I can't be responsible for any more deaths. Every time he follows me to a city and I read about a serial killer in the papers, I feel as if I had brought him there. Let me do this, Falcon. Don't look so stubborn and intimidating. I know you understand why I have to do this."

Falcon's hard features slowly softened. His perfectly

sculpted mouth curved into a smile. He framed her face between his hands and bent his head to kiss her. "Sara, you are a genius." He kissed her again. Slowly. Thoroughly. "That is exactly what we will do. We will use you as bait and trap ourselves a master vampire."

She raised an eyebrow, not trusting the sudden grin on his face.

Chapter Ten

Sara sat on a boulder, dipped her hand into the small pool of water, and looked up at the night sky. The clouds were heavy and dark, blotting out the stars, but the moon was still valiantly attempting to shine. White wisps of fog curled here and there along the forest floor, lending an eerie appearance to the night. An owl sat in the high branches of the tree to her left, completely still and very aware of every movement in the forest. Several bats wheeled this way and that overhead, darting to catch the plethora of insects flying through the air. A rodent scurried through the leaves, foraging for food, drawing the attention of the owl.

Sara had been out for some time, simply inhaling the night. Her favorite perfume mingled with her natural scent and drifted through the forest so that the wildlife were very aware of her presence. Sara stood up slowly and wandered back toward the house. Rare night blossoms caught her attention and she stopped to examine one. Her fresh scent mingled with the fragrant flower and was carried on the breeze, wafting through the forest and high into the trees. A fox sniffed the air and shivered, crouching in the heavy underbrush near the boulder where the human had been.

There was a soft sound in the vegetation near her feet.

Sara froze in place, watching the large rat as it foraged in the bushes quite close to her. Too close to her. Between her and the house. She backed away from the rodent, back toward the interior of the forest. She glanced toward the boulder, judging its height. Vampires were one thing, rats quite another. She was a bit squeamish when it came to rats.

When Sara turned back, a man stood watching her. Tall. Gaunt. With gray skin and long white hair. The vampire stared at her through red-rimmed eyes. Eyes filled with hatred and rage. There was no false pretense of friendship. His bitter enmity showed in every deep line of his ravaged face. "After all those wasted years. At last I have you. You have cost me more than you will ever know. Stupid, pitiful woman. How ridiculous that a nothing such as you should be a thorn in my side. It disgusts me."

Sara retreated from him, backing the way she had come until her legs bumped against rock. With great dignity she simply seated herself on the boulder and watched him in silence; her fingers twisting together were the only sign of fear. This was the monster who had murdered her family, taken everyone she had loved, virtually taken her life from her. This tall, gaunt man with hollow cheeks and venomous eyes.

"I have nearly limitless power, yet I need a little worm like you to complete my studies. Now Falcon's stench is all over you. How that sickens me." The vampire laughed softly, tauntingly, spittle flying into the air, fouling the wind. "You did not think I knew who he was, but I knew him well in the old time. A stooge to do the Prince's bidding. Vladimir lived long with Sarantha, yet he sent us out to live alone. His sons stayed behind, protected by him, yet we were sent to die alone. I did not choose death but embraced life, and I have studied much. There are others like me, but I will be the one to rule. Now that I have you, I will be a god and nothing will touch me. The Prince will bow to me. All hunters will tremble before me."

Sara lifted her head. "I see now. Although you think yourself all-powerful, a god, you still have need of me. You have followed me for fifteen years, a puny human woman, a child when you found me, yet you could not catch up to me."

He hissed, an ugly, frightening sound, a promise of brutal retaliation.

Sara frowned at him, sudden knowledge in her eyes. "You need me to find something for you. Something you can't do yourself. You killed everybody I loved, yet you think I will help you. I don't think so. Instead I intend to destroy you."

"You do not have any idea of the pain I can inflict on you. The things I can make you do. I will derive great pleasure in bending you to my will. You have no idea how powerful I am." The vampire's parody of a smile exposed stained, jagged teeth. "I will enjoy seeing you suffer as you have been a plague to me for so long. Do not worry, my dear, I will keep you alive a very long time. You will find the tomb of the master wizard and the book of knowledge that will give me untold power. I have acquired several of his belongings, and you will know where the book is when you hold these items. Humans never know the true treasures for what they are. They lock them up in museums few people ever visit, and none see what is truly valuable. They believe that wizards and magic are mere fairy tales, and they live in ignorance. Humans deserve to be ruled with an iron fist. They are cattle, nothing more. Prey only, food for the gods."

"Perhaps that is your impression of humans, but it is a false one. Otherwise how could I have evaded you for fifteen years?" Sara asked mildly. "I am not quite so insignificant as you would like me to believe."

"How dare you mock me!" The vampire hissed, his

features contorting with hatred as he suddenly looked around warily. "How is it you are alone? Are your keepers so inept they would allow you to walk around unprotected?"

"Why would you think they are not guarding me? They are all around me." She sounded truthful, sincere.

His eyes narrowed and he pointed one daggerlike fingernail at her. Had she denied it, he would have been far more wary, but she was too quick to give the hunters away. "Do not try my patience. No Carpathian hunter would use his lifemate to bait a trap. He would hide you deep in the earth, coward that he is, knowing I am too powerful to stop." He laughed softly, the sound a hideous screech. "It is your own arrogance that has caused your downfall. You ignored his orders and came out into the night without his knowledge or consent. That is a weakness of women. They do not think logically, always whining and wanting their way." His dagger-sharp finger beckoned her. "Come to me now." He used his mind, a sharp, hard compulsion designed to hurt, to put tremendous pressure on the brain even as it demanded obedience.

Sara continued to sit serenely, a slight frown on her soft mouth. She sighed and shook her head. "That has never worked on me before. Why should it now?"

Cursing, the vampire raised his arm, then changed his mind. The vibration of power would have given him away immediately to the Carpathian hunters. He stalked toward her, covering the short distance between them, his strides purposeful, his face a mask of rage at her impertinence.

Sara sat perfectly still and watched him come to her. The vampire bent his tall frame, extending his dagger-tipped bony fingers toward her. Sara exploded into action, only it was Falcon's fist slamming hard into the chest cavity of the undead, as he returned to his true form. As Falcon did so, the vampire, with a look of sheer disbelief, stumbled back so that the fist barely penetrated his chest plate. Overhead, Jacques, in the shape of the owl, launched himself from the branches and flew straight at the undead, talons outstretched. The small fox grew in stature, shape-shifting into the tall, elegant frame of a male hunter, and Mikhail's hands were already weaving a binding spell to prevent the vampire from shifting or vanishing.

Pressed from the air, caught between the hunters and unable to flee, the vampire launched his own attack, risking everything in the hopes of defeating the one Carpathian whose death might force the other two to pause. Calling on every ounce of power and knowledge he possessed, he slammed his fist into Falcon's elbow, shattering bone. Then he whirled away, his body replicating itself over and over until there were a hundred clones of the undead. Half the clones initiated attacks using stakes or sharp-pointed spears; the others fled in various directions.

Jacques, in the owl form, drove talons straight through the head of a clone, going through empty air so that he was forced to pull up swiftly before hitting the ground. The air vibrated with power, with violence and hatred.

Each of the clones on the attack was weaving a different spell, and sprays of blood washed the surrounding air a toxic crimson. Falcon's mind shut off the pain of his shattered elbow as he assessed the situation in that one heartbeat of time. It was all he had. All he would ever have. In that blink of an eye the centuries of his life passed, bleak and barren, stretching endlessly until Sara. *This is my gift to you.* She was his life. His soul. His future. But there was honor. There was what and who he was, what he stood for. He was guardian of his people.

She was there with him. His Sara. She understood that he

had no other choice. It was everything he was. Without regret, Falcon flung his body between his Prince and the vampire moving in for the kill. A multitude of razor-sharp spears pierced Falcon's body, taking his breath, spilling his life force onto the ground in dark rivers. As he toppled to earth, he reached out, slamming both open hands into the scarlet fountain on the vampire's chest, leaving his prints like a neon sign for the other hunters to target.

Sara, sharing Falcon's mind, reacted calmly, already knowing what to do. She had made good use of Falcon's knowledge and she shut down his heart and lungs instantly, so that he lay as still as death on the battlefield. She concentrated, holding him to her, a flickering, dim light that wanted to retreat from pain. She had no time for sorrow. No time for emotion. She held him to her with the same fierce determination of the Carpathian people's finest warrior as the battle raged on around him.

Mikhail saw the ancient warrior fall, his body riddled with holes. The Prince was already in motion, snapping the spears like matchsticks as he drove forward, directing Jacques with his mind. The clones tried to regroup to throw the hunters off the scent, but it was too late. The vampire had revealed himself in his attack, and Mikhail locked onto Falcon's marks, as certain as fingerprints.

The undead snarled his hatred, shrieked his fury, but the holding spell bound him. He could not shift his shape and it was already too late. The Prince buried his fist deep, following the twisted path the ancient warrior had mapped out. Jacques took the head, slicing cleanly, a delaying tactic to give his brother time to extract the black, pulsating heart. The sky rained insects, great stinging bugs, and pellets of ice and rain.

Mikhail calmly built the charge of energy in the roiling clouds. All the while, the black heart jumped and crawled blindly, seeking its master. Blisters rose on the ground and on their arms as the scarlet spray embedded itself in their skin. The fury of the wind whipped them, moaning and hissing a dark promise of retaliation. Mikhail grimly continued, calling upon nature, directing a fiery orange ball from the sky to the pulsing heart. The thing was incinerated with a noxious odor and a cloud of black smoke.

The body of the vampire jerked, the head rolled, the eyes staring at Falcon's still form with a hatred beyond anything the hunters had ever witnessed. A hand moved, the dagger-tipped claws reaching for the fallen warrior as if to take him along on the path to death. The orange ball of energy slammed into the body, incinerating it immediately, then leaping to the head to reduce it to a fine powder of ashes.

Jacques took over the cleansing of the earth, and then their own skin, erasing the evidence of the foul creature which had gone against nature itself.

Raven met her lifemate at the door, touching his arm, sharing his deep sorrow, offering him comfort and warmth. "Shea has gone ahead to the cave of healing, opening the earth and taking the candles we will need. Jacques has brought Falcon there. The soil is rich and will aid her work. I have summoned our people to join with us in the healing chant." She turned to look at Sara.

Sara stood up slowly. She could see compassion, even sorrow, on Raven's face. Tears streaked Raven's cheeks and she held out both hands. "Sara, they have brought him to the best place possible, a place of power. Shea says . . ." She choked back a sob and pressed a fist to her mouth even as she caught Sara's hand in hers. "You must come with us quickly to the cave of healing."

Mikhail stepped back, avoided her eyes, his features a mask of granite, but Sara knew what he was thinking. She touched his arm briefly to gain his attention. "I was sharing his mind when he made the decision. It was a conscious decision, one he didn't hesitate to make. Don't lessen his sacrifice by feeling guilty. Falcon believes you're a great man, that the loss of your life would be intolerable to him, to your people. He knew exactly what he was doing and what the cost might be. I am proud of him, proud of who he is. He is an honorable man and always has been. I completely supported his decision."

Mikhail nodded. "You are a fitting lifemate for an ancient as honorable as Falcon. Thank you for your kindness in such a bleak hour, Sara. It is a privilege to count you among our people. We must go to him rapidly. You have not had time to become used to our ways, so I ask that you allow me to take your blood. Falcon's blood runs in my veins. I must aid you in shape-shifting to get to this place of healing."

She met his black gaze steadily. "You honor me, sir."

Raven's fingers tightened around Sara's as if holding her close, but Sara could barely feel the contact. Her mind was firmly entrenched in Falcon's, holding him to her, refusing to allow him to slip away despite the gravity of his injuries. She felt the prick of Mikhail's teeth on her wrist, felt the reassuring squeeze of Raven's hand. Nothing mattered to Sara but that flickering light so dim and far away.

Mikhail placed the image of an owl in her mind, and she actually felt the wrenching of her bones, the contorting of her body, and the sudden rush of air as she took flight. But there was only Falcon, and she didn't dare let go of that fading light to look at the world falling away from her as she winged her way to the cave of healing.

Deep beneath the earth, the air was heavy and thick with the aroma of hundreds of scented candles. Sara went to Falcon, shocked at the terrible wounds in his body, at his white, nearly translucent skin. Shea's body was an empty shell. Sara was vividly aware of her in Falcon's body, valiantly repairing the extensive damage. The sound of chanting—ancient, beautiful words in a language she recognized yet didn't know—filled the chamber. The ancient language of the Carpathians. Those not present were there nonetheless, joined mind to mind, sending their powers of healing, their energy, to their fallen warrior.

Sara watched the Prince giving his blood, far more than he could afford, yet he waved the others off and gave until he was weak and pale, until his own brother forced him to replenish what he had given. She watched each of the Carpathians, strangers to her, giving generously to her lifemate, reverently, paying a kind of homage to him. Sara took Falcon's hand in hers and watched as Shea returned to her own body.

Shea, swaying with weariness, signaled to the others to pack Falcon's terrible wounds with saliva and the deep rich earth. She fed briefly from her lifemate and returned to the monumental task of closing and repairing the wounds.

It took hours. Outside the cave the sun was climbing, but not one of the people faltered in their task. Sara held Falcon to her through sheer will, and when Shea emerged, they stared at one another across his body, both weary, both with tears shimmering in their eyes.

"We must put him to ground and hope that the earth works its magic. I have done all I can do," Shea said softly. "It's up to you now, Sara."

Sara nodded. "Thank you. We owe you so much. Your efforts won't be wasted. He'll live. I won't allow anything else." She leaned close to her lifemate. "You will not die, do you hear me, Falcon?" Sara demanded, tears running down her face. "You will hold on and you will live for me. For us. For our children. I am demanding this of you." She said it fiercely, meaning it. She said it with her heart and her mind and her soul. Gently she touched his beloved face, traced his worn features. *Do you hear me?*

She felt the faintest of stirrings in her mind. A warmth. Soft, weary laughter. *Who could not hear you, my love? I can do no other than comply.*

The house was large, a huge, rambling home built of stone and columns. The veranda wrapped around the entire structure on the lower story. A similar balcony wrapped around the upper story. Stained-glass windows greeted the moon, beautiful unique pieces that soothed the soul. Sara loved every single thing about the estate. The overgrown bushes and thick stands of trees. The jumbles of flowers that seemed to spring up everywhere. She would never tire of sitting on the swing on her porch and looking out into the surrounding forest.

It was still difficult to believe, even after all these months, that the vampire was truly out of her life. She had been firmly in Falcon's mind when he assumed her shape. Her thoughts and emotions had guided his disguised body. Falcon buried deep, so that the vampire would fail to detect him. The plan had worked, the vampire was destroyed, but it would take a long while before she would wake without being afraid. She could only hope that the book the vampire had been searching for would remain hidden, lost to mortals and immortals alike. The fact that the undead had gone to such lengths to find the book could only mean that its power was tremendous. In the wrong hands, that book could mean disaster for both mortals and immortals.

Falcon had told Sara he'd known the vampire as a young boy growing up. Vladimir had sent him to Egypt while Falcon had gone to Italy. Somewhere along the way, Falcon had chosen honor, while his boyhood friend had wanted ultimate power. Sara rocked back and forth in the swing, allowing the peace of the evening to push the unpleasant thoughts from her mind.

She could hear the housekeepers in the kitchen talking quietly together, their voices reassuring. She could hear the children, upstairs in their bedrooms, laughing and murmuring as they began to get ready for bed. Falcon's voice was gentle as he teased the children. A pillow fight erupted as if often did, almost on a nightly basis.

You are such a little boy yourself. The words appeared in Falcon's mind, surrounded by a deep love that always took his breath away. Sara loved him to have fun, to enjoy all the simple things he had missed in his long life. And she was well aware Falcon loved her for that and for the way she enjoyed every moment of their existence, as if each hour were shiny and new.

They attacked me, the little rascals. Sara could see the image of him laughing, tossing pillows as fast as they were thrown at him.

Yes, well, when you are finished with your war, your life-mate has other duties for you. Sara leaned back in her swing, tapped her foot impatiently as a small smile tugged at her soft mouth. Deliberately she thought of her latest fantasy. The pool of water she had discovered by the waterfall in the secluded cliffside. Tossing her clothes aside. Standing naked on the boulder stretching her arms up in invitation to the moon. Turning her head to smile at Falcon as he came up to her. Leaning forward to chase a small bead of water across his chest, down his belly, then lower, lower.

The air shimmered for a moment and he was standing in front of her, his hand out, a grin on his face. Sara stared up at him, taking in his long silken hair and his mesmerizing dark eyes. He looked fit and handsome, yet she knew there were still faint scars on his body. They were etched in her mind more deeply than in his skin. Sara went to him, flowed to him, melted into him, lifting her face for his kiss, knowing he could move the earth for her.

"I want to check out this pool you have discovered," he whispered wickedly against her lips. His hands moved over her body gently, possessively.

She laughed softly. "I had every confidence you would."

At Avon Books, we know your passion for romance—once you finish one of our novels, you find yourself wanting more.

May we tempt you with . . .

- **Excerpts** from our upcoming releases.

- Entertaining **extras**, including authors' personal photo albums and book lists.

- Behind-the-scenes **scoop** on your favorite characters and series.

- **Sweepstakes** for the chance to win free books, romantic getaways, and other fun prizes.

- Writing **tips** from our authors and editors.

- **Blog** with our authors and find out why they love to write romance.

- **Exclusive content** that's not contained within the pages of our novels.

Join us at
www.avonbooks.com

AVON

An Imprint of HarperCollins*Publishers*
www.avonromance.com